A Lesson Hard Learned

Wendi Sotis

A Lesson Hard Learned

By Wendi Sotis

First draft was posted serially on BeyondAusten.com
from May 2015 through July 2016

Cover art by Matthew Sotis

ISBN-13: **978-1537155579**

ISBN-10: **1537155571**

Includes short passages paraphrased from *Pride and Prejudice* by Jane Austen (1813) and brief excerpts from *Camilla or A Picture of Youth* by Fanny Burney (1796.) Both are in the public domain.

This book is dedicated to all my readers

who urged me to expand the short story,

A Lesson Hard Learned,

into a novel.

Chapter 1

Fitzwilliam Darcy bolted upright in his seat. Taking several deep breaths to calm the storm of anxiety pumping through his veins, he surveyed the chamber.

He was in his study in London, *not* the library at Pemberley.

Thank God!

His abrupt awakening apparently caused a portion of the ink pot's contents to spill, ruining the journal entry he had been writing a few hours earlier. As Darcy used his handkerchief to mop up any ink the paper had not already absorbed, Parkman charged through the door.

The butler's stance told all. Darcy must have shouted during his terrifying dream, causing his loyal servant to fear the master was in danger. Face white and eyes opened wide, Parkman held a large silver tray as if he would be expected to use it defensively. After a fleeting glance around the room, without hesitation, Parkman transformed his countenance as smoothly as if hearing his master scream were an everyday occurrence. The man straightened his spine, tucked the tray under his arm, and adjusted his expression to his usual stoic demeanour.

"Are you well, Mr. Darcy?"

"Yes," Darcy blurted, though he was not well at all after that dream.

Needing to move about, he pushed himself from his chair and crossed to the window. He clasped his trembling hands together tightly so Parkman would not notice.

Darcy usually looked out the window to think, but at this moment, mulling over his nightmare was the last thing he wanted to do. Requiring a distraction, he pivoted to observe the butler cross to the hearth and rekindle the fire.

Once his respiration calmed, Darcy cleared his throat. "Inform Mrs. Martin I will take a light meal in my chambers in one hour." Stiff from sleeping at

1

his desk, he rolled his head, rubbing his neck with his hand. "I would prefer coffee this morning."

Parkman bowed. "Very good, sir."

"Oh, Parkman?"

The man stopped and turned. Darcy moved to the desk and used his letter-opener to lift the ink-saturated handkerchief. "Will you see what Hughes can do with this, please?"

Darcy almost laughed when Parkman's eyebrow twitched. Hughes was as fastidious about his master's clothing as was any valet, but he seemed to have an unnatural desire for making absolutely certain Darcy's handkerchiefs were in perfect condition.

"What do you recommend, Parkman? Shall I burn it instead?"

The butler's colour drained, his face becoming pastier than when he had entered the room. Hughes would have a fit if he knew Darcy had even suggested it.

"Then take it to Hughes, will you?" He dropped the handkerchief on the tray and returned the letter opener to his desk. "I give you permission to blame me *before* he sees it."

"As you say, sir."

The door closed with a thump behind Parkman, and Darcy returned his gaze to the window. The full moon hung low in the sky, just above the slight hint of a glow marking the eastern horizon.

The exchange with Parkman was exactly what he had needed to recover enough reason to contemplate his dream.

As a boy, he often had endured nightmares. His mother had encouraged him to examine his dreams, believing they were a veiled awareness or a concealed dread that was difficult to put into words—as if one's deepest sense of right and wrong advised a person of the truth while he slept.

He had usually found this assumption to be correct, using his nightmares to enlighten him as to strengths or weaknesses of one facet of his character or another. But as bits of *this* dream floated back to him, he was not as certain.

In tonight's nightmare, he had seen himself as a bitter, angry man in the cold dark winter of his life, who had, for many years, been obsessed with Elizabeth Bennet's refusal of his marriage proposal, certain it was at the core of his numerous regrets.

With a flash of insight, the much older version of himself realized the cause had not been her refusal at all. He had been too proud to admit she was correct about his faults and too self-righteous to be properly humbled by her reproofs. Ironically, he had lived the remainder of his life in such a way that proved her accusations correct in every respect.

His dream-self opened his fisted hand and smoothed out the letter he had crumpled with rage upon first reading. He stared at the one-lined missive stating that Elizabeth Bennet was deceased. Somehow, he knew she had died alone—as alone as he had been since the day of her refusal decades earlier. And although he had not seen her since that day, he could not imagine continuing in a world where the only woman he had ever loved no longer drew breath.

The dream had ended when he awakened in a cold sweat.

Even now, merely recollecting the nightmare caused his heart to pound as if it would smash through his ribs.

Was it possible that his mother had been right? Were his opinions warring with his principles, predicting what his future would hold if he continued along his present course? Were his attitudes sparring with his scruples, cautioning him of the insufficiency of his pretensions?

Were Miss Elizabeth Bennet's assertions about him correct?

After his excessive prodding for the reasons behind her simple refusal, she had said, "Your manners impress me with the fullest belief of your arrogance, your conceit, and your selfish disdain of the feelings of others."

Although he had been consumed by her accusations over the past fortnight, he had not been aware of any measure of self-doubt. Had he been questioning whether her charges were accurate all this time?

And now, unexpectedly, he distrusted all of the preconceived notions that had taken root with such determination to direct his life and dictate his actions.

Two weeks ago, when he proposed to Elizabeth, he had harboured no question as to how she would answer. Years of evading society matrons who brandished their daughters before him at every opportunity had taught him his hand was highly prized. Their focused attentions pumped him full of vanity, self-importance, and pompous superiority. He had assumed that, like every maiden of his social sphere, Elizabeth sought his good opinion. In his estimation, no one in her right mind would refuse a proposal of marriage if he offered it, if not for his personal attractions, then for the wealth and consequence that would naturally accompany such an event. Even now, he suspected none would—except Miss Elizabeth Bennet.

Striking him like a bolt of lightning, understanding hit him full force.

She was superior to all of them in every way that truly mattered. This was the very reason she had caught his attention.

No other lady in his acquaintance would have held fast to her principles the way Elizabeth had done. Even most men would fear to reveal aloud their honest opinion of him, and yet Elizabeth had held nothing back.

Or at least he hoped she did not think him lower than the assessment she had voiced when he proposed, the night before he left his aunt's estate.

He closed his eyes. His face heated.

No, he had not simply *left* Rosings Park.

Fitzwilliam Darcy—master of the sprawling estate of Pemberley, owner of an elegant house in coveted Grosvenor Square, landlord of several other properties, gentleman investment pioneer, and a man responsible for the livelihood of hundreds—he had *bolted* from Kent with his tail between his legs in order to avoid the possibility of seeing Elizabeth once again.

A Lesson Hard Learned

Elizabeth Bennet. Yes, she was a lovely, vivacious, amusing, and intelligent lady, with the finest eyes he had ever seen, but still, she was only a country miss, daughter of a gentleman with little income and even less import in society.

He had never run from any other challenge in the course of his eight and twenty years; yet, *he* had fled *her* presence.

That he allowed her to hold such power over him was mortifying.

The moment he returned to London, he wasted no time in venting his spleen into his journal.

His journal! He spun around to face his desk.

Memories of the resentful and indignant speeches he had poured out into this book over the last few days flooded his mind. The words he had used, the expressions, the philosophies…

Heaven help me. Elizabeth was right.

Suddenly, it was not unwelcomed that a number of the entries were now illegible due to the spilled ink.

Four steps across the room brought him to the hearth with his journal in hand. He drew aside the hearth-screen his sister, Georgiana, had painted for him. Ripping the last sheet from the journal, he cast it into the fire.

The edges browned then glowed red. With a flash, the page burst into blue and amber flames.

His nose wrinkled in protest as the acidic stench overpowered that of the burning coal and paper. Logic dictated the wet ink was responsible, but in his heart he knew it was the very scent of the previous evening's exceptionally virulent, bitter, and unjust entry.

He tore another page from the book and tossed it into the flames. The next was promptly followed by another until every last harsh judgement he had recorded over the past fortnight was reduced to charred embers.

He nodded. Elizabeth *had* been correct in her refusal.

Returning to the window, he took strength in the new day as it broke over the horizon. Along with it came the opportunity to right his wrongs.

A few minutes later, he removed a key from his pocket, moved to his desk, and locked what was left of his journal in a lower drawer.

If he was to transform himself into a better man, one who might someday be worthy of Elizabeth's affections, his efforts and reflections deserved a fresh volume, untarnished by his previous pride and prejudice.

Chapter 2

As Elizabeth Bennet placed the last of her gowns in her trunk, she was startled by a knock. She turned to the vanity mirror and pulled at the long, ebony curl that had escaped its pin. Tucking it into the knot of hair at the back of her head, she was satisfied she was as presentable as possible on such short notice before calling out, "Come."

Jane opened the door. A thin, listless smile was pasted on her pale features. No pleasure shined from her now-hollowed eyes. Happiness had abandoned her sister four months ago, at the same moment she had realized Mr. Charles Bingley would probably never return to Netherfield Park.

Elizabeth successfully bit back the gasp that threatened every time she saw her sister since the gentleman departed. She forced a reciprocal grin, gestured for Jane to enter, and bent over her trunk to return to her packing. It was essential she keep herself occupied long enough to stifle the urge to react as she had ten days ago, when she first arrived at their aunt and uncle's house in London after visiting their friend, Mrs. Charlotte Collins. Her elder sister had been mortified when Elizabeth rushed to her side and fussed, begged to know the truth about her state of health, and insisted Jane go above stairs to rest.

Without looking up from refolding the gown she had only just consigned to her trunk, Elizabeth asked, "Maria is not with you?"

Jane shook her head. "She has emptied her trunk and is busy repacking it. Apparently, Lady Catherine de Bourgh described the way a lady's gowns should be placed. Our aunt's maid did it incorrectly."

A sense of relief settled over her. Without Maria Lucas in the room, perhaps she and Jane could discuss more openly Elizabeth's holiday with their friend Charlotte, Charlotte's marriage, and her new residence. They certainly could not do so in front of Charlotte's sister.

Elizabeth chuckled. "Charlotte's patroness is quite firm in her assertions. The only *right* way of doing anything is *her* way. Maria was impressed by

1

Lady Catherine's opinions far more readily than I was. Charlotte defers to Lady Catherine's wishes, but I think it is to keep the peace."

Should she tell Jane about Mr. Darcy's proposal?

Jane was quiet for too long. Elizabeth straightened and turned to face her sister, who sat staring at a letter in her hands.

"This came for us today, Lizzy. It is from Mama."

"What does she say?"

"She suggests we remain in London."

To linger in Town would be a happy alternative to having to listen to their mother's tirades, and it might be healthier for Jane, too. At least being here in London under their Aunt and Uncle Gardiner's care seemed to have helped her sister recoup a small portion of the alarming amount of weight she had lost in recent months. However, though Jane was still the most beautiful of the five Bennet daughters, her heartbreak had now turned to melancholy. Would returning home be more beneficial than the demands of society in Town? Elizabeth prayed her dearest Jane would sink no deeper.

Elizabeth raised one eyebrow. "For how long?"

"At least until…" Jane's soft voice trailed off. It must have something to do with Bingley since she flushed so deeply.

"May I see it, dear?"

Jane handed her the pages without lifting her eyes.

Elizabeth's muscles tensed as she scanned past her mother's criticism of *her*, which covered both sides of a sheet of paper. At seeing Jane's name, she read more carefully. Elizabeth gasped. Their mother ordered Jane to remain in London until she saw Mr. Bingley? The missive went on to reminisce about the gentleman's stay at his leased home in their neighbourhood, cataloguing every attention he had paid Jane for another two sheets.

How would Jane ever recover if their mother would not stop speaking of the man? Mayhap Elizabeth should ask Aunt Gardiner to talk to her mother about her harping on the subject.

"Did you not tell Mama about Miss Bingley's, um… *reserved* manner when she finally returned your call?"

She stopped herself from repeating what their aunt had told her of the visit and from adding her own comments. According to Mrs. Gardiner, Miss Bingley's behaviour was a clear insult to Jane and her. Bingley's other sister, Mrs. Hurst, had not even accompanied Miss Bingley.

Jane shook her head. "I did not have the heart to tell her, Lizzy. You know how Mama was set on my marrying… *him*." Jane sighed.

Poor Jane could not even say Mr. Bingley's name!

Elizabeth said, "Papa would not have sent his carriage if he meant for us to stay."

Jane nodded and returned her gaze to the letter. She furrowed her brow—probably dreading their mother's reaction to their arrival at Longbourn late this afternoon. Jane's expression was the as close to voicing an unkind opinion as she had ever come.

With the intention of changing the course of their conversation, Elizabeth shuffled the pages to the beginning of the message and handed it to Jane. "Perhaps I should not have spoken so generously of the Hunsford Parsonage when I wrote home."

"I am sorry Mama does not understand why you refused Mr. Collins, Lizzy."

Elizabeth shrugged. She would probably never hear the end of being the cause if they *were* turned out into the hedgerows when their father died—in the far distant future, God willing. She bit her lip. She hoped it would not happen as her mother feared, but after coming to know their cousin Mr. Collins, she expected the heir would claim possession of the estate soon after their father was buried.

"Mama is afraid, Lizzy. That is all."

"Yes, I know."

Jane whispered, "Had I not failed in my duty, she would have forgotten your refusal of Mr. Collins by now."

"Oh, Jane!" Elizabeth stepped closer to take her sister's hand in hers. "Please trust me—you have failed no one."

Should she inform Jane of what Darcy told her? It would be helpful if Jane could understand she had done nothing wrong—that Bingley *did* love her, but his family and friends had intervened. It would also be beneficial to erase any doubt in her mind about the intentions of Caroline Bingley and Mrs. Hurst. They had befriended Jane due to their boredom whilst in the country, and nothing more. Elizabeth suspected neither lady ever held a warm emotion for anyone in their lives, including their good-natured brother. However, if she did apprise Jane of all this, she would have to admit to Darcy's part in the scheme. She did not want Jane to think badly of him.

But why? She *was* sure he would rectify his error now that he knew of it, but there was something more. What was it?

Jane sniffed and wiped a tear from her cheek, recapturing Elizabeth's attention. Guilt clenched at her heart. She had to tell her gentle sister *something*.

"What do you think Mama would say if she learned I refused Mr. Darcy, too?"

Her sister opened her eyes so wide, Elizabeth feared they might pop out of her head. But then she smiled genuinely for the first time in months. "You tease me, Lizzy."

She shook her head. "He proposed to me in Kent. I refused him."

Jane's grin melted away, and she covered her open mouth with her hand.

Frowning, she replied, "It was not a romantic proposal. His manner of speaking shocked me so much, I am afraid I reacted unkindly. I accused him of things which I regret—especially concerning Mr. Wickham."

"Lizzy! Tell me you did not confront him with Mr. Wickham's tale of how Mr. Darcy abused him and acted against his father's last will and testament?"

Elizabeth nodded. "I did. Knowing what I do now, I will never forgive myself for voicing such charges." She pressed her lips together. No, she would not tell Jane about Mr. Darcy's impropriety in writing her a letter, even if it was only to answer her accusations. "Mr. Darcy explained the truth to me, and I believed him. He did nothing wrong, just as you and father suspected. Additionally, to warn me of Mr. Wickham's true character, he told me of a most unfortunate circumstance." Elizabeth explained how the previous summer, Mr. Wickham had convinced Mr. Darcy's sister to elope with him so he could gain control of her dowry, and how Mr. Darcy stopped it from happening.

Jane's voice trembled when she cried out, "Poor Miss Darcy! But was Mr. Darcy certain Mr. Wickham's affections were not sincere? When Mr. Wickham was among us in Hertfordshire, he seemed like a pleasant young man. Mayhap his part in the situation was misunderstood?"

Elizabeth chuckled. "No, Jane. It certainly was not. Even *you,* who never speaks a negative word against anyone, cannot believe it. Mr. Darcy was wholly in the right." She shook her head. "It shames me to think of how I trusted Mr. Wickham only because his estimations of Mr. Darcy reinforced my own hastily formed first impressions. I never once thought of how improper it was for Mr. Wickham to reveal those opinions to the entire neighbourhood."

She hesitated. Was Mr. Darcy also correct to advise Bingley against proposing to Jane? Something Charlotte warned her about while Bingley resided at Netherfield came to mind. Their friend had said Jane was so shy, it would be impossible for anyone who did not know her well to recognize her regard for Mr. Bingley.

And Mr. Darcy *did* say he had not detected Jane's preference for his friend.

If Bingley had behaved as reservedly as Jane, would she have advised Jane to steer clear of Mr. Bingley?

Perhaps.

Elizabeth continued. "I am afraid I misjudged both gentlemen completely. I am thoroughly ashamed of myself, Jane."

Could she be wrong about Mr. Darcy still? She had always imagined a man in love enough to propose marriage would think of nothing but a happy future together. After hearing his reservations enumerated, she had assumed he did not really care for her. She had even expected he would have little difficulty overcoming his regard if he concentrated on them again, and suggested he do so.

But what if he, like Jane, did not wear his emotions on his sleeve? Was it possible Mr. Fitzwilliam Darcy truly loved her?

She tried to swallow past the knot forming in her throat.

After the insults she had flung at the gentleman, she could no longer hold his angry response against him. He had mentioned her family's conduct at many of the neighbourhood outings they had attended together—behaviour that had also embarrassed her at the time. Had she assumed love was blind, that a gentleman of intelligence would not notice her family's faults, as she did herself?

The more she replayed their argument in her mind, the more she realized that, although he seemed to be angry at the time, his replies could have been fueled by distress, as well. How deeply had her reproofs wounded him?

Had she wronged him so badly she could not expect to earn his forgiveness?

A feeling akin to panic rose in her chest.

Jane cleared her throat, and Elizabeth flinched. She had forgotten her sister was in the room.

Jane asked, "Do you regret refusing him, Lizzy?"

Elizabeth stared at Jane. *Do I?*

A knock on the door interrupted her thoughts. Jane rose and opened it. Their aunt stepped into the room.

"The men from your uncle's warehouse are here to help load the trunks. Did you finish packing?" Mrs. Gardiner asked.

Jane nodded.

Elizabeth answered, "I only have to lock my trunk."

Mrs. Gardiner smiled. "Shall we collect Miss Lucas and take a short walk down the street to the churchyard while they complete their task?"

Both young ladies agreed.

Jane followed Mrs. Gardiner from the room. As Elizabeth slipped into her pelisse and bonnet, she expected to spend quite a few more sleepless nights questioning her behaviour.

Chapter 3

As Darcy hurried through his ablutions, he planned his day. He had allowed too much time to pass since he discovered his error in judgement concerning Bingley and Miss Bennet. A longer delay was unacceptable. He would set things to rights this very day.

The butler found him preparing to leave the house. "Sir, the post just arrived."

Darcy reached for the letters and moved into a parlour off the entry hall, seeking the light of a window. The missive on top came from his aunt and uncle's estate in Derbyshire, and he recognized the script as that of his aunt, Lady Adelaide Fitzwilliam. She wrote that the earl's health had worsened again. Darcy's heart sunk heavily in his chest.

Next, he opened a letter from his cousin, the former Lady Bianca Fitzwilliam, who was currently with her new husband in Virginia on their wedding trip, arranged so she could meet the family of her husband's American mother. Could the newlyweds return in time to see Bianca's father before it was too late?

Lady Bianca wrote:

> *Dear Fitzwilliam,*
>
> *I thank you for your recent communication informing me of my father's illness. I regret to inform you that while Bartholomew was in the process of hurrying our return, he suffered an unfortunate accident. After several days of suffering, my husband passed on.*
>
> *Now that Bartholomew is gone, my situation here is unendurable. I would like to come home, but I fear travelling by ship without a gentleman's protection. While Bartholomew's family would be happy to be rid of me, they are unwilling to offer me assistance in any way.*

A Lesson Hard Learned

I realize my brothers are unable to escort me home. I beg of you to come for me, dear cousin.

Yours, etc.,

Bianca

The news of the death of Darcy's friend came as a shock. He dropped into a nearby chair. A number of memories of pleasant times they had shared on the debate team at school, fencing, and at gatherings with friends came to mind. Bartholomew would be sorely missed by many.

He examined Bianca's note once again, briefly wondering why she did not call on her brother Richard to come for her. Yes, he had recently taken a leave from the Army to visit with their Aunt Catherine in Kent, but surely his general would have understood and granted another leave of absence for a family emergency such as this. Perhaps Bianca was afraid he would not be given time enough with the family when their father passed away?

It was no matter. Of course he would attend Bianca.

He shook off the shock of his friend's death and turned over the third letter. The sender could not be mistaken—only Bingley would scrawl the direction this poorly. It was a wonder the letter was delivered at all.

The news Bingley imparted was frustrating at best. He had penned his note just before he left London this morning, gone to Scarborough to visit family. Relieved his friend indicated his relation's address, Darcy decided to send Bingley news of Bartholomew's passing and inform him he must delay their house party at Pemberley until he returned from America. He dared not relay the information about Miss Bennet through a letter, though he would mention he wished to speak to Bingley as soon as was possible.

Perhaps it was better this way?

When they both returned to Town, if his friend continued to show signs of being affected by the loss of Miss Bennet, he would gladly admit to the failure in his conclusions regarding the lady's affections. If it meant his friend's aching heart would heal, as well as Miss Bennet's, he would concede to his mistake.

But mayhap he would not have to tell Bingley at all? Bingley would have opportunities to spend time with other ladies. If he was no longer interested in Miss Bennet by then, so much the better. Why risk such a long-standing acquaintance?

Darcy gasped and rose from his chair. The effects of the dream were already fading. If he was not careful, he would fall back into old habits. He could not allow it!

No matter what happened—even if Bingley was engaged to someone else when Darcy returned from America—Darcy *would* tell Bingley of his errors in judgement during their time in Hertfordshire. Even if it meant losing Bingley's friendship in the process.

Darcy stared out the window for several minutes, planning all he would have to accomplish before he departed for America. He had a few stops to make this morning, and the sooner, the better. Whenever his man could get him on a ship leaving harbour, he needed to be prepared. And he would have to arrange permissions for his steward to handle all his business matters while he was away.

Making his way to his study, he rang for the butler and began writing. When Parkman appeared, Darcy held up a finger indicating he should wait as he signed his letter.

"This is for Lady Adelaide; send it express to Matlock as soon as possible. Also, Hughes should pack my trunks appropriate for a voyage to America. Dispatch a man to the docks to procure passage on the first ship going to the general area of Virginia. Speed is of the essence, not comfort. I am unsure as to when I will return, though I shall not dally in America. If I must, I will wait for more comfortable accommodations for our return trip, as I will be escorting Lady Bianca home. Miss Darcy and Mrs. Annesley shall go to Matlock to stay with our aunt and uncle whilst I am away. Have my sister's maid commence their packing. When Miss Darcy returns from the modiste, please inform her and her companion I must speak to them as soon as I return from my business in Town." He rose from his chair and picked up his gloves. "I planned to walk to my attorney's office, but since there is little time, have the carriage readied."

"Sir, your attorney is not in his office on Fridays."

Darcy closed his eyes and took a deep, calming breath. He dashed off a quick note to his attorney, informing Mr. Lynsey he would like to take advantage of the man's offer to stop by his home whenever necessary. "Will you send a man to Lynsey's house on Gracechurch Street with this letter immediately? I will return here to hear his answer after I make a few stops." Once the note was sealed, he began another. "And send a boy to the Clayworths' home with this. I must decline their invitation to dine tonight." He looked up at Parkman. "Send in Mrs. Martin."

Parkman bowed and left the room as Darcy wrote another note to Cassidy, his steward in London. Mrs. Martin knocked just as he sealed it.

"Ah, Mrs. Martin, have you been brought up to date on what must be done?" He waited for the housekeeper to answer in the affirmative before continuing. "Since I have business which I cannot delay until I return from America, Mr. Cassidy and I shall take a tray in my study this evening." He waved his hand, gesturing to the mounds of papers on his desk and raised his eyebrows. "Keep us well supplied with coffee and tea. We shall work well into the night so he may know how to act while I am away." He took up one stack. "Respond to these invitations. Tell them I will be unable to attend for I have been called out of the country unexpectedly."

Mrs. Martin took the correspondence. "Yes, sir. Will Hughes accompany you to America?"

Darcy vacillated. He hated to drag his valet with him across the Atlantic, but he might need him. "Yes. Please inform him that he should pack a trunk for himself, as well." Glancing at the clock, he pulled on one glove. "I must not linger any longer."

"Yes, sir." Mrs. Martin curtsied. Following her from the room, Darcy quit the house.

After visiting shops to acquire a few things he might need while away, he had his driver pull up at Darcy House. The footman approached the carriage directly, delivering a note from Mr. Lynsey, which said he was always welcome to call on him at his home. He tapped the roof three times with his cane, and the carriage lurched to a start.

The rhythmic clip-clop of hooves was mesmerizing. As Darcy stared out the window, he saw nothing.

Several weeks ago in Kent, as he was waiting to be announced at Hunsford Parsonage, he had happened to see a letter on the table in the entranceway addressed to Miss Jane Bennet in London. The exact address had stood out to him because he recognized it as being on the same block as his attorney's home. It was not in Cheapside, where Miss Bingley and Mrs. Hurst often insisted the Bennets' relations in trade resided, but near to it.

Guilt pinched at his soul as the coach made its way across town to Lynsey's residence. He could have easily written what needed to be said in a note and left it at the attorney's office, but if he went to Lynsey's home, there was a slight possibility he would catch a glimpse of Elizabeth. It would ease his mind a great deal if that were so, for he knew he would not be comfortable without seeing her—alive—after that dream.

Chapter 4

Darcy's eyes searched the street as his carriage moved past the address he remembered from Elizabeth's letter to her sister. The residence was well-maintained and substantially larger than he anticipated for a man in trade. Mr. Gardiner's business ventures were clearly successful.

He felt Providence had smiled upon him at seeing there was nowhere for the carriage to stop in front of Lynsey's home. Darcy knocked on the ceiling and directed the driver to circle the block, stating he would exit the carriage at the head of the road. Darcy leaned back against the seat and sighed. The tactic would force him to walk past the Gardiners' home. It was the best he could manage on short notice.

Disembarking, he paced slowly down the opposite side of Gracechurch Street without diverting his attention from the Gardiners' residence, where a carriage now stood. Two men were occupied with loading and securing trunks atop the conveyance.

A lady, a few years older than himself, exited the house, trailed by Miss Bennet and Miss Lucas. Relief filled him, and his breath caught at the most beautiful vision he had ever seen—Elizabeth—as she followed the young women. Behind her was a gentlemanly-looking man who he assumed was her uncle.

The sight of Elizabeth acted upon him like a magnet, and before he knew what he was about, Darcy had already crossed the street.

Elizabeth's emerald-coloured pelisse matched her eyes exactly, enhancing a sparkle of good humour as she spoke to her sister. He approached the curb as Elizabeth turned to face him. Her gaze locked with his own, and his heart rejoiced.

He could not make out the emotions that flitted across her face before she averted her eyes. She looked at everything but him. Perhaps that alone was enough to confirm her opinion of him. After reading his message, written with such venom, how could Elizabeth do anything but despise him even more than she had before?

He should not have approached her.

His chest ached with his apology, impossible to voice at present.

Mr. Gardiner cleared his throat. Darcy turned towards the remainder of the party and bowed. "Good morning, Miss Bennet, Miss Elizabeth, Miss Lucas."

All three ladies of his acquaintance curtsied, but their expressions varied. Elizabeth blushed. Miss Lucas stared with wide-eyed astonishment. Miss Bennet smiled.

A pang of remorse spread through him as he noticed Miss Bennet's physical state—pale and considerably thinner than the last time he saw her.

After an uncomfortable silence, Jane Bennet replied, "Good morning, Mr. Darcy. May I introduce to you my aunt, Mrs. Madeline Gardiner, and my uncle, Mr. Edward Gardiner? We have been staying with them whilst in London." She glanced at the house from which they just stepped away.

The newly introduced members of the party bowed and curtsied. He stepped forward and shook Mr. Gardiner's hand.

The usual stiffness that crept through his person when amongst those he did not know came over him. In an effort to stay true to his resolution, he struggled to push it away. "The pleasure is mine." He gestured down the street. "I was just on my way to speak to my attorney, who is at home today..." His breath failed him when Elizabeth met his gaze.

"Ah, Mr. Lynsey?" Mr. Gardiner asked with good cheer. "A fine fellow. I benefit from his services myself."

Darcy nodded. All conversation seemed to be at an end, a sure signal he should make his farewells.

His heart pounded as he drank in Elizabeth's visage one last time, unsure of when, or even *if*, he would see her again.

14

Her enchanting voice pronounced his name. "Mr. Darcy, we were about to take a short stroll before boarding the coach to return to Hertfordshire." Elizabeth smiled at him. "Would you care to join us?"

He could not resist the opportunity to spend a few minutes more in her company.

~%~

Elizabeth's heart stopped beating when she found Darcy standing before her. After the way she had treated him, she had not thought they could ever be friends... not until she looked into his eyes. A pleasant warmth spread throughout her being, and she had to look away lest her knees turn weak.

Was there a chance he still cared for her, or was she only seeing what she wished to see?

The thought surprised her. How had her opinion of him changed so suddenly?

The answer came unbidden. He had caught her interest the moment she first laid eyes upon him at the Assembly Ball in Meryton, but she was hurt too deeply by his rejection to admit her attraction. She had spent the next several weeks fascinated with the gentleman, examining his every look, his every word, his every gesture, sketching his character in an attempt to convince herself he was the last man on earth she could ever be prevailed upon to marry… all because she overheard him say she was not handsome enough to tempt him to dance.

Good heavens! Her first impression had clouded every subsequent encounter with him from that day forward.

She felt herself blush furiously and had to work to keep these thoughts from showing on her features—at least for now. There would be plenty of time to examine her feelings while on her daily walks once she arrived home.

When it seemed as if Darcy was about to make his goodbyes, panic enveloped her. Elizabeth asked if he would join them for their walk. He seemed pleased by her request and accepted.

Mr. and Mrs. Gardiner crossed the road first, with Jane and Maria close behind them, leaving Elizabeth with Darcy. When she had made the invitation, she had not thought of how they would split up. Though this arrangement was agreeable to her, she was afraid he would think she had managed it this way on purpose. As they crossed the street, she clasped her hands behind her back and looked away from him to hide another blush. Before long, Jane and Maria were beyond hearing distance.

The two began to speak simultaneously. Darcy gestured that she should go first.

Unable to look at him, she stared ahead as she spoke. "Mr. Darcy, I read..." She hesitated when a couple passed them on the walkway, headed in the other direction. She should not directly mention his letter. "Please, allow me to apologize for what I said the last time we met. I understand much better now."

His step faltered, and she turned slightly as he caught up. "I was about to apologize for the things I said to *you*, and for the tone of the—"

She turned abruptly to warn him not to speak of it, and he seemed to change what he was going to say.

"I should have waited until my temper cooled before attempting to justify my opinions. It was badly done."

She shook her head. "It may be that, at first, I did not accept your explanations with grace, but now, all is clear. I believe I needed to hear it in exactly that way to come to understand myself, sir."

"To understand *yourself*?"

"Yes." She did not elaborate.

They reached the end of the street and followed the others into the churchyard. A group of trees overhung a lawn, an informal flower garden, and a path leading around a small pond—a bit of the country in the middle of a bustling city. When visiting her relations, Elizabeth brought the Gardiners' children here as often as time and the weather made possible.

From of the corner of her eye, she could see Darcy was staring at her. He spoke again. "I must leave England—to collect my cousin from Virginia."

She turned her head to meet his gaze. "America?"

He nodded. "Yes. She married a long-time school friend of mine. Since his mother was an American, he took her to meet that half of his family for their honeymoon trip. Unfortunately, he recently died as the result of an accident, leaving my cousin stranded there. I will escort her home."

Elizabeth was surprised at the sudden unhappiness that settled over her. She knew it was not in bereavement of a man she had never heard of before. Her sorrow was for the loss of Darcy—he was leaving England just when she realized she might have made a terrible error in refusing him!

But then, perhaps it was for the best they lose touch again. What gentleman would swallow his pride and propose a second time after such a refusal?

This overwhelming desire for him to do so astonished her.

She drew in a deep breath and said, "Your cousin is fortunate to have you as a relation. Many would not be willing to travel across the sea, even in a time of need."

He coloured. "There is no one else who can manage it at this time. After being away from his duties to the Crown for so long while in Kent, Colonel Fitzwilliam cannot go quite yet. His elder brother must tend to his father's business since the earl is very ill."

"I am sorry to hear it. The Earl of Matlock is a good man."

Darcy seemed surprised. "You know my uncle?"

"Not personally, but I read my father's newspapers whenever I can. Your uncle has supported many good causes in Parliament."

Darcy stared at her.

She looked away from him. "Yes, I know it is shocking that a lady should follow politics."

"On the contrary. I find it impressive."

She turned at once to examine his countenance. His expression proved his words were in earnest.

After a few moments of silence, he said in an awkward tone, "Miss Elizabeth. I must tell you... I have not met Bingley since returning from Kent. He is spending some time with relatives in Scarborough." He paused. "I am afraid I shall not be able to speak to him until I return to England."

Elizabeth nodded in response. It warmed her soul to know he would correct his error. To change the subject, she asked, "Do you know the village of Lambton?"

"Yes, it is but five miles from Pemberley."

She gestured towards where Mr. and Mrs. Gardiner had stopped near the entrance to the churchyard. "My aunt spent her childhood there."

The smile that spread across his features made her heart take flight. Struck by how handsome he was, she had to look away.

"When you introduced Mrs. Gardiner, she seemed familiar. I must have seen her in the village."

They caught up to the remainder of the party, and Darcy asked, "Mrs. Gardiner, Miss Elizabeth tells me you hail from Lambton?"

"Why, yes, Mr. Darcy, I do. Actually, when I was very small, my father leased a tenant farm at Pemberley, but when his older brother passed, he took over my grandfather's shop in the village. I have not returned to the area since my marriage, but I still have many connexions there. Mr. Gardiner and I will travel to the Lake District this summer, and we plan to stop at Lambton for a visit."

The two continued to discuss the area surrounding Lambton and Pemberley for a minute or two.

Mr. Gardiner joined in. "My father-in-law used to boast that the fishing near Lambton was the best to be had. It has been far too long since I have had the opportunity to cast a line. I am looking forward to spending some time there."

"I have never experienced better sport than at Pemberley. My sister and I usually summer at our estate, but I fear this year, we will be quite late in our visit as I will be away from England. Mr. Gardiner, you are welcome to take advantage of the lakes and streams at Pemberley. I will send a note to my groundskeeper, Mr. Jones, informing him to expect you. He can provide the proper equipment if you do not wish to carry it along with you on your journey."

Mr. Gardiner smiled widely. "That is kind of you, sir. If time permits, it will be a great pleasure."

Jane caught Elizabeth's gaze and raised one eyebrow almost imperceptibly. Elizabeth widened her eyes. When she again looked at Darcy, she realized he had been watching her. Her cheeks burned.

Darcy made his goodbyes to everyone, ending with Elizabeth. "I wish you a pleasant trip home, Miss Elizabeth."

"And I hope you have an uneventful voyage. May you return to England safely, Mr. Darcy."

He seemed to hesitate for a moment before holding out his hand. Taking the hint, Elizabeth placed her hand in his. He bowed over it. A shiver passed up her spine, but she was unsure whether it was from the slight pressure he applied to her fingers before letting go or the hunger and yearning in his eyes when he did so. She could not look away from his form as he tipped his hat and turned to walk in the direction of Mr. Lynsey's residence.

Mr. Gardiner cleared his throat. "Well, that was a very interesting *stroll*, Lizzy."

"Yes..." she whispered, still staring after Darcy. At her uncle's chuckle, Elizabeth blinked to clear her thoughts. "We met Mr. Darcy last winter when he stayed at Netherfield Park with his friend, Mr. Bingley."

Her uncle exchanged a knowing look with his wife. "We will meet you back at the house." He held out one arm to Jane and the other to Maria.

As he escorted the two young ladies out of the churchyard, her aunt threaded her arm through Elizabeth's and held her back. The light in her aunt's eyes danced with amusement. She gestured to the path, and the two began another turn around the pond.

"We heard all about Mr. Bingley through several communications from your mother, in which she described Mr. Darcy as proud, indifferent, and quite unpleasant. Yet this morning, his behaviour was unlike we were led to expect—generous, even, offering your uncle access to his grounds for sport. We were also informed of your opinion of Mr. Darcy, but *that* account was quite different from what we have just witnessed, dear."

"What do you mean?"

"Lizzy, if that gentleman is not in love with you, I will never trust my judgement again."

"Aunt!"

"Do you have an understanding with Mr. Darcy?"

"I..." she swallowed hard. "No, I do not." She shook her head. "My mother was correct about my opinion of him last winter. But at Easter, he was visiting his aunt, Lady Catherine de Bourgh, who is Mr. Collins's patroness."

"And you were staying with the Collinses," her aunt observed.

Elizabeth nodded. "As a result of further... *exploration* of his character, I find my opinion of him has greatly improved. He is not the man I thought him to be last year."

"If it is of any consequence, I must say your mother's description of the gentleman puzzled me exceedingly. As you can imagine, the village of Lambton is quite dependent upon Pemberley for its livelihood. I have heard only that the current Mr. Darcy is kind, generous, and fair. Many in the surrounding area thank God every day for his being the master of the estate. Even Jane was not as liberal in her praise as is she usually her custom. It was almost as if you all were writing to me of a different man. The tales I received in letters from Longbourn did not match any description that I have ever heard from my friends. But then, sometimes people act so differently when amongst strangers… though I saw no evidence of that today."

Elizabeth stared off into the distance for a moment, her aunt's last words reminding her of a conversation she had had with the gentleman himself while dining at Rosings. He had said he could not speak easily with strangers, and in a round-about way, she had told him that discomfort did not excuse him from being civil to others.

She stifled a gasp. Had he taken her advice?

Elizabeth took a deep, calming breath before speaking again. "Today, his behaviour was everything that is good and right."

Mrs. Gardiner smiled. As they rounded the pond, she gestured towards the exit to the street, and they headed in that direction. "Perhaps you should freshen up before departing. We shall have plenty of time to discuss this further in June when you accompany us on our trip to the Lakes."

Elizabeth beamed. "I am certain Father will write to uncle soon with permission for me to go with you. I so look forward to it."

Chapter 5

~SIX WEEKS LATER – Longbourn Estate, Hertfordshire

Jane glanced at the closed trunk and opened her eyes wide. "Oh, you are finished. I am sorry I was unable to offer my assistance earlier, Lizzy. Mama had need of me."

Elizabeth crossed the space between them and took Jane's hands in her own. "Are you certain you do not mind if I go along on this trip to Derbyshire with Aunt and Uncle Gardiner?"

"Lizzy, please go. I accompanied them last summer to the shore. It is now your turn. Besides, I will be so busy looking after our young cousins, I will barely have time to miss you."

Elizabeth knew their mother would, at least, have less time to discuss Jane's *loss* of Bingley as she would keep to her rooms to avoid the noise of the children. Perhaps being engaged with the Gardiner children would do Jane some good after all. "Do you have everything you need in the old schoolroom?"

Jane nodded. "Yes. Our young cousins are such dears, and I am certain Mary, Kitty, and Lydia will be of assistance in entertaining them."

In an effort to stifle the urge to disagree, Elizabeth turned away and busied herself with locking her trunk. She knew from experience the previous summer that seventeen-year-old Mary would be stricter than mild-mannered Jane, but still a great help with the children. On the other hand, their youngest sisters, Kitty and Lydia, were spoilt by their mother and misbehaved more often than the Gardiners' much younger offspring. Although Kitty was sixteen and Lydia was a year younger, Elizabeth feared when they *helped*, Jane would have five to look after instead of only three. She expected that as long as they stayed in the school room, all would be well. Elizabeth had spoken to Mary once about accompanying Jane and the children when they took their daily exercise, but she would make it a point

He tightened his eyes. There must be more under the surface of what she said, but he could not detect what it was. "We shall return as soon as possible."

"The first month we were here was difficult enough when Bartholomew was in good health. Though they accepted Bartholomew as family through his mother, his relations despised the British and refused to tolerate my presence. My title meant nothing to them. My lineage seemed to infuriate them. I wished to stay in my rooms, but my husband refused to go anywhere without me, trying to force their acceptance." Her frown deepened. "Now, with Bartholomew gone, his family will not even make an attempt at civility."

He had heard a similar tale from an acquaintance who had returned to England recently. Perhaps he had been wrong to suspect her. Still... there was something in her countenance telling him she was holding something back. "They asked you to leave the plantation?"

Bianca shook her head. "No, but it was torture to remain amongst them, which is why you find me here, at the hotel. I have remained in my rooms most of the time since Bartholomew's manservant warned me the villagers speak of a war brewing between our countries."

"I am sorry you suffered abuse, Bianca, but that will continue no longer. You are now under my protection, and I will not stand for any mistreatment."

"I must return home, Fitzwilliam—to my own people. Everything here is tainted... spoiled." She placed her hand on his arm. "I must spend time with my father, before it is too late..." Her voice trailed off. "First Bartholomew... and now I will lose Father, too? Am I to be alone in the world?" Her tears began falling anew.

His heart ached for her grief. If it had been Georgiana, he would have embraced her, but having no idea what to do to pacify a grown woman exhibiting such hysterics, Darcy simply handed her his handkerchief and waited.

She calmed too suddenly, making him suspicious once again. Just in case, Darcy felt he should say something to distract her. "When I arrived in Virginia, I left a man at the port town of Alexandria, seeking return passage. We shall leave here the day after tomorrow and stay in Alexandria until we find a suitable conveyance to England."

"Thank you, dearest Fitzwilliam. I do not know if I could have survived much longer without you."

~%~

The Gardiners' coach pulled up the drive to Longbourn with several trunks loaded atop, and the Bennets came out to meet them. The children disembarked and hurried directly to greet their cousins while the parents lingered, speaking to their contemporaries.

Mrs. Bennet fanned herself with a handkerchief. "You are so late, Brother! I was sure you had met with some sort of accident on the road."

Mr. Gardiner chuckled. "With your own girls now grown, you forget that one is never on time when travelling with young children. I will warn you now to plan quite a bit of extra time before getting them out of the house to attend church, or else you will miss the service all together."

Since the adults would be staying only one night while the children would be in residence for several weeks, Mr. Gardiner and Mr. Bennet moved off to direct the servants as to which of the trunks should be unloaded. Lydia accompanied her mother into the house while Jane, Mary, and Kitty took the children for a march around the garden to dispel some of their pent-up energy after having been confined in the coach for so long a time.

Elizabeth remained behind with Mrs. Gardiner to watch the children play with Elizabeth's sisters. The gentlemen approached when they were no longer occupied.

Mr. Gardiner said, "I must apologize to you, Lizzy, for shortening our trip. I hope you are not too disappointed."

Elizabeth tried her best not to allow her smile to dim. Even though she had had a few days warning by letter, she still felt disappointment tugging at her heart. "After hearing so much of Derbyshire's beauties from Aunt, I am looking forward to seeing it. It shall be a delightful holiday, and we three shall make a very pleasant party."

Mrs. Gardiner took Elizabeth's hands and gave them a light squeeze in thanks.

Mr. Bennet chimed in, "Although I would not prevent Lizzy from going with you, I, for one, welcome the change in your plans if it means she will return home sooner." He turned to Elizabeth. "During your trip to Kent in the spring, I barely heard two words of sense spoken together. There is only so much silly conversation a man can tolerate with equanimity."

Mr. Gardiner clapped a hand onto his brother' shoulder. "I am certain spending more time than usual amongst your books was a hardship for you, Thomas."

Knowing her father would enjoy nothing more than spending all his free time in his library, Elizabeth fought back a grin.

Mr. Bennet nodded. "The only hardship I had to endure related to that subject was having to listen to my wife complain about it whenever I ventured out of my rooms."

"Perhaps the children would enjoy hearing you read to them, as you did when I was young." Those times were among her favourite memories from childhood. He had done so with Jane and Mary, as well, but had given up the practice when her youngest sisters could not sit still to listen. Recently, he had confided to her that he wondered if Kitty and Lydia would be less 'silly' now if he had continued his efforts.

Mr. Bennet raised one eyebrow. "Perhaps."

Chapter 6

Mr. Darcy entered the dressing room. "My cousin wishes to visit her husband's gravesite before we leave the area. The church is at least three-quarters of an hour drive from here, but I am unsure how long she will wish to remain there. We should return in time for our evening meal."

Hughes approached his master to assist with his greatcoat, then positioned a black mourning band to lay *just so* around his upper arm. "I have arranged for dinner to be served in Lady Bianca's sitting room, sir."

Mr. Darcy nodded. Although it seemed hotels here did not supply a sitting room for their guests, he had rented extra rooms on this floor so it would be more like home for his cousin. "I shall change when we return. Leave out what we will require in the morning, but see to it the remainder of my things are packed—except my writing desk. I will attend to that myself."

"Yes, Mr. Darcy."

"Since it may be several days more before we find passage on a ship suitable for a lady, please make certain the two letters on the platter in my room are posted to England. I am sure there is a ship leaving before we will be ready to do so—there were a few in port when we passed through. One message is to my steward and the other is to Georgiana. If there are any fees, have them added to the bill for the rooms. I will settle the account later today."

"Very good, sir."

Hughes saw his master leave his rooms before returning to his work. A while later, there was a knock upon the dressing room door and a maid entered. One of the women in the kitchen had explained that this servant girl's family had come to Virginia from Prussia. Although at times there had been some difficulties making themselves understood to one another, the maid spoke and comprehended English well enough for them to get by. "Post letters?" she pronounced carefully.

Hughes could not stop what he was doing without ruining the work he had spent the past quarter of an hour preparing. He answered, "Yes, on the table by the door." He gestured towards the bedchamber.

She curtsied before disappearing.

Hughes noted the sound of the door to the corridor closing as he continued with his packing.

An hour later, he came into the room and found the two letters remained where his master had left them.

Thinking the girl had not understood him after all, Hughes brought them down to the front desk personally.

~%~

His task taking longer than expected, Darcy found their meal waiting for them when they returned. Once changed into a clean set of clothes, he joined his cousin to dine. After the meal, he made his excuses and retired to his rooms.

Time spent with Bianca was rapidly becoming a burden to be borne.

Over the past two days, he had listened patiently to his cousin speak in detail of her wedding trip. Before she had married Bartholomew, Bianca had seemed in love with his friend, but now her discourse was filled with constant criticism of her late husband and statements bordering on ridicule. Darcy now believed Bianca's behaviour during their engagement had been an act. Mayhap she had been in love with the notion of becoming a countess instead of with the earl himself?

As she went on and on cataloguing her misfortunes, each phrase she uttered uncomfortably reminded him that, since this journey interrupted an opportunity—perhaps even his last chance—to begin anew with Elizabeth, the marriage of convenience Bianca described might be all *he* had to look forward to in life.

At the end of these sessions, Darcy could find no relief except during that brief interlude while penning all that gnawed at his mind and heart, as he intended to do now.

Discovering a statement of costs incurred at the hotel in place of the journal pages he had written during the sea voyage and the days since he had arrived in America, he moved towards the dressing room.

"Thank you for collecting the bill, Hughes, but I told you I would pack my writing table myself. Where did you put the pages that were on top?"

Hughes maintained his stoic expression. "I would never touch your private papers, sir. The desk was clear when I left the bill there."

Darcy re-entered the bedchamber and searched through the drawers of the writing desk, but still did not find the papers. His heart began to beat faster. "Hughes!"

The servant approached.

"There was a stack of papers right here, tied with a ribbon. Where are they?"

"I saw them this morning as I dusted, sir, but they were not there later in the day. I thought you had put them away before you went out."

Darcy shook his head. "I lost track of the time and was late in meeting my cousin, so I left them right here. Who else was in this room today?"

"The maid came in to get the post," Hughes took a quick breath. "She left without taking the two letters, which I thought strange at the time, since collecting them was her stated purpose. I took your correspondence down myself." He blinked. "Sir, did you send a parcel by post today?"

Distracted, Darcy searched through the drawers in his portable desk. "No, why?"

"Have you examined the bill, Mr. Darcy?"

A sense of doom raced down Darcy's spine. He snatched up the bill. A parcel was charged on today's date. Realization hit him like a blow to his gut—the maid had taken his journal pages along with the letter atop them instead of the missives he meant to post.

In too much of a panic to do it himself, he commanded, "Get down there and retrieve that parcel. NOW!"

Darcy stopped pacing the room when Hughes returned an hour or so later, in a surprisingly dishevelled state.

"I am sorry, sir, but I could not recover the parcel. When I tried to stop the late post, I was accused of being a bandit and almost shot. After the innkeeper rescued me, I explained the maid's error. It took quite a bit of convincing, as well as a few coins to persuade him, but the post collector allowed us to search through the bags. I am sorry to report your parcel must have been in this morning's post. It is gone, sir."

Darcy closed his eyes. Even though he took several deep breaths, he could not calm his mind well enough to think. He gestured for Hughes to leave him.

Hughes obeyed without delay.

Darcy stood at the window for a long time, staring out into the darkness in the general direction of England.

Heaven help him! Had the maid really sent his *journal*, of all things, to Elizabeth?

Elizabeth's opinion of him was low enough already. Judging by what she had said upon their opportune meeting in London, he felt he had been forgiven for the impropriety of handing her a note at Rosings. But what would she think of him when she received a parcel such as this, containing all of his personal writings?

He had left England in a hurry and had forgotten to pack his new journal book. Alternatively, he had begun to keep it on single sheets of paper. These sheets were kept bound along with a note he had written the night after he had seen Elizabeth in London.

Within the document, he explained all that he had not been able to say that day in London. He apologized for his poor judgement and lack of manners he had displayed during his shameful excuse for a proposal at Hunsford cottage at Easter, as well as in his previous letter. Most importantly, he explained it was of vital importance to him that she knew he was attempting to mend his ways.

On a whim, he had addressed the missive to Miss Elizabeth Bennet, Longbourn Estate, Hertfordshire, but in the next moment, he knew it could never be posted. She being a single lady, and he, most definitely not her fiancé, if a letter were discovered, it would only cause a scandal—and it certainly would be discovered if it went by post. Doing so would ruin her reputation.

If he had had the pleasure of meeting with her again after returning to England, he would have found a way of passing it to her undetected, as he had dared to do once in the past just after she had refused him.

Now the missive had, in fact, been posted.

Worse yet, along with it went his journal pages, filled with his most intimate thoughts and dreams, and his hopes for the future—most of which involved her. The dream which had convinced him to change his ways had been detailed as well.

With a heavy sense of mortification, Darcy fell into a nearby chair.

How could this have happened?

Perhaps she had only sent the letter addressed to Elizabeth, but left the other pages here somewhere in the room?

He searched his writing desk once more and found nothing but blank pages. He proceeded to tear apart the room, moving furniture and all. Rushing out into the hallway, he opened a closet where he had seen a maid store a broom, and he took it. Kneeling on the floor, he used the broom to search under the bed. Nothing but a bit of dust. He stood in the middle of the room and ran a hand through his hair.

It was gone—all of it—gone to England. Posted to Miss Elizabeth Bennet.

Exhausted, Darcy righted the mattress, lay upon it, and closed his eyes. Sentences, phrases he had written appeared in his mind, unbidden. His eyes snapped open, and he stared at the ceiling.

One of the things he loved most about Elizabeth was her quick and intelligent mind. He imagined her conscience and her determination to do what was right battling with her curiosity to read what he had said about her.

Which would win?

Would she continue reading?

What would he do in her position... if he had somehow obtained *her* journal? He groaned with the realization that after a struggle against temptation, in the end, he would read it.

But what would be her reaction?

Would she turn the parcel over to her father?

He swallowed. If so, Mr. Bennet would, no doubt, insist they marry, and Darcy would have Elizabeth as his wife.

What would be her response to being forced into a marriage with him? Would she despise him? Would she fear him because of what he had written?

Had he no hope of winning her once he returned to England?

And the ribbon! The ribbon tied around the pages had been one he found just outside her room last autumn while they had both been staying at Netherfield Park, the home of his friend Bingley.

After all this time, it still had the slightest trace of her scent, but even if it had not, he would have cherished it forever.

His soul ached to have lost it. Now he had nothing of her save the memories that haunted him day and night.

Darcy shook his head. Time would tell, and until it did, there was nothing more to be done.

"So be it."

He hugged a feather pillow to his chest and drifted off into a restless sleep.

~%~

~ Two weeks later

While Mr. and Mrs. Gardiner preferred to tour churches and the manor houses of the great estates, the couple were well aware that Elizabeth would rather walk the estates' grounds and gardens or visit places which boasted of natural beauty, such as Baslow, Curbar, and Heathersage. Therefore, the trio alternated where they would stop.

During their stay at a village near Matlock, they were told the house was not available for tours since the earl was ill and the family in residence, but they would be allowed to tour the grounds. When Mr. Gardiner applied to the groundskeeper, the man recommended they take a specific footpath from the main garden in order to view a beautiful waterfall. As the small group strolled along, Mrs. Gardiner, not being as good a walker as Elizabeth, fell behind, leaning heavily upon her husband's arm. They were about to turn back when Elizabeth declared she could hear the waterfall. She turned a corner in the path and there it was, quite grand, standing at least five times the height of the tallest man she had ever seen.

"It is beautiful!" She dashed on ahead of them.

Mrs. Gardiner called out, "Lizzy! Please, wait for us."

Elizabeth was too enthralled to take heed.

She stepped onto a relatively dry boulder jutting into the stream and carefully made her way out to stand directly across from the waterfall. The direction of the breeze changed, blowing a mist across her face. She closed her eyes. Her skin tingled as the tiny droplets fell, hypnotizing her. She filled her lungs with the scent of the woods all around her.

A Lesson Hard Learned

This was life!

"Lizzy," Mr. Gardiner yelled over the thunderous sound of water dropping into the pool below. "Come down, dear. How did you manage to climb up there? Do be careful—"

Elizabeth turned too abruptly, and her heavy walking boots slipped on the rock face. She righted herself and looked around her. When the breeze had changed direction, not only had her skin been misted by the water, but the boulders had, as well. It was quite wet and slippery now.

She locked gazes with her uncle. "It was dry before."

"Stay where you are. I will find some way to assist you." Moving hurriedly, he disappeared into the woods and returned holding a long branch. "Here, take hold of this."

As Elizabeth reached for it, all became a blur of confusion, everything tumbling around her.

Pain exploded as her ankle snapped

Icy cold water splashed over her.

Her aunt screamed.

Blackness enveloped her.

Chapter 7

"When we talked 'afore, ye' said ye' didn't wanna come wit' us, Mista' Darcy, since we ain't got no fancy lodgings on board." Captain Mott spit some tobacco over the side of his ship into the water. He lifted a hand, darkened and weathered from the sun and sea, running his fingers through what little thinning grey hair he had left in a half-halo around his head, and then moved his hand to shade his eyes.

Darcy's gut tightened. There had been problems between the British and Americans, and the scent of war hung thick in the air all around them. Almost nobody would accept British citizens into their places of business. They had been fortunate Darcy had enough gold with him to bribe the hotel manager in Alexandria or they would never have found a place to shelter them.

Not only was Bianca depending on him, but Hughes, Bianca's maid, and Bartholomew's valet, as well. It was imperative they leave American soil before the war began in earnest.

"Captain Mott, I beg of you... at this point, I shall welcome any British accommodations I can find. As long as Lady Bianca, the Countess of Lashbrook, has private quarters to share with her maid, I will sleep anywhere, as will my valet and the lady's manservant. We *must* return to England with all due haste."

Captain Mott's pale green eyes were clear and sparkled with intelligence. Darcy wondered why this man had not gone into some other line of business. There was a sense of kindness and humour about him which comforted Darcy, but he reminded himself to remain on his guard. These were smugglers, after all.

Mott chuckled. "Why not? We're usually takin' goods back and forth, but we take people now and then—as long as ye' pay the price we talked about. Gotta' be in gold, too. But we'll be expectin' you men to help out if you're needed. Everyone's on edge with the war brewin'. Who knows what'll happen at sea."

Darcy held out his hand. "Agreed."

Mott shook it, sealing the deal.

"We're gonna take a round-about way back to England, Mista' Darcy. This time, everythin's on the up-and-up, but we know how to avoid bein' boarded. Don't want me whole crew bein' *convinced* to join the Navy and me supplies and ship *donated* to their cause." Mott winked. "It'll take longer for us to get to port, but we ain't run into any Navy ships goin' this way yet. They might 'o changed things up with war in the wind, though, so I can't promise nothin'. We'll land in Liverpool."

Darcy said, "That fits perfectly into my plans, Captain. It will be a shorter trip to Matlock from there."

Mott raised his eyebrows. "Matlock? 'Tis you or the lady any relation?"

"Lady Bianca is the earl's daughter."

Mott nodded. "You?"

"The earl is my uncle."

"Ye' should'a told me that 'afore." A broad smile spread across Mott's features. "The earl's one of our best customers."

Darcy widened his eyes with surprise.

"We'll have *two* cabins for ye', then. The ladies can stay in mine. Ye' and those other men can take the first mate's. We won't mind splittin' the extra gold ye'll be givin' us to get 'em." He winked again.

Darcy agreed, "That would be appreciated. Do you know where we can hire a cart to bring our trunks? There are not many locals who will do business with an Englishman at the moment."

"Aye, don't I know it." Mott turned to the largest man Darcy had ever seen—all muscle—and motioned that he should join them. The bear of a man bowed his head in greeting.

"We have a cart. Jeremiah here'll meet ye' at the hotel tomorrow 'afore sun up to get yer things. We sail at first light."

Darcy held out his hand once more. With the deepest of sincerity, he thanked Captain Mott for providing their passage home.

~%~

Lady Adelaide, the Countess of Matlock, and Miss Georgiana Darcy were strolling through the rose garden close to the house when they heard a number of raised voices.

Lady Adelaide let go her niece's arm and lifted her skirts, rushing towards the main house. Georgiana was considered tall, and her legs were long, but she struggled to keep up with her aunt, who towered over her. Both ladies halted when a maid hastened to meet them. She stopped short, making a slight curtsey.

Breathless, the maid began, "Beggin' your pardon, my lady—"

Lady Adelaide interrupted, "Is it the earl, Sarah?

"No, my lady. Lord Matlock's restin'. The head groundskeeper says a lady tourin' the estate got herself hurt down by the waterfall, ma'am. She hit her head, and her party can't wake her. The groundskeeper got a cart to bring her up to the house, but Mrs. Evans wants to know if that's all right and what you'd like to do with her."

"Oh, dear!" Georgiana cried.

Lady Adelaide closed her eyes and took a deep breath to compose herself, relieved her husband had not taken a turn for the worse. By the time she opened her eyes, she had a plan. "Of course. Run down to the stables and send a boy into the village for Mr. Brown. I will pass along instructions to Mrs. Evans myself."

Sarah curtsied and scurried off towards the stables.

"Come, Georgie. We will go in through the servants' door." As the ladies entered the bustling kitchen, all noise ended and a dozen kitchen maids curtsied low. The housekeeper rushed in to see what had caused the abrupt change in volume of the chatter and clatter.

"Ah, there you are, Mrs. Evans." Lady Adelaide hurriedly crossed the kitchen. "I have sent for the doctor. Have the men take the injured lady up to the Red Room in the guest wing. Find out how many are in her party and have rooms readied for them, as well. If there are ladies of the *beau monde* among them, we might have several women swooning by the end of the day." She turned to Georgiana and rolled her eyes. "You know how they all love to make a display, especially if another lady is garnering all the attention by having the audacity of becoming truly injured."

Georgiana pressed her lips together to stifle a smile.

The housekeeper said, "She is accompanied by a married couple, my lady."

Lady Adelaide turned back to the housekeeper. "Good. Place them in the Yellow and Blue Rooms across the hall from the Red Room. In the meantime, put water to boil, prepare bandages, and have the healing herb satchel sent up to her rooms, as well. Do we know the injured lady's name, Mrs. Evans?"

"Mr. Harris said her name is Miss Bennet, mistress. The others are Mr. and Mrs. Gardiner."

Georgiana gasped. "Miss Elizabeth Bennet? From Hertfordshire?"

Mrs. Evans shook her head. "I know not from where she hails, Miss. Excuse me." She began giving instructions to the kitchen maids to carry out their mistress's orders, and the usual noise of the kitchen resumed.

"Come, Georgie." Lady Adelaide moved towards the doorway to the corridor. Once they were in the house proper, the countess continued on in the direction of the front door, through which she expected the butler to bring the injured lady, since that staircase was not nearly as steep or narrow as the servants' staircase. "Do you know Miss Bennet, dear?"

Georgiana answered, "If she is Miss Elizabeth Bennet from Hertfordshire, I do not know her personally, but my brother spoke highly of her in his letters to me whilst he stayed at Mr. Bingley's estate, Netherfield Park. I believe her father's estate is called Longbourn. It is my understanding she has four sisters. Fitzwilliam was in company with her again when visiting Aunt Catherine at Easter."

Lady Adelaide raised an eyebrow. "How interesting. I had also received a note from him at that time, and she was mentioned, though I did not remember her name. At the time, I recall being shocked since I had never heard Fitzwilliam speak highly of any lady besides you."

Georgiana nodded emphatically, the blonde curls arranged to frame her face bouncing. "I have heard so much about her; I feel almost as if I know her."

Now Lady Adelaide raised both eyebrows. "*Very* interesting." She blinked a few times in quick succession. "And who are the Gardiners?"

"Brother never mentioned them."

The front door opened. The butler was followed by two men carrying a high-backed chair, held at such an angle, the lady was nearly lying down. A blanket was tucked around her, and a sheet was tied about her chest, lashing her to the chair so she would not fall as they carried her. Blood ran from her wet hair down one side of her face, and her raven-coloured curls were matted with it.

A couple followed. The man's clothing was wet, and his coat was stained with blood. The lady was quite pale and carried the injured lady's bonnet, her husband's hat, and a blood-soaked handkerchief.

After directing the butler to take Miss Bennet to the proper room, Lady Adelaide approached the couple.

"Mr. and Mrs. Gardiner? I am Adelaide Fitzwilliam, and this is my niece, Miss Georgiana Darcy. I have sent for the doctor. Rooms are being readied for your use, as well."

The Gardiners greeted the countess with a bow and curtsey. Mr. Gardiner spoke, "Thank you for your kind attentions, Lady Matlock. We apologize for the inconvenience."

Lady Adelaide gestured with her hand as if she were shooing away a fly. "It is no inconvenience. Since the housekeeper is busy at the moment, Georgiana and I will show you to your rooms."

Mrs. Gardiner said, "Thank you, Lady Matlock, but you must not go to any trouble to make up a room for me. I must go directly to Elizabeth. I will stay by her side until I am assure of her complete recovery."

Lady Adelaide exchanged a look with Georgiana at hearing the injured lady's name.

A tear escaped Mrs. Gardiner's eye. She almost wiped her face with her handkerchief but stopped just in time. Her eyes filled with tears again as she stared at the blood-soaked cloth. Georgiana retrieved another from a pocket of her pelisse and handed it to Mrs. Gardiner. She nodded her thanks.

"Of course you would wish to nurse your niece, Mrs. Gardiner, but you will require rooms, for you must also rest. Mr. Gardiner must change into something dry immediately. We do not want another illness to contend with." Lady Adelaide began to climb the stairs. "I will show you the way to the rooms where Miss Bennet will be staying."

Mr. Gardiner helped his wife up the staircase behind Lady Adelaide. Georgiana followed them up the two flights of stairs. The men who had carried Elizabeth were leaving the room as they approached. Lady Adelaide led the group inside.

Elizabeth was already laid out on the quilt which protected the bedcovers from her wet, bloody clothes, while two maids bustled around her, situating her more comfortably.

Lady Adelaide turned and said, "I am sorry, Mr. Gardiner, but you will have to leave now. We must undress Miss Bennet to prepare for the doctor's arrival. The footman stationed outside the door will show you to the Blue Room across the hall."

Mr. Gardiner frowned as though he loathed leaving his niece's side. His gaze locked with Mrs. Gardiner's. His wife nodded. He thanked the countess once again and quit the room, closing the door behind him.

Lady Adelaide began directing the maids immediately. Mrs. Gardiner shed her pelisse. Georgiana followed suit. Mrs. Gardiner moved to help the maids undress Elizabeth. Lady Adelaide stood by, taking Elizabeth's soiled clothing from them as required.

"May I do anything to assist, Aunt?" Georgiana asked. "Perhaps I can fetch one of my nightgowns so Miss Bennet may be changed into something dry?"

"Yes, dear Georgiana. That would be a great help."

~%~

As Georgiana left the room, she was surprised to find Mr. Gardiner already in clean clothing, pacing the hallway.

He stepped closer. "Is there any improvement, Miss Darcy? Has Elizabeth awakened?"

She shook her head. "No, sir. I am sorry, she has not. Excuse me, please. I am on an errand and must return without delay."

She hurried off to get her nightgown, thinking how lucky Miss Elizabeth Bennet was to have people who cared so much for her.

When she herself had fallen ill after all that had happened last summer, her brother, cousins, aunt, and uncle had behaved quite like Mr. and Mrs. Gardiner were doing now. Since then, she had deduced that knowing she was loved was a vital part of her recovery.

Miss Elizabeth Bennet was highly thought of by her brother. The sheer frequency of the lady's being mentioned in his letters proved she was important to him. Therefore, Georgiana was determined every attention should be paid to Miss Bennet to make sure the lady knew that all the people at Matlock cared for her.

Miss Bennet *must* recover, for her brother's sake, if nothing else.

At first, Georgiana chose her best nightgown, but thinking of all the blood she had seen, she realized it would be better to take the lady something less elaborate for now.

Upon her return, she said to Mr. Gardiner, who stood in the hallway outside Elizabeth's room, "I am sorry, Mr. Gardiner, but with all the confusion, I must assume no one has told you the Red Room has a private sitting room." She opened the door next to the bedchamber where Miss Bennet was staying. "Through this door." She turned to the footman stationed a few feet down the hall. "Roger, will you send for tea for Mr. Gardiner and a larger tray for Miss Bennet's room?" She turned back to Mr. Gardiner. "Perhaps some reading material? A newspaper?"

"Thank you, Miss Darcy. I feel rather helpless. If there is anything I can do..."

Georgiana shook her head. "At the moment, I do not think so, but I promise to send word if there is any change, sir."

She slipped through the door to Elizabeth's bedchamber.

Mrs. Madeline Gardiner cleaned the wounds on Elizabeth's arm and leg as the maids cleaned the blood and dirt away from the injury to Elizabeth's head. Mrs. Gardiner would never say so aloud, but she was surprised the countess and Miss Darcy remained in the room and even assisted in their efforts. She was impressed when Lady Adelaide even tried to empty the soiled water from the basins herself, only to have a maid insist that she be allowed to accomplish the task for her.

Mrs. Gardiner had heard only good of Lord and Lady Matlock. Experiencing the countess's behaviour herself proved it all true. For a member of the peerage to wish to personally take on menial tasks was a curiosity, but to do so for an injured stranger... the lady obviously had a singular personality.

The only other member of the upper crust she could think of who would have behaved in a similar manner was Lady Anne Darcy, this lady's late sister-in-law, and the mother of the other lady in the room.

Mrs. Gardiner glanced up from her task, her gaze brushing over Lady Adelaide and Miss Darcy before returning her attention to Elizabeth's wounds.

She expected Lady Anne would have gotten along well with this sister, and she most certainly would have been quite delighted with her daughter.

Chapter 8

Darcy stood at the rail of the *Gypsy's Promise*, beside the rest of his party. Although the voyage to America had been less than ideal for him, he had become accustomed to the sway of the ship with little effort on this crossing, as did his cousin's maid and Hughes. Bianca and her manservant, Fleming, had not adapted so well, and they had spent most of the day above board, keeping an eye on the horizon to help settle their stomachs.

Darcy deeply inhaled the sea air and stared across the calm water at the sunset. It was exquisite. The sky was clear except for a few wisps of clouds that seemed swept away from the sun with a broom. He marvelled as the red-orange light transformed into a deep rose, which eventually changed to lavender further away from the burning sphere. The ocean seemed afire with the reflection.

Georgiana, who appreciated a sunset or sunrise as much as he did, would have loved this scene. Being a lover of nature, Elizabeth, he suspected, have enjoyed it, as well.

The thought brought a wrinkle to his brow. What would she think of him for sending her a parcel?

The moment his cousin had been situated in the hotel in the city of Alexandra, he had sought out the postmaster. The man had remembered his letters and parcel because there had been a cargo ship leaving for England that afternoon. He had sent a man to rush them to the dock before they left port.

Though Darcy did not wish misfortune to fall upon anyone, and while he hoped his messages to Georgiana and his steward made it to England, he also longed for the parcel addressed to Elizabeth to somehow fall into the sea.

If his return address had been on the package, he doubted Mr. Bennet would hand it over to his daughter, though he was sure the gentleman would have read it himself. The thought made him shudder.

But the manager of the hotel had said he addressed the parcel himself. The man had not added a return address since he did not know from which room the maid had taken it. He had wrapped them in paper and written the address from the letter on the entire lot.

So, Darcy reasoned, with no return address, it was likely Elizabeth would assume the bundle was from a friend or relative. She would open it.

He prayed she would recognize his handwriting immediately and discard every page.

He shook his head. There was no sense in worrying, for it would be at least another month before that ship even docked off the shores of England. Indeed, he might never know her reaction.

He had made some strides at their meeting on his last day in England. The way she reacted to his presence at Gracechurch Street had been both a surprise and relief to him. She was more than civil... even friendly. It had given him hope.

But if Bingley did not decide to return to Netherfield, he did not know whether they would ever have reason to meet again.

Unless, of course, he purchased the lease on Netherfield from Bingley.

What reason could he give for doing so, other than to pay court to a woman who had previously refused him? That would seem insane.

Yet, he would find a way to woo her.

~%~

Mr. Gardiner, Lady Adelaide, and Georgiana all rose as Mrs. Gardiner and the doctor entered the sitting room.

"How fares my niece?" Mr. Gardiner asked the doctor.

Mrs. Gardiner moved to her husband's side. She shook her head in an attempt to get her frayed emotions under control.

Georgiana asked, "May I go in and sit with Miss Bennet until you are able to return to her?"

Mrs. Gardiner took a deep breath. "That would ease my mind a great deal, Miss Darcy. Thank you."

Lady Adelaide said, "I shall join my niece."

"Please stay, Lady Matlock. I believe you should hear what the doctor has to say since it concerns your household."

The countess nodded.

As soon as the door closed behind Georgiana, the doctor began, "Miss Bennet has suffered a severe blow to the head. Since she is unconscious, I have not been able to complete an evaluation of her speech and behaviour. At this point, I cannot even guess as to the extent of damage that has been done to her brain. I will not rule out that there may be bleeding within her skull, but there is also the chance that there may be very little injury at all. She has suffered a break in her ankle bone, but the leg itself and foot are sound. She should not be removed from here, at least until she regains consciousness, when I can assess her injuries further."

"Well, of course she will remain at Matlock. As will Mr. and Mrs. Gardiner," The countess raised her chin. "Do not dishonour me, Brown, by suggesting that I would order an injured lady from my home."

Mr. Brown's eyes almost popped from his head.

The countess narrowed her eyes at Mr. Brown for a moment, and then her expression transformed to one of sympathy as she met Mrs. Gardiner's gaze. "Your family are welcome to stay with us as long as is necessary, Mrs. Gardiner."

Mrs. Gardiner replied with a relieved smile. "I thank you. Will you please excuse me?" She turned to her husband. "I should change my clothing and return to my niece."

"Of course, my dear," Mr. Gardiner said. "Our trunks have been unloaded and brought up. I will show you our rooms. I must also write to my brother of Lizzy's accident, though I am not at all certain what I should say."

"It is during the few days after an injury like this that the patient's condition is the most..." Mr. Brown hesitated. "...*changeable*. Mrs. Gardiner tells me Miss Bennet's parents live several days' ride from here. It does not make sense to cause them undue concern. I suggest you wait to write your letter until we know more."

Lady Adelaide asked, "Are you saying Miss Bennet is not yet out of danger?"

Mr. Brown nodded. "Exactly so, your ladyship."

~%~

Georgiana moved aside a damp lock of hair that curled over the bandage across Elizabeth's forehead.

The scent of blood was much less apparent now that the lady had been washed, changed, and bandaged. Such a large amount of blood loss had been frightening to witness, but Georgiana knew from experience that a head wound bled more than did other injuries. Last summer, when her brother had confronted Mr. Wickham, accusing him of trying to elope with Georgiana only for her dowry of thirty thousand pounds, the villain had hit Fitzwilliam over the head with a vase before escaping out of the house and away from Ramsgate.

Georgiana shivered at the memory of that horrible day and pushed it from her thoughts.

As she studied Elizabeth's features, she tried to distract herself by remembering all the lovely things her brother had said about the lady in his communications to her. It was obvious Fitzwilliam had feelings of a romantic nature for this lady.

Georgiana's gaze wandered around the room. The maids were near the fireplace, sorting through Elizabeth's clothing and the linens they had used to clean her. It seemed they were sorting them into piles of what was ruined and what they thought they would be able to save. She leaned in to whisper, "Miss Bennet, I am Georgiana Darcy. It is a pleasure to meet you. Please, be well. My brother would be heartbroken if you do not awaken."

Just then, the door leading to the sitting room opened, and Mrs. Gardiner returned.

"Thank you for keeping watch over Lizzy, Miss Darcy."

"It was no trouble. I hope she recovers quickly... I have long been looking forward to meeting her."

Mrs. Gardiner raised her brows. "Have you?"

Georgiana said, "My brother has spoken of her in his letters."

Mrs. Gardiner smiled. "I had the pleasure of making Mr. Darcy's acquaintance when we met by chance in London, just before he left England. You both look so much like your parents."

Georgiana's countenance brightened. "Did you know them?"

Mrs. Gardiner pulled a chair close to the bed and sat near Georgiana. "I was reared at a tenant farm on the grounds of Pemberley, and then later at Lambton. I saw your father only from a distance, but I spent quite a bit of time with Lady Anne. To this day, I think of her often… and always with fondness. I was a student and later a teacher at the school for girls she established in the village. At least, I was until I married Mr. Gardiner. I understand you have continued her work?"

"Yes, I have," Georgiana said.

"Through my friends who still live in the area, I have heard that you and Mr. Darcy have carried on your parents' traditions of fair-mindedness and goodwill towards those who depend on the estate. I believe your parents would be proud of both you and your brother."

Tears filled the young lady's eyes. After spending some minutes feeling too emotional to speak, Georgiana excused herself.

Chapter 9

Over the past two days, Georgiana had re-read all of the letters she had received from her brother over the last several months, paying special attention to those penned while he was visiting at Netherfield and Rosings. He had not written nearly as often of any other lady as he did of Miss Elizabeth Bennet—ever—not even of relatives. Another noticeable abnormality was that everything he said of Miss Elizabeth had been in praise.

She clapped her hands excitedly. Now absolutely convinced that Fitzwilliam was in love with Miss Elizabeth, she was determined to get to know her once the lady awakened.

With renewed interest, she reviewed her cousin Richard's notes written during his stay at Rosings Park at the same time as her brother. He said his stay had been much more interesting than those in the past, mostly due to Miss Elizabeth's presence.

Since the lady had the approval of both her guardians, her own approbation of Miss Elizabeth was almost guaranteed. Would not her brother be surprised when he came home and found his lady-love and she were already good friends?

Georgiana folded the pages and returned them to her drawer. After selecting a favourite book to read aloud to her patient, she made her way to the guest wing.

Upon her entrance, Georgiana noted Mrs. Gardiner rising from her seat with difficulty, seeming stiff from having spent the night in the chair.

"Good morning, Mrs. Gardiner. Has there been any change in Miss Bennet's condition?"

The lady shook her head. "No, I am afraid not, but she has not developed a fever, at least."

"That is good news! Please go and rest for a while. I will stay with her."

Mrs. Gardiner paused briefly, but then she seemed resigned. "If the doctor comes before I return, would you send word, please? I would like to be here when he makes his examination."

"Of course." Georgiana smiled and escorted Mrs. Gardiner to the door. "He usually comes every afternoon to see Uncle, but if he comes any earlier, I will send one of the maids for you."

"Thank you."

Georgiana closed the door and looked around the room. One maid dusted while another came in through the service corridor with a pitcher of fresh water. When they were finished, Georgiana dismissed them, assuring them she would ring if they were needed.

Settling into the chair next to Miss Elizabeth's bed, she began to read.

~%~

Pulsating pain in her head, left arm, and right ankle greeted Elizabeth as she swam up from the depths of the darkness that surrounded her. An unfamiliar voice prompted her to open her eyes. Though her vision was blurry, and the light stung, she made out the shape of a lady sitting in a chair to her left. When she turned her head slightly to get a better look, the bed seemed to buck and spin viciously.

She closed her eyes and listened to the girl read.

> *...I feel it to have excited in me the most lasting attachment, from my fixed admiration of your virtues and talents, I cannot endure to run the risk of incurring your aversion. Allow me then once more, under the sanction of that excellent lady in whose care I have had the honour of seeing you, to entreat one moment's audience, that I may be graced with your own commands about waiting upon Sir Hugh, without which, I should hold myself ungenerous and unworthy to approach him; since I should blush to throw myself at your feet from an authority which you do not permit. I beseech you, madam, to remember, that I shall be miserable till I know my doom;*

51

but still, that the heart, not the hand, can alone bestow happiness on a disinterested mind.

I have the honour to be, Madam, your most devoted and obedient humble servant, Alphonso Bellamy.

At the pause in speech, Elizabeth worked up the courage to open her eyes again. After blinking several times to clear her vision, she found the pretty young lady sitting in a chair nearby was looking down at her book with one hand on her chest. Obviously genteel, she was well-dressed and perfectly groomed. "To receive such a letter as this!" She sighed so deeply, the golden ringlets surrounding her face were set to bobbing.

The girl moved to trace one finger across the page as she read aloud:

The idea also of exciting an ardent passion lost none of its force from its novelty to her expectations. It was not that she had hitherto supposed it impossible, she had done less—she had not thought of it at all. Nor came it now with any triumph to her modest and unassuming mind. All it brought with it was gratitude towards Bellamy, and a something soothing towards herself, which, though inexplicable to her reason, was irresistible to her feelings.

The wistful expression on the young lady's face slowly faded. She raised her head to look at the fire, so Elizabeth could only see her in profile. In the next moment, her shoulders sagged as if she took the weight of the world onto her back.

Wishing to bring the girl comfort, Elizabeth held her hand out to her.

The girl's head turned to look at her, and then a beautiful smile spread across her features. "You are awake!"

Elizabeth attempted to speak, but she choked on a dry throat instead. The young lady helped her to sit up a bit, then took a glass of water from the bedside table and offered it to Elizabeth. Elizabeth tried to take it from her, but her hands shook so forcibly, the contents would have spilled, so she allowed the young lady to cater to her. After a few small sips, Elizabeth nodded her thanks. The girl moved to rearrange the pillows behind

Elizabeth. Once she had reclined more comfortably, Elizabeth found voice enough to thank her, then asked, "What were you reading?"

"I was keeping you company while you lay unconscious, reading aloud from the novel *Camilla*. It is written by the same author who wrote *Evelina* and *Cecelia*. Have you read any of them?"

"The titles sound familiar, but I do not remember the particulars just now." Elizabeth shivered and pulled the covers up higher.

The young lady closed her book and placed it on the nearby table. She rose and brought Elizabeth another blanket that had been placed across the foot of the bed. "Your aunt and uncle have been worried about you. They will be so happy to hear you have awakened." She walked over to the hearth and pulled the bell pull hanging near it.

Following the girl's movements around the room with her gaze, nothing seemed familiar. Confused, she frowned. "May I ask where I am?"

"You are at the estate of the Earl of Matlock. While touring the grounds here, you slipped and were injured. The doctor was not certain whether or not you would awaken at all."

"Matlock?"

"Yes."

Elizabeth blinked several times. "I do not remember becoming injured."

"I am Miss Georgiana Darcy, niece to the Earl and Countess of Matlock." She curtsied. "It is a pleasure to finally meet you. I believe you are acquainted with my brother, Fitzwilliam—"

Just then, a maid entered through the servants' door. Georgiana said, "Bessy, please inform Mrs. Gardiner and Lady Matlock that Miss Bennet has awakened."

As Elizabeth turned her head to follow the maid's progress across the room and out through a different door, she was overcome by another wave of lightheadedness. She closed her eyes and swallowed hard.

"Miss Bennet? Are you feeling worse?"

"Dizzy…" was all Elizabeth could manage to say.

A few moments later, the door to the hallway opened. Mrs. Gardiner rushed to her bedside more swiftly than Elizabeth had ever seen her move before.

"Lizzy! Thank the good Lord!" She took both of Elizabeth's hands in hers. "You *will* be well again!"

Chapter 10

Elizabeth's eyes widened as she felt the weight of the doctor's pronouncement darken every corner of her soul. "Are you saying I should not walk at all?"

"Yes, exactly so, Miss Bennet. You will put no pressure on your right leg what so ever. If you do, it will displace the bones I have set, and the ankle will not heal correctly. If you must move from one place to another, someone must carry you."

Elizabeth placed her hand to her temple. It seemed when she became upset, her head pounded more painfully. She, who would not put off taking a walk unless the weather was at its worst, could not even walk from her bed to a chair? How would she survive the next few weeks without going mad? Since she had awakened, she could barely keep still for the hour it took for the doctor to arrive.

Mrs. Gardiner spoke up, "I am certain your uncle will carry you into the sitting room or wherever is necessary, my dear."

"Thank you, Aunt." Elizabeth tried to smile her appreciation of the offer, but at the moment, even that task was difficult to manage.

Looking at Elizabeth over his spectacles, Mr. Brown continued, "I understand you do not wish to take laudanum. Many of my patients feel the same way. Instead, please mix these powders in cold water and drink it in its entirety whenever pain prevents you from sleeping, Miss Bennet. You need rest most of all. A lump on the head, a sprained arm, and a broken ankle are lesser evils than what *could* have resulted from such a fall," the doctor declared. "A knock to the head of that severity could have ended in many complications." He cocked his head to the side. "But after today's examination, I may safely say that *if* you follow my instructions—to the letter—you will suffer no worse consequences."

"Is it safe to move her at this time, Mr. Brown?" her aunt asked. "We have rooms available to us at the inn at Lambton. We do not wish to trespass on the generosity of our hosts any longer than necessary. Perhaps she would do better at home, but that is a three-day ride even with no complications."

Mr. Brown answered immediately, as if he anticipated the question. "A few more days of rest will be required before Miss Bennet may be moved even so much as the short distance to Lambton. However, I must prohibit travelling any further than that for quite some time."

The doctor turned away and began returning the tools of his trade to his bag.

"Of course, we will do as you recommend." As if the high neckline of her morning gown was too tight, Mrs. Gardiner pulled at it and cleared her throat. "But will Lizzy be able to travel by the end of June? My husband is due in London by the third day of July. His business—"

Mr. Brown interrupted. "Miss Bennet's ankle must be fully healed before I would advise she travel such a distance. If my directions are followed, perhaps two months. If not, it may be longer."

Two months! Elizabeth's eyes widened with alarm.

"I understand." Mrs. Gardiner's brow furrowed.

Elizabeth said, "I am sorry, Aunt."

Her aunt smiled politely. "You did not injure yourself on purpose, dear. What is done is done. Think no more about it." She turned to the doctor. "May my husband contact her family at this time, doctor, and tell her father of your recommendations?"

"Yes, he may feel free to do so now."

Mr. Brown lifted his bag and bowed to the ladies. Elizabeth's aunt led Mr. Brown into the sitting room, where her uncle waited.

The heavy weight of guilt pressed down upon Elizabeth. She closed her eyes and sighed. Would this incident affect her uncle's livelihood? And the inconvenience to her young cousins and her own family. The Gardiner children would have to remain at Longbourn until her aunt and uncle returned. The children would be distraught, missing their parents. Mayhap she should tell her aunt and uncle to leave her at the inn at Lambton with a maid.

She shook her head, knowing they would never do so.

Poor Jane would be overworked trying to keep the children occupied for so long. Her mother's nerves would be stretched to their limits. Her father might never forgive her for causing such an uproar.

How could she have been so foolish as to climb out onto that rock? That one impulsive decision gone wrong would have far-reaching consequences.

~%~

~Five days later

Lady Adelaide, Mr. and Mrs. Gardiner, and Georgiana were visiting with Elizabeth in her sitting room when a knock came upon the door, promptly followed by the entrance of Colonel Richard Fitzwilliam.

"Richard! You did not send word you were coming," Lady Adelaide exclaimed. "I thought you were unable to come so soon?"

"As soon as my mission was complete, I was granted leave. I was to travel with Reginald, but business delayed him, so I rode on ahead. I am certain my brother will follow within a day or two. Perchance it was Providence since I came upon Mrs. Annesley returning from her stay with her sister when I stopped at an inn on the first night. For the remainder of the journey, I rode alongside the carriage Darcy had arranged for her in advance." Richard greeted his mother and cousin with a peck on the cheek.

"That was good of you, Richard. I thank you," Georgiana said.

"It was my pleasure." He turned to his mother. "I have seen Father. He is resting now."

A serious look passed between mother and son.

Elizabeth glanced at her aunt and uncle. They all felt as if they were intruding, and the guilt weighed more heavily every day. Mr. Gardiner had heard from the innkeeper in Lambton. Her uncle had paid in advance, and the innkeeper ensured their rooms would be held until their party could relocate there. She hoped when the doctor came to see her tomorrow afternoon, he would give her leave to travel to Lambton.

Richard's face took on a more pleasant expression as he turned to Elizabeth.

"I suspected I would find you here, Mother. You are always drawn to charming company such as Miss Bennet's." Richard's eyes twinkled as he bowed his head to Elizabeth.

After introductions to the Gardiners were made, Richard said, "It is a pleasure to find you here at Matlock, Miss Bennet, though it is unhappy news that you should find the need to convalesce." He gestured towards the sofa, where she sat with her legs up, covered with a blanket. "I hope you are feeling better."

"I am afraid it will be quite a while before I am returned to normal, Colonel, but I have made some improvements. It is good to see you again."

"I understand you met my son at Rosings Park this past spring?" Lady Adelaide asked.

Elizabeth smiled. "Yes. My good friend, Charlotte Lucas, had recently married my cousin, Mr. Collins, who, as I am sure you know, is Lady Catherine's rector. I was staying with them at Hunsford Cottage at the same time Colonel Fitzwilliam and Mr. Darcy were at Rosings Park with their aunt."

"Having Mrs. Collins and Miss Bennet in the area made it a most pleasant visit." Richard bowed his head to Elizabeth.

Georgiana said, "In my brother's correspondence written while at Rosings, and from his time at Mr. Bingley's residence in Hertfordshire, as well, he often spoke of how much he enjoyed hearing you play the pianoforte, Miss Bennet. I hope to hear you play one day."

Both Lady Adelaide and Elizabeth asked at the same moment, "Did he?"

Georgiana nodded.

Elizabeth raised her eyebrows in surprise. She answered with mirth in her tone, "If my vanity turned towards my musical talent, I would allow Mr. Darcy's exaggerations to remain without dispute, but I am afraid your brother has excited your anticipation for naught. As I am certain Colonel Fitzwilliam will remember, Lady Catherine often voiced a much more sobering opinion of my ability."

At noticing Georgiana's newly furrowed brow, Elizabeth continued, "Oh, do not allow it to distress you, Miss Darcy. I wholeheartedly agree with Lady Catherine's appraisal. I do not have the patience required to become a true proficient, though I have heard that you *do*. I should enjoy hearing you play."

"You have been correctly informed, Miss Bennet." Lady Adelaide beamed proudly at her niece. "Our Georgiana outdoes even my own daughter, Bianca. Her performance will be the just the thing when she debuts next Season. Of late, though, she has not practiced as much as she normally would since the earl is unwell."

"Thank you." The young lady blushed. "I do practice as often as I can..." she hesitated. "But I have found that a technically perfect execution may not be as enjoyable as a piece played and sung with true feeling."

Elizabeth had felt so about Mrs. Hurst's and Caroline Bingley's performances, in which every note was played to perfection and yet were still lacking somehow. She wondered if Miss Darcy was thinking of the same.

"Fitzwilliam highly admires the latter in your performance, Miss Bennet."

"Georgiana speaks the truth," Richard added. "He mentioned as much to me, as well. Several times, in fact."

With all eyes on her, especially considering the countess's expression of renewed interest in her person, it was Elizabeth's turn to blush. "Thank you."

She was at a loss to say more. The other day, as Miss Darcy read to her, she had worried a novel might not be to her liking since, in his letters, her brother had admired her taste in books. Now this?

And the Colonel—what was he about, confirming all of Miss Darcy's assertions of what he had heard Darcy say about her?

She blanched. Were either of them, or both, aware of Darcy's proposal?

~%~

"Oh, Fitzwilliam!" Lady Bianca sobbed and leaned heavily on his arm. "What am I to do without a husband?"

Darcy looked out to sea as he reached into his pocket to retrieve a handkerchief, knowing his valet would be furious that he did. His cousin never returned them. Just this morning, Hughes mentioned he would have to speak to Bianca's maid, for this was his last one, and there was nowhere to purchase more on a ship such as this.

"I will deliver you safely to your family, Bianca."

Bianca stepped closer to him—so close that the swell of her bosom pressed against his chest. Darcy pivoted his body away from her.

He could not ignore her sorrow, whether it be real or fabricated to gain his sympathy, but he would not be accused of placing her in a compromising position, either.

He glanced to confirm Bianca's maid was nearby, as he had ordered, then he looked down at his cousin. She now patted tears from her cheeks as she stared up at him with an expression of disappointment. He averted his gaze. He would not encourage her in case she expected anything more from him than to see her safely home.

How he wished he could escape this scandalous new behaviour his cousin had begun to display the moment her seasickness had subsided, but the only place to go on this ship was the deck or his cabin.

A Lesson Hard Learned

The first mate's cabin, where he was staying, was stiflingly small. At night, it was crisscrossed with hammocks now belonging to Hughes, Fleming, and himself. Once the day began, they would fold them away, but even then, with his trunks and those of the two valets stored in the cabin along with another trunk containing the first mate's belongings, there was barely enough room on the floor to stand and dress properly.

From the hallway, he had peeked through the open door of the captain's cabin. Bianca had a bed to sleep in, and a table and chair for her use. If that were his cabin, he would pass quite a bit of time there, but Bianca preferred to spend her day on deck attached to Darcy's arm. Every time he encouraged her to speak of her late husband, she changed the subject to something about himself. He soon stopped trying.

She nestled closer again, and Darcy took another step to his right. He would soon have to change tactics as he was quickly running out of deck space.

Just before her debut to society last season, her brother Richard had warned Darcy to be careful around Bianca, lest he end up shackled to her for a lifetime. Once Bianca had become engaged to Lashbrook, Darcy had thought Richard had been mistaken. Now, he was not so sure. Had Richard been correct?

He sighed.

He longed to truly understand love… to live it. He would be willing to do anything to attain the goal of marrying Elizabeth. His cousin's aspirations would not get in his way.

Chapter 11

~The next day

Mr. Brown removed his spectacles, huffed a breath onto each lens, and rubbed them clean with his handkerchief—a sequence of movements Elizabeth had come to recognize was something he did when he was making a decision about her condition. After repeating the same series of actions several times, he slid his glasses into his breast pocket and carefully folded his handkerchief.

Elizabeth felt as if she might faint in anticipation of his verdict.

Once his handkerchief was satisfactorily stored away in another pocket, the doctor folded his hands before him. His gaze settled first on Elizabeth, and then on Mrs. Gardiner. "I believe it is safe for Miss Bennet to travel to Lambton."

Elizabeth released the breath she had been holding during his dramatic proclamation and thought she heard her aunt do the same. "Thank you, Mr. Brown."

Mrs. Gardiner rose from her chair. "Mr. Gardiner is waiting to speak to you in the sitting room. Will you come this way, please?" She moved towards the connecting door.

The doctor gathered his things and stopped next to the bed, bowing his head to Elizabeth. "It has been a pleasure treating you, Miss Bennet. I am certain the physician at Lambton will agree with my recommendations." He held up a letter. "I will give this to Mr. Gardiner to pass along to Mr. Smythe."

Mr. Brown followed Mrs. Gardiner into the sitting room.

A moment after the door closed, it opened again, and Georgiana entered. "Mrs. Gardiner said you might welcome company, but if you are too tired, I can return later."

"Please come in, Miss Darcy. I think I have rested enough to last me through the remainder of the year!" Both ladies giggled. "I am not accustomed to inactivity. Your visit will keep my mind occupied, at least, though I would rather take a walk through a park as we converse."

"Thank you, Miss Bennet. My brother mentioned in his correspondence that you take delight in walking."

Elizabeth blinked in surprise. Miss Darcy was always turning the conversation to speak of Darcy, almost as if she were reminding her of his existence since he could not be with them himself.

Elizabeth gestured to the chair beside the bed. Georgiana took the seat.

"Yes, your brother had ample evidence of my indulgence in the exercise whilst he was in Hertfordshire."

Elizabeth almost laughed at recalling his expression when he met her as she arrived at Netherfield. A day earlier, Jane had been caught in heavy rains on her way to dine with Miss Bingley and Mrs. Hurst at Netherfield Park and had fallen ill. Since the carriage was unavailable, Elizabeth had walked three miles in order to see her sister, and by the time she arrived, her skirts had been splashed with quite a bit of mud. Surely any time her name had been mentioned during Darcy's stay at Netherfield, Miss Bingley and Mrs. Hurst would have reminded anyone who would listen of her appearance that day. They would probably continue doing so for all eternity.

Elizabeth continued, "Mr. Darcy also came across me several times as I took pleasure in the grounds at Rosings Park."

"Rosings Park does have lovely gardens and woods, Miss Bennet." Georgiana seemed pleased to have another point of common reference.

"Will you call me Lizzy? Or Elizabeth if you prefer."

"I will call you Lizzy if you will call me Georgie."

Elizabeth smiled brightly. "I would be happy to, Georgie."

"Lizzy," Georgiana said her name slowly, as if she were trying it out. "While the doctor was examining you, Mr. Gardiner received a letter from his business partner." Georgiana paused awkwardly. "It seems there are further problems with Mr. Gardiner's business ventures. He must return to London even sooner than he expected. In fact, it would be best if he began his journey tomorrow."

Elizabeth's cheerfulness faded. Her uncle would not be able to escort them to Lambton?

"Unaware as we were of the doctor's arrival, Richard—my cousin, Colonel Fitzwilliam—and I had hoped to discuss something with you all and entered the sitting room a few minutes after Mr. Gardiner had received the communication. Once he informed us he would have to leave, it seemed our plan would be an even better idea than when we had conceived it. Your uncle has agreed to our proposal, depending on whether you and your aunt concur, of course."

Curious, Elizabeth raised her eyebrows and cocked her head to the side, waiting for Georgiana to continue.

"As I think you are no doubt aware, my brother and my cousin share my guardianship. The doctor states that my uncle's condition is stable for the time being, and Richard does not feel I should remain here at Matlock now that Mrs. Annesley has returned. Tomorrow, my cousin Reginald will arrive, and two or three days later, Richard will escort Mrs. Annesley and me as we remove to Pemberley, where he will remain with us. Pemberley is not more than an hour by horseback across the fields, you see, and if my uncle's condition worsens—that is, if Richard should be needed at Matlock—my aunt can send a servant for him." Georgiana looked at her with expectation.

What does she wish for me to deduce from that speech? Elizabeth asked aloud, "Has Colonel Fitzwilliam offered to escort my aunt and me to the inn at Lambton?"

Georgiana stared at her hands folded in her lap. "Not quite... Oh, I am afraid you will think me presumptuous for having suggested it—" she broke off, clearly distressed.

"Georgie, these past few days, I have come to see in your manner that you have nothing but the best of intentions. Please go on."

The younger lady toyed with a long ribbon hanging from the bow tied at her waistline. "Would you come home with me, Lizzy?" She looked up from her lap.

"I am sorry, Georgie. I am afraid I do not understand..."

"I have enjoyed your company immensely... We thought you would be more comfortable. And now that your uncle will not be in attendance—he was so distressed about leaving two ladies unprotected! Richard felt this would be a perfect solution for everyone concerned. Pemberley is quite safe, after all."

Elizabeth's chest tightened with anxiety. "Pemberley?"

"My home." Georgiana nodded. "Your uncle said he would be more at ease knowing you and your aunt were at Pemberley instead of at the inn at Lambton, but he wished to speak to you both before agreeing to our plan."

Live at Pemberley for two months? How could she possibly—

"We have an excellent library." Georgiana's tone was now one of persuasion, and her obvious excitement grew with each word spoken. "I am certain Mrs. Reynolds will order the rolling chair my father used years ago brought down from the attics. I look forward to taking you on a tour of the house. When I broke my leg three years ago, it was great fun to be pushed around, and the chair fits nicely under the pianoforte, so I may hear you play. Perhaps we could learn a duet to entertain Mrs. Gardiner and Mrs. Annesley? And I will take you through the gardens surrounding the house. And... Oh! But you will never guess." Georgiana smiled brightly. "I can drive a gig! I am sure a ride around the grounds when the weather is pleasant would be permitted as long as a footman accompanies us. Please say you will come, Lizzy?"

Elizabeth looked away from Georgiana. She had to admit Georgiana's enthusiasm was infectious. She truly enjoyed the girl's company. And she *was* curious to see Pemberley. Georgiana had confided in her earlier in the week, saying since she was not yet out, she became quite lonely when her brother left her alone in Derbyshire with only Mrs. Annesley for company. It did seem an ideal situation now that she and her aunt would have to remain in Derbyshire without Mr. Gardiner.

She did not wish to insult her new friend, but *Pemberley?* Darcy's home... the very house where she might have been mistress by now had she accepted his proposal?

What would Darcy think of her when he heard she had stayed there while he was away? And—goodness! What if he should return from America before she was well enough to travel? How could she possibly explain away such impudence if he should come home and find her there?

No! Even if she had to break with convention and explain her reasons to her aunt and uncle in order to convince them, they *must* refuse Miss Darcy's offer. Her uncle's footman could surely remain with them at the inn as protection. Georgiana could come to see them there as often as she liked. It would have to be enough.

Georgiana's pleading expression almost broke her resolve, but something about the light shining from the young lady's eyes reminded Elizabeth of Darcy, and her determination strengthened. As she opened her mouth to speak, a knock came from the door leading to the sitting room, and her aunt passed into the room. Her gaze examined the two young ladies, and then she waved her husband through the doorway.

"Lizzy—have you heard the news?" Mrs. Gardiner asked excitedly as she crossed to the bed. "Miss Darcy has generously requested we stay at Pemberley until you are well again. Your uncle has accepted. Is it not ideal?"

Elizabeth's eyes opened almost as wide as her mouth was at that moment. Thankfully, everyone was looking at Georgiana.

As she attempted to regain control over her countenance, Mr. Gardiner asked Georgiana, "Are you certain it is not an imposition, Miss Darcy?"

"Of course not, Mr. Gardiner. I am looking forward to having your wife and niece as my guests."

The relief that softened Mr. Gardiner's features was too pronounced for Elizabeth to ignore. She closed her mouth and bit her tongue to remain quiet.

Mr. Gardiner sighed. "Thank you, dear girl. I was growing sick with worry at the thought of leaving the ladies at the Rose and Crown alone. I shall never be able to repay your kindness."

Georgiana's smile widened as she glanced at Elizabeth, then back to Mr. and Mrs. Gardiner. "There is no need, sir. Your wife and niece do me a courtesy by accompanying me. The pleasure will be all mine."

Elizabeth's heart beat forcefully against her ribs. The entire situation was all her fault. If not for her error in judgement, she and her aunt would be able to return to London with her uncle. She could not deny either of them this peace of mind, no matter her discomfort at staying at Darcy's estate.

To Pemberley they would go.

Chapter 12

Spending the night in a hammock had taken some getting used to. But certainly, it was better than stretching out across uneven crates in the cargo hold amidst the rats that infested most ships, as he had pictured himself having to do when desperation caused him to beg Mott to allow them on board.

Two weeks into their voyage, it was well into the night when Darcy heard the chorus of shouts coming from above deck. Although he could not make out what was being said, the tone of the men's raised voices sounded urgent. His first reaction was to jump out of bed, and yet, he was soon reminded that haste was ill-advised when one was inexperienced in dismounting from a rope hammock. Hughes was almost instantly by his side helping him untangle his limbs from the ropes.

Once free, Darcy narrowed his eyes. "How did you remove yourself from your hammock without any trouble?"

Hughes made no answer and moved to help Fleming, Bartholomew's former valet, from his hammock. His avoidance of the question made the gentleman wonder whether his valet had disclosed his complete background upon being hired.

Without wasting a moment's time, Darcy rifled through his luggage, then glanced up at Fleming. Though the man still seemed a little green around the gills, he sprang into action with renewed energy as Darcy pulled two pistols from his trunk. He handed both weapons to Hughes, who had already anticipated his master's actions and retrieved the ammunition from another trunk. Hughes began loading both pistols.

"Fleming, go next door and knock on Lady Bianca's door to wake her and Ellen. Tell them to dress but remain below in their cabin. Stand guard at their door unless you hear differently from me. Understood?" Darcy handed a pistol to Fleming. With a nod, the man headed out the door to keep watch over his mistress.

When the other pistol was ready, Hughes held it out to his master, but Darcy shook his head. "Hold onto it, Hughes."

Hughes followed Darcy above.

The waxing moon cast enough light to ascertain what had caused the commotion.

Indeed, there were ships closing in on them, but they were not pirates as Darcy had feared. The sight of three vessels flying English colours and swiftly approaching the *Gypsy's Promise* would have been awe-inspiring and quite welcome under different circumstances. But in this case, the scene before Darcy made every muscle stiffen. Though Mott had assured Darcy they were carrying only legal supplies on this trip, Darcy knew these men were usually smugglers. If any of the crew members of the Navy ships recognized Mott's ship, they might be blown to bits.

Looking around for Mott, Darcy easily spotted Jeremiah, who stood at least a head taller than most of his shipmates. Since he had noticed the two were usually in each other's company, he headed in that direction. Mott stood nearby, calling out orders to his men.

"You cannot think of outrunning them," Darcy declared.

Mott gestured to Jeremiah, who took his place. He then pulled Darcy out of the way of the men carrying out their duties. "Nothin' else we can do. Me brain ain't addled enough to stand and fight it out wit' three of 'em."

"Of course not, but if we run, they will fire upon us, will they not?"

"They'll try, but *Gypsy's Promise* is fast. I'm hopin' we'll be too far away for them to get a piece of us."

"And what if we are still in range? Each of those ships has at least twice the firepower of this one. Did it slip your mind just *whom* you have on board? I advise you to stop the ship, Mott. Do not fire one shot. Trying to evade them would seem like an admission of guilt to the commander."

Mott shook his head. "You don't understand, Mista' Darcy. Half o' my men ain't from England—they be from Denmark. They happened on us in port one day afta' they escaped the Navy ship they'd been *pressed* into workin'. Turns out the Navy boarded their ship and accused 'em o' being deserters. Most o' 'em didn't even speak English nor never stepped foot on British soil 'afore, but none of it mattered. Navy crewmen came forward and said they knew 'em from their home county, so the British cap'n pressed 'em into service 'afore their own commander could make it to his cabin so he could show 'em the proof he had they all be from Denmark." He pointed out to sea. "Ships that size need lots o' sailors and are always lookin' to do the same. My men would rather die tryin' ta fight than risk bein' pressed into service again. If you 'eard the stories I have of how they were treated, you wouldn't wonder why neither."

Darcy took a deep, calming breath. "Let me talk to the party that boards your ship, Captain. I give you my word that not one man from this ship will be forcibly placed into service. Not one." Darcy relied on his best Master of Pemberley expression to cover the uncertainty he felt about the plan he hastily conceived while Mott spoke.

Mott crossed his arms over his chest and examined Darcy closely. Something about the way the smuggler eyed him made him think Mott recognized his doubts.

He took in a deep breath and glanced high above them at the men moving through the riggings, then met Darcy's gaze. He snarled out, "You'd betta' be right, Darcy, or this'll be the bloodiest press gang boardin' in history. Every one o' my men is armed an' ready ta use 'em. I ain't about to tell 'em ta do otherwise."

The captain turned and started calling out orders again, rescinding all his previous commands. The men were to lower their sails instead.

A few astonished gasps and one or two oaths made their way to Darcy's ears. After a tense moment's hesitation, the crew obeyed. It was obvious they believed in their captain.

Darcy hoped the tournament-winning debating skills he had perfected in his university days would not fail him now. Each one of these men depended on it.

He turned to move towards the rail and almost bumped into Hughes, who was staring at the naval ships as if he had seen a ghost. "What is it, Hughes?"

"'Tis the *Caledonia*, sir, the flagship of Admiral Croft, along with the *Boyne* and the *Galatea*."

"Croft, did you say?"

"Yes, Mr. Darcy."

"That is good news, Hughes." Darcy regarded the naval ships, then met Hughes's gaze. "Shall I ask how you knew these ships by sight?"

Hughes shook his head. "'Tis too long a story for our present circumstances. As it is, Mr. Darcy, my presence here may *complicate* things. It may be best if I remain below with the ladies. Perhaps Fleming can assist you in my stead?"

"I thought as much." Darcy sighed. "Go."

Several minutes later, first light broke the horizon as Darcy stood at the rail watching the naval ships make their final approach. If naval personnel came on board, it could create problems. What if one of the crewmen recognized one of Mott's men? Whether they joined the Navy under their own volition or were pressed into it, Mott's men would be considered deserters. If one man were to draw a weapon, all would.

If a battle did occur and, by the grace of God, his party were spared, what would happen to them? Most likely, Hughes and Fleming would be pressed into service—if Hughes was not taken into custody, and judging by his reaction to seeing these ships, he just might. Bianca, Ellen and himself would be required to live aboard a naval ship until they docked in a friendly port. They would remain there until they found a ship returning to England, which could take years if war began as the rumours in Virginia indicated.

What would Georgiana do without him? Would she think him dead? And Elizabeth—by the time he returned, she would have surely married someone else.

The risk was too high. He had to prevent them from coming aboard the *Gypsy's Promise*.

He felt someone come up alongside him. Assuming it was Fleming, he looked to his right, and his eyes widened. "Bianca!" He turned to see Fleming and Ellen standing behind her. Ellen seemed terrified. "Fleming, return them to their room and keep them there—"

"I know where you wish me to be, Fitzwilliam." Bianca folded her hands before her. "But here is where I *should* be. Hughes has explained the situation. The sight of ladies on board might prevent any battle that might ensue. Besides, if the ship sinks, it will make no difference whether we are above deck or below it."

Darcy searched his cousin's features and shook his head. She had an all too familiar stubborn look about her. If they had come across pirates, keeping the females hidden would be best, but in this case, it would be a waste of time to argue with her. "I was just thinking; I will ask Mott to have men take me over to the *Caledonia*. It will be less risky to meet with the commander there." His tone was firm when he said, "You will stay here."

She raised her chin. "I will do as you say, but I will remain above deck, in full view." She hesitated a moment. "When you explain who is being transported home, you may tell them I carry the possible heir to the title Earl of Lashbrook."

Darcy took his cousin's hand, squeezing it slightly. "I am happy for you."

She bowed her head in thanks but displayed no emotion. "It may give them the incentive they need to allow these men to take us home without further interruption."

"It should." He nodded. "I have previously met Admiral Croft. A cousin on the Darcy side of my family was serving under him as Captain when he was killed in a battle with pirates near the Indies. Let us hope he remembers me."

Chapter 13

Four oarsmen were good enough to volunteer to take Darcy across to the *Caledonia*, although they refused to leave their longboat. In fact, the men insisted on moving the boat away from the side of the ship as soon as Darcy was safely on board.

Darcy was greeted by two burly officers carrying rifles, who instructed him to wait and took up positions along the rail a pace or two from either side of him. Darcy raised his Master of Pemberley façade before boldly meeting the curious gazes of several other men on deck, for he was disinclined to allow any of the crew to sense the uncertainty of the situation. The men promptly returned their attention to their duties.

Uncomfortable with the tense atmosphere surrounding him, he turned his back to the crew and watched Mott's men move their longboat to about half-way between the *Gypsy's Promise* and the *Caledonia,* where they would await his signal to retrieve him.

Seeking a way to distract himself from the gravity of the situation, he reviewed what he remembered about Admiral Croft.

More than two years ago when Darcy had met then-Captain Croft, the naval officer was a robust man—a gentleman in behaviour, quite willing to share tales of his adventures when an enquiry was made. Croft was an excellent storyteller, though his experiences would have fascinated Darcy even if another had told them. What he recalled most clearly about the man was his good-humour and his open, amiable manner. In fact, at the time they met two years ago, Darcy had taken an instant liking to him, especially since the admiral strongly reminded him of what he expected Bingley to be like twenty years hence, though perhaps Bingley would not be quite so weather-beaten. He stifled a chuckle at the thought.

Hearing heavy footsteps on the deck, he turned to find Admiral Croft approaching. Relief spread through him at seeing the smile displayed on the admiral's face.

"Ah! Mr. Darcy, is it you? I had not thought we would come across *you* on that ship. Well, how d'ye do, sir?" The admiral extended his hand and shook Darcy's heartily.

"I am well, Admiral, and I can see you are the same. It is good to see you again."

"Being at sea always suits me very well. Yes, very well indeed."

"And how is Mrs. Croft, sir?"

"Ah, Sophy is in Deal, but I like to think she is well. We were just returning to England when the call came to patrol this area. Sophy would have been delighted to see you again. I shall write to her this evening."

"Congratulations on your promotion, Admiral. I read about it in the newspapers," Darcy said.

"Yes, yes, thank you." He waved it away as if the thought were a pesky fly. "The promotion came after an especially *interesting* engagement in the North Seas. I have not even seen Sophy since it happened." The admiral looked off to sea towards England and frowned. After a few moments, he returned his attention to Darcy. "Can I be of any use to you, Mr. Darcy?"

"In fact, you can." Darcy considered all the men scattered around the deck. Though they kept busy with their work, judging by the way they held themselves, he assumed they were paying close attention to what was being said between the admiral and himself. Croft gestured to a ladder leading up to the fore-deck, where they could be alone. Croft followed him up and dismissed the two men stationed there. Darcy waited until they had gained their privacy to speak again. "Admiral, we are in need of your services—"

Admiral Croft interrupted, shaking his head. "We are not returning to England any time soon, Mr. Darcy. The best we could do is to leave your party at the next safe harbour we encounter."

A sudden fear seized Darcy's gut. "It was not that of which I was about to ask. I am sure you have been informed of the presence of ladies aboard the *Gypsy's Promise*. It is my cousin, Countess Lashbrook and her maid. The countess was in America when her husband passed away."

"I am sorry to hear of your cousin's loss. Please give her my condolences."

"I will. Thank you, sir."

"But that ship," he nodded towards the *Gypsy's Promise*, "is not suited for passengers. In fact, it has been recognized as one belonging to smugglers."

Darcy raised his chin just a little. "Admiral, I travelled to America in order to escort the countess home. With the talk of war, we had some trouble gaining passage on any ship bound for England. Captain Mott stepped up when no one else would, and he and his first mate have given up their quarters for our party's comfort. I ask you to allow us to pass so we may complete this journey successfully. Captain Mott does not believe he can deliver us safely home without his crew at a *full* complement..." Darcy left the idea hanging in the air.

Admiral Croft's gaze settled on the *Gypsy's Promise,* and he knit his brow.

"There are no illegal goods aboard that ship at this time, Admiral."

Darcy hoped his expression and tone did not betray his doubts. Perhaps he should have asked for a look into the cargo hold so he could have said that sentence with more conviction, but he had not dared. Darcy searched his feelings about Mott. Did he trust the captain?

Mott was a smuggler, but smugglers were not the same as pirates. Smugglers were business men, in a sense. They procured goods that might be less than legal to transport, but were highly sought after by the upper crust of British society. Mott had even said Darcy's uncle was one of his best customers.

Quickly sorting through a list of gentlemen and other men he had known throughout his eight and twenty years, he had to admit that one's profession, or lack of one in the case of gentlemen, did not always dictate whether or not the man could be trusted.

Darcy scanned the deck of the *Gypsy's Promise* and could make out Mott standing next to Bianca along the port rail. If it had been another man in this situation, Darcy could easily imagine the captain might hold Bianca ransom if things went bad, but he could not see Mott doing so. He could only expect Mott was ready to protect Bianca from harm if circumstances dictated.

Yes, Mott might be the son of nobody in particular, and yes, he might be a smuggler, but he was a good, trustworthy man.

Darcy stood a bit straighter. "I give you my word as a gentleman, Admiral. All is on the up and up aboard the *Gypsy's Promise*. You are welcome to inspect the cargo hold if you would like."

He could see Admiral Croft remained undecided.

Darcy said, "Admiral, I must inform you that the Earl of Matlock is ill. The Countess of Lashbrook is his only daughter and would very much appreciate being able to see her father before he passes on, sir. If one of your ships will not break away and return us to England themselves, I ask you to allow us to pass."

Croft shook his head. "It is against my better judgement, Mr. Darcy."

Georgiana! "I am sure you remember my sister, admiral… who accompanied me to our cousin's family's home the first day we met in London?"

Croft rubbed his chin. "Yes, your sister is everything a fine young lady should be."

"Thank you, sir. You may also remember meeting our cousin, Colonel Richard Fitzwilliam, as well? I believe you dined with him that same day."

Croft nodded.

"Perhaps you are not acquainted with all the facts concerning my sister and cousin, sir. Georgiana has been left to the guardianship of Colonel Fitzwilliam and me. With my cousin being in the service to the Crown, he is away from England for extended periods of time, much like you are now. When this happens, Georgiana's welfare is left entirely up to me. If I am not in England, I would be leaving her alone…" He stopped before he said, *as alone as Mrs. Croft is now.* He hoped the admiral filled in that part himself. "If we divert to another port, it may be years before I can return. I do not know how my sister would fare, if that were the case, Admiral."

The admiral still did not seem to be swayed. Should he ask Admiral Croft to return with him to the *Gypsy's Promise* and meet Bianca and her maid? It was possible Bianca's talent for tears would be of some use. No, there was something better.

"There is an additional matter you must consider." Darcy took a deep breath. For the sake of propriety, he did not like having to reveal his cousin's condition, but it had come to the point where he could not avoid it. "I hesitated to mention this in order to respect the lady's privacy, but my cousin has given me permission to inform you of the situation if there is no other alternative. The countess is carrying the child of the Earl of Lashbrook. It is quite possible we have the heir to the title aboard the *Gypsy's Promise* at this very minute. Not only would the countess prefer to spend her confinement in England, but she had already notified the earl's family by letter of her husband's death before she realized..." Darcy cleared his throat. "I am certain you can imagine that unless we return to England without delay, the earl's relatives will appoint a successor to the earldom. If this happens, when we do return eventually, the situation could become quite uncomfortable." Darcy watched the admiral's eyebrows rise high upon his forehead. "Admiral, I must respectfully request you allow us to continue. We *must* return to England as soon as possible, sir."

"Yes." Admiral Croft nodded. "Yes, indeed, you have convinced me, Mr. Darcy. Allowing this ship to continue on to England is, in a sense, a service to the House of Lords, and in turn, to the Crown."

Darcy felt a great deal of tension drain away as Admiral Croft shook Darcy's outstretched hand.

"Thank you, sir. My family will never forget your kindness."

"Nonsense, it is nothing." Croft glanced once more at Mott's ship. "You are certain, are you not, that there is nothing illegal going on?"

"Yes, Admiral, I am."

"Then you had best be going, Mr. Darcy, as should we. But before you do, I would like to give you some letters I have written to Mrs. Croft. Will you post them when you reach England?"

"I would be happy to, sir. I will take all letters your crew may wish to entrust to me."

The Admiral bowed and left to gather his dispatches and those of the crew.

The wind played with Darcy's hair. He turned into it, allowing the salty breeze to brush his curly locks away from his forehead. Realizing he faced the same direction Croft had turned when thinking of his Sophy, he recalled how they behaved towards each other when he had seen them together. Mrs. Croft was more than simply a wife to the admiral—she was the love of his life.

Darcy searched the horizon. England might still be distant, but in less than three weeks, he would be on her shores again. After delivering Bianca to Matlock, he would take Georgiana to Pemberley for a few days, where he would do his best to devise a way to convince Elizabeth that *she* was the love of his life, as well.

~%~

As soon as Darcy climbed the rope ladder and had two feet firmly planted on the deck of the *Gypsy's Promise*, Bianca threw herself into his arms and sobbed into his chest.

Darcy's eyes widened. He took his cousin by the shoulders, stepped back, and said to Bianca's maid, "Ellen, please take care of Lady Bianca's needs."

Ellen stepped forward and handed the pouting Bianca a handkerchief.

Bianca sniffled. "Oh, Fitzwilliam! You were gone so long; I was not certain you would ever return."

He shook his head. It was not as if he had boarded a pirate's ship. He had been among civilized men. He turned and found all of Mott's crew staring at him. He addressed the captain, "As I hoped, Admiral Croft has given us permission to continue on our journey. You may raise the sails, Captain Mott."

A little more than half the men smiled and patted each other on the back. A couple cheered. One of the men translated what Darcy said into what must have been Dutch. Several others seemed quite relieved.

Mott called out, "All right, men; git back ta work." He gestured to Jeremiah, who took over giving orders. Mott held out a hand to Darcy. "Thank ye, Mr. Darcy. Couldn't 'o done it wit'out ye."

Darcy shook Mott's hand. "You are welcome, Captain. It took a bit of convincing. I was not sure I would be successful when the admiral offered to take Lady Bianca and me to a friendly port and leave us there for heaven knows how long."

Mott glanced from Darcy to Bianca's retreating form and back again. His eyes sparkled with mirth as he said, "Ah, but she is a beauty. Would that be such a terrible arrangement?"

Darcy straightened his spine. "She is my cousin, Mott. Nothing more."

Mott spoke in a quiet voice. "Ye got a lady back home waitin' for ye then?"

Darcy stopped himself from voicing his reproach of the question, realizing Mott's inquiry was kindly meant. "I have hope."

Mott ran a hand over his beard as he glanced again at Bianca. He stuck a finger into Darcy's chest. "Ye betta watch out then, Darcy. I been watchin' the two 'o you on deck. I don't think gettin' stranded in a foreign land would'a been as much a punishment to *her* as it would'a been for you."

Darcy nodded solemnly. "Thank you for the warning, Captain."

Chapter 14

Lord Reginald arrived at Matlock the following day, as scheduled. After agreeing it would be best if Georgiana returned home and promising to send word immediately if Richard was needed, three days later, the viscount and his mother waved off the remainder of the party as they departed for Pemberley.

Although a rider could effectively reach Pemberley in an hour if he rode across the fields following several shortcuts, while travelling along the roads fit for a carriage, the trip usually took two. However, allowing for Elizabeth's comfort and the doctor's orders to travel slowly, the caravan consisting of a carriage transporting Georgiana, Mrs. Gardiner, Elizabeth, and Mrs. Annesley, along with a less ornate carriage carrying servants and two carts hauling luggage, made the journey in a little more than three hours. Colonel Fitzwilliam escorted the procession from the back of his horse.

Georgiana jested that he did so in hopes that just the sight of the deep crimson of his uniform would scare away any highwaymen who happened to see them while they were still far away. Elizabeth shared a look with her aunt and could tell she agreed. Though the younger lady thought it was a joke, in truth, there was merit behind the idea.

Elizabeth was quite sore by the time her aunt pointed to a farmhouse in the distance and said, "You will be able to rest soon, Lizzy. That was the tenant farm my family leased at Pemberley before my father took over my grandfather's shop at Lambton. The road to the manor house lies just around the next bend in the road."

Georgiana said, "My excitement to be coming home always increases when I see that farmhouse. It is the outer rim of our grounds."

The cavalcade turned right through the gates and rode for some distance. The carriage began to climb a hill.

"All of this is part of Pemberley?" Elizabeth asked.

Georgiana nodded, smiling.

Elizabeth continued, "It is quite a grand estate."

As the carriage approached the crest of the hill, Georgiana pointed out the window on the left and said, "It will be just there, when the trees break."

Elizabeth turned to look out. The coach moved beyond the trees, and Pemberley came into view. On the opposite side of a valley, the stone building stood at least four stories tall on rising ground. The manor overlooked a small, natural lake, fed by a stream. Her gaze traced it up into a ridge of high, woody hills framing the house. It was more wonderful than she could have possibly imagined.

Elizabeth had to stifle a gasp. No, *house* was not the correct word at all. Pemberley was more like a castle!

And the grounds... she had already ridden through fine woods, spacious fields, and extensive groves. They had experienced one of the smoothest rides she had ever had, proving the road was in the best condition possible. They had crossed two small bridges, which were well maintained, and were about to traverse a third, more expansive bridge in order to approach Pemberley House. Even from here, she could see formal gardens, lawns, and paths leading off in several directions into the woods.

Pemberley was stunning.

And Mr. Darcy asked me to be mistress of all this? I could never have imagined that he had confidence enough in my abilities to lead a staff the size of the size of a village. Georgiana said the grounds are ten miles around. I had thought she might be exaggerating, but after seeing this, I know she was not. Did he really believe I would be the right person to care for the many tenants of such a sprawling estate? Me, a simple country squire's daughter?

My aunt was correct. He truly must have been in love with me to offer me all this. It could have been nothing else.

"Lizzy?" Georgiana sounded concerned. "Lizzy?"

Startled, Elizabeth turned to her and almost whispered, "It is resplendent, Georgie. Exquisite. I have never seen a place better situated in all my life."

Georgiana smiled brightly. "I am glad you like it."

"How could I not?" Elizabeth laughed. "I did not hit my head *that* hard, my friend!"

~%~

Elizabeth surveyed her bedchamber and grinned at the memory of Mrs. Reynolds explaining this was the Rose Room. She need not have. The bedchamber, dressing room, and sitting room were adorned in varying shades of pink, cream, and light yellow.

The walls were papered with bouquets of roses of different colours, embellished with garlands of rose vines in between. In each room, a large, plush carpet matched the wallpaper so closely, Elizabeth assumed they were woven for that purpose. The curtains on the windows and bed were a solid colour matching the deepest maroon that appeared in that design. Her bedding was of the lightest blush, edged with green piping, one shade darker than the vines embroidered on the quilt.

All in all, the suite was elegant without being ostentatious.

Upon their arrival two days ago, Elizabeth had been so mortified at her need to be carried up the stairs by a strange servant, she had not noticed details concerning the interior of Pemberley House. After having so little activity for so long, the journey had exhausted her so completely that Aunt Gardiner had tucked her into bed immediately and refused to allow her to leave it for most of the next day. Even when Georgiana had visited her in her rooms for a short amount of time, Elizabeth remained in bed. The doctor from Lambton, a Mr. Smythe, came to see Elizabeth in the afternoon, then later in the day, her aunt ordered trays to be brought up.

Earlier in the morning, Hannah, the maid Georgiana had assigned to her for the duration of her stay at Pemberley, had been surprised when she entered the room to bring a pitcher of fresh water and found Elizabeth was sitting up, reading by candlelight. Hannah helped her wash and dress before the sun made its full appearance for the day.

Now, Elizabeth felt so much recovered that she was anxious to be doing something, and she found herself eager to discover whether or not the rest of the house was decorated as tastefully as was her suite of rooms.

When a knock sounded, without the pain in her head to remind her of her injuries, out of habit, she almost sprang out of bed to answer the door. Fortunately, Hannah had done so before Elizabeth could manage the undertaking.

"Good morning, Lizzy!" Georgiana sang out as she entered the room. "You will be happy to see what James has for you today."

Behind Georgiana, James, the footman who had carried her from the coach to her bedchambers, wheeled in a rolling chair.

"It is the chair my father and I both used in the past." Georgiana continued. "Mrs. Reynolds found it in the attics the day before yesterday. I did not mention it since we were afraid to raise your hopes too high before the carpenter finished his thorough examination of the wood."

Elizabeth smiled widely. "Oh, Georgie, you have no idea how much I have been looking forward to getting out of bed, especially if it does not mean I have to move to a couch!"

"I cannot promise you will never be confined to a bed or couch again for the next two months, but as your hostess, I will do my best to prevent it from being for long. Our carpenter has replaced any wood that was not in good condition. He even made an alteration to the lower area so you can elevate either one leg or both."

Georgiana pulled up both sections of the leg-rest and pushed them in towards the seat so they would remain outstretched; then she tugged each outward and allowed the leg-rests to hang down again.

"There are wooden wedges in a leather pocket across the back of the chair. We shall place them around the wheels when you need the chair to remain still, such as when you get in and out of it."

She took one out to show Elizabeth and the footman put one in place at the front and back of each wheel.

"Thank you so very much, dear Georgie," said Elizabeth. "This chair is heaven-sent, as are you."

Georgiana blushed. "Your aunt should be here momentarily." She gestured at the footman. "James will push the chair as I give you and Mrs. Gardiner a tour of a few of my favourite parts of the house." Her forehead furrowed. "You *are* feeling well enough for an adventure today, are you not?"

Elizabeth smiled. "After sleeping so soundly in this comfortable bed for two days, I am quite recovered from the fatigue I experienced from travelling. This room is lovely, Georgie—in fact, I think it is the most beautiful room I have ever been in in my life—but I am looking forward to seeing something other than these four walls. I would enjoy seeing your home. And if James is up to pushing me that far..." Elizabeth raised her eyebrows expectantly. "...I would love a breath of fresh air."

Georgiana giggled. "I think that can be arranged."

"As long as you do not grow too tired, Lizzy," Mrs. Gardiner said as she entered the room.

"Good morning, Mrs. Gardiner." Georgiana tilted her head to the side. "It is breezy this morning. Perhaps we should take shawls and bonnets with us now and go out into the garden first."

"Yes, please, that would be wonderful." Elizabeth agreed enthusiastically.

"After our walk," Georgiana went on, "We will take tea; then I shall show you the music room and the portrait gallery before we return you to your rooms to rest." She glanced at Mrs. Gardiner, who nodded her thanks. "We will have plenty of time to go over more of the house in upcoming days. Of course, if you feel well enough after your rest, James will take you downstairs to dine. Just ring the bell once for Hannah and twice for James at any time, Lizzy. Either of them will be at your service if you wish to get in and out of the chair. You are both welcome to join me at all times, no matter what I may be doing."

"I dislike being such a bother," Elizabeth said, glancing at both the maid and footman, and then at her aunt's scolding expression. "But do not worry, Aunt, if I *must* be a bother to heal properly, I *will* be a bother."

Chapter 15

Elizabeth took one last breath of fresh air and looked over her left shoulder. "Thank you for pushing me around the gardens, James."

James bowed his head slightly and rolled her chair through a French window on the side of the house and into a parlour, then halted the rolling chair diagonally across from the sofa so Elizabeth could see out the windows as well as anyone in the other chairs.

A maid took shawls and bonnets from Georgiana and Mrs. Gardiner, and then she stood waiting for James to anchor the chair's wheels so she could help Elizabeth from her outerwear. Georgiana ordered tea and asked the girl to inform Colonel Fitzwilliam of their location. The maid and James retreated into the corridor as Georgiana invited Mrs. Gardiner to have a seat.

Colonel Fitzwilliam entered the room a minute later, smiling. "Ah, Miss Bennet, it is good to see you are making use of my Uncle's chair. You are looking well."

"Thank you, Colonel. Pemberley's gardens are truly a bit of paradise on earth!" Elizabeth turned to Georgiana. "I am grateful for the suggestion of going out first, Georgie. Nothing else could have done me as much good."

"I am glad our gardens meet with your approval," Georgiana said. Elizabeth wondered why she blushed.

"Being out of doors does seem to have revitalized you, Lizzy. Your colour has returned fully." Mrs. Gardiner smiled widely. "I will be happy to relay news of your continued recovery to your uncle in my letter this evening. He has been quite concerned about you."

Several maids came in with a tea service and plates filled with biscuits, cheeses, and cold meats. After Georgiana finished serving, another maid entered carrying a missive on a salver.

Georgiana straightened her form, her interest apparent in her expression. "Is it from my brother, Alice?"

Alice curtsied and said. "No, ma'am. 'Tis an express for Mrs. Gardiner. Mrs. Reynolds tol' me to bring it right away." She turned towards Mrs. Gardiner and held out the tray.

"An express? For me?" The colour drained from her aunt's face as she reached for the communication with a trembling hand. With all eyes on her, she took a deep breath and then broke the seal. One hand moved to her throat as she began to read. A moment later, relief spread across her features. "It is from my husband. All is well…" Her voice trailed off as her gaze scanned the letter. "He stopped at Longbourn to collect the children and their nursemaid. They should be in London by now."

Mrs. Gardiner continued reading. She opened her eyes wide then looked up at Elizabeth. "No wonder he sent it express! It seems your father insisted Mr. Gardiner send it in this manner, Lizzy. Even though Mr. Bennet and Jane have both received messages from you and Mr. Gardiner has assured them you are healing well, my husband tells me that Mr. Bennet is quite worried about your welfare. He will not feel comfortable until he sees you himself."

Elizabeth opened her mouth to speak, but her aunt continued.

"Although he did not wish to impose while we were at Matlock, now that you are at Pemberley with an inn so close by, he and Jane will take rooms at the Rose and Crown in Lambton for a few days." She held up her letter. "In fact, according to this, your father and Jane will leave Longbourn on Monday, the twenty-ninth of June. Your uncle says it will take two and a half days to make the journey. We should expect them to come directly to Pemberley on the second of July so they can ease their minds immediately by seeing you before they continue to the inn."

"Oh, dear," said Elizabeth. "They need not come such a distance. Perhaps if you send a return express to my father, we can catch them before they leave."

Mrs. Gardiner shook her head. "Your uncle states that Mr. Bennet would brook no opposition, Lizzy. He would come, and that is the end of it. If he had not had important business with a tenant, he would have been on his way before now. Mr. Gardiner was surprised when Jane *insisted* that she would make the journey with him."

Mrs. Gardiner raised her eyebrows in a certain way that confirmed her suspicions. Her parents must have had quite the disagreement over her father's coming. Elizabeth expected the addition of Jane to the plans must have caused even more of a ruckus. She could well imagine her mother would have been adamant that Jane remain at home, and her father would have supported Jane's wishes in order to have her company. Elizabeth nodded her understanding.

When she looked away from her aunt, she noticed Georgiana and Colonel Fitzwilliam were having a quiet discussion.

Georgiana said to Elizabeth, "They must be very concerned to come all this way, Lizzy. Of course, they are welcome to visit you here, but please do send an express to Mr. Bennet and inform him that I insist they stay with us at Pemberley instead of at the Rose and Crown."

"You have already been so generous, Georgie. We could not impose further—"

"It would be no imposition," Colonel Fitzwilliam joined in. "Mrs. Reynolds keeps the guest rooms in readiness at all times. I am sure she would be delighted to have someone use them." He chuckled. "And I would not mind some male company around the house, especially after supper in Darcy's study for cigars and brandy."

Elizabeth laughed. "But are you certain *Mr. Darcy* would not mind, Colonel?"

Georgiana's tone was anxious when she answered, "My brother would certainly welcome your family to Pemberley, Lizzy. I believe he would be pleased if he found you all here when he comes home."

Georgiana's enthusiastic belief in her words was plain to hear, but Elizabeth doubted the young lady comprehended the situation well enough to recognize that her statement was incorrect.

At the reminder that Darcy would be coming home to find her and members of her family in his home, Elizabeth's anxieties were renewed. She attempted to push her worries aside, but she could not.

Goodness, what would he think of her? It was too much! Her headache returned in full force, pounding along with each heightened pulse.

"Mrs. Gardiner," Georgiana said as she rose from her chair and crossed to a small table. "There is a writing desk just over here. As soon as you are finished penning your note, I can have someone take it to the post office in Lambton and send it express. Then we will continue our brief tour."

Mrs. Gardiner took a seat at the writing desk. "Thank you, Miss Darcy. I shall be only a few minutes."

"Where are you ladies off to next?" Colonel Fitzwilliam asked before popping a biscuit into his mouth.

Georgiana's brow puckered into a concerned frown. "We were going to spend some time in the music room, but Lizzy seems suddenly pale. Perhaps Mrs. Gardiner was correct in supposing she should not do too much before taking a rest."

Mrs. Gardiner turned in her chair. "Are you all right, Lizzy?"

"Yes, it's just a bit of a headache," Elizabeth said. "Would you all be terribly disappointed if we visited the music room later?"

In the space of a moment, Georgiana wilted, blinked, and then recovered fully. "Of course not. Later would be fine—or even tomorrow or the next day. We will have plenty of time together." Georgiana rose. "I will walk with you as James returns you to your rooms." She turned to Colonel Fitzwilliam. "Cousin, will you take Mrs. Gardiner's letter to Mrs. Reynolds when she is finished writing?"

"I'll do one better," said Colonel Fitzwilliam. "Since I was planning to take a ride, I will change into my riding clothes while Mrs. Gardiner finishes, and then take the express to the post office in Lambton myself."

Chapter 16

Because Elizabeth's headache continued into the evening, she remained in her rooms. Georgiana sent up a book she thought Elizabeth might enjoy, but she was unable to concentrate on reading.

The following day, she awakened feeling much better.

Hannah entered with a tray with bread and jam, a small tea cosy, a pitcher of water, and fresh linens folded over her arm. Hannah curtsied. "Good mornin', Miss Bennet."

Elizabeth noted the page she was reading and then put her book aside. "Good morning. Thank you for bringing a tray up here this morning, Hannah. I hope to be well enough to join the others downstairs in a few days."

"'Tis my pleasure, miss." Hannah approached and placed the bed-tray over Elizabeth's legs. Leaving the linens on the chair next to the bed, she then took the pitcher of water from the tray and crossed to the washstand. "Oh, I 'ave somethin' for you." She pulled a letter from the pocket of her apron and began to cross the room again.

"Has my mail caught up with me? I had written to my sister asking her to forward it to Matlock before we planned to relocate to Pemberley. I was afraid she might have written before she knew I had come here."

"Sorry, miss. 'Tis from Miss Darcy. Marie, her maid, gave it to me last evn'n. Said I was to give it to you as soon as can be this mornin' and let her know your answer." Hannah handed the note to Elizabeth and took the clean linens into the dressing room.

Elizabeth opened it immediately. When Hannah re-entered the room, Elizabeth said with a smile, "You may inform Marie that I will join Miss Darcy in the music room at ten o'clock."

"Yes'm. I'll return as soon as I deliver your message." Hannah left the room.

~%~

When Georgiana finished the piece she had been practicing, Elizabeth signalled James to roll her into the room. "That was lovely, Georgie! Your brother did not exaggerate your talent."

"Thank you." Georgiana blushed. "He usually does tell the absolute truth, though he does seem a little too kind when he speaks of me." She rose and pulled her bench to the side. "Please come sit with me, Lizzy. I have found a few duets among my sheet music. I would like you to help me decide which we should practice together."

"Certainly." She nodded at James, and he pushed her to the pianoforte. Once she was there, she wiggled her fingers. "Perhaps if we sit close, some of your skill will rub off on me."

The two ladies giggled.

"Truly, Georgie, my musical abilities are nothing compared to yours. I do not know if I can keep up with you."

Georgiana raised her eyebrows. "In the short time I have known you, I have learned that you do not give yourself enough credit, Lizzy; therefore, I will not take no for an answer. As I said, my brother does not lie, and he has mentioned more than once how well he enjoys your playing and singing." She pulled a piece of paper out of her skirt pocket. "I have even come prepared. I have one of his letters with me. Would you like to see his actual words?"

Elizabeth kept her hands folded firmly on her lap as she eyed the letter. Did she wish to know exactly what he had said about her? To know what he was thinking about her all those times he stared at her stoically whenever they had been out in society together? Was the missive written while he was staying at Netherfield or was it from Rosings? Had he been thinking of her while he had been away from her during those months in between, or was the letter written just before leaving England—after they had met again in London and made such progress towards making amends—but only received by Georgiana after he sailed to America? Was he aware that he was falling in love with her when he wrote it, or by this time had he decided to propose and wrote this note more or less to introduce her to his sister?

In all her life, she had never been so full of curiosity as this. But her conscience dictated that she should not give in. The correspondence was private... thoughts relayed in confidence from a brother to a sister. His words were not meant for her eyes; after all, he had written it never imagining she would have occasion to read it.

It was also possible she could be injured by his prose. Perhaps *she* would be able to detect a hint of sarcasm in his phrasing that his sister had never suspected.

And certainly the letter would not be only about herself. Would he have written something complimentary about another lady in the same document? If he wrote of another, she *could* pass over it without reading. But no, she knew she would not. She would be too interested in his opinion of another lady to avoid attending those paragraphs, even though it would wound her. Deeply.

Just the possibility of it being so caused a burning sensation to tighten her chest and rise up her spine. She blinked in confusion.

This was jealousy!

Was it true that absence makes the heart grow fonder? Was she falling in love with Darcy?

She swallowed hard. Since the morning she had received his letter—no, if she were honest with herself, it had been since she met him—she had borne a particular regard for the gentleman, different than any she had ever experienced with another.

That was the reason why his comment at the assembly ball had wounded her so. That was why she had pushed him away at every opportunity. That was why she had become so angry when he proposed and insulted her in every way possible. After the statement she had overheard, it was too much to hope for—he could not mean he *wished* to marry her. She feared there must be some other reason. She had always wanted to marry for the deepest love, and if he could not even be tempted to dance with her, he could not love her!

What was it he had said?

Against my will. Against my better judgement...

But in the days that followed, what confused her most was asking herself if not for love, why else would he have offered for a simple country squire's daughter, unknown to the upper crust of the *ton*—the circle in which he socialized? Why would he have risked displeasing all his family and becoming the ridicule of all his friends unless he had been so in love with her that he had felt he could not live without her? A deep, lasting love, the kind she had always desired.

It had been the main subject of her thoughts during the weeks between his proposal and seeing him again in London. In fact, she had been reviewing that situation again before Jane had entered the room and distracted her—just minutes before stepping out of the house and meeting him. All through April and May, and during the many hours spent in carriages with the Gardiners in June, she tried to think of another reason. But every time, she had come to the same conclusion: She had practically no dowry and no glorious connexions to speak of. Marriage to Elizabeth Bennet of Longbourn could have offered nothing, save the possibility of love. She was doubly convinced after seeing Matlock and meeting the countess and viscount—two of the relatives who would most likely oppose the match.

Her Aunt Gardiner was correct. Darcy *was* in love with her, or at least he had been.

And no, she was not falling in love with Mr. Darcy. She already *was* in love with him!

Although she had done her best to hide her emotions, even from herself, he had somehow detected them. They had given him reason to hope for a successful outcome to his proposal.

She had dashed his hopes to ashes, enumerating the reasons for her rejection—each turning out to be mistaken assumptions borne of her own wounded pride—ruining her chances of ever living a life of love.

She had refused him. She had insulted him. She had broken his heart.

And now, of all things, she was living in his home!

No matter the progress they had made before he left England, if he returned to find her here, would he not think her new opinion only *professed*?

Would he not feel she had been impressed by his possessions, his wealth, and the prestige that would naturally go along with being his wife, and not with him?

Would he not think she schemed her way into Georgiana's good graces—something similar to what Miss Bingley would do?

Would he not come to congratulate himself on his escape?

It would be completely unfounded, but conceivable… even probable!

No! Whether what he wrote in the note to his sister was all good news or all bad, she could not read it. Reading a letter that was not meant for her eyes was too high a risk, no matter how strong her curiosity might be.

Georgiana touched her arm. "Lizzy, are you all right?"

Elizabeth's stare moved from the paper, up Georgiana's arm, past her shoulder, and now she met the younger lady's gaze. The concerned look on her face brought Elizabeth to her senses. How long had she been silent? She blinked several times in quick succession and took a deep breath, clearing her mind.

Elizabeth forced a smile. "Yes. Yes, I am fine, Georgie."

Georgiana pushed the letter towards her. "Shall I read the letter aloud?"

"No, Georgie. I cannot." Elizabeth averted her eyes and reached for a sheet of music. "Now, which of these pieces were you thinking of trying?"

~%~

The first few days they were on board, the group ate their meagre fare separately according to gender. Later, as Lady Bianca insisted they not abandon all the good manners of society, they established a routine where Darcy's and Lady Bianca's servants brought trays of food to the captain's cabin. The masters would eat first, sitting with their trays on the captain's table, as the others served what little there was to be served. Darcy and Lady Bianca would then walk on deck as the servants took their meals.

Each day, Bianca clung closer to Darcy's person. And each day Darcy felt less comfortable.

Through Hughes, Darcy requested that Ellen dine in the first mate's cabin at the same time that the masters ate in the captain's quarters, which would leave Ellen free to accompany them on their stroll.

Tonight, as Darcy and Bianca settled onto their benches, Lady Bianca said to the two manservants, "Leave everything on the trays this evening. You may go."

"Very good, madam," said Fleming so hastily, Darcy thought he must have been told to expect this. Fleming bowed and headed to the door.

Darcy opened his eyes wide as he looked to Hughes. Hughes remained in place, standing at attention.

"I said you may go, Hughes," Bianca said haughtily. "And close the door behind you."

Having repeatedly been told all his life that *the genteel never argue before servants*, the tradition was too well ingrained in Darcy's manner to say a word until the door closed behind Hughes. Darcy stood, crossed the room, and opened the door half way.

In hushed tones he said, "I do not care if we are not among our peers in society on board this ship; it is not proper for us to be left alone, Bianca. There will be talk…"

Bianca waved her hand. "Oh, pish, posh, Fitzwilliam. We will order the servants not to speak of it."

"What of the sailors?"

Bianca laughed as she set down her silverware. "Just who would they tell? I wish for some private time with you. Close the door and come sit down to eat."

Livid, Darcy left the door open and remained standing.

Bianca raised her chin. She picked up her fork and began eating again.

Darcy said, "Say what you need to say to me in private, Bianca, for I am leaving in a moment."

She sniffed and her lower lip started to tremble. A tear made its way down her cheek.

Darcy made no attempt to stop himself from rolling his eyes. He knew her too well to take her sudden emotional state seriously. From the time Bianca was a child, she had always been able to cry at will. For years, he had watched even the strongest gentlemen's will melt at the sight of her tears. He had hoped that as she matured, she rid herself of the annoying habit, but more recently, he suspected she had only learned to use it more sparingly.

When he had come upon her in Virginia, he thought she had been truly upset, but since coming aboard ship, she had been turning on the tears much more quickly and, at times, without any provocation other than she had not gotten her way. It proved to him that she was still the spoiled brat she had been before her coming out, before her marriage. He wondered how many times Bartholomew had fallen for this.

"Bianca, we may be cousins, but we are not children. I am a single gentleman, and you are a widow." He raised one eyebrow. "And you propose we remain alone in a bedchamber without even a servant present?" He took a step towards the door and then turned again to face her. "I have no interest in whatever it is you would like to *do* during this private time you have arranged."

He opened the door all the way and stepped through it.

"Wait!" she called after him.

With one foot in the hall and one in the room, Darcy stopped and turned his head to look at her.

She blotted her tears with her napkin, and all evidence of her distress vanished. "I am alone, Fitzwilliam." She placed a hand on her stomach. "Whether my child is a girl or boy, it will need a father. You have never shown an interest in any lady of fashion, and yet, you *must* marry to provide an heir. Aunt Catherine seems to think you will marry Anne, but I know I am more attractive as a wife than Anne could ever be. A marriage between us would make our family so happy—" She hiccupped. "If my child is a boy, you could live as luxuriously as an earl, only without any power in the House of Lords. If it is a girl, I am certain my husband provided quite well for a daughter and for myself. At the very least, I know that my dowry of sixty thousand was to be mine if Bartholomew died before me."

Darcy took a step back into the room, leaving the door open. "Bianca, your brothers will be more than happy to offer guidance to a son or provide protection for a daughter. Last season, you were the belle of every ball. You will have plenty of opportunities for another marriage, if that is what you wish. *I* have no interest in a marriage of convenience."

"But I have *always* wanted…" her voice trailed off when Darcy shook his head.

"I have found someone—a lady I wish to become my wife." He sighed. "I am sorry to disappoint you, Bianca, but nothing you say will convince me to submit to any other arrangement."

As he left the room, he could have sworn he heard her say, "We shall see about that."

He shuttered involuntarily.

Chapter 17

After his confrontation with Bianca, Darcy lay awake for much of the night, wishing he could toss and turn in a hammock. Eventually, he abandoned all hope of sleep and rose. Dressing as best as he could without waking the others, he made his way above to pace the decks. He always thought better with a little fresh air.

Once on deck, he nodded to a passing crew member and studied his surroundings. There were lanterns lit here and there, but once one moved away from them, it was very dark. Fearing he might trip over something and end up falling overboard, he stepped to the rail to stare out at the sea.

The wind had kicked up since he had gone below, and it was now almost cold. He looked up at the crescent moon peeking through the thickening, fast-moving clouds. Perhaps a storm was brewing? Pulling his coat tighter around him, Darcy wished he could go below deck and unpack his overcoat, but he could not do so without waking Hughes and Fleming.

Yes, he needed to think, but there was no way he could remain out here long.

When they returned to England, if Bianca lied, declaring he acted with improper intentions towards her during their journey—and he would not be surprised if she did—he could not condemn his family for taking her side. He would be blamed, without a doubt, of taking advantage of a grieving, newly-widowed, expectant lady, whose father was on his deathbed.

They would pressure him to marry her

He shook his head with frustration.

If it happened as he feared, he would do his best to withstand their arguments, but he knew if he endured too long, they would make his "transgression" known. All within the *ton* would be required to show him the *cut direct* in society. Unless Georgiana took sides with the remainder of the family, she would be isolated as well, and his aunt, Lady Adelaide, would surely refuse to sponsor his sister's debut. Nobody would dare go against the Countess of Matlock's wishes. If Georgiana had no sponsor, she would not be presented to the Queen.

If such a thing came to pass, he would have to advise his sister to speak against him and go to live with Aunt Adelaide.

Darcy swallowed hard.

And if all this happened, even if he were lucky enough to gain Elizabeth's favour, he would never be able to offer for her.

His hands fisted.

No!

Never again would he be tricked into being left alone with Bianca. He could not risk losing the two women who meant more to him than his own life!

He would take his meals in his own room, along with the manservants, for the remainder of the voyage—or perhaps, since the manservants were bound to obey her orders, it would be safer to dine with the crew. Mott would understand. After all, the request would prove that the captain's warning was warranted.

He chuckled. If this journey had taken place before his meeting Elizabeth—before he had received her honest appraisal of his character and decided to change—would he ever have thought of dining with the crew?

Something flashed out on the sea. A moment later, it was gone. Darcy stared at the spot, squinting, hoping that, if it was not his imagination, he would see it again. A minute later, it flashed again. He continued to watch the spot for several minutes. It reappeared a few times, intermittently.

Hearing footsteps, he hailed a crewman as he passed.

As the crewman approached, Darcy realized it was Jeremiah. "Mista' Darcy?"

"I am sorry to distract you from your duties, but what is that flash of light I have been seeing out in the water?"

100

"Flash, sir?"

"Yes, about there…" Darcy pointed out to sea. "It does not seem to be a reflection of the moon for the clouds have thickened and the light is tinted red."

"Red?" Jeremiah hunched down to Darcy's eye level. He shook his head. "I ain't seen nothin'."

"Wait for it. It comes and goes."

Jeremiah leaned on the rail and watched the spot that Darcy had pointed out. The pair studied the area longer than he had before, so long that he began to question whether he had seen it at all. Just as he was about to tell Jeremiah to continue with his duties, it flashed again.

"There!" Darcy said triumphantly.

Jeremiah straightened abruptly.

"It seems to be getting larger every time I see it," Darcy observed.

The clouds parted momentarily. Even in the low light emitted from the waxing moon, Darcy was able to make out the outline of a ship, so close that the light reflected off the white figure on the flag they were flying. A skull and crossbones!

The clouds blocked the moon once again, and it seemed as if the ship disappeared.

Jeremiah rushed away from Darcy, scrambled up a rope ladder, and tugged on rope attached to an alarm bell. Darcy followed him. Half-dressed crewmen piled out of the door from the lower levels of the ship.

Jeremiah cupped his mouth with one hand and called out over the clang of the bell, "The light ain't gettin' *bigger*, Mista' Darcy; it's gettin' *closer!*"

~%~

As Elizabeth slowly regained her endurance, the little group settled into a routine. Elizabeth and Georgiana practiced two duets as well as several other songs, half of which Elizabeth sang and Georgiana played, and the other half in the opposite configuration.

During the hours in which the young ladies practiced, Mrs. Gardiner went to see her friends at Lambton and Colonel Fitzwilliam rode to Matlock. Both enjoyed hearing the results of their practice sessions when they played and sang for them in the evening after they dined.

The doctor gave permission for Elizabeth to ride in Georgiana's gig. Later that day, she took Elizabeth for a short ride. Colonel Fitzwilliam rode alongside. After seeing that fresh air did Elizabeth only good, the younger lady suggested that perhaps the following week they could visit the nearest tenant. While Elizabeth was quite used to carrying out similar duties at Longbourn and was happy to assist Georgiana, she wondered whether they would be able to do so once her father and sister arrived on the morrow.

As they pulled into the drive at Pemberley, they found Mrs. Gardiner returning from her visits. Once they were all in the entry hall, Georgiana said, "I never did show you the portrait gallery, Mrs. Gardiner, Lizzy." She turned to Elizabeth. "Are you feeling up to seeing it now?"

"Yes, in fact, I am. Aunt?"

Mrs. Gardiner agreed.

"Would you mind, James?" Elizabeth asked the footman who carried her.

"'T'would be my pleasure, miss." James turned up onto the short staircase leading to the second floor and turned right, waiting for the footmen who carried Elizabeth's chair to catch up to them. As soon as the chair was set up with the blocks in place so it could not roll, James set her down.

"Thank you." Elizabeth was sure to nod to James and each of the other footmen, who took up stations on either side of the staircase as she said it. They would be needed again when they finished here to take her up one more flight of stairs.

She blushed. No matter how often she had been carried since she was injured, it still embarrassed her to have to inconvenience others. How she longed to be able to walk again so she could go wherever she liked and see what she wished without having to rely on anybody.

Then it struck her: When that day came, she would leave Pemberley. She would not be able to see anything at all of this beautiful estate. The thought sobered her.

James pushed her down the corridor slowly. They stopped at each painting as Georgiana identified each of them, placing them in historical context and the family lineage. Her young friend had been taught well—she had an interesting or amusing story to tell about the person or persons in each portrait.

When they arrived at the fourth or fifth painting, they met up with Mrs. Reynolds and Mrs. Annesley, who continued on with them.

Elizabeth had met the housekeeper upon their arrival, when she had supervised her being carried to her rooms and made comfortable, and several times when Mrs. Reynolds came to ask if there was anything more the staff could do for her. Even in those short intervals, the woman had made quite an impression upon Elizabeth. Her pride in being at Pemberley was almost palpable, and there was a glitter in her eyes, which could only be affection, whenever she spoke of the family. Elizabeth liked her very much.

As the group approached a painting of a couple, Elizabeth said, "Goodness, this *must* be your parents, Georgie. While your brother seems more a combination of both, your resemblance to your mother is quite remarkable!"

Mrs. Gardiner agreed wholeheartedly.

"Do you really think so?" Happiness spread across Georgiana's face.

Elizabeth said, "Absolutely! If you were a few years older, I would have thought this was a painting of you…"

The volume of her voice dwindled on the last two words, for when she turned her head, her attention was captured by the next picture.

A younger version of Mr. Fitzwilliam Darcy stared down at her.

In the painting, Elizabeth judged him to have as much as ten younger than he was now.

His expression was carefree. Contented. Pleased. Serene.

There was a hint of a smile—more in his eyes than on his lips.

He was young enough for her to assume this was painted well before he took over as master of the estate and guardian of his sister. His features displayed none of the tension that was there in present-day, after an abundance of responsibility had been heaped upon him when his father passed away. She wondered if his mother had still been alive at the time.

With a flash of insight, she recognized the expression, and she understood him much better. This same mien often had been directed at *her,* usually during their conversations and debates, and especially when she teased him.

So much that had confused her suddenly made sense. *This* was why he had fallen in love with her!

Wishing to know *exactly* how old he had been when it was painted, she looked for a plaque below the frame, but there was none there.

Mrs. Reynolds must have noticed the direction of her gaze, for she said, "I am sorry, Miss Bennet, a new plaque is being carved. It was painted when Mr. Darcy was fifteen years of age." She grinned widely. "Was he not a fine-looking boy?"

Elizabeth simply nodded, for the breath in her lungs seemed to expand with all she felt but could not say.

Georgiana interrupted her thoughts. "He is the best of brothers."

"True," Mrs. Reynolds agreed. "And he is the best of masters, as well. Ask any of his servants or tenants. Not one would say anything against him."

"All my friends in Lambton have many good things to say of Mr. *and* Miss Darcy," Mrs. Gardiner joined in.

"Mrs. Reynolds?" Georgiana asked. "You said a new plaque is being carved. What happened to the one that was there before?"

"It fell off the wall last evening, Miss Darcy. Nobody knows how."

Georgiana paled significantly. "Fitzwilliam?" She staggered, putting her hand out to lean on the wall.

"Georgie!" Elizabeth cried, almost rising from her chair.

Mrs. Reynolds steadied her mistress and was soon joined by Mrs. Annesley on the other side. James left Elizabeth's side, steering Georgiana and her escorts to a window seat across the hall. Mrs. Gardiner crossed, leaving Elizabeth alone. Elizabeth grabbed hold of the wheels of her chair and pushed downward, slowly moving the chair to Georgiana's side.

"Do you think something has happened to him in America? Or on the ship?" Georgiana asked, looking first to Mrs. Reynolds, Mrs. Annesley, then Mrs. Gardiner, her gaze settling upon Elizabeth. A tear rolled down her cheek.

Mrs. Reynolds shook her head, "No." Her hoarse voice and pallor were not very convincing, informing Elizabeth that the housekeeper must be as superstitious as Georgiana seemed to be.

Mrs. Reynolds took Mrs. Gardiner aside and said something in a low tone.

Elizabeth searched her feelings. Somehow, she felt she would *know* if he had passed from this world to the next. With confidence, Elizabeth said, "Mr. Darcy is fine, Georgie."

"Truly, Lizzy?"

"Yes. He is in perfect health. I am absolutely certain of it." She patted Georgiana's hand.

Georgiana nodded. "Then I will put trust in your intuitions about him over my fears."

Elizabeth blinked in surprise. Was her affection for the gentleman *that* obvious?

Mrs. Gardiner and Mrs. Reynolds rejoined Mrs. Annesley and the young ladies. Mrs. Gardiner said, "We are all a bit tired, and I trust will feel better once we have rested. Let us finish the tour of the gallery another day."

"Yes. Yes, we shall." Georgiana stood.

Mrs. Reynolds came to her side. "Mrs. Annesley and I will see Miss Darcy returns to her rooms to rest. James will see you upstairs, Mrs. Gardiner, Miss Bennet."

Once Georgiana and the others were out of earshot, Elizabeth asked, "Aunt, what did Mrs. Reynolds say to you?"

"None of the servants could explain how the plaque could have fallen from the wall since there were *two* nails holding it in place." Mrs. Gardiner held up two fingers. "Mrs. Reynolds did not think about what it could mean until Miss Darcy mentioned her fears."

A shiver passed up Elizabeth's spine.

Chapter 18

While there was little chance Elizabeth's father and sister would arrive earlier than mid-day, she had left word with Hannah that she would have her morning meal in the breakfast room Thursday morning—for the first time since coming to Pemberley—so she would be readily available when they came down the drive.

Elizabeth awakened so early, she had plenty of time to review all that occurred the previous evening. After supper, Mrs. Gardiner suffered a headache and retired. Colonel Fitzwilliam had correspondence which required his immediate attention, and so the young ladies were left to themselves. At one point, Georgiana had burst out crying, blurting out all of her fears for her brother—disease, wild natives, shipwreck, storms, pirates—the list went on. Elizabeth had done her best to console her friend. While it was true nobody had heard from Darcy from the time he left England, seeing that the trip to and from America was at the very least five weeks each, this was to be expected.

Hannah entered, pulling Elizabeth from her recollections. As she went through her bath and toilette, Elizabeth convinced herself she had been wholly correct in all she said to Georgiana the previous evening, and her mind drifted to her family.

While she was filled with anticipation to see her father and Jane, at the same time, misgivings for causing such inconvenience tugged at her conscience.

Her father was taking much time away from the estate to come so far, and the rest of her family would have to do without him for the remainder of his visit here. She hoped her father had put their housekeeper, Mrs. Hill, in charge of the household funds, because if he had not, without Jane and herself there to curb her mother's, Kitty's, and Lydia's spending, the family could be without any funds at all when her father returned! Or perhaps he had turned over the household funds to Mary's charge, which would most probably result in no spending at all and a houseful of frustrated ladies and servants.

And the Gardiners, who had forgiven her so completely for taking an unreasonable risk, had been the ones who suffered the most hardships in the wake of her accident.

One person's reckless decision was all it took to turn so many lives upside down.

Spontaneity had been thoroughly ingrained in her manner. She had always been proud of her quick intellect, her ability to instantly size up a situation, form prompt opinions, and make rapid decisions. Stubbornly, she would defend her original conclusions, no matter what new information proved them wrong.

No longer!

After all, had not her refusal of Darcy's proposal ultimately been the result of her impetuosity? If she had thought through what she overheard at the assembly ball, as she had done every day since his proposal, she would have surmised that Darcy's comment to his friend might have been the result of something other than herself—other than her own shortcomings. Not only did he not dance with *her* that evening, but also he had not danced with Jane, who was by far the most beautiful girl in the room. She would have realized his comment had coloured her opinion of him so thoroughly that she could not even give him an opportunity to prove himself anything but the last man in the world whom she could ever be prevailed upon to marry.

And at Matlock, she should have known not to climb out onto that boulder! What had possessed her to do such a thing?

She was convinced that, from now on, she must carefully consider all consequences before she acted, no matter how trivial the situation seemed at its onset.

Her muscles tensed with anger at herself, and the ache in her ankle swelled. Her life had been made up of a series of careless, imprudent decisions, pure and simple.

In a way, she was glad this injury might ache a little every day for the rest of her life. It would serve as a lesson hard learned—a reminder of what she must do.

And yet, even knowing this, she could change nothing of what had previously come about.

In an attempt to move on, she tried to think of some good that might come from her most recent impulsive behaviour. Jane would benefit from the distraction and hopefully cease contemplating Bingley's abandonment. And she had met Georgiana, though the circumstances had also caused inconvenience to her new friend and her staff.

Hannah informed her that her hair was finished, pulling Elizabeth from her musings. After helping her into the rolling chair, the maid rang for James to assist Elizabeth in joining the others in the breakfast room.

It was one hour after noon when Elizabeth heard the crunch of gravel indicating the arrival of a coach. She leaned forward onto the stone rail surrounding the balcony outside the front parlour. With her legs out straight to help keep the swelling of her ankle down, her position was awkward. Excitement rose in her breast as she watched the hired coach pull to a stop on the drive near the front of the house.

Two footmen preceded Georgiana, Colonel Fitzwilliam, and Mrs. Gardiner down the steps to greet the travellers. One footman opened the door, and the other lowered a carpeted box to the ground and moved back.

Mr. Bennet descended first and looked up, examining the stone face of Pemberley. He chuckled and shook his head, then shaded his eyes, his gaze directed towards her. She waved; he returned the gesture and then stepped aside. Elizabeth could then see Jane inside the coach. Jane's eyes were open as wide as an owl's as she stared at the house. Elizabeth had to wave her entire arm to catch her sister's attention. Jane smiled and held up a hand in greeting. Elizabeth recognized her father's voice, though she could not hear what he said. Jane took her father's hand and allowed him to help her out of the coach.

As Mrs. Gardiner stepped forward, Elizabeth distinguished the gestures associated with an introduction. The group ascended the front steps. Jane looked once more in her direction before they entered the house.

Forgetting James had anchored the wheels so the rolling chair would not move, Elizabeth tried to turn the chair herself so she could push it into the parlour, as she had learned to do in the portrait gallery, but to no avail. She called out. James and a maid must have been in the corridor just outside of the room for they came to her aid a few moments later. The maid lowered her legs, and then James pushed her into the room just in time for the others to enter. The grouping now including Mrs. Annesley.

"Papa! Jane!" she cried out.

The faces of both her father and sister lit up as they quickly walked towards her. Mr. Bennet leaned down and kissed her forehead. Jane stepped in and hugged her sister.

"Oh, it is so good to see you both!" Elizabeth exclaimed.

Mr. Bennet raised both eyebrows. "Well, well, Lizzy. First Matlock, now Pemberley. Could you not have chosen a more convenient location to injure yourself, as well as to convalesce? A bit closer to home, perhaps?"

Elizabeth glanced at the others in the room. Mrs. Gardiner and Colonel Fitzwilliam seemed amused, but Georgiana had turned pale.

Elizabeth chuckled, partly from amusement at her father's familiar teasing; partly so Georgiana would see she was not upset by his impertinent questions, and mostly to relieve Georgiana's shock at witnessing his unconventional humour for the first time. "Believe me, Papa, if possible, I would not have chosen to become injured at all. Miss Darcy has been a gracious hostess, as was Colonel Fitzwilliam's mother, Lady Adelaide, Countess of Matlock."

Elizabeth's gaze moved to Jane. Although she continued to smile, Jane remained quiet.

"I supposed as much," said Mr. Bennet. "I have heard nothing but good of the Matlocks." He bowed his head at Colonel Fitzwilliam before turning his attention to Georgiana. "I thank you for the hospitality you have shown my daughter."

Georgiana's voice was barely above a whisper. "It has been our pleasure, Mr. Bennet. Would you not take a seat? Shall I call for tea?"

The trace of approval crossed Mrs. Annesley's features.

Elizabeth realized the effort that short speech must have taken for the young lady, and she was sure Mrs. Annesley had spurred it on. It was evident to her that with the introduction of new society, Georgiana's shyness had made a reappearance and was battling with her sense of propriety. Rightly so, propriety had won out.

"Thank you, Miss Darcy, but we are much too dusty from the road and would soil your furnishings." He redirected his attention to Elizabeth. "Where has Mr. Darcy been through all this?"

"I am surprised my husband did not inform you, Thomas," Mrs. Gardiner said. "Mr. Darcy had to sail for the Americas on business of import."

"Ah, yes. So he did… so he did." He nodded, a mischievous gleam in his eye.

Elizabeth wondered what he was thinking. He turned back to her. "You are looking a good deal better than I had expected."

"Thank you, sir. While I am happy to see you both, you need not have come so far. The doctor informs us I am recovering well. My arm has healed completely, and my head is much better."

Jane cleared her throat. "My uncle did tell us the same, Lizzy, but we felt the need to come and see you ourselves. We shall not stay long. Three days, most likely."

"Oh," Georgiana said. "Please, both of you are welcome to continue at Pemberley for the remainder of Lizzy's recuperation, if possible."

Her father smiled at Georgiana. "I appreciate the offer, but I will begin my journey home no later than Monday. I must return to Longbourn to oversee repairs on a tenant's home."

"Whose?" Elizabeth asked.

"The Clays. Apparently the inspector I hired to examine the tenant homes did not have a talent for detecting problems with the roof. Theirs partially collapsed several days ago when we received a great deal of rain. I am afraid the inspector might have been deficient in additional areas as well, so I am interviewing others."

"Oh! Was anyone injured?" Elizabeth asked.

Jane answered, "Mrs. Clay broke her arm while shielding the babe. Papa saw to it the Johnstons took in Mrs. Clay and the child for the time being until all has been repaired. Mary is making certain all is taken care of."

"Mr. Bennet, while you are here, you may wish to have a discussion with Darcy's steward," offered Colonel Fitzwilliam. "I understand both my father and Darcy use the same trusted inspector. If he will not travel to Hertfordshire, he might be able to recommend someone who will."

"Perhaps..." Mr. Bennet answered, looking doubtful. Elizabeth suspected he worried Matlock and Pemberley would be able to pay a great deal more for an inspector than Longbourn could afford.

Mrs. Reynolds entered the room and addressed the newly arrived guests. "May I show you to your rooms, Mr. Bennet, Miss Bennet?" She glanced at Georgiana, who blushed. "Your luggage has been brought up and is now being unpacked."

It was at that moment Elizabeth realized that, since Mrs. Darcy had passed on when Georgiana was an infant, the young lady had never had the benefit of a mother's teaching. Nor did she have an older sister, like Jane, to instruct her. She was sure this was the first time Georgiana had hosted guests at Pemberley without her brother's being here to take charge of all the arrangements. So many things that Elizabeth had learned from her mother and sister must have been left up to servants to teach to Georgiana as these recent events unfolded.

"Yes, the last few days of travelling have been trying, to say the least," Mr. Bennet said. "Will you come up with us, Lizzy? I would like to have a few words with you."

Elizabeth blushed. "It is not a simple matter for me to go above stairs and come down again, Papa." She asked Georgiana, "Will their rooms be near to mine?"

Georgiana looked to Mrs. Reynolds, who replied, "Miss Bennet's rooms are on the other side of yours, Miss Elizabeth. In fact, there is a door adjoining your sitting room with her chambers. If you would like, we could unlock it. Mr. Bennet will be in the rooms just across the hall from yours."

"Well, then, perhaps you should go up and take a rest after you speak with your father, Lizzy," Mrs. Gardiner suggested.

"Yes, that is an excellent idea, Aunt. Thank you."

Mrs. Reynolds disappeared from the doorway, and James came through it just as Mr. Bennet moved around the rear of the chair. James stepped aside, and Mr. Bennet pushed Elizabeth through into the hallway. Mrs. Reynolds led the way to the staircase at the rear of the house, for it was closer to her rooms. Once they arrived, Elizabeth said, "I am afraid I will have to bother you to take me up the stairs again, James."

Mr. Bennet shook his head. "*I* will be carrying you whilst I am here, Elizabeth, not a servant."

"It is three floors, Papa. I would never forgive myself if you became injured on my account."

"Nonsense, Lizzy! It is my fatherly duty." James held the chair as Mr. Bennet picked her up. "And you are light as a feather, my dear. All that walking, I suppose." He chuckled as Mrs. Reynolds preceded him up the stairs. Jane came after him, followed by James and another footman carrying the chair. Mr. Bennet's pace slowed on the second set of steps, but he continued on, and he seemed a bit relieved when they reached the third floor as James held the chair ready for him to put her in it. Elizabeth glanced at Jane, who seemed to be stifling a giggle.

They proceeded down the hallway until Mrs. Reynolds stopped and showed Mr. Bennet into his rooms. He stopped at the doorway and said, "I will meet you girls in your sitting room in a few minutes." He then disappeared into his chambers, and James took over pushing her chair.

Mrs. Reynolds came out again and showed Jane and Elizabeth into Jane's room. She introduced Jane's maid, Dorothy, and unlocked the door to Elizabeth's sitting room. The housekeeper proceeded to explain where each door led.

Jane's room was all lavender and bluebells, with a pink rose and white daisy here and there. Again the design in the wallpaper matched the rugs.

"Thank you, Mrs. Reynolds. These are the grandest rooms I have ever had the pleasure of staying in," Jane said, wide-eyed.

Mrs. Reynolds nodded before excusing herself and departing through the door to the corridor.

Dorothy said, "I can 'ave a bath drawn if you'd like, miss."

Jane smiled. "Yes, that would be lovely. Will you help me out of this dress, please? I will remain in my chemise until you are ready."

The maid did so and then folded the dress over her arm. "I'll 'ave your travellin' dress cleaned as soon as can be, Miss Bennet." She curtsied and exited into the dressing room.

When the door closed behind Dorothy, Jane moved closer to Elizabeth and took her hand. "Oh, Lizzy, we have been so worried! How are you, really?"

"I am healing, Jane. Everyone has been so helpful and obliging. Lady Adelaide was quite pleasant and accommodating, but I think our presence there was an additional burden since the earl is so ill. I do believe that is what was behind our moving to Pemberley, though I suspect they did not want Georgiana there if Lord Matlock should pass away, as well. She has already seen enough death in her lifetime. Additionally, her habit is to practice the pianoforte for hours a day as it gives her much pleasure, and the doctor did not want her to do so at Matlock, for the earl's sake."

Elizabeth closed her eyes and sighed. "Jane I am angry at myself for putting everyone through so much trouble. This was supposed to be a holiday for our aunt and uncle, but it became duty and drudgery instead. Poor Aunt, having to nurse an injured niece as an alternative to spending time with her friends and enjoying herself, and Uncle with nothing to do but wait for news and pay the doctor's fees."

"Lizzy, I am certain they did not mind. It was an accident."

"An accident which should have been avoided." Elizabeth shook her head. "One that would not have happened at all if my behaviour had not been reckless and impulsive! I should have known better, Jane, and I am determined you shall never see such foolishness from me again."

"I am sure you exaggerate, Lizzy." Jane squeezed Elizabeth's hand.

"Unfortunately, I do not." Elizabeth sighed. "But, on a more pleasant note, I have gained a new friend in Georgiana. She is sweet and kind, and I think you will like her as much as I do. Although she might seem quiet at first, she will open up to you once she knows you better.

"Colonel Fitzwilliam is as amiable as when I met him in March at Rosings, and all the staff at Pemberley is very attentive. I have caused much trouble to many people, yet no one complains. I have often compared my treatment here to what it would have been like if this had occurred at home, and when I do, I realize, quite selfishly, it is better it happened here." Elizabeth chuckled.

She expected her mother had experienced numerous fits of nerves upon hearing she was injured—and especially when her father had told the family they were not *all* coming to Pemberley—but with her being away from home during her recovery, her mother's fits would pass quickly. Kitty and Lydia would be jealous and would make certain their mother's focus was soon redirected back to themselves. Whether she was at Longbourn or Pemberley, their sister Mary would voice many speeches in an attempt to instruct—and Elizabeth was expecting to hear them repeated once she was home.

While she could tell that Jane was thinking about the same thing she was, she knew Jane would never comment on the subject.

"And how are my mother and my sisters?" Elizabeth asked.

"They have been concerned, but they are well. Lydia was miserable when Papa forbade her from going to Brighton."

Goodness! What an uproar must have ensued for Jane to raise her eyebrows!

"But I thought Papa gave her permission…" Elizabeth's voice trailed off when Jane shook her head.

"The express from Mr. Gardiner arrived the night before she was to leave. Papa was afraid uncle made your condition sound better than it was to ease our worries, and he did not want the family 'spread to the four corners of the winds' if we should need to travel suddenly. He truly feared the worst, Lizzy."

"But why?"

"Do you not remember the story about what happened with Papa's brother John?"

Elizabeth gasped. "I do recall it, now that you have mentioned it. I had forgotten." Apparently, their father's younger brother had been staying with a friend's family in the north when he fell ill. Mr. Bennet was told by letter that all would be well, but then a few days later, he received an express requesting him to come. John Bennet had died before his brother was able to get there.

"And your handwriting was not the same as usual, Lizzy—even your style of writing was different. I have never seen Papa so worried in all my life.

Elizabeth frowned. "I had twisted my left arm, so it was difficult to hold the paper when I wrote. I thought I had done well with my penmanship, but apparently not! Also, until these past few days, I had a terrible headache. Most likely, I was not paying as close attention to the content as I usually would."

"That would explain it." Jane smiled. "I am so happy you are well!"

Dorothy came in to tell Jane her bath was ready.

"I should go rest for a few minutes or Aunt will never forgive me."

At Elizabeth's request, the maid pushed her chair through the sitting room and into her own bedchamber, where Hannah took over her care.

Chapter 19

An hour later, Elizabeth joined her father and aunt in the Rose sitting room.

"Well, well," said Mr. Bennet. "This is quite the estate. The furnishings are so fine, I am afraid to touch anything! And I suspect one could get lost for days in the house without seeing another living being. Perhaps it is a bit easier to forgive Mr. Darcy his elevated pride after seeing Pemberley, eh, Lizzy?"

Mrs. Gardiner said, "Mr. Darcy has every right to be proud of his estate, Thomas, but we saw nothing of undue pride when we met him in London, did we, Lizzy?"

"No, but..." Elizabeth paused. "My opinion of Mr. Darcy has improved a great deal since we saw him in Hertfordshire, Papa."

"Really, Lizzy, I would never have suspected *you* would change your opinion and think the man more *tolerable* only after seeing the wealth of his estate."

"You misunderstand my meaning. I have come to know him better. Whilst visiting Charlotte in Kent, I spent time in his company, and then we met again in London. I do not mean that either his mind or manners were improved, but that, from knowing him better, his disposition is better understood. You will see it for yourself if he returns from his journey while you are here, sir. I am sure you will agree."

Her father peered at her with a grim intensity which was rarely seen upon his features. "I must ask... will Mr. Darcy request an audience with me when he returns from America, Lizzy?"

Elizabeth averted her gaze in an attempt to hide her deep blush. She whispered, "I – I do not believe so, sir."

"I am glad this subject came up while your aunt was in the room, because judging by the look Madeline is giving me, she supposes otherwise."

Elizabeth quickly looked at Mrs. Gardiner. An expression of apology accompanied her saying, "I think he deserves some sort of warning, Lizzy, after all."

Elizabeth shook her head. "He will not, sir."

An uncomfortable silence came over the room until Mr. Bennet spoke again. "Let us play the supposing game we used to amuse ourselves with when you were a child, Lizzy. Suppose Mr. Darcy *was* to come to me to ask for your hand? I always thought you despised the man, so up until a few moments ago, I had not even thought twice about what my answer would be, but now..."

"It is of no consequence, sir. He will not come to you."

Mrs. Gardiner rose from her seat. "I think I will check on Jane. She is through this door here?"

Elizabeth nodded.

Mrs. Gardiner was half-way across the room when the door opened and Jane entered the sitting room.

Mrs. Gardiner said, "Will you please show me your room, Jane? I—"

"You both might as well stay," said Elizabeth with a chuckle. "That way I will not have to explain this three times."

Mrs. Gardiner returned to her seat as Jane asked, "What is it, Lizzy? You are so pale."

Mr. Bennet looked at his eldest daughter and motioned towards the sofa. Jane sat next to her aunt.

Mr. Bennet said, "Satisfy my curiosity and play along, my dear. *Suppose* Mr. Darcy does ask for your hand. What would you wish me to say?"

Elizabeth stared at her lap.

"Do you like him, Lizzy?" he asked.

She did not look up. "Yes."

"Enough to marry him?"

She nodded.

"You would not be doing this as a result of your mother's comments after I refused permission to Mr. Collins, would you? Her saying she will be turned out to the hedgerows and all that? I would not have you marry where there was not mutual respect and admiration. My greatest wish is that you, Jane—and all my daughters—have a happy life."

Elizabeth examined her father's concerned expression. "No, Papa. Mama has nothing to do with it. I do like him, very much. In fact, I love him."

Mr. Bennet's shocked appearance made Elizabeth's stomach tighten. He looked at Jane, who smiled widely.

Mrs. Gardiner was nodding. "I saw evidence of it myself, Thomas, in London. You should also know that Mr. Darcy is in love with Lizzy."

"Aunt, as I already explained, he will not ask for my hand again."

"Again!" Mr. Bennet exclaimed.

Elizabeth felt her face heat. "I was *angry* at him when he proposed, sir, and I refused him."

Mr. Bennet laughed out loud. "You rejected Mr. Darcy's proposal of marriage? Well, well! I wonder what your mother would say to *that*!" He chuckled for another few seconds until his gaze landed on Jane. "Jane, you do not seem surprised to hear any of this."

Jane's eyes opened wide.

"No need to explain, dear Jane. I understand. Elizabeth has spoken to you of this before." Mr. Bennet turned to Elizabeth. "Are you certain your affections are of the lasting kind, my dear? Not infatuation or that you are impressed with all this?" He waved his hand around, indicating Pemberley.

"I am sure, sir. I already regretted my refusal before I returned to Longbourn in the spring."

"I thought something was bothering you when you came home, but I dismissed it as having spent so many weeks in the company of Mr. Collins." He chuckled again. "Well, I certainly do hope Mr. Darcy returns to England before Monday so I may see for myself if my opinion improves upon longer acquaintance. But if he does not, and your aunt is correct, I am sure I will see him again soon. From what I have seen of this house thus far, the gentleman has excellent taste—which should mean he would recognize your worth. If he *is* in love with you, Lizzy, he will offer for you again. Mark my words."

"And mine," Mrs. Gardiner added.

"I agree," said Jane.

"Goodness! I am afraid you all will be terribly disappointed when he does not! How could anyone expect a man such as Mr. Darcy to offer for the same lady *twice*? He has probably forgotten me by now."

Mr. Bennet rose and took his second daughter's hand. "If he has, he would not deserve you, my Lizzy."

He leaned down and kissed her forehead, then looked at the other ladies and took a deep breath, as was his way whenever he dismissed one subject and wished to begin another.

He turned back to Elizabeth. "Mrs. Hill sent your mail with us, but I forgot to bring it in with me. Since you will be here a while, I have told her to forward anything else that comes in. I will return in a moment." He left through the door to the corridor.

The door closed behind him and left the three ladies sitting in silence. Elizabeth tried to think of something to say so neither Jane nor Mrs. Gardiner would revive the previous discussion, but her mind was blank.

What an embarrassing conversation that had been! And had her father actually said he would grant permission for Mr. Darcy to marry her if he solicited his approval? As she reviewed the exchange, she realized he had not, but he had certainly implied it.

Elizabeth was called back to the present when she heard Jane make a noise. She glanced up—both her aunt and sister were trembling with stifled laughter. Before long, Elizabeth was giggling right along with them, and the other two ladies laughed out loud. The tension eased, Jane spoke of their journey, seemingly to fill the time—and avoid the subject they were probably all three still thinking about. Mr. Darcy.

Mr. Bennet returned holding a stack of letters and a thick parcel. He crossed to Elizabeth. "It was not until you went away to visit with Mrs. Collins that I realized how many correspondents you have, Lizzy. I am sure you asked permission to correspond with all these people at one time, but I cannot remember who some of these people are." He put the stack on the table next to Elizabeth.

Elizabeth picked them up one by one and explained—one was from Charlotte, another from her mother, her sister Mary, a young lady she had met through Mrs. Gardiner, a former neighbour who had married and moved away, and so on, until she came to the parcel. "This has no return address. I wonder who it is from."

"Open it and see," her father suggested. "I would like to see who sent something that took up so much room in my luggage."

She ripped off the brown paper and removed a page from within. "It is the book I was sure I had left at Hunsford Cottage. It seems the maid found it, assumed it was one from Mr. Collins's library, and placed it on a shelf there. Charlotte came across it and has returned it." She picked up the book and handed it to her father. "I was going to look for a replacement for your library while we have been travelling."

"Ah, I was looking for this the other day," Mr. Bennet said.

"May I finish reading it first, Papa? I had only a few pages left. I shall read it tonight and give it to you tomorrow so you can read it on the way home."

"Certainly. Which reminds me... I have been thinking..." he began. "I believe the best course of action on Monday would be for Madeline to return with me—along with your maid, of course, to make everything proper." He nodded to her. "We will take a more direct route to London than the one we took here. You will reunite with your husband and children by Wednesday, after which I will return directly to Longbourn. Jane shall remain here with Lizzy." He hesitated. "That is, if Miss Darcy approves the plan, of course."

Elizabeth said, "I am sure she will."

~%~

The next several days passed quickly. After speaking to the doctor himself on Friday, Mr. Bennet was satisfied Elizabeth was healing as well as could be expected, though the doctor still would not allow her to travel.

As Elizabeth had predicted, Georgiana and Jane got along splendidly and were calling each other by their Christian names before the weekend had passed. Therefore, Georgiana was happy to agree to Jane's staying on at Pemberley. Jane had brought along her embroidery, for which she had a special talent, and she kept busy with that whilst listening to the other two young ladies practice on the pianoforte.

Mrs. Gardiner took leave of her friends at Lambton after attending church there on Sunday.

Surprisingly, Mr. Bennet and Colonel Fitzwilliam spent quite a bit of time together in Darcy's study and also in his billiard room. Whenever they rejoined the ladies after supper, the two would be guffawing over some jest Elizabeth was sure only gentlemen would understand.

Monday morning, Mr. Bennet met his daughter in the Rose sitting room, with the intention of escorting Elizabeth downstairs to break their fasts together before he and Mrs. Gardiner departed.

"Jane came to see me a few minutes ago," Elizabeth said. "She will meet us downstairs."

"Fine." Mr. Bennet walked over to the bell-pull and rang twice to call James to transport the rolling chair, then turned to face Elizabeth. Amusement twinkled in his eyes. "I am sorry, my dear, that I cannot stay any longer and continue to carry you about, but I must return to Longbourn. I have to say I did not think I would enjoy my time here as much as I have. It is a shame none of my girls have a large enough dowry to satisfy Colonel Fitzwilliam's requirements, for I would not mind having him as a son-in-law."

Elizabeth laughed. "I will miss you, Papa. Thank you for coming such a distance to make certain I was as well as Uncle Gardiner said I was."

Two hours later, as Mr. Bennet handed his sister-in-law into his hired coach, Mrs. Gardiner turned to wave goodbye one more time to Jane, Elizabeth, and Georgiana, who were together on the front parlour balcony. Once Mrs. Gardiner was safely inside, Mr. Bennet did the same. The three girls remained until the coach was out of sight, and then Jane pushed Elizabeth back inside.

A minute later, a maid entered with a letter on a salver, crossing to Georgiana. As Georgiana picked it up, delight brightened her countenance. "It is from Fitzwilliam!" she declared, and she broke the seal immediately. Elizabeth and Jane sat in silence, hoping to hear Georgiana's news.

Her gaze continued to scan the words as she said, "He arrived in Virginia safely." Her hand fluttered to her throat. "My cousin Bianca was in a bad way when he found her. They were to return to the port town within three days and take the first return ship they could find." She examined the top of the missive again. "If they found passage soon after they arrived at Alexandria, Fitzwilliam could be home in a week!"

Jane furrowed her brow. "I am sorry to disappoint you, but do not get your hopes up too high. It seems this dispatch made the crossing on a very fast ship, Georgie."

Elizabeth joined in, "When one of our neighbours made the trip, it took longer than six weeks."

"That is what I thought as well, but this letter's arrival in five weeks proves it is possible. Perhaps they were even on the same ship!" She practically bounced out of her chair. "He might even be home today!" She rushed across the room to the window and out onto the balcony, but returned shortly, blushing. "That was a silly thing to do, was it not?"

Elizabeth smiled. "It displays your affection for your brother in a way words cannot." She gestured to Jane. "We have never had a brother, but I will tell you a secret. When Jane and my father were expected, if I had been able, I would have been rushing to and from the window the same way you did just now."

"And when we made the turn into Pemberley's drive..." Jane giggled. "I was so excited to see Lizzy, I began fidgeting in my seat. By the time we saw the house, I was ready to get out and run the rest of the way. In fact, our father told me he had never seen me behave so much like our sisters Kitty or Lydia before!" Jane stopped a moment. "Oh! They are very energetic."

Georgiana and Elizabeth were already smiling.

"Georgie has heard quite a few stories about all of our sisters. I am sure she knows more about Kitty and Lydia than they do of themselves."

The three young ladies had a good laugh.

"There," said Elizabeth. "So you see, we wholeheartedly forgive you for running away from us." She hesitated a moment. "With Mrs. Gardiner and my father on their way home, Mrs. Annesley in Lambton, and Colonel Fitzwilliam gone to Matlock, we are fresh out of distractions for you. However, we should do something to keep you occupied. Perhaps Jane could sit near the window as she does her embroidery and keep watch on the drive while we practice a new duet?"

"And later, we may go for a ride in the gig," Georgiana said. "Oh, but it only sits two. Do you ride, Jane?"

"Jane is an expert horsewoman and loves to ride."

"But I did not bring my riding habit," Jane said.

"We are almost the same size. You can borrow one of mine," Georgiana answered.

"Well, then. We have our plan for the day."

"Only if you rest after we take some air, Lizzy," Jane said. "Aunt Gardiner made me promise you would."

"I will, Jane. Do not worry."

"Poor Richard," said Georgiana. "It is too bad Mr. Bennet could not remain longer. I am sure my cousin would be more comfortable if we had another gentleman at Pemberley."

"And I am sure he will survive. Our father has been surrounded by his wife and five daughters on a daily basis for many years, and he has lived through it, though the colonel may be happy to return to his troops eventually."

"While I love my brother and cousin very much, after spending most of the past five years with Fitzwilliam and Richard, I have enjoyed so much spending time with the both of you. I have always wanted a sister..." Georgiana looked at Elizabeth, blushed, and averted her eyes. "I am thankful you had to stay at Matlock and came to Pemberley, Lizzy. And that Jane came to stay." She gasped. "Oh! But I am *not* glad you were injured!"

"No need to worry, Georgie! I understood what you meant." Elizabeth said. "If we are for the music room, will one of you ring for James, please? I would do it myself, but I cannot get to the bell-pull."

Georgiana bit her bottom lip sheepishly. "Since no one else is around, would you mind if I pushed you myself?"

Jane shrugged and smiled.

"As it is on the same floor, I do not see why not. It would be a relief not to take anyone else away from their duties."

Chapter 20

Two days later, the ladies, along with Mrs. Annesley, were in the front parlour once again, their task being to mend clothes from the poor box. Jane and Mrs. Annesley chatted amiably together as they sewed, while Georgiana had taken a seat by the window with Elizabeth beside her. The younger of the two had spent more time looking out at the driveway than sewing. Though she did not say so, all knew she hoped her brother would arrive at any moment.

Ever since they had been to the portrait gallery, Elizabeth often found Georgiana staring at nothing in particular, thinking. Worrying. Usually, Elizabeth would try to distract her, but, she thought, perhaps it was time to address her fears again.

"Georgie," she said quietly enough so Jane and Mrs. Annesley could not hear. "Are you thinking about the plaque again?"

Georgiana turned her head and opened her mouth to speak, then closed it and nodded.

"I have been thinking about it, too. I am sure a servant bumped into it and loosened it, and it fell later without anyone around to hear it. I feel confident it does not mean anything dreadful happened to your brother."

"I know it does not make sense to think it was an indication something terrible has occurred, but until I see him, I will worry. It is my nature."

Elizabeth asked, "I understand, but what do you feel in here?" She put her hand on her chest. "In your heart? Search your feelings. Does anything feel *different*?"

Georgiana shook her head. "No. If anything, I am happier at having you and Jane here. I do not feel at all sad, Lizzy."

"Well, hold onto that, Georgie." She put her hand on Georgiana's and squeezed as Jane crossed the room towards them. "It will get you through until he does come home."

Jane approached. Handing a child's dress to Georgiana, she said, "I am not sure this one can be repaired without adding new fabric at the hem…" Her voice trailed off as she abruptly turned her head to look out the window. "Look, Georgie! A coach has just now come over the hill."

Georgiana rose and rushed through the open French doors, out onto the balcony. Mrs. Annesley crossed and followed her.

"Help me up, Jane! Quickly," Elizabeth said.

"Lizzy, you should not."

"Oh, I will stand only on my good leg and lean on the doorway. Please? I need to see if it is he," she whispered. "I promise not to put any weight on my injured leg."

Jane helped her up but stood by with a hand on her sister's back to steady her.

As the coach crossed the bridge, Mrs. Annesley said, "It is a gentleman's coach, not a hired coach as Mr. Darcy would have had to use."

"That is true," Georgiana said with disappointment, though she still watched its approach. "Since we do not know the name of the ship he is on, we do not know where it will land."

Elizabeth was about to ask Jane to help her sit down again when she realized Jane's hand was trembling against the small of her back. She studied her sister. "Jane?"

Jane pointed at the approaching coach and said hoarsely, "It…" She cleared her throat. "It is Mr. Bingley's coach."

Elizabeth held the doorway more firmly and leaned forward, attempting to move up onto the toes of her good foot. Yes, she could see it more clearly now. It *was* the Bingley coach. Once she regained her footing, she turned back to her sister, grabbed hold of her free hand and squeezed. "Jane! It will be well," she whispered. "Help me back into the chair, please."

Georgiana said, "Mr. Bingley and his family were *supposed* to arrive today, but Fitzwilliam told me he wrote to delay the gathering until he returned to England."

"It seems Mr. Bingley did not receive the letter, Miss Darcy," Mrs. Annesley answered. She returned to the parlour and began to collect their sewing supplies.

Georgiana proceeded to help her.

Jane pushed Elizabeth's chair further into the room, situating it so she could see all of the chairs and sofas arranged in the sitting area and moved to assist the others.

Wishing she could help, but confined to her chair, Elizabeth gathered her own materials while she reviewed everything she knew about the current state of affairs in an effort to prepare herself for what might happen once the superior sisters and Bingley entered the room.

Elizabeth shook her head. *Poor Jane! What she must be going through!*

Although Darcy had admitted to telling Bingley he believed Jane did not care for him, Elizabeth had deduced Mrs. Louisa Hurst and Miss Caroline Bingley were primarily responsible for Bingley's departure from Hertfordshire so suddenly last fall. His sisters must have realized they could not convince him Jane did not care for him if Jane was present at every gathering and lived an easy visiting distance only three miles away, so they had carefully designed to have their brother abandon Hertfordshire, in turn, breaking Jane's gentle heart.

And since Bingley had so obviously returned Jane's regard, it was probable he was in a similar state of misery.

But now, with them all living in the same house for as long as the Bingleys and Bennets remained at Pemberley, Bingley would have daily proof of Jane's affections! Her delighted smile, her loving gaze, her delicate blushes, and her sweet conversation would serve as a constant reminder that the truth contradicted the ideas his sisters had worked so hard to embed in his mind. Jane *had* truly loved him when they were all together in Hertfordshire, and she loved him still.

And yes, it would be the immediate assumption of Mrs. Hurst and Caroline that they had best prevent the two from ever conversing, even from looking at each other if they could manage it. If their plan ever had a chance of success, they would be forced to attack sweet Jane and break down her confidence the moment they entered the room.

Suddenly, the contents of the note Caroline wrote to Jane upon the Bingleys leaving Hertfordshire last November came flooding back to her.

Caroline Bingley had implied her brother would soon marry *Georgiana!*

Goodness, how could she have forgotten such a thing?

Darcy had made it clear to Elizabeth that there were no tender feelings between Georgiana and Bingley. But Jane did not know this. She could not have explained it to her sister. Jane would have been humiliated to know her heart had been a topic of conversation between Elizabeth and Darcy. The last thing Elizabeth had wanted to do was to cause Jane to feel worse than she already did.

The worst of it was that right now, poor, poor Jane would be expecting to have to watch the gentleman she loved try to impress another lady until Elizabeth healed.

What a predicament! How could she ease Jane's mind?

This initial encounter would not be pleasant, but it would be more important than any future gathering of the same players, for it would set the stage.

Could she manage to stand up to Mrs. Hurst and Caroline, to give Jane and Bingley a second chance at the happiness they deserved without insulting Georgiana's guests in any way, in turn offending Georgiana?

Elizabeth took a deep, bracing breath. She simply *had* to!

The ladies finished tidying up their work and sat down just in time for the butler to open the double doors and announce the new guests.

"Mr. Bingley, Mr. Hurst, Mrs. Hurst, and Miss Bingley," he said formally, standing aside to allow them to pass through.

All who could stand, did. Elizabeth saw Mrs. Annesley shift a bit closer to Georgiana and touch her elbow. Georgiana nodded once, straightened her spine, and moved forward a few steps.

Jane shifted a step to her right, closer to Elizabeth, so Georgiana was standing between her and the door. Elizabeth assumed that from the door, one could see someone was standing there, but not be able to identify the person immediately.

It pained her to see that both Georgiana and Jane were trembling.

Briefly, Jane glanced at Elizabeth. Her eyes were open wide in fright. Elizabeth reached out and squeezed Jane's hand. Her sister blushed deeply but seemed to relax a little. She wished she could do a similar service for Georgiana.

Poor Georgiana. Although Elizabeth was certain the girl's brother would not have allowed it, she could only imagine the Bingley sisters must take advantage of her sweet nature in every way possible whenever he was not present. Elizabeth would not allow that to happen in his absence this time. Elizabeth cleared her throat, hoping it would be enough to remind Georgiana she was not alone.

After a few seconds' delay, which was probably aimed at heightening Georgiana's anticipation of their entrance, Mrs. Hurst appeared first, followed closely by Caroline.

Georgiana, Jane, and Mrs. Annesley all curtsied, as did the Bingley sisters.

With a great deal of pomp, Caroline extended her right arm and moved forward, crying out, "Dearest Georgiana! It has been *ages* since I saw you last!"

A glance to her hostess's right resulted in Caroline's spying Elizabeth. Her stumble was so quick, Elizabeth almost missed it. She corrected herself instantly, but it was too late--Caroline's display of absolute perfection as she crossed the room was ruined. Her arm dropped to her side. "And Miss Eliza." Her tone fell flat as her nostrils flared.

Bowing at the waist being the closest thing to a curtsy she could manage just now, Elizabeth did so, which served her well as she did not think she could look upon the authors of her sister's misery for one moment longer without sneering. "I apologize for not standing, but I have broken my ankle." She gestured to a wheel on the chair.

Jane stepped to her left, now into full view of the newcomers. "Good day, Mrs. Hurst. Miss Bingley." She curtsied once more.

The Bingley sisters did not return the consideration. Their shock and dismay upon seeing Jane at Pemberley was almost palpable. Mrs. Hurst looked back at the door, still open, the entryway empty except for the butler who remained in place, evidently still waiting for the two gentlemen to enter.

Mrs. Hurst exchanged a look with her sister, and then addressed Elizabeth. "Whatever are you doing here? Is it not a bit far from Longbourn for one of your long walks?"

Elizabeth blinked. At least at Netherfield, their dislike for her had been veiled, not such blatant hostility! Her presence here must have shocked Mrs. Hurst more than she had anticipated. "I was travelling with my aunt and uncle. My aunt spent her childhood in the area."

"Ah! Were you travelling with the relatives in trade, who live in Cheapside, or perhaps with the uncle who is an attorney at Meryton?"

Was this flagrant attitude for Georgiana's benefit—to prove to her that Elizabeth was not worthy of her friendship? "With Mr. and Mrs. Gardiner, who live in London."

The newcomers did not hide their satisfied smiles.

Yes, her aunt had grown up in a tenant farmhouse instead of the manor house of the estate, but Mrs. Gardiner was ten times a lady in behaviour than either of the Bingley sisters were.

Georgiana's pallor turned into a blush.

Elizabeth saw Jane's hands fist, attracting her attention. Gone was the expression of embarrassment and fear that had been there only a moment before. In fact, she had never seen her elder sister so furious in all her life!

Georgiana said, "Will you sit down, please?"

Once all of the ladies found a seat, Elizabeth asked, "Are not Mr. Bingley and Mr. Hurst with you? I thought the butler announced—"

"They were right behind us. I do not know... They have disappeared," Mrs. Hurst answered. "How are your family, Miss Eliza?"

Again Elizabeth was addressed without even acknowledging Jane.

"They are well. You have just missed seeing my father by two days. He came with Jane to speak to the doctor. On his return trip, he took my aunt with him, so she could be reunited with her husband and children in London. In fact, you may have passed them on the road or seen them at an inn—"

"I doubt we would stay at the same inns," Caroline said, turning up her nose. "Miss Eliza, it is very *convenient* that you should become injured at Pemberley. I find it strange that whenever a member of your family is at a house grander than Longbourn, you two seem to find a way to remain there in order to convalesce. Will you be leaving soon?"

Georgiana's gasp was audible. Her colour had risen higher.

"Elizabeth is improving as well as can be expected. Thank you for your concern in asking," Jane said forcefully, raising her chin.

Elizabeth had a difficult time keeping herself from laughing. Jane was quite mild-mannered unless someone insulted a member of her family. The next proved the same could be said about Georgiana when someone disrespected her friends.

Georgiana's tone was firm when she said, "Lizzy was injured at Matlock, where I was staying in my brother's absence, and not at Pemberley. My aunt, Lady Matlock, saw to it that her *guest* was well taken care of. When she was able to travel a short distance, I invited her to complete her recovery here."

"Why, of course she would be recovering well…" Mrs. Hurst sputtered out, apparently realizing she had offended Georgiana. "After all, I am certain Lady Matlock and Mr. Darcy have seen to it that Miss Eliza has received only the best of care."

"My brother is not at home. In fact, he is not even in England at this time," Georgiana said.

Both Mrs. Hurst and Caroline raised their eyebrows. Elizabeth noticed Georgiana press her lips together as if hiding her amusement. Her young friend knew, as she did, that their only aim in coming was to make a good impression on Darcy, and with him not here… Well, Elizabeth decided, they would probably not turn down the hospitality Pemberley could offer even if Caroline's target was out of the country.

"But I am certain he would approve of the plans for Lizzy's recovery, as does my other guardian, Colonel Fitzwilliam. My cousin is out just now, but he will rejoin us later."

Just then, Bingley entered through the open doorway and stopped before the door to bow.

At first glance, Elizabeth's impression was that he had lost a great deal of weight since she had last seen him and he seemed much older than he actually was. The smile that graced his handsome face everywhere he went in Hertfordshire was gone completely now. He did not look well at all.

Mr. Hurst followed a moment later, bowed slightly, and plopped himself down next to his wife. The butler left the room, closing the door behind him.

Looking only at Georgiana, Bingley said, "Good day, Miss Darcy. I apologize for the delay. I forgot something in my coat—"

A movement on the sofa diagonally across from Georgiana made him look in that direction. His speech stopped short, and literally before Elizabeth's eyes, he transformed from the wretched creature who had entered the room into the Bingley she had known the previous fall. His features slowly reorganized into one of the widest smiles Elizabeth had ever seen upon his face, proving once and for all that his grins last autumn had been for Jane.

Jane was smiling at Bingley as well, but she could also see that her sister's eyes glittered in the sunlight as she blinked back tears.

"Miss Bennet! How good it is to see you!" Bingley bowed low, rising again as he deliberately absorbed every inch of Jane's countenance. "Indeed, this certainly *is* a pleasure. I had no idea you would be at Pemberley! Darcy never said a word."

The last was said under his breath as he searched the faces in the room, probably looking for Darcy. He noticed Elizabeth.

"And Miss Elizabeth! I am glad to meet with you again." He moved towards her and bowed again, not quite as fully as he had to Jane. Noticing the rolling chair she sat in, his brow furrowed. "Oh! You are injured? I am sorry to hear it." He glanced back at Jane.

"Yes, thank you, Mr. Bingley. It is nice to see you again, as well. I am afraid that, although Mr. Darcy had asked that we visit Pemberley to tour the house and take advantage of the grounds while he was away, he had no inkling we would be staying here, so he would not have been able to inform you of such."

"Ah!" Bingley said, fixing his eyes on Jane once again. He seemed too distracted to think of anything further to say. His gaze darted from one empty chair to another.

Elizabeth recognized his dilemma. If he sat across from Jane, he could drink in her features as much as he liked, but if he sat next to her, he could speak with her.

Elizabeth was happy when he chose the latter and applied both strategies at once. When he took his seat, he turned towards Jane as much as he could without seeming rude to the others.

Happy day! Mr. Bingley still loves Jane!

Jane beheld him through her lowered lashes, blushed, and looked down at her lap again.

With Georgiana's right side to Mrs. Hurst and Caroline, when she turned to look directly at Elizabeth, it was plain to see the former could not perceive the left side of her young friend's face. Georgiana glanced at where Jane sat with Bingley, then back to Elizabeth. Elizabeth almost laughed when Georgiana proceeded to wink at her with her left eye.

Mrs. Annesley, who was now sitting directly across from Georgiana, cleared her throat. When the two young ladies looked her way, Elizabeth expected to receive some sort of reprimand, but instead, Mrs. Annesley smiled.

It seemed Jane had two more allies!

The door to the corridor opened again, and several maids entered with an elaborate tea service. Colonel Fitzwilliam came in as the servants scurried out of the room. After greetings, Bingley immediately regained his seat next to Jane. The colonel pulled up a chair between Mrs. Annesley and Mrs. Hurst.

"Georgiana, dear," Caroline said loudly, obviously hoping to distract her brother, to no avail. She spoke even more forcefully when she continued, "You mentioned Mr. Darcy had gone away from England. May I ask where he has gone?"

"Virginia."

"The colonies?"

"They are not colonies anymore, Miss Bingley," Colonel Fitzwilliam joined in.

Georgiana nodded. "Yes, my cousin Bianca—the Countess of Lashbrook—required my brother's assistance to return home after her husband passed away."

Caroline paled and turned to her sister, whose eyes were open wide. "Are you saying Lady Bianca is a widow? So soon? And she is *alone* on a ship with Mr. Darcy?"

Elizabeth examined the silent exchange of looks between the sisters. Interesting. Caroline seemed in a panic at this news.

"Yes, Miss Bingley." Colonel Fitzwilliam raised his chin. "My *sister* is now a widow and in mourning. If you are suggesting there is some sort of misconduct occurring on board ship between my sister and cousin, please say it plainly, madam, for I would dearly love to hear it."

Caroline's high-pitched titter betrayed her anxiety. "No! Colonel, I assure you that you misunderstood my meaning."

Mrs. Hurst chimed in, expertly diverting the attention from her sister. "And when is Mr. Darcy expected home?"

"I should think they will be home within the next few days." Georgiana smiled. "I received a communication from Fitzwilliam two days ago. He said he—and his party…" She glanced at Mrs. Hurst and Caroline. "…would be on the next ship leaving for England."

"And it is a good thing, too," said Colonel Fitzwilliam. "I do not know how much longer the earl will be able to put things off."

Although the Bingleys and Hursts did not understand the meaning of that statement, the remainder of the company understood all too well. Elizabeth hoped Lord Matlock would be able to see his daughter one last time.

"It is a wonder Darcy did not write me and delay our visit," Bingley said, proving he *had* been paying attention to something other than Jane.

The colonel cleared his throat of any emotion remaining after uttering his last statement. "I was told that he did, Bingley, but I can see by your presence here that you must not have received it."

Bingley raised his eyebrows. "No, I did not." His apprehensive gaze wandered to the couch across the way, where his sisters sat.

Did he suspect one of his sisters had hidden or destroyed the letter? Goodness, this meeting was turning out to be quite enlightening!

Caroline remained quite upset, and being so, when she directed her attention to her brother, who was yet again busy speaking in quiet tones with Jane, she narrowed her eyes. Elizabeth knew she had to do something to turn the sisters' mind elsewhere.

"Miss Bingley, I understood you were in London for the holidays. London must be lovely at that time of year…"

Elizabeth did her best to continue to distract them, asking questions about anything and everything that might have happened between the day they had left Hertfordshire until their arrival here. After a few minutes, Georgiana and Colonel Fitzwilliam seemed to catch on and joined in. One time, even Mrs. Annesley redirected the conversation. Between them all, they kept one or the other sister speaking until tea was finished and Mrs. Reynolds came in and nodded to Georgiana.

Georgiana stood. "Mrs. Reynolds will show you to your rooms now. I am sure you must be tired after your journey. Shall we expect you to join us for supper?"

Mr. Hurst voiced his first opinion of the day, "Absolutely!"

Based on past experience, Elizabeth guessed he would not miss a meal for the world.

Mrs. Hurst and Caroline added their agreement, as well, and they all followed Mrs. Reynolds from the room.

All except Bingley, who evidently missed the exchange.

Colonel Fitzwilliam chuckled. "Bingley, old boy! Time for us to change out of our dusty travel clothes, I think."

Bingley stood and bowed to the ladies. "I will see you all at supper, then."

The two gentlemen took their leave.

As Bingley walked through the doorway ahead of him, Colonel Fitzwilliam turned and caught Elizabeth's eye, glanced quickly at Jane, and returned his consideration to Elizabeth. He nodded thoughtfully and then left the room.

Had he realized the young lady he had told her of at Rosings was Jane? The one Darcy spoke of helping to separate from Bingley? If so, she looked forward to hearing his opinion on the matter now that he had met her and had seen the two together with his own eyes.

What an eventful afternoon!

~%~

Darcy scanned the ocean. Nothing. Perhaps they had given up the chase?

He rubbed his weary eyes and cast his gaze as far to the left as he could, studying the horizon once more.

They had first sighted the pirate ship two weeks ago, and the crew thought they lost it only to have it reappear on two different occasions. When the *Gypsy's Promise* had stopped to try to restock their fresh water, the pirates caught up with them.

If Mott's ship had not been as fast as the captain boasted, they would have been captured by now.

Darcy prayed the wind kept up. In fact, they had been making such good time, they would arrive in England sooner than expected.

How did the pirates know which route they would take? Was it a coincidence or was someone aboard the *Gypsy's Promise* sending signals of some sort?

The level of tension amongst the crew was high and arguments regularly ensued at least once each day. A few ended in full-out brawls.

Mott had recommended all three of his male passengers carry guns and even sold Darcy an additional firearm. Either Hughes or Fleming stood guard at Bianca's cabin at all times.

Darcy bore the unenviable task of forbidding Bianca and her maid from coming above deck for more than an hour a day. When they did, he, Hughes, and Fleming would remain close by—armed and alert.

Mott had said he recognized the ship, and had had trouble with these pirates before. He promised the pirates would give up as soon as they entered heavily patrolled waters. It was a good thing Darcy had asked Admiral Croft for a memorandum with his seal, granting the *Gypsy's Promise* safe passage.

Some of the crew wished to go to their home port, which was much closer to the open sea. As smugglers, they had a safe harbour at Broadstairs, near Ramsgate. Darcy well understood that, but Mott's business partner had insisted he should land at Liverpool so they would be nearer to whomever was to receive delivery of their goods, and so they would. At least with Croft's letter, the route they would take was shorter than if they had been obliged to avoid the British Navy.

With any luck, they should land within a few days. If the weather cooperated, it would be a journey of one and a half days' on land to see Bianca safely at home with her parents at Matlock. Subsequently, two hours later, he should be at Pemberley, planning how his life could begin again.

Chapter 21

Elizabeth finished dressing and asked Hannah to wheel her to the sitting room. She knocked on Jane's door.

"Come in, Lizzy," Jane responded.

Hannah opened the door and pushed her through, curtsied, and left the room.

Jane was sitting on her bed in her dressing gown.

"Why are you not yet dressed?"

"I do not know what happened, but there are several buttons on my gown that have worked themselves loose, Lizzy. Dorothy would not allow me to help mend them, so I wait." She took a deep breath and let it out slowly, a sure sign she was nervous.

Elizabeth raised her eyebrows. "Well?"

"Well?" Jane gawked at her with feigned innocence.

"Oh, Jane!" Elizabeth giggled. "How are you after seeing Mr. Bingley again?"

"I was anxious when he sat next to me. At first, I thought I might have a fit of nerves that would rival Mama's, but after a few moments of awkwardness, our conversation flowed so naturally, I felt much better." Jane blushed as she looked away. "From now on, we will be able to meet as common and indifferent acquaintances."

"Indifferent?" Elizabeth laughed out loud. "Jane! Even you cannot believe it."

Jane's colour deepened. She stared down at her lap.

"Oh, Jane, do not worry. Mr. Bingley loves you more than ever."

She regarded her with pleading in her eyes. "Lizzy, please do not tease me. I am *trying* to be indifferent." She looked down at her now trembling hands. Her voice lowered to a whisper. "Please, do not raise my hopes."

Elizabeth reached out and put her hand on her sister's. "I will speak of it just once more, and then I will not mention it again unless you bring it up. I know for a fact that he *did* love you, Jane, and I can see quite plainly he still *does*." Elizabeth straightened in her chair. "And that is the end of the subject. Now, shall I wait for you and your buttons, or shall I go down and make your apologies to Georgiana for being delayed?"

"I would not make you late, too, dear. Go ahead. I shall be down as soon as I can."

"Will you push me back through the sitting room, then, Jane? I think Hannah returned to my chambers."

~%~

Elizabeth sighed as she watched two footmen set the chair down at the bottom of the stairs. Hannah removed the blocks of wood from the pocket in back and handed them to a footman.

Roger, she thought, *and the other is John.* She was getting to know the entire staff of Pemberley by name.

It had been quite some time since she had been left alone for more than two minutes together. At the very least, she usually had Hannah hanging on her every movement. Whenever she needed to go from one room to another, one footman was required, and if another lady were not present, Hannah or some other maid—for it would not be proper for Elizabeth to be left alone with a footman, especially one with his arms on her person. If the stairs were a necessary part of her destination, James would carry her, and two additional footmen were required to move the chair, plus a lady or maid.

As James carried her down, Elizabeth said, "Honestly, I think the moment the doctor says I can walk again, I might run mad instead."

One corner of James's mouth twitched, but no more—he showed no emotion, just as a good servant should. Elizabeth could not help thinking

142

James would be a good butler when Barnes retired. She hoped Darcy saw his potential.

"I warn you, James, it has become a personal challenge to get you to laugh, or at least smile someday. When I do succeed, have no fear; I will not tell a soul!"

"Miss Elizabeth," Colonel Fitzwilliam said as he hurried down the stairs. "May I speak with you briefly?"

The two extra footmen set the blocks of wood in place around the wheels of the chair, bowed, and left. As Hannah held the chair steady, James placed Elizabeth in it and stood at attention. Hannah lingered nearby.

Elizabeth said, "Yes, Colonel. James, Hannah, will you wait for me a moment over there, please?"

If it had just been only Georgiana and Jane in the house, she would have felt quite safe to dismiss James and Hannah entirely and be left alone with the colonel to have the discussion she knew was about to take place—but not with Caroline Bingley and Mrs. Hurst lurking about. Who knew what they would think, and to whom they would voice their opinion, if they found her alone with the gentleman. While she liked him, she certainly did not wish to be considered compromised and forced to marry Colonel Fitzwilliam.

When James and Hannah were out of hearing range, but still within view, she asked quietly, "What is it you wished to discuss, sir?"

Colonel Fitzwilliam bowed. "I feel I must apologize for what I said last spring, Miss Elizabeth. It was wrong of me to inform you of Darcy's business with Bingley. It never occurred to me..." his voice trailed off. He cleared his throat.

Although Elizabeth was wondering how he would pry himself out of the corner he had talked himself into—for she could see on his face it had just struck him that perhaps *she* had never thought it could be her own sister of whom he had spoken of months ago—she decided to save him the discomfort.

"That the lady Mr. Darcy objected to marrying Mr. Bingley might have been my sister?"

"Yes." The colonel actually blushed. "Yes, quite. And yet, Darcy never did name her, so I still do not know for certain of whom he spoke. But…"

Elizabeth said, "Today's events made you suspect it might have been Jane."

He nodded.

"Do not trouble yourself, Colonel Fitzwilliam. Even before you mentioned the subject at Rosings, I had already suspected Mr. Darcy was involved in separating Mr. Bingley from Jane. I do admit it was a shock to hear you say it straight out as you did, but it was for the best. Mr. Darcy has since realized his error and promised to make amends as soon as he comes back into the country. But as you saw for yourself, the blunder might be in the process of being rectified."

Colonel Fitzwilliam raised his eyebrows. "You mean, after we had spoken, you confronted Darcy?"

It was Elizabeth's turn to blush. From many of the things the colonel had said over the past weeks, she had assumed he knew of the proposal and her rejection. Was it possible her assumption was wrong?

Yes, she had done it again. She had jumped to conclusions without having any proof to verify them.

She answered, "I did speak to Mr. Darcy about it. Let us just say it was unavoidable. Mr. Darcy admitted what he had done, which was not as nefarious as I had assumed. His opinion had been sollicited and he gave it, however mistaken it was—and ultimately, it was harmful towards both parties. But that is the nature of opinions, is it not? As it turned out, the bulk of the *obstruction* was from another source."

"After this afternoon, I, too, believe I know from which direction those obstructions came," he agreed. "I also wished to confirm that, as far as I am concerned, there are *no* objections to the lady. In fact, I hold a high opinion of her, as well as of her sister…" He bowed to Elizabeth. "And their father, for that matter."

She smiled. "I am glad to hear it, Colonel, for I know I speak for the others when I reply that all three hold you in high regard, as well."

The colonel bowed again. "May I escort you into the sitting room, where we shall await the others? I am afraid my cousin's new guests will not be as prompt as you are."

"Yes, you may, sir."

Colonel Fitzwilliam turned to the servants and said, "James, you are dismissed. Hannah, will you accompany us to the sitting room?" James bowed and left them as Colonel Fitzwilliam pushed Elizabeth's chair down the hall.

Georgiana, Mrs. Annesley, and Bingley were already there, so Hannah was dismissed.

"Jane sends her apologies for being delayed, Georgie. She had some trouble with a loose button or two. Her maid was seeing to it when I left her."

Bingley's expression faltered, but he soon rallied. The four spoke of subjects of little consequence until Jane arrived. After her greetings, Bingley commanded Jane's attention. The others discussed music until Caroline and the Hursts arrived, after which, the whole of the company moved to the dining room.

Elizabeth stifled a moan when she realized her seat would be sandwiched between Caroline and Mrs. Hurst, but her mood lifted when she saw Georgiana had seated Bingley on one side of herself with Jane next to him. Mrs. Annesley was on Jane's other side with Mr. Hurst next to Colonel Fitzwilliam, who occupied the seat Darcy would have taken had he been present. Caroline was next to him.

All in all, Elizabeth could not have seated herself any better without separating Jane and Bingley, so she heartily forgave Georgiana for the arrangement of her own dinner partners. The more she thought about it, the more she realized Georgiana had done well, providing a friendly buffer—or at least a cushion of guests willing to distract those who disapproved of a more intimate connexion between Jane and Bingley—and at the same time, allowed the two to reacquaint themselves with one another.

She caught Georgiana's gaze and grinned appreciatively at her friend. The smile dancing in Georgiana's eyes showed she returned the sentiment.

The meal went as expected, and Elizabeth was relieved Caroline's and Mrs. Hurst's disparaging comments were veiled, more like they had been in Hertfordshire.

After supper, while the gentlemen separated from the group, Caroline and Mrs. Hurst began cataloguing the accomplishments of the young ladies they—and their brother—had been exposed to since they had last been together.

At her first opportunity, Georgiana interrupted with a compliment to both Mrs. Hurst and Caroline on their talent on the pianoforte and begged them to play for them all this evening, effectively keeping them from speaking again.

Both were asked to play again once the gentlemen returned. When they were finished with their performances, the Bingley sisters asked Georgiana to take a turn.

Georgiana confided in Elizabeth that while she was happy to sing before her family, Mrs. Annesley, Elizabeth, and Jane, she would rather not sing for other company. Elizabeth suggested she play a song she had heard Georgiana practice, given that Elizabeth was familiar with the vocals. Of course, the Bingley sisters praised Georgiana's talents to the skies and had barely a word for Elizabeth. Though it did not bother Elizabeth in the least, their slight left both Georgiana's and Jane's feathers ruffled. Even the colonel seemed quite annoyed. They and Mrs. Annesley went over and beyond what was necessary in their admiration of Elizabeth's singing. Even Bingley seemed to catch on and joined in, though Mr. Hurst slept through the entirety.

As the ladies announced they would retire, the gentlemen proceeded to the billiard room.

Mrs. Hurst was clearly tired and wished to turn in. Before leaving the room, Caroline asked, "Dearest Georgiana, will you not accompany me to my rooms? It has been so long since you and I had a tête-à-tête."

Georgiana answered, "I thank you, Miss Bingley, but I shall wait for the footmen to arrive to escort Lizzy to her rooms."

Caroline directed her best glare at Elizabeth, and then returned her gaze to Georgiana. "How gracious of you, dear. You are an excellent hostess. Tomorrow?"

Georgiana blinked. "Perhaps. Good night to you, Mrs. Hurst. Miss Bingley."

When the door closed behind them, all was quiet for several beats before Georgiana declared, "You know, it may be wicked of me to say so, but I have never liked them. Their comportment is always as if they were above all in their company, no matter who is present. Towards Mrs. Annesley…" She turned to her. "They have always acted as if you do not exist at all. They have no right! It is unpardonable." She turned back to Jane and Elizabeth. "And they speak to the servants with such boorish disrespect; it is shameful. Even my aunt and uncle do not display this behaviour even though they usually *are* above everyone in their party."

She shook her head. "And during this visit, Mrs. Hurst's and Miss Bingley's behaviour towards Jane and Lizzy has been absolutely appalling."

She raised her chin. "Therefore, I have decided that I like them even less than ever before. I would enjoy asking them to leave Pemberley in the morning, and I am certain my brother would condone these actions. If not for Mr. Bingley being their brother, I would do it, too. But Mr. Bingley is all goodness and amiability, and would probably feel he had to leave with them. My brother has always kept his opinion of them from their brother for that very reason. Therefore I shall not say a word—to them." She crossed her arms. "But oh, how I would like to!"

Surprising them all, Mrs. Annesley burst out into a fit of giggles worthy of a schoolgirl. She promptly attempted to regain control, though her eyes were tearing with the effort. As she did so, Jane's hand moved to cover her mouth, and her shoulders began to shake. Elizabeth did not hold back—she laughed aloud.

Before long, all four were crying with laughter.

"Oh, thank you, ladies," Mrs. Annesley said, wiping her eyes with her handkerchief. "On occasion, silliness is a necessary relief. Good night." She crossed the room to the door and opened it, finding James standing in the hallway. "Good night, James," she said and continued on her way.

James entered, a hint of a smile on his lips.

Elizabeth said, "Let me guess, you have been keeping watch on the door whilst we had our bit of hilarity, have you not, James? Making sure no one else should witness our undignified and shocking behaviour?"

James raised one eyebrow almost indiscernibly.

"Thank you for your loyalty, James," Elizabeth said. "Ladies, mayhap we should continue our discussion in a more private location, such as the Rose sitting room. What do you think?"

Jane agreed.

Georgiana said, "Yes, please. That sounds lovely."

~%~

"Land Ho!" the crewman high up in the crow's nest called out. Darcy looked up. The man examined the horizon through a spyglass.

Though Darcy strained, he could not see it with the naked eye for another ten minutes. When he did, he closed his eyes and whispered a prayer of thanks. They had been running away from war, away from pirates, and for him, away from Bianca. Now, England was in sight, at last. He was almost home!

Hughes came up beside him. "By the grace of God, sir, we have made it."

"Yes, indeed."

"Shall I bring up the countess and Ellen?"

Darcy nodded. "I think they would like to see this." He reached into his pocket to make sure he had his gun. He lowered his voice to say, "Although I do not believe we will have any problems now, bring Fleming with you, just in case."

The valet began to walk away but then turned back. "Perhaps it is not my place, Mr. Darcy, but I feel I must say that once we are on dry land, there will be even more opportunities for Lady Bianca to..."

Darcy rolled his eyes. "Yes, I am quite aware of that. Once we find a hotel, I will look for the local port admiral's office to hand off the post entrusted to us by Admiral Croft and his men, and then find the post office and send an express to Matlock saying we will arrive in two days. You will find a coach and cart for hire for our journey." He sighed. "Although I would like to leave the moment we set foot on land, I must allow Lady Bianca a night in Liverpool to recover what sailors call their 'land legs.' One night only, though, Hughes—I will not tolerate a longer delay! We begin our journey to Matlock at first light tomorrow."

"Would you like me to sleep in the room with you tonight, sir, as we've done on board?"

Darcy chuckled. "It may be necessary, Hughes."

"How long will it take to get to Matlock, sir?"

"A day and a half at most." He took in a deep breath. "I will stay a short while, but we will spend no more than two hours at Matlock. We will collect Georgiana, and we will be on our way to Pemberley. I can always ride over to Matlock the following day to spend more time with my uncle and aunt. If my sister's maid cannot pack her things in such a short time, they will have to be sent on later. We *will* sleep in our own beds two nights from now, Hughes. I guarantee it."

"Yes, sir." Hughes was off to bring the rest of their party above deck.

Chapter 22

"There has been no swelling at all this week, Mr. Smythe." Elizabeth studied him hopefully.

He made a non-committal grunt in response.

Elizabeth met her sister's gaze. Jane shrugged.

After some time passed while the doctor wrote in a journal he carried with him, he said, "I am quite satisfied with your progress, Miss Elizabeth." Mr. Smythe looked at her over his glasses. "In a week or two, you may graduate to crutches, but not quite yet. I will return in a few days to see how you are coming along."

Elizabeth nodded. So much for her hopes of hobbling into the gardens to escape Caroline and Mrs. Hurst anytime soon. She sighed.

A few minutes later, Jane followed Hannah, who pushed Elizabeth into the Rose sitting room, where Georgiana awaited them.

"It looks like I will be in the chair for another few days at least, Georgie."

Georgiana did not seem surprised. "I thought you might enjoy spending the day outside in the fresh air. Mrs. Reynolds and Cook have prepared a picnic for us. I can take you out to the lawn near the lake in my gig. The others may walk if they wish to join us."

"That would be lovely, Georgie," Jane said.

Elizabeth smiled. "From the veranda, I thought I saw a path from the house to the lake."

"Yes, we would usually walk to the lake. It is not far."

"If it is all right with you, and James of course, I would not mind taking the path."

Georgiana and Jane voiced their agreement.

Elizabeth grinned mischievously. "It is unfortunate Miss Bingley and Mrs. Hurst will be with us, or I'd roll the chair myself. I am getting quite good at turning the chair and pushing the wheels."

"Lizzy! You will ruin your hands," Jane said, wide-eyed. "Mama will never forgive me if I allow you to acquire calluses."

"I know, Jane, and I will not do it so much as that. It was only a wish. I am not used to allowing others to do *everything* for me." Elizabeth sighed.

Elizabeth took a book from her lap and handed it to Georgiana. "Georgie, I have finished the book you gave me the other day. Is the library ready for guests, yet? After hearing so much about it, I would like to see it."

Every time Elizabeth brought up the library, Georgiana blushed, and this time was no different. Since they had arrived, anytime Jane or Elizabeth needed a book, Georgiana or Colonel Fitzwilliam got it for them, and now she was keeping the Bingley family out, as well. At first, Elizabeth had assumed the library was undergoing renovations—after all, why else would her young hostess be keeping them out of that room—but then why did Georgiana colour every time it was brought up? She had asked James and Hannah about it, and even Mrs. Reynolds, but they had all avoided the question by saying only that the mistress would supply any books she needed. Elizabeth suspected something was afoot, but she could not imagine what it was.

"Not yet, Lizzy. If you give me an idea what subject you would be interested in reading, I will bring you a few selections to choose from."

Elizabeth nodded and named a few titles she had been thinking of reading for a second time. "At home, I often go for a walk with a book and find somewhere to sit and read. I have several favourite places to do so. There was also an exceptionally pretty little grove near Rosings where I used to go to read whenever Mrs. Collins was busy with parish business. I miss doing that." She contemplated the French doors on the other side of the room which overlooked the natural garden. If she could find a corner of the garden where she could hide and find a little peace from the Bingley sisters, it would be heaven. Feeling Georgiana's and Jane's eyes upon her, she shook herself from her bout of melancholy. Turning to them, she forced a smile. "Soon enough, I suppose." She sat up straighter. "When shall we leave for the picnic?"

"I am ready. While you were in with the doctor, I spoke to Mr. Bingley, Miss Bingley, and Mr. and Mrs. Hurst about it." Georgiana pulled her watch from her skirt pocket and checked the time. "I believe they should be ready to leave soon. I will send someone to retrieve your books and meet us in the front parlour so that you may take one along with you, Lizzy."

"Will the colonel join us?"

Georgiana shook her head. "He was afraid to miss a day at Matlock."

The ladies observed a moment of silence over the earl's condition.

Jane stood. "If you will excuse me, I need to change into my walking boots." She left through the door to her rooms.

"Given that I am allowed to walk nowhere, I do not need to change. I am ready now." Elizabeth rolled her chair over to the bell-pull and signalled for James to come. She held her first finger up to her lips, indicating Georgiana should keep the secret of her moving the chair around herself.

Georgiana giggled.

~%~

"May I see it, Georgie?" Elizabeth held out her hand for the younger girl's sketchbook. Georgiana had done an excellent job of drawing a cluster of flowers growing near the lake. "Nicely done."

Miss Bingley and Mrs. Hurst were following Georgiana's lead, both sitting with sketchpads. Seeing as Elizabeth was unable to draw a stick figure accurately, she had brought a book, but with such a lovely view to claim her attention, she was not disposed towards reading.

"I am determined to learn the names of all the flowers and plants that grow at Pemberley," Georgiana said, "and their uses, if any."

Elizabeth said, "If I have learned nothing else from speaking to the farmers, tenants, and villagers near Longbourn it is that most plants are useful in some way but some should be avoided. It is always good to know which is which."

Mrs. Hurst and Caroline tittered and sent mocking glances her way. Elizabeth rolled her eyes. When Caroline had been the mistress of Netherfield Park, she never visited the tenants—yet another reason she was unfit to be the wife of a gentleman who owned an estate. Meanwhile, Caroline would think Elizabeth's conversing with the tenants was evidence she was a hoyden.

Georgiana cleared her throat. "I will be starting my monthly visits to the tenants tomorrow, calling on one or two families each morning. Would anyone like to accompany me?"

Elizabeth tried not to laugh at Georgiana's obvious set-down directed at her guests for their derision of such a duty. "Yes, I would. I believe Jane would, as well." Elizabeth looked at Jane, who sat on the same blanket, but whose attention was fully involved in a conversation with Bingley, who stood near her. "It is an obligation of being the daughter or sister of an estate owner that we both enjoy."

Caroline Bingley and Mrs. Hurst suddenly paid an inordinate amount of attention to their drawings.

Elizabeth was glad the Hursts did not own an estate. If Caroline married a land-owner, she would be quite shocked when she learned all of the things she considered were "far beneath her" that her husband would expect her to do on a regular basis.

Although James stood on the back of the gig, there was no room for the chair, so Elizabeth had to remain seated in the vehicle. Since a few of the servants who worked at the manor house were children of tenants, most of the tenant families were aware of her injuries by now, so it was no surprise that when Georgiana's gig pulled up to the farmhouse, Mrs. O'Malley, Hannah's mother, came out to see them. As James took a basket of food into the house, the ladies chatted with Mrs. O'Malley.

Wendi Sotis

Elizabeth was the only one facing in the direction of a large stand of pine trees when black clouds rolled into view from behind it. She glanced up and gasped. "Georgiana, we had best return to the house. A storm approaches!"

"Aye, yes, I knew there be a storm comin'. My knee's been achin' all day," said Mrs. O'Malley. "Please 'scuse me, ma'am. I mus' be bringin' in the washin' 'afore it gets ruined."

"Of course," Georgiana said and gestured to James to help her.

"No, no, Mizz Darcy. I thank ya, but ye betta' be goin'. None of us wants any of you ladies to be ailin', miss. My girls'll 'elp me." She hurried away, calling to her daughters who were inside the house, most likely putting away the food Georgiana had brought them.

Jane mounted her horse as Georgiana and James returned to the gig. They went as fast as the vehicle could manage, but it was not fast enough. Although the rain slowed as they pulled into the stables, the four were soaked thoroughly by the time they arrived at Pemberley.

An hour later, after she had changed into dry clothing, Elizabeth arrived first at the ladies' meeting place, the Rose sitting room. Hannah pushed her to sit near the windows so she could watch Mother Nature's violent display. It was almost as dark as night. Lightning illuminated the sky, signalling the beginning of another storm. The rain began to fall so hard, it poured off the rooftop in sheets. A roar of thunder boomed deafeningly. The panes of glass shuddered; the echo rumbled through every fibre of her being. It was one of the angriest storms she had ever witnessed—as frightening as it was magnificent.

With the next flash of light, a door slammed behind Elizabeth, startling her. She turned; Jane stood just inside the door, her face pale and drawn. As long as Elizabeth could remember, her older sister had been terrified of thunderstorms. The current look of panic on her face proved her fear had not diminished.

"Come closer, Jane. Watch the storm. Perhaps it will help. If you simply accept the noise, it can be beautiful."

154

A Lesson Hard Learned

Jane took a seat as far from the window as possible.

Elizabeth pushed herself across the room to Jane, who was in such a state, she forgot to scold her for doing it herself.

A few minutes later, when Georgiana joined them, Jane hid her fear, though she still seemed preoccupied.

Georgiana looked worriedly at Jane as she said, "I hope neither of you suffers any ill effects from being caught in the rain."

Elizabeth shook her head. "None! I enjoy the rain. This storm is glorious to behold, Georgie. Thank you for arranging it for my entertainment," she teased.

Jane startled with the next thunderclap. Her posture remained rigid.

Georgiana met Elizabeth's gaze and nodded. "Would you like to practice, Lizzy?"

"Yes, that seems like a good idea." She could see in her young friend's eyes that she had the same thought: if Jane sat near the pianoforte, the song might drown out the noise of the storm. "I will push myself to the staircase."

"Lizzy!" Jane exclaimed.

Elizabeth smiled mischievously. Ah, she was more herself!

Georgiana rang for James.

A few minutes later, as they approached the music room, Elizabeth, Jane, and Georgiana stopped to listen. Apparently Mrs. Hurst and Caroline were already there, and one or both were performing a song Elizabeth and Georgiana had presented together the evening before, this time with Caroline singing.

The ladies and James waited in the corridor until they had moved on to another tune, then they entered. As Elizabeth suspected, Mrs. Hurst accompanied Caroline's song. The newcomers settled themselves in to listen. Before James left, Georgiana asked him to let Bingley and Mr. Hurst know where they were.

When the song ended, the Bingley sisters forfeited the pianoforte to Georgiana, who played a tune. At the end of the song, Colonel Fitzwilliam, Mr. Hurst, and Bingley entered.

"Richard! I thought you had gone to Matlock," Georgiana said, rising from her chair and crossing to him. "I did not think you would be able to return until tomorrow."

Colonel Fitzwilliam shook his head. "If old injuries are good for anything, it is supplying forewarning of bad weather approaching. I did not wish to be caught in the rain; my mother would not have allowed me to leave for a week." He chuckled. "I understand some of you ladies were wet through when you returned from visiting a tenant."

Bingley's eyes nearly popped from his head. "I hope you are all well?" His attention settled worriedly on Jane. "At Netherfield, you became ill after being caught in the rain. I hope you have not felt any consequences today, Miss Bennet?

She gazed into his eyes and smiled pleasantly. "I appreciate your concern, sir, but I am quite well."

A crack of thunder sounded out, but this time, Jane did not seem to notice. Elizabeth turned her face away from the company to hide her amusement.

Georgiana regained her seat at the pianoforte and asked Elizabeth to add her voice to the next composition.

Towards the end of the piece, Georgiana hit the wrong key. If any other pianist had done so, Elizabeth would have ignored it, but she had learned Georgiana rarely missed a note. She turned to find the young lady aglow with happiness as she missed another note. Elizabeth continued singing as she shifted to see what held Georgiana's attention.

Chapter 23

After asking Hughes and Fleming to join Bianca, Ellen, and him inside the coach, Darcy re-entered and shook out his hat as best he could in such cramped quarters. He banged on the roof to signal the driver to continue.

"How long until we reach Matlock?" Bianca asked. "Or will we have to stop at another inn this evening?"

Darcy shook his head. "It is only drizzling now, but the sky is dark and threatening, and the winds have picked up again. I just spoke to the drivers. Pemberley is much closer. We shall have to stop there for the night."

Bianca's wicked smirk made him squirm in his seat and look away.

Good Lord! What does she have planned for tonight?

He was glad he had taken Hughes's advice and asked him to sleep in his room at the inn at Liverpool. Well after midnight, Bianca had knocked on his door. He wished he could have seen her face when Hughes answered it, after which she had made up some excuse for needing the valet's services.

Apparently determined, she tried it again at the small inn they had stayed at last night, but this time Ellen came to ask for Hughes's help. A minute after Hughes left with her, Bianca knocked, not realizing he had also asked Fleming to stay with him, with the promise of a glowing letter of recommendation *and* an interim position at Pemberley should Bianca let the man go for spoiling her plans.

Although Fleming did not say as much to Darcy, it seemed he was not especially *fond* of his mistress. While aboard ship, Fleming mentioned to Hughes that the countess would most likely return to England to find many of her servants had left her employ soon after she and her husband had left for America. So it was no surprise when Fleming requested to be considered for any openings at Pemberley whether Bianca dismissed him or not.

As they passed a certain landmark, Darcy's attention returned to the present. His heart leapt with excitement. They were very near Pemberley! He leaned out of the window and called up to the driver to make the next turn.

About half-way up the drive, the skies opened up again, this time with thunder and lightning. The horses were spooked and fought against their restraints—something his own steeds would never have done—but it only encouraged the driver to urge them on faster, which Darcy did not mind a bit.

He hoped Bianca would remain in her rooms once they arrived so he could spend a quiet afternoon and evening at home.

Alone!

No Hughes or Fleming to bump into every time he turned around. No trunks or ropes or extra sails to trip over. No swinging hammocks. No irate sailors everywhere he looked. No gun hidden on his person. No threats from traitors or pirates or American ships. No lumpy beds at unfamiliar inns. And no Bianca to avoid.

All he wanted to do was to take a long, hot bath, choose a book from his library, read while sipping a fine brandy, and sleep soundly in his own bed.

He sighed deeply with contentment and closed his eyes. When he felt the coach begin to climb a hill, he opened his eyes just in time to see the house through the break in the trees.

Home! Pemberley.

A moment of sorrow passed over him. Back in March, just before he had asked Elizabeth to become his wife, he dreamt of the next time he came home, for he expected she would be by his side. Above anything else—well, *almost* anything—he had wanted to see her expression when he escorted her into the library. Confident she would love the gardens and grounds even more than the house, he wished to show her every inch of Pemberley.

In a few days, once he knew what was happening with his uncle and felt it was safe to leave Derbyshire, he and Georgiana would return to London. He would contact Bingley and tell him what he must. He hoped they would all return to Netherfield.

Would Bingley forgive him? Although the prospect of Bingley refusing to pardon his lapse in judgement weighed heavily on his conscience, it mattered not when it came to his plans. If Bingley would never see him again, Darcy would still go to Hertfordshire, even if he had to stay at the inn in Meryton.

But if Bingley did grant forgiveness and allowed him to stay at Netherfield, he would take Georgiana with him this time. He had never confessed to his regard for Elizabeth to Georgiana, but she had hinted in her letters that she already knew. And he expected Elizabeth and his sister would get along splendidly.

He would court and win the woman he loved.

And *next* time he arrived at Pemberley, he hoped it *would* be with Elizabeth by his side.

A particularly loud clap of thunder jarred Darcy from his musings. The coach pulled up in front of the entrance, but nobody came out to greet them. Though disappointed, he understood. No one was expecting visitors in this pouring rain, and the noise of the storm would have drowned out the crunch of gravel caused by the wheels.

Hughes opened the door and stepped out first. As he lowered the steps, Darcy turned to Fleming and chuckled. Fleming seemed quite impressed with his new home. A moment later, Fleming remembered himself and stepped out, holding out his hand to assist Ellen. Darcy followed her, then helped Bianca descend the steps. As Darcy escorted Bianca up the stairs and into the house, he turned back to see Hughes directing the drivers to go around to the stables.

Still no one came to meet them, so once they were all inside, a dripping wet Fleming went to work, taking their coats and hats. The wind quieted for a moment, and Darcy could hear the strains of the pianoforte.

"Georgiana must be home," he said to Bianca, fearing that meant they were too late for Bianca to see her father before he passed away.

When Hughes came in, Darcy turned to him. "Will you go to the kitchens and find Mrs. Reynolds, please, Hughes? Arrange for our luggage to be brought up and have quarters assigned to the drivers, Ellen, and Fleming—and of course, for Lady Bianca. Mrs. Reynolds can find us in the music room. We shall go up and see Georgiana directly before we retire to dry off."

He hesitated, noticing Bianca's sly smile. He would have to post footmen in the corridor outside his bedchambers, as well as the guest wing where Bianca would stay. He nodded to himself. Perhaps in the servant corridors, as well.

"Also, Hughes, please inform Mrs. Reynolds I must speak to her as soon as possible."

Hughes bowed and left them. Again the wind died momentarily, and he could hear the tinkling ivories.

Now thinking only of seeing Georgiana, he began to walk away, but Bianca cleared her throat. He returned and held out his arm, then escorted her up the staircase. As they reached the landing, someone began to sing, and his steps faltered. Recovering immediately, he walked faster down the hallway.

It could not be Elizabeth. It was simply impossible. His mind must be playing tricks with him, but he had to find out. Immediately!

James, the footman, was standing outside the door. As they approached, his face lit up with recognition. James opened his mouth to speak, but Darcy placed a finger to his lips. He would surprise Georgiana. James reached to open the door, but Darcy waved him away and opened it himself, slowly... and then froze in place.

Georgiana sat at the pianoforte playing. There sitting next to her, singing, was none other than Miss Elizabeth Bennet.

Elizabeth leaned over and turned the page of Georgiana's music.

Was he dreaming—asleep in the coach on the drive leading to Pemberley?

Had he gone mad?

Or was Elizabeth Bennet truly *here*, at Pemberley?

He pulled in a deep breath as his heart swelled with the resonance of her voice. The image before him was delightful—the two women he loved most in the world smiled at each other. He released his breath slowly, afraid to make a sound, afraid to move, or this vision might be disrupted.

But Bianca had no such fears. She pushed past him and walked into the room.

The movement attracted Georgiana's attention, and she turned. Her face lit up with happiness.

His awareness locked on Elizabeth. His heart stopped as she turned to see who had come in. She smiled with more brilliance than he had ever seen upon her countenance—and it was directed at *him*.

Warmth filled every corner of his being.

Elizabeth!

Georgiana rose suddenly and rushed across the room. As she threw herself into his arms, he was forced to pull his gaze from his beloved.

Whispering greetings to his sister, out of the corner of his eye, he saw movement and looked up.

He blinked and raised his eyebrows in surprise. *What is going on here?*

Many voices welcomed them. Richard, Miss Bingley, the Hursts, Bingley, Miss Jane Bennet, and Mrs. Annesley all stood. The gentlemen approached him.

Caught in what he could only call a death-stare with Miss Bingley, Bianca quite forcefully reattached herself to his arm. He rolled his eyes.

Whispering to Georgiana, he told her he needed to speak to the others and would spend some time with her alone later. Richard approached and shook his hand.

"We were on our way to Matlock," Darcy said, "but the storm was too violent to continue." He tilted his head, silently asking about his father.

Colonel Fitzwilliam cleared his throat. "My mother and father greatly appreciate your sacrifice in going so far to escort their daughter safely home, Darcy."

Relief spread through Darcy—they had returned in time.

The colonel turned to his sister then looked at Darcy again. "However, you *should* go tomorrow."

Darcy nodded. Although he knew, with Elizabeth here, leaving Pemberley even for a few hours tomorrow would be much more challenging than it had ever been before, he would go to see his uncle before he passed on.

Darcy escorted Bianca to a chair and invited her to sit. She had little choice but to do so. He said to the others, "Please, everyone, take a seat and be comfortable."

He turned to Elizabeth. She had not risen with the others. Was she using his father's rolling chair? He could not stop himself; he moved towards her. "Miss Elizabeth, you are injured?"

As he approached, he saw her eyes were filled with tears, and yet she smiled. His chest expanded with hope. Was she overcome with emotion on his arrival—relieved that he had returned home safely?

She averted her eyes and cleared her throat before looking at him again. "I was touring Matlock with the Gardiners when I fell near the waterfall. At about the same time the doctor said I could travel to our rooms at the inn in Lambton, my uncle was recalled to London to deal with an emergency. Georgie brought me home with her." She examined her hands. "I hope it is not too inconvenient, sir."

His breath hitched. *Inconvenient? Never!* Given the fact that his voice stuck in his throat, he only shook his head.

She was here, and she had become close enough with his sister not only for them to use first names, but nicknames? The situation was far better than any he could have imagined.

Finally, he found his voice. "You are more than welcome to remain as long as you wish, Miss Elizabeth." Internally, he added, *Anywhere I am, you are always wanted. Forever.* He blinked and turned, remembering the others in the room. "As are Miss Bennet and the Bingleys and Hursts." He could not stop himself from returning his attention to Elizabeth.

Outdoors, lightning struck nearby, and the roar of thunder came almost immediately. Elizabeth held his gaze without flinching.

Georgiana came up beside him and threaded her arm through his. "I would like to hear all about your adventures, but you are soaking wet, Fitzwilliam. I will order you a hot bath." She turned to Bianca. "For you as well, cousin. We cannot have either of you become ill." Suddenly her eyes flew open wide. "Oh, cousin, I apologize for not thinking of it sooner. I am so sorry for the loss of your husband."

Others murmured the same. Bianca nodded and touched her nose with a handkerchief.

Darcy stared at his sister, marvelling at how much Georgiana had recovered while he was away. Intuition told him he had Elizabeth to thank for that.

Nearby, Bingley cleared his throat. "Darcy, I say, it is good to have you home safely. I am sorry we came while you were away. Apparently you sent a letter that I never received." He glanced at Jane Bennet.

Bingley does not seem sorry at all. "Yes, I did send a note delaying your arrival, but it seems it all worked out well." He looked at Georgiana. "A bath does sound perfect, Pigeon." He felt his face heat a bit, then whispered, "I apologize, Georgie, I am tired and was not thinking."

Georgiana smiled. "I have longed to hear you call me anything at all, Fitzwilliam, so I will forgive you. I have missed you so!" She hugged his arm and beamed up at him, whispering, "But tomorrow, you will not get away with it."

He chuckled. "I am glad I have an excuse for today, at least."

A glowing Mrs. Reynolds came into the room and curtsied. "Welcome home, Mr. Darcy! Your rooms have been kept ready for you every day since your letter arrived. Your trunks are being brought up at this very moment." She turned to Bianca. "Countess, if you will follow me, I will show you to your rooms. I believe Ellen is unpacking what you will need."

"I assume I will be in the Rose Room, as usual?" Lady Bianca asked.

"Ah… no, my lady, as the Rose Rooms are already occupied by Miss Elizabeth." She gestured to the correct lady. "You will be in the Green Room, my lady."

Bianca's eyes narrowed, and she threw a look that could kill at Elizabeth.

Darcy watched the exchange with foreboding. A look like that could not only be about the rooms. Had his affections for Elizabeth been that obvious?

"Oh! How rude of me," Darcy said. "Please forgive me for not making proper introductions." He proceeded to introduce all who were present to Bianca.

Miss Bingley came forward and said, "We are so happy you have arrived, Mr. Darcy. Except for dear Georgiana's presence, Pemberley has seemed an empty shell without you here."

Why would she believe insulting his guests would cast her in a more favourable light in his eyes? He raised one eyebrow as Caroline Bingley attached herself to his arm.

Bianca moved forward and took his other arm, saying, "Fitzwilliam, will you show me to my rooms? I am so tired. I need a sturdier arm to assist me than that of Mrs. Reynolds."

Feeling almost as if the two ladies were playing tug-of-war, with him as the rope, Darcy looked at Richard for assistance. His cousin was obviously stifling a smile.

The thought occurred to him that he would be happier if Elizabeth was one of the ladies fighting to be on his arm, but he was also glad she was as far away from him as she was at this moment. Although he had washed as thoroughly as possible in salt water every day aboard ship, they did not have the facilities for a bath. The first inn in Liverpool had offered him a bath, but Bianca had also ordered one, and he was too tired to wait up for her to finish and the servants to move the tub and heat more water. The inn they had stayed at last night did not even own a tub, which made him wonder about the facilities in general.

Richard said, "Come, Bianca. Darcy is tired, as well. I will escort you."

Bianca gave her brother a nasty stare, but she took the arm he offered. The two left the room.

Darcy stepped back—and most decidedly away from Miss Bingley—and bowed to the company. "Please excuse me, but I fear Georgiana and Mrs. Reynolds will both be displeased if I do not get out of these wet clothes. I will see you all at supper."

He regarded Elizabeth one more time before leaving the room. A sudden thought occurred to him—had she received his journal? He examined her countenance a moment longer. If she had, she did not seem to hold it against him. Without thinking, he bowed to her again before leaving the room.

As he walked down the corridor towards the stairs leading to his chambers, a smile spread across his face.

Elizabeth is here!

This homecoming was much better than he could have hoped.

Chapter 24

Two hours later, Darcy was much more comfortable; a short rest had revitalized him, and now he was washed and dressed in a clean suit of clothes that had not accompanied him on what had seemed like a very long journey. Barnes, the butler, helped Darcy dress since Hughes was given two days off to rest and spend with his family. As Barnes shaved him, he informed Darcy that Georgiana was waiting for him in his sitting room. As soon as could be, Darcy joined his sister.

"How are you *really*, Fitzwilliam?"

"I am fine, Pigeon." He grinned playfully. "You did say you would forgive me for calling you that for the remainder of the day."

She giggled. "I will." she kissed his cheek. "But not in company again, please. And I *did* notice how you avoided giving me a thorough answer to my question."

He nodded. "I am tired. The journey did not go as well as it could have, but also, it could have been much worse. I shall tell all of you about it at supper—so that I do not have to say it all twice. But, there is one issue that I must speak to you about in private. Bianca seems determined to secure me for her husband."

"Oh, no! Fitzwilliam, please do not marry Bianca!" She reddened and took a moment to school her features. "I apologize. I should have asked if that is what you wish, as well?"

Darcy chuckled. "I feel the same about the idea as you do, Pigeon. I have been forced to become quite crafty in avoiding her, and even enlisted both Hughes and Fleming—Bartholomew's valet—in the endeavour. As a matter of fact, Fleming will be joining our staff as a result."

He examined her features as she poured tea for him.

She seemed to be almost a different person than the heartbroken, timid girl he had left behind. He accepted his tea with thanks. "You are looking well."

"I *am* well. Lizzy and Jane have become good friends; I am so glad I met them, Fitzwilliam. We have had such fun together. I only wish it had not been necessary for Lizzy to be injured to make our meeting possible." She raised both eyebrows. "Lizzy *is* the lady you wrote to me about on numerous occasions, is she not?"

Darcy choked on his tea. "Georgiana!"

His sister brought up her chin. "You cannot tell me she is not the same Miss Elizabeth Bennet of Longbourn you have written to me about and spoken of. I have reviewed all of your letters time and again, dating from when you met her at Mr. Bingley's estate. I know it is she—and I have Richard as a witness to your spending time with her at Rosings, I might add. You have never written of any other lady as highly or as often as you did of her, Brother. Even Aunt Adelaide noticed you mentioned her with frequency in your letters to her. With that in mind, our aunt made an effort to get to know Lizzy." She smiled. "I thought you would be interested in knowing Aunt Adelaide liked her—she was always seeking out Lizzy's company. Aunt also enjoyed Mr. and Mrs. Gardiner's company so much that she seemed to forget Mr. Gardiner was in trade, which is quite the accomplishment. Richard approves of her family, or at least the ones he has met, and since he goes to Matlock every day, I am sure Aunt has heard all about them." She paused. "I love Lizzy as a sister. I want you to know I would like it very much if you decided to bring her home permanently one day."

During her speech, Darcy's heart nearly leapt from his chest.

He would not yet admit these were his wishes as well. He did say, "It seems you have my entire life planned out for me." He furrowed his brow. "Please tell me you have not discussed these plans of yours with *her*."

"No, but I do suspect I have helped you along."

He closed his eyes. Richard had also tried to make him look good in Elizabeth's eyes when he told her of how he had assisted Bingley in escaping what he thought had been a match of convenience on the lady's side. Elizabeth had immediately recognized her sister Jane's situation, and she had been quite angry with him. He hoped Georgiana had not done something similarly damaging.

"Fitzwilliam, I did not say anything that should not be said. I only told her I knew a few things about her already from your letters: how she likes to walk, dance, how enjoyable you found her playing and singing, and the like." She blushed again. "I did lie to her about one thing, though."

"You lied?" He frowned. "About what?"

"Oh, nothing really. Or that is to say, it is not important. You had once told me you thought of Lizzy as a great reader, and you wished to show her the library at Pemberley." She looked away, brushing lint from her skirt. "Because you had expressed that wish—and you rarely voice a desire for anything—I wanted to allow *you* to give her the tour of that particular room. I told our guests they could not go into the library." She cleared her throat. "They have assumed we were making renovations. I did not correct them, and I have sworn the servants to secrecy."

Relieved it was nothing worse, Darcy found the situation much to his liking. He started to laugh.

Once he quieted down, Georgiana asked, "Did I do well, then?"

He nodded. "Yes, you did well, Pigeon." He took a deep breath. He had to find out if his fears these past weeks were for nothing. "Do you know—that is…" He swallowed hard. "Is Miss Elizabeth having her mail forwarded to Pemberley?"

She furrowed her brow. "Yes, I believe she is."

"Has she received any parcels?"

Georgiana's tone was suspicious now. "I think she did receive one package. Her father brought it when he and Jane travelled here to see Lizzy. Mr. Bennet wished to speak to the doctor, as well. Why?"

Darcy felt the blood rush from his face. "Mr. Bennet was at Pemberley?" *He came all the way here? Has he read the journal? Did he come thinking he would see me?* "Did he seem… angry?"

"No, not at all." Georgiana's eyes widened. "Why would he be angry?"

Darcy did not answer.

Georgiana continued, "He was only relieved Lizzy was not as ill as he had imagined. Brother, what is wrong?"

He shook his head and waved away her question. "Did Miss Elizabeth mention who had sent the parcel?"

Georgiana nodded. "I believe it was from her friend, Mrs. Collins, containing a book from Mr. Bennet's library Lizzy had left behind when she visited Kent."

Darcy closed his eyes and let out the breath he had been holding. If Elizabeth had not yet received his journal, perhaps he could intercept it when it did come. He should speak to Mrs. Reynolds and Barnes about bringing him all mail as soon as it arrived.

Georgiana was staring at him. He smiled politely and took his last sip of tea, then rose and placed his cup on the tray.

Georgiana asked, "Is there something I should know, Fitzwilliam?"

He walked to the window. It was not raining any longer, but lightning flashed in the distance, indicating there was more to come. Diverting to Pemberley had been the correct decision, for more than one reason. If they had gone straight to Matlock, yes, he would not have had to deal with Bianca any longer, but he probably would have been told that Elizabeth had been there and was now at Pemberley. Would he have been able to ride home safely this afternoon? Probably not. But he would have been so anxious to get here to see her, he would have taken the chance, which might have ended in an accident of his own. No, this was better.

Elizabeth. Should he just tell her there was a parcel sent to her by mistake, so if it slipped past him, she would not open it? But then, how could he explain how her name and direction came to be written on the parcel? When it came in, he *could* remove the letter and give that to her, then she would understand. However, now that he was here, there was a chance he could tell her all those things in person instead of relying on the missive. That would be preferable.

"Fitzwilliam?" Georgiana repeated. "Is there something you should tell me?"

He turned to face her. Should he mention the journal mishap to his sister? If he did, he would have to explain it *all* to her: the proposal, Elizabeth's refusal, his breach of propriety in handing her the first letter, his further impropriety in writing the second, the journal being sent by accident, and his continuing desire to have her become Mrs. Darcy. It was too much.

"No, there is nothing you need to know at this time, Georgiana." He cleared his throat. "I must speak to Mrs. Reynolds and Barnes about a few things, and I should check the desk in my study for any urgent business before we dine. Shall I call for you at the usual time and escort you to supper?"

Georgiana shook her head. "When I can, I go down with Lizzy so she does not have to worry as much."

He tilted his head. "Worry?"

"She becomes upset thinking she is taking servants away from their duties. She needs one footman to carry her down the stairs, two to carry the chair, and if Jane or I are not present, a maid as a chaperone."

Envy and resentment raged in his breast as he nodded. Were all the footmen in the house more familiar with Elizabeth's form than he was, or was there one particular footman who always did the duty? At least it was not Bingley or Richard.

"Which footman carries her?" His tone was much harsher than he meant it to be.

Georgiana squealed with excitement. "You *are* in love with her!"

"What?"

"You are jealous!"

He knew he could not deny it. His nostrils flared. "*Which* footman?"

"James." Her expression changed to one of concern. "But Fitzwilliam, please do not punish James for doing his duty. Lizzy was mortified she had to be carried at all, and I felt it would be less embarrassing if it was the same footman every time. He has been thoroughly professional. In fact, Lizzy has made it a personal challenge to get him to smile before she leaves Pemberley."

He knew that last statement was meant to make him feel better, but it did not. "I will carry her from now on."

"You cannot, Brother. Even if you were engaged to her, you could not. Not with Mr. Bingley's sisters in the house. It is not proper. She would be considered compromised."

He arched an eyebrow. "And it is proper to have a servant carry her?" He paced to the window and back. "As a female, you cannot understand my concerns, Georgiana." He stopped and took a deep breath. "Fortunately, after spending months in the same household on numerous occasions, I know for a fact Bingley's sisters do not come down until the last possible moment before we dine. When Elizabeth spent a few days at Netherfield, she was usually ready much earlier than anyone else. In fact, I once found her pacing the hall outside the dining room, and her object seemed to be to delay her arrival at meals so she was not alone with the gentlemen.

"After supper tonight, I will wait until the Bingleys have gone to their rooms to bring Elizabeth up."

He was so upset, he did not realize he had used only her Christian name until after he had finished speaking. Georgiana did not seem to notice.

She answered firmly, "*Only* if Lizzy agrees to it, Fitzwilliam. If she does not, I will call for James. I will not allow you to make her feel uncomfortable just to appease your *misguided* jealousy."

Her eyes popped open wide, as if she had surprised herself by standing up to him.

Darcy felt himself mirror her expression. *Georgiana is growing up.*

He smiled in spite of himself. "Thank you for reminding me *her* comfort should be my paramount concern, not my own."

"I felt you needed the reminder," she said shyly. "You are too accustomed to telling people what to do and having them all jump to do exactly as you bid."

He shook his head. "Ah, but I hope I am learning. Unfortunately—or maybe I should say *fortunately*—over the past few months, there have been a great many things that have *not* gone according to my own wishes."

"Fortunately?"

"I have come to realize the things most worthy of having must be earned or else they will be taken for granted. I might not have learned this if not for…" *Miss Elizabeth Bennet* "…some recent impediments."

"Happenstances during your journey to America?"

He nodded. "Along with other events which occurred before I left England." He straightened his jacket. "I hope I am learning to be a better man."

Georgiana blinked. "*I* think you have always been the best of men, Brother."

A wave of regret passed over him. The only other woman in the world whose opinion mattered as much as Georgiana's did not feel the same way. "Thank you, Georgiana, but I believe I can improve."

He crossed to his sister and kissed her furrowed forehead. "You are correct. I should allow James to bring Miss Elizabeth down. If Miss Bingley or Mrs. Hurst should see me carrying her, within an hour after the next post reaches London there would be gossip about Miss Elizabeth spread all around the *ton*." He sighed. "I will see you at supper."

He left the room in a hurry.

~%~

Darcy examined his study, his gaze settling on the raindrops running down the window pane.

He had expected to feel, at the very least, comfortable and relieved to be home.

Why then were his thoughts centered outside of this room, with the others? He grunted. They were not with *all* the others. They were only with Elizabeth.

Richard cleared his throat, no doubt to remind him he was in the room. When he had Darcy's attention, he said, "After seeing Miss Elizabeth deal with Aunt Catherine the way she did, I had no doubt that she would handle Miss Bingley and Mrs. Hurst without any problem. I was not here when they first arrived, but Georgiana tells me Bingley was so distracted by the mere presence of Miss Bennet, he did not even notice his sisters were continually insulting both of the Bennet ladies. Once I did arrive, from what I understand, they acted a little better, but came to behave themselves more appropriately once they realized Georgiana was displeased with their antics. I expect they will conduct themselves even more properly now that you have returned."

"I am not so sure about that. So what did you wish to warn me about if not Miss Bingley?"

"Bianca," Richard stated, leaning back in his chair. "I told you more than a year ago, before her debut, that she had always had her cap set at marrying you. It puzzled me when she went after Bartholomew so soon after coming out, and I could not account for it until I realized she accepted him only to outdo the girl who had always been her biggest rival *and* who wanted him for herself.

"The moment you and she arrived this morning, I began watching her carefully. Judging by Bianca's behaviour thus far, I gathered she knew Miss Bingley was trying to impress you—though that is not surprising

173

since most of the *ton* have also realized marrying you is Miss Bingley's goal. Miss Bingley did not concern Bianca, though. Most of my sister's glares were aimed at Miss Elizabeth."

Yes, Darcy had noticed it, too, but... "Richard, do you think because you and I know my history with Miss Elizabeth that we see more to it than Bianca possibly could have guessed?"

Richard shook his head. "I am not certain what gave it away—something you did or said—but Bianca *knew*. I am sure of it."

Darcy took in a quick breath. "I told her."

Richard sat up at attention. "You what?"

"Whilst we were aboard ship. Your sister attempted to sedu—" Was he mad, saying such a thing to her brother, even if it was Richard? "To *explain* her wishes for the future. I told her there was no chance for a marriage between us as there already was a lady that I want to marry."

Richard nodded. "Then she only had to see the way you looked at Miss Elizabeth to know it was her." His brow furrowed. "What concerns me most is *what* Bianca will do with this knowledge. She has never been one to play fair at anything. You know as well as I do that she cheats at cards and other games, even if the outcome does not matter, just to prove she can get away with it. When the prize is this important, there is no telling what she might do."

"Do not worry, Richard. Whilst we were aboard ship, I was able to avoid her. When we arrived today, she was exhausted; I doubt she will even come down for supper this evening because she is in mourning. She will stay here only one night. I believe all will be well."

"You do not think my sister can accomplish anything in that little time, I suppose." Richard laughed. "But I recommend you do not let your guard down. I can only liken her to a barracuda, Darcy. She loves to strategize—to plan and plot—and success is the only acceptable outcome no matter what rules she must break to achieve that end. I have often thought Bianca would have been a fantastic general in service to the Crown."

"A *mother* barracuda."

"Mother?"

Darcy picked up a letter opener off of his desk and fidgeted with it. "Actually, her condition saved us from one difficult situation, which we will speak of later."

"So, not only has she always wanted you, but she will do what she feels she must to gain a father for her child. She will not play by the rules, Darcy, and she knows tonight will be her last chance. She *will* take it."

"Do you think Bianca will move against Elizabeth, or will she try again for me?"

"We had best prepare for both possibilities."

"I have posted two footmen in the family wing corridor, two in the guest wing—which I always do when the Bingleys are at Pemberley, anyway." He rolled his eyes. He did not need to explain to Richard about Caroline. "But I have added two in the *servants'* corridor leading to my rooms. All have orders not to leave their posts unattended. One will not leave on an errand unless the other has returned. Perhaps I should add two to the servants' corridor leading to Miss Elizabeth's chambers."

Richard sighed. "Bianca must have been busy during your journey if you already have such a plan in hand, Darce. I was just thinking along the same lines. However, I had not recollected the servants' corridor. Do you think she might attempt it?"

Darcy nodded. "And it is my own fault. It is how I used to get into your chambers to play tricks on you and your brother years ago when you all stayed here. One time, she caught me entering the servants' corridor through the nursery. I swore her to secrecy, to which she agreed only after I promised she could come with me and assist in setting up the prank."

"Ah, ha! So that is how you did it? I used to set up traps at the door to the corridor, but you never tripped them." Richard laughed. "In that case, for our purposes, it might be easier to place someone in the servants' corridor outside *her* rooms, instead of Miss Elizabeth's chambers and your own. If someone is there, she could not leave that way."

"Good. I was wondering where I would find all these footmen and still keep the rest of the house staffed."

Richard chuckled. "And, I have one more ploy to suggest that would ensure nothing could happen."

A knock sounded out.

"That is probably Bingley. On my way here, I stopped by his room to ask him to come speak to me when it was convenient for him."

"Then I will explain later," Richard said.

Darcy called out, "Come!"

Bingley entered the room. "Ah, Darcy. I am glad to find you alone—" He stopped when Richard stood from the high-backed chair that hid him from view from the doorway. "Oh! And it is good to see you, as well, Colonel."

His uncomfortable appearance betrayed his words were not exactly correct.

Richard understood the hint. "I was just leaving, Bingley. I will see you both at supper." Richard exited the room.

Darcy rose and walked over to his brandy tray. Even the thought of speaking to Bingley about Miss Bennet made him feel as though he would need a bracer. "Would you like one?"

"Yes, I believe I would. Thank you."

Darcy handed him the glass and invited him to sit, and then took his own chair behind his desk.

Bingley sat, crossed his legs, uncrossed them, and popped back out of the chair. He walked to the opposite end of the study, then approached the desk again and placed his glass on it. He straightened his back and said firmly, "Although you might not be pleased to hear it, Darcy, I am quite happy to inform you that you were *wrong*!"

Darcy sat back in his chair. "I know, Bingley. It is what I wished to discuss with you."

Bingley arched his brows. "It was?"

"Yes."

"Do you even know of what subject I speak?"

"Miss Bennet." He rose and came around to Bingley's side of the desk. "I have it on good authority that the opinion I gave you last fall was utterly and completely mistaken. I apologize."

Bingley's mouth dropped open, and he stood staring at Darcy with an expression of shock.

"When I – uh…" Darcy took a breath and gathered his thoughts. How much should he say? "I was about to go to your house in London to speak to you on the subject when I received your note saying you had already left for Scarborough. I did not think it was proper to explain through the post, so I decided to speak to you when you we met again, here at Pemberley this summer. And here we are."

Bingley stepped forward. "I wish you had explained it through the post, Darcy. I spent the past months in a bad way."

"Again, I apologize. But just think, if you did not receive the letter I *did* send, most likely you would not have received that one, either, and who knows who might now have the knowledge that Miss Jane Bennet does, in fact, care for you."

A grin slowly spread across Bingley's face. "I had only suspected it in Hertfordshire, but now that I see her again, I am absolutely certain of it. I must say it sounds much better when said aloud than it did only in my thoughts." He narrowed his eyes. "May I ask who is your 'good authority'?"

Darcy looked down at the glass in his hand. "No, you may not."

"But this person is reliable?"

Darcy chuckled. "I thought you said you now have no question of her feelings for you?"

"Well, yes, I am certain. But I would like to hear it from another source just the same."

"My informer is completely reliable." Darcy hesitated. "Do you forgive me for my faulty advice?"

"Forgive you? I asked your opinion. You gave it. You did not force it upon me. And though my sister Caroline might not agree with the following proclamation, I have never believed you are without fault, Darcy. In fact, you have proven to me on multiple occasions you are wrong more often than right when it comes to judging matters of relationships."

A great weight lifted from Darcy's shoulders. Amusement twitched at his lips. He raised his glass. "To Miss Bennet. I hope you may find felicity together."

Bingley reached for his brandy and took a sip. "Thank you, Darcy. If she does accept me—eventually—I can guarantee your wish will be fulfilled for I will be the happiest man on earth, and I will work every day towards ensuring she will feel the same. I only hope you may find an equal measure of happiness."

Was Bingley's smile a bit on the impish side, or was it his imagination playing tricks with him?

"Thank you." He would gladly pay homage to that prospect.

Chapter 25

Darcy knocked on Georgiana's door. Her maid answered, and he handed her a note. "I will wait for her answer."

She closed the door.

He nodded to the two footmen guarding the corridor, and then walked over to a painting and pretended to examine it. His thoughts did not relate to it, but on someone in another wing of the manor.

Not five minutes later, Georgiana came out into the corridor. "Since I was almost ready, I thought I would come out straight away instead of sending an answer. Jane, Lizzy and I usually meet long before supper begins. I was just heading to their sitting room now. Will you join me?"

Tempted as he was, he shook his head. He did not wish to witness James carrying Elizabeth down the stairs. "Will you ask them if they would meet me in the second drawing room? I will take your advice and escort them on a tour of the library before we meet everyone else for supper."

Georgiana said, "This is excellent news, Brother. I do not know how I have kept Lizzy out of there for this long as it is."

~%~

Elizabeth smiled with excitement at Jane and Georgiana as James pushed her past them and down the hallway. She would finally get to see the famed library at Pemberley!

The door to the second drawing room stood open, and James took the turn without delay. Darcy stood by the window, his hands folded behind him, looking out at the continued rain. He was a bit thinner than he had been when she saw him before he left for America, and she wondered what troubles he had experienced along his journey.

Most likely sensing her advancement into the room, he turned. A grin formed upon his lips. Her breath failed her. He was still as incredibly handsome as he ever was. He stood looking at her for a moment before reacting with a start and crossing to them. Stopping before Elizabeth, he bowed.

"Miss Bennet, Miss Elizabeth. Good evening. I am glad you could join Georgiana and me for a look around the library before we dine. As soon as Georgie told me you had not yet been shown that room, I made certain it was ready for you to see it tonight. The others have all been there before, and I suspect they would not be interested in another tour."

He looked at James. "Thank you, James. I will push Miss Elizabeth's chair from here. We will ring for you if you are needed."

Darcy moved around behind Elizabeth and asked, "Are you ready, Miss Elizabeth?"

She peered over her left shoulder and met his gaze. "I have been ready to see the illustrious library at Pemberley ever since it was first mentioned at Netherfield, Mr. Darcy."

His eyes sparkled with something she could not identify. "I am glad to hear it."

Darcy propelled the chair through the doorway and into the corridor. Jane and Georgiana followed. When they arrived at the library, he stopped, opened the door, and then pushed her through it.

Once inside the library, Elizabeth gasped. Bookcases jutted out perpendicularly from the interior wall, each ending half-way to the outside wall at a column most likely placed where part of the structure had been removed to make the room into one mammoth chamber.

They made their way further into the library. She looked down the aisles and realized most of the doors in the corridor must be false. Instead of there being doors on this side of the wall, there was shelving. Her eyes followed the bookcases upward, and her mouth dropped open. The library took up *two* stories of the house. Every shelf of books was perfectly placed so that, during the day, the light from one of the room's sixteen windows—eight on each floor—illuminated every aisle.

A Lesson Hard Learned

Shelves of books climbed every wall, breaking only at large windows on her right, and on the left, intricately carved woodwork lined the underside of an approximately six-foot-wide walkway which bordered three walls of the chamber. After a moment, she realized the walkway was probably what remained of the floor of the room above. There was a door at each end of the lower level, directly below two on the second floor.

At each end of the room were identical enormous stone hearths around which stood a sitting area made up of inviting stuffed leather chairs and a few low tables. Between the chairs stood tall torcher candelabras. She assumed they had been placed there for the convenience of those who indulged in night-time reading.

At the heart of the room, instead of a bookcase, a beautiful circular staircase wound around the column, leading to the second-floor walkway.

"I have never seen anything like it!" Elizabeth exclaimed in a reverent whisper. "So many books!"

Darcy stopped and came around to stand before her. "It has been the work of many generations," he said quietly.

Elizabeth remembered his using that exact phrase at Netherfield in answer to Miss Bingley's comments concerning the library at Pemberley. Although in most cases, when speaking of anything concerning a Darcy, Miss Bingley tended towards exaggeration, in this instance, the lady had made an understatement of such proportions, Elizabeth found it absurd. She chuckled.

Darcy raised an eyebrow.

Once she regained her self-control, Elizabeth smiled at him. "I just recalled a time someone described your library as *delightful*." She shook her head. "That comment did your collection quite a disservice, sir. It is nothing short of magnificent. I doubt there is another library in all of England as grand as this. One could spend every day of his lifetime in this chamber and never have to read a book twice."

Goodness! Had she just implied she would like to spend the rest of her life at Pemberley?

Without taking his eyes from her face, Darcy straightened his form. It was a gesture she recognized, one that was usually accompanied by his ridding his mien of all emotion. But this time, he did no such thing, and she could not look away. She could swear he coloured slightly as he continued searching her eyes in a way that made her breath catch in her chest.

Nearby, Georgiana cleared her throat.

Darcy blinked, breaking their intimate gaze, and he looked away, taking a deep breath. He addressed the entire party when he explained how the books were laid out in general subjects and brought them to a small pedestal that held a diagram of the room.

Again, he moved her chair to where she could see everything more easily. "The library is at your disposal, ladies. Feel free to visit at any time to select a book or to come here to read."

"Thank you, sir. I will take you up on that offer," Elizabeth said.

Darcy raised one eyebrow.

Realizing the phrasing she had used, Elizabeth blushed.

Darcy's delight shone from his eyes instead of his lips. "I *do* hope so, Miss Elizabeth."

She felt as if her heart stopped beating. Had he implied he would—

He averted his eyes. "While we are here, is there anything I can get for you? I will have someone bring it up to your rooms."

Jane shook her head. Elizabeth regained her senses in time to tell him Georgiana had gotten her a book to read only yesterday. "Perhaps tomorrow?"

"I shall be at Matlock tomorrow, but Georgiana or any of the servants can assist you in my brief absence."

A Lesson Hard Learned

~%~

When everyone had arrived at the drawing room—including Bianca, to Darcy's surprise, considering she was in mourning—Georgiana rang the bell, and they went in to dine. Again, Darcy pushed Elizabeth's chair himself, escorting her in. He held back a smile when he saw his sister had placed her next to him, though Caroline Bingley was on his other side. Bingley took in Bianca and Jane Bennet, who sat on either side of him. Bianca did not seem at all pleased to have been escorted in by and seated next to Bingley, though she was sitting in a seat of honour at Georgiana's side. Mr. Hurst escorted his sister-in-law, and Richard offered his arms to Mrs. Hurst and Mrs. Annesley.

"It is so good to have returned to England," Bianca said. "Nothing is done properly in the Americas. We were treated abominably."

Darcy raised his eyebrows. How could she complain about nothing being done properly in another culture as she was sitting at table with his other guests while she was mourning her husband? He had no doubt Caroline Bingley and Mrs. Hurst would spread this information all over the *ton* within minutes of next arriving in Town. Perhaps even sooner by letter.

He replied, "I have been to America before. It was all done properly according to their customs. The way we were treated, though inconvenient to us, seemed understandable considering they were about to declare war with England. We were forced to find passage in a hurry."

"And how was the crossing?" Georgiana asked Bianca.

"My journey there with Bartholomew was in the best of comfort, but on the way home, the conditions aboard ship were deplorable," Bianca answered. "It was dirty and cramped, and there was no society what-so-ever. I had to share a cabin with my maid."

"It was almost impossible to find passage." Darcy looked directly at Georgiana. He realized his tone was defensive, and he made an effort to sound more informative than as if he were scolding his cousin. "Though the *Gypsy's Promise* was not a passenger ship, when I explained the circumstances, Captain Mott kindly took us on board. He and the first mate gave up their cabins for our use so we could be more comfortable."

"The crew was crude and coarse," Bianca said.

"Ordinary men who were well-skilled and hard workers."

"They were smugglers—"

"They usually supply items from France to the upper crust, who feel they cannot do without them, such as the lace you are wearing, Bianca, the wine you enjoy at home, and the brandy your father keeps in his study." He switched his gaze to Elizabeth. "They were not smuggling any goods from America; instead, they were transporting legal commodities to England, as I assured the British Navy when they came upon us."

"We were overtaken by pirates!" Bianca announced.

"Pirates?" Georgiana's alarm was unmistakable in her voice and upon her countenance.

"Darcy?" Richard regarded him with some amusement. It was evident he knew if they had been taken by pirates, they would not be at Pemberley now.

Darcy took in a deep breath and let it out slowly. "The *Gypsy's Promise* is a fast ship. Captain Mott and his crew kept us ahead of them. They abandoned their quest soon after we entered the more heavily patrolled waters nearer to England. Not one shot was fired the entire time we were on board, though we felt it necessary to keep the ladies below deck much of the time to ensure they were out of the path of danger."

"And to protect us from the crew," Bianca said in a superior tone.

Darcy sighed quietly. "Captain Mott felt there was a chance one of the men might have been signalling the pirate ship, for the pirates seemed to know where we were and caught up to us twice even though the captain changed course several times in an attempt to evade them."

"And how was that resolved?" Richard asked.

"The crew was on edge for days, every man knowing *he* was not a traitor, but uncertain of those around him. None but the captain and one other crew member trusted us. Hughes, Fleming, and I began making it obvious that we carried pistols, hoping the sight of them in our belts would avert the need to use them for our own protection."

Darcy cleared his throat and tried not to glare at Bianca. "Though the crew and most of the passengers had taken pains to make certain the ship was in complete darkness at night, since that is when we would change course, it so happened one of the *passengers* ignored instructions and kept a lantern lit in the captain's cabin at night. That chamber is at the rear of the ship and had large windows." He turned to Elizabeth and explained, "The sea at night is very dark. During the day, the pirates could sight the ship by a looking glass, but at night, if the ship had been in total darkness, they would not have been able to follow us."

Elizabeth's brow furrowed. "But in this case, all they had to do was follow the light left on in the captain's cabin."

"I told you, the ship was filthy." Bianca sniffed. "There were rats aboard. I only wished to make certain my maid could see them so she could chase them away."

Mr. Hurst laughed heartily. Bianca scowled at him.

"There are rats aboard every ship," Richard said. "And *you* are terrified of them. Are you saying you forced Ellen to stay awake at night to keep watch for rats?"

"Ellen did not mind. She slept for a little while each day."

"So your maid has barely slept in weeks?" Richard asked, and then said under his breath, "It is a wonder Ellen is still alive." Then louder, "It is a wonder *any* of you are still alive."

Bingley asked, "Darcy, how did you discover the problem?"

"When Ellen asked Captain Mott for more oil for the lantern, the captain's suspicions rose. The windows in that cabin are more than large enough so there was no need for a lantern during the day. After Ellen answered a few questions, the problem became clear."

Darcy did glare at Bianca this time. Bianca raised her chin and looked away.

Elizabeth said, "We are all relieved the ship was fast enough to remain ahead of the pirates and you have returned safely."

He met her gaze. She truly seemed happy he was home. He fought the urge to take her hand in his. "Thank you."

After supper, the group moved into the music room. Caroline sang and Mrs. Hurst played the same song Elizabeth and Georgiana had been practicing earlier in the day—in fact, at the very moment Darcy had arrived. Elizabeth met Darcy's gaze. There was amusement in his eyes that she understood perfectly. She could see he, too, suspected they chose the song on purpose with the intention of displaying their superiority. Elizabeth bit her lip and stifled her amusement. Although she was warmed by the shared confidence, she looked away, knowing if they continued this exchange any longer, she would be laughing before long.

Elizabeth was wheeled to the pianoforte next, and Georgiana sat next to her, working the pedals as Elizabeth played.

Afterwards, as Georgiana searched through the music for the song she was to play next, Bingley remarked, "I have not heard that song since we were at Netherfield, which puts me in mind of the families we met. How are all our neighbours?"

Jane answered, "All is as it was in the fall, though the militia has left the neighbourhood. I believe they are camped in Brighton for the summer."

"Ah, what a loss that must have been for your family, Miss Bennet. Especially for Miss Eliza, it must have been quite a blow."

"I cannot imagine what you mean, Miss Bingley," Elizabeth replied, though she knew what—or more precisely, to whom—Caroline referred.

A Lesson Hard Learned

"I thought you had a favourite among them… a Mr. Wickham, if I remember correctly."

Georgiana stiffened beside her. Darcy moved half-way out of his seat, but he hesitated when he heard Elizabeth speak.

"You are mistaken, Miss Bingley. The true characters of all men are revealed eventually."

From the corner of her eye, she could see Georgiana was now trembling.

From where the Hursts and Bingleys were seated, they could not see their hands, so she took Georgiana's hand in hers and gave it a little squeeze.

Georgiana gasped softly.

Elizabeth turned her head and met Georgiana's confused gaze.

The younger girl's brows twitched questioningly.

Elizabeth smiled reassuringly. She would have turned over the instrument to Georgiana, but her hands were still shaking, so she said softly, "Shall we work together while I play another, dear friend?"

Georgiana's eyes moistened with tears.

Elizabeth squeezed her hand again.

The younger girl let out a trembling breath, and the pain in her eyes turned to gratitude and relief. She nodded.

Elizabeth turned her attention to the music and, paging through, chose a song that meant something to both her and her hostess. "How is this one?"

It was a song Elizabeth had practiced quite a bit when she first arrived— one they had laughed over as Elizabeth had made one mistake after another. Fortunately, Elizabeth had become much more proficient at the song with repetition, but she suspected that was the day Georgiana had learned it was possible to forgive one's own blunders instead of constantly agonizing over them.

Georgiana answered, "That is perfect."

As Elizabeth began to play, she glanced at Darcy and her gaze became caught in his. His smile communicated such depth of emotion, she could look nowhere else. The remainder of the company melted away as if the two of them were alone in the room.

Her heart rejoiced.

He loved her still.

~%~

After Elizabeth was already in bed, there was a knock on her door. Unable to answer it for Hannah was gone by now, she called out, "Enter."

Georgiana walked in and lingered by the door. Elizabeth asked her to come in.

Georgiana approached the bed. "How did you know, Lizzy? Did Wickham tell you?"

"No, Georgie. It was your brother," Elizabeth admitted.

"But he forbade me from speaking about it to anyone. Why would he tell you?"

Elizabeth patted the bed next to her. "Come and sit with me."

Once Georgiana had made herself comfortable, Elizabeth began, "Miss Bingley was right, in a way, though I did not really favour Mr. Wickham in the way she meant. I found him charming and attractive, so I allowed his attentions because I was flattered. It was wrong. Many people thought I cared for him when I did not, though I empathized with him after he told me a story which I later found out was a lie."

She looked down at her hands. "About me?"

Elizabeth shook her head. "No, he did not say much about you—no more than a passing mention of your name. The lie was about his relationship with your father and your brother's mistreatment of him through his administration of your father's will."

"Oh! It is probably the same story he told me."

"It could be. But I will not repeat it now as I know it is not true."

"How did you find out he had lied?"

Elizabeth chuckled. "I confronted your brother with it, and he told me the truth."

"Did you believe him?"

"I am ashamed to say I did not, at first. I think he told me about what happened to you so I would better understand that Mr. Wickham was truly a scoundrel. Mr. Darcy thought I had a tendre for Mr. Wickham and assumed I would not trust his speaking against Wickham's character. And yet, he wished to protect me from being taken advantage of by him."

"And it worked?"

Elizabeth nodded. "Yes, it worked. I might not have liked your brother at the time, but I knew he would not make up a story like that about his sister. It helped me to understand Mr. Darcy better, too. I saw I had misjudged him. In fact, his telling me that story changed my life in many ways."

"For the better?"

Elizabeth thought about it for a moment. It had been difficult to face up to her faults, but as a result, she was a better person. "Yes."

"Then I am glad he told you."

"Thank you, Georgie. It is generous of you."

They sat in silence for a minute, and then Georgiana asked, "Lizzy, can I tell you about what happened in my own words? I was too ashamed to talk about it openly with Fitzwilliam and Richard. But seeing that you already know..."

Elizabeth said, "You can tell me anything, Georgie. I have always felt better after telling Jane my troubles."

"Oh! Does Jane know about me, too?"

Elizabeth cringed. "I am sorry, but I felt so foolish, so naïve for believing Mr. Wickham when there were so many inconsistencies in his speech, I needed to talk it out. Jane would never reveal it to anyone."

Georgiana swallowed hard. "You both knew, and yet you did not hold it against me... You sought to become friends with me anyway."

Elizabeth took Georgiana's hand. "We both knew Wickham in Meryton, Georgie. He duped us all—everyone. The entire village. Since the militia has left Meryton, stories have surfaced displaying his true character. He ran up gaming debts and lines of credit at the shops and the tavern, and he has repaid none of it." She would not mention the shopkeeper's daughter he had ruined. "He is good at deceit. Very convincing. We could not blame you for being deceived by a man when so many others, who were older and should have been wiser, were taken in by him, as well."

Georgiana set her shoulders as if she were convincing herself she had the courage to reveal what had been kept hidden for so long. "He came to see me at Ramsgate, where I was staying with my companion, Mrs. Younge. I was unaware at the time, as were Fitzwilliam and Richard, that Mrs. Younge was acquainted with him from before she came to work for my brother. Mrs. Younge said that because he was a friend of the family, it was acceptable to invite him to dine with us, to walk with us, and the like. He acted as if he loved me, and he told me he did. He asked me to marry him."

She wiped a tear away from her cheek.

"He said he did not want to wait to marry me and convinced me to elope with him to Scotland. I was foolish enough to think of it as an adventure and assumed my brother and Richard would approve because Wickham was their childhood friend. We planned to leave the next day, but then Fitzwilliam came to see me as a surprise. Of course, I told him of my happiness, my joy of finding I was loved by a man as charming and handsome as Wickham."

A shadow fell over her face. She shook her head.

"Instead of wishing me joy, my brother became panicked. I had never seen him so upset. When I told him that nothing had happened between us—Wickham had never touched more than my hand, you see..." She blushed. "...he relaxed a little, but then he became angry. Wickham came to the house to see me and was shown in, only to find my brother in the parlour." She blushed again. "I will admit to you, Lizzy, that I listened from the next room. I wanted to hear Wickham defend himself and say he loved me." Her shoulders fell. "But he did not. He called me terrible things and said he never loved me, and then he admitted he was after my dowry to repay him for what my brother stole from him."

Tears were freely flowing down her face now.

Elizabeth pulled her into her embrace. Georgiana sobbed for a while. When she calmed down she whispered, "I thought I loved him, Lizzy, but now I know I did not. I was flattered. I had not thought I was pretty enough to cause anyone to fall in love with me, but he kept telling me how beautiful I was. As you said, he was charming and very good at lying to get what he wanted."

"Wickham is not an honourable man, Georgie. I despise he did this to you... that he made you feel unworthy," Elizabeth said. "You are beautiful, not only on the outside, but more importantly, on the inside as well. Someday you will meet a man who is worthy of you, and he will not be able to stop himself from falling in love with you. Please believe me. I would not say it if it were not true."

Elizabeth waited a moment before continuing. "You do know now that any man who will not wait to be married properly and wishes to elope probably has ulterior motives?"

"Yes, *now* I understand he did not wish to ask for permission from my brother because he was aware Fitzwilliam and Richard would not grant it. He is a scoundrel, as you said."

"So you have learned a great deal from this experience."

"I have, and it helps to know that hearing of my experience saved you from him, as well."

Elizabeth smiled. "Let us think of it this way: *Your brother* saved us both."

"Fitzwilliam is the best of men, Lizzy." Georgiana studied her expectantly.

Should she tell her what she felt? She did not wish to lift Georgiana's hopes, but she did want to speak the truth.

"I agree, Georgie. Mr. Darcy *is* the best of men."

Chapter 26

So much for sleeping in my own bed tonight.

Darcy fluffed a pillow and tried to find a position where he could coax his long body into sleep. It embarrassed him to know that Richard had been placed in a room with such an unpleasant mattress. As soon as he made his way downstairs in the morning, he would seek out Mrs. Reynolds and order it re-strung.

Or perhaps it was not the mattress? Mayhap it was his uneasy thoughts that kept him awake? And worry.

It was difficult to stop thinking of the reason he was sleeping here tonight, in Richard's room. Bianca. At least he was safe from her here, and tomorrow that risk would be gone completely. He would take her to Matlock, fulfilling his duty to his aunt and uncle.

Richard informed him the earl had taken a turn for the worse. The doctor had reluctantly revealed his uncle would live a few more days, but no longer. They had returned to England just in time.

And yes, he could not stop thinking about Elizabeth. Did she see any improvement in him? Could he manage to keep his journal from her? Had he made progress towards her finally accepting him, making him the most fortunate man on earth?

He rolled over and stared at the door. Elizabeth was somewhere in the guest wing. He hoped she slept comfortably and healed well, though healing quickly might lead to her leaving Pemberley sooner.

He pulled the covers up over his head. Better not to think about how close she was.

Something touched his shoulder. He froze.

"Richard? I am glad you are awake."

Bianca! How did she get in here? She is craftier than Richard and I put together.

If she mistakenly took him for her brother, maybe he could further the ruse and get her to leave. She would recognize his voice, but Richard was not the most cheerful person when he first awakened. Darcy grunted.

"You have always loved Fitzwilliam like a brother. Did you ever think of what it would be like if he truly *became* your brother? I could arrange it."

He made a non-committal noise.

"Fitzwilliam has laid down a challenge for me. You know how I love contests of wit and will. It is a game we have been playing the entire time we were away. In order to win, I must find a way into Fitzwilliam's rooms. Will you help me?" She shook his shoulder. "Richard! Answer me."

Darcy scrambled off the bed, away from Bianca. Grabbing the sheet, he wrapped it around himself like a cloak.

"Fitzwilliam!" Her smile was wicked. "How very convenient."

Darcy shook his head. "How did you make it past the footmen posted outside your rooms?"

She did not answer. Instead, she looked at him seductively and moved slowly around the bed, untying the top tie of her robe.

"Stop! I have had enough of this subterfuge, Bianca." Darcy marched to the door, opened it, and exited into the hallway.

"Fitzwilliam!" she called out loudly.

He had to keep her from shouting, or she would awaken the entire household.

Darcy took a few steps down the corridor and stood under a lantern on the wall. The footmen three doors down stirred. Darcy raised his hand to stop them from approaching. He wanted witnesses, but he did not want them to be able to hear what he said to her.

He hoped they would not see Bianca exit from the chambers where he had been sleeping, but there was little he could do about it now. He had a feeling they understood the *reason* they were posted there, so they should know nothing had happened between him and Bianca.

Bianca eventually followed him into the corridor. Once she caught up to him, he turned to her, speaking softly. "Must you force me to say it again, Bianca? I thought I had explained it well enough while we were aboard ship, but now I see I must be blunt. No matter what you try, I will not marry you. Give up. I am in love, and it is *not* with you."

"Yes, I know." Somehow she managed to look down her nose at him, though she was at least eight inches shorter than he. "You are in love with Miss Elizabeth Bennet. It was plain to see in your every look this evening."

He was not certain whether it was Bianca's expression or the shadows that played across her face which made her look so hateful.

She continued. "She is so far below you, it is a disgrace to the names of both Darcy and Fitzwilliam if you even *think* of marrying her."

"I am a gentleman. She is a gentleman's daughter. It is all I require."

"Ellen has made inquiries with the maids who are serving her and her sister. And Miss Bingley's girl knows even more about them since the Bingleys lived in the same neighbourhood as the Bennets for several months. Are you aware that neither of the Bennets has a maid accompanying her, Fitzwilliam?" She snorted. "Their family cannot even afford an abigail for each of their five daughters. They *share* one. And she has practically no dowry at all. Her father's income is but two thousand a year." She narrowed her eyes. "I am sure you could not have known any of this. You cannot marry someone so low, Fitzwilliam. You simply cannot do it!"

Darcy sighed heavily. "It is not for *you* to decide. These things do not matter to me. Do you ever listen when I speak? I am *in love* with her, Bianca."

"Love! What difference does that make?" she scoffed. "Marriage is for increasing one's wealth, connexions, and consequence. If you marry *me*, you may not be able to attend Parliament, but you will *live* like an earl. You will further strengthen the connexion between our families and increase the Darcy accounts with my dowry, which will be returned to me upon the reading of Bartholomew's will." Her face smoothed as if she had come up with a brilliant idea. "Love is for affairs and mistresses. You can always keep her on the side, Fitzwilliam. I would not mind."

Darcy flared his nostrils. "I would never dishonour Miss Elizabeth in such a way." He shook his head in disgust. "And believe me, love makes all the difference in the world when *you* are the one in love. Your parents love each other, Bianca. Mine did, as well. Between those couples, you had excellent models. Where did you get these ideas?"

"From you, Fitzwilliam."

He pulled back as if she slapped him. Several moments and a few recollections later, he nodded in defeat. "You are correct. At one time, I did think as you do. But that was before I met Miss Elizabeth Bennet." He tried his best to use a kind tone, but it came out as if he pitied her. "I do hope you find love someday, as well, Bianca."

She harrumphed. "If finding love should make me as weak as you are now, I would never want it. It can only lead to degradation."

"We can never agree. I will discuss this with you no longer. I will speak as plainly as I know how so you will put an end to this scheme of yours once and forever." Darcy straightened his spine in an attempt to appear as intimidating as was humanly possible when one was wearing a bed sheet as a robe. "I do not want you, Bianca. I have no interest in you in that way. None whatsoever. I will not take you to my bed—ever—and I will certainly not marry you. There is nothing you can do, and there is nothing your father or your mother or your brothers can say to convince me. I will *not* have you." He gestured as if he were sweeping her out of his life. "Do not make another attempt for I do not wish to humiliate you before your family, but if you do try anything again, I warn you that I will not hesitate to do so. The only reason I will go with you to Matlock on the morrow is to visit my uncle. Once I deposit you on your parents' doorstep, I will have nothing more to do with you. After this experience, I know I cannot trust you. You will not be welcome at Pemberley again. Is that clear enough?"

She straightened her spine and lifted her chin. "Perfectly clear. You are a complete fool, Fitzwilliam Darcy."

Darcy started laughing. "I could not care less about what you think of me, Bianca. Shall I call the footmen and ask them to remove you to your own rooms or will you return of your own accord?"

Bianca stamped her foot like a frustrated child who was not getting her way.

Determined, he began walking down the corridor towards the footmen.

She huffed and swept past him as she headed to the guest wing.

Watching her until she turned the corner, he returned to Richard's bedchamber, closed the door, and leaned his back against it.

Thank God that is over.

~%~

"She's here, sir!"

Elizabeth opened her eyes. Georgiana was fast asleep in the other half of her humongous bed. Who had called out?

"Down here, sir."

Elizabeth turned over and saw a girl she recognized as a scullery maid standing just outside the open doorway to the corridor, pointing into her bed chamber. The maid turned to look down the hall in the opposite direction and rushed away.

A few moments later, Darcy stepped into view. He stopped short; his eyes widened until Elizabeth thought they would pop out of his head.

"Elizabeth!" he cried.

"Mr. Darcy!" she answered.

Startled, Elizabeth sat up quickly, and her nightgown slipped down one shoulder. She looked down at herself. Good Heavens! Part of her chest was exposed. Thoughts of fastening the strings that always came untied during the night flitted through her mind, but it would take too long. She leaned over and pulled up her sheet to cover herself. Her hair was loose—she had been so busy speaking to Georgiana last night, she had not braided it. She must look a mess!

He still stared at her in shock. "This is *your* chamber?"

She nodded.

He was standing just outside her room—her bed chamber!—hair tousled as if he had just awoken, dressed in what seemed to be bed slippers and trousers. Her eyes roved over him as he stood before her, and she took in a deep breath when she noticed a few dark hairs peeking out of the top of the open V-shaped neckline of his lawn shirt.

Her pulse rate increased tenfold as her gaze flicked back up to his face.

The look he gave her made her breath catch. He had caught her ogling him!

Her face heated thoroughly. "Can I help you, Mr. Darcy?"

"The maid said…" He finally blinked. "Do you know where Georgiana is?"

Still holding the sheet up to her chin, Elizabeth pointed at the other side of the bed. "She came in here to talk to me last night and fell asleep."

He closed his eyes and leaned his shoulder against the door frame.

"Are you well, sir?"

He opened his eyes. Seemingly remembering himself, he turned suddenly to face the corridor. "My valet woke me and passed on word from my sister's maid saying Georgiana was missing. We have been searching the entire house for her."

"I am sorry. Back home, my sisters and I talk into the night and fall asleep in each other's beds. Quite often, in fact. If I had known it would cause such worry and trouble, I would have awakened her and sent her back to her own rooms instead of covering her with a quilt so she would not catch chill." Elizabeth examined Georgiana again. "She certainly sleeps soundly! Shall I wake her so you can say goodbye before you leave for Matlock?"

Am I actually having a conversation with Mr. Darcy from my bed? Stop talking, Lizzy!

She started laughing. "I apologize; I tend to ramble on when I am…"

"Nervous, Miss Elizabeth?" His voice had a touch of humour in it.

She pulled the sheet away from her and looked down. Thank goodness her nightgown had not slipped down too low. He could not have seen more than he would have had she been wearing an evening dress. "Well, I *am* in bed, Mr. Darcy!"

"Yes, I *did* happen to notice you are in bed, Miss Elizabeth." He shook his head. "Just tell Georgiana I said goodbye and I should return before dark. Excuse me; I must call off the search."

Still in the hallway, he straightened and turned around abruptly to face her. "And I should finish dressing before I go." He smiled rakishly.

Her mouth dropped open. Since her hands had lowered a little, she pulled the covers back up to her chin.

"I will see *you* when I return, Miss Elizabeth."

He stepped into the room, took hold of the doorknob, and closed the door firmly behind him.

The bed began to shake. Elizabeth turned to look at her bedmate. "Georgie?"

Georgiana laughed out loud.

Elizabeth pulled the covers off her friend. "You were awake through all that?"

"I awakened about the time my brother asked where I was." She giggled for several more seconds before she could catch her breath. "I was too busy chaperoning to say anything." Her fit of giggles started anew.

"I cannot believe the maid left the door open."

Georgiana sat up. "Who was it? I should have her reprimanded." She wiped her eyes.

"I am not sure of her name…I think she is a scullery maid. But Georgie, do not dismiss her; I am certain she did not mean any harm. She was only relieved she found you."

"My brother does all the hiring in this household, and I am confident *he* will not dismiss her." She started giggling again.

Elizabeth asked, "I could not stop myself from prattling on and on."

"I would not worry about it, Lizzy. He did not sound at all *damaged* by the experience." She rose from the bed. "I should return to my rooms before anyone else awakens. I will see you later."

~%~

Darcy rinsed his face with the water in the basin.

This cold water is a blessing.

He needed more of it. Much more.

Cupping the water in his hands, he rinsed his face again, raking his fingers through his hair repeatedly. Water trickled down his neck and back, cooling his body, but not his thoughts.

He leaned his hands on the table on both sides of the basin and stared at himself in the mirror above it.

Once he had spied Elizabeth in bed, all thoughts of his purpose for being there fled his mind. Elizabeth, in a nightgown made from a material so sheer, it was almost transparent.

He would never forget the enticing way the open neckline slid down her shoulder. Time stood still as her skin was slowly exposed. The way her soft curls flowed down, down, forever downward. The appraising manner in which she had regarded his person made him aware of the pulse in every inch of his body. When she blushed, his imagination had gone wild.

Those few minutes would haunt him for all eternity!

When he recalled his objective, he should not have stood there talking to her, but after the scare he had just been through—Georgiana missing—he needed the comfort of hearing her voice. He could not force himself to leave.

And though he knew he should not have done so, still, he had to turn, had to look at her one more time, for he did not know if he would ever have another opportunity to do so.

*I **am** in bed, Mr. Darcy!*

He chuckled.

Yes, she had been in bed. Tempting him. Her gaze wandering over the length of his form, caressing him.

He dipped his hands into the water again, and splashed it over his head.

Yes, cold water *is* a blessing!

~%~

The sun was low in the sky when Georgiana met Darcy in Pemberley's entry hall as he handed the footman his gloves.

"You do not look well, Fitzwilliam."

"I am fine, but it has been a long day." He sighed. "A long few months, actually."

She furrowed her brow. "How is Uncle?"

He shook his head. "The doctor thinks we returned to England just in time, Georgie. He was lucid, and we talked a little, but he became tired quickly. The doctor asked me to leave him. I sat with Aunt Adelaide for a while, but there was nothing else I could do, and she wished to sit with her husband. I am glad I got to see him and say my goodbyes. Richard will remain at Matlock until he is no longer needed."

Georgiana asked, "Shall I go to see him, too?"

He answered, "Uncle told me he would rather you remember him as he was the last time you saw him, not as he is now." He noticed she was wearing a shawl. "Where were you off to at this hour?"

"Mr. Bingley, Jane, and I were just about to take Lizzy out to stroll in the garden and watch the sunset. Would you like to come with us?"

"Yes, I would like that very much. Thank you." He looked down at his dusty clothing. "Give me a minute to change."

Georgiana nodded. "I will wait for you here."

~%~

When the door opened, Georgiana entered, and her brother followed her.

He looked so tired.

"How is the earl, Mr. Darcy?" Elizabeth asked.

He bowed and then met her gaze. "Not well, Miss Elizabeth. I do not believe he will be with us for much longer."

"I am sorry to hear it, sir."

Jane and Bingley added their regrets, and Darcy acknowledged their sentiments, but he did not look away from Elizabeth. She felt her face heat and averted her eyes from his piercing gaze. Was he thinking of this morning, too?

He said, "I understand you are going to the gardens to observe the sunset."

Georgie said, "Yes, Lizzy gets rather irritable if she does not get some fresh air every day."

Elizabeth smiled at the tease. "That is very true! You know me well."

"We should go now if you are to get the full effect." Darcy turned to Bingley. "Your sisters and brother do not wish to join us?"

"Hurst has no interest in nature unless he can shoot at something, and my sisters… well, not when *I* asked them."

Should they discover Darcy had returned, they would likely change their minds and declare themselves most anxious to view the gardens. Elizabeth hoped no one would suggest they ask again. No one did.

Darcy stepped behind her chair. "May I, Miss Elizabeth?"

His tone made her heart skip a beat—he made it sound as if it was a privilege to push her chair. Why did she feel as if it was an intimate gesture when he offered to assist her, but not when it was anyone else?

She glanced over her shoulder at him. "Yes. Thank you, sir."

Chapter 27

Darcy wheeled Elizabeth to the best place available within the lower garden to view the setting sun and remained near her. Observing the sunset was something he and Georgiana enjoyed every evening, if the weather allowed. It was a pleasure to share this special time of the day with friends like these, especially Elizabeth.

Whenever he had imagined witnessing this with her, she was standing in his arms, leaning into him, with her back pressed tightly against his chest. His arms were wrapped around her, their hands entwined. He would lean down to press his cheek to her temple, experiencing what she did, or at least as closely as was possible.

While his heart ached for such a tender scene this evening, he would be content with being in the same vicinity as Elizabeth.

She fidgeted as if distracted, and he realized at her lower angle, the wall of the garden must block her view of the horizon.

As if Georgiana were privy to his thoughts, she said to nobody in particular, "There *is* a better place to see this miracle. It is above the steps that lead to the lawn, just there." She pointed. "However, Lizzy cannot climb the steps."

Elizabeth blushed. "I would be perfectly content to remain here alone if you all wanted to continue without me."

Although Darcy could think of an alternative, he dared not make the suggestion lest he be deemed presumptuous.

"No, Lizzy, we will not leave you. But I have been thinking." Georgiana's playful tone and her glance towards him made him suspect she had the same idea as he did. "If someone carried you up the steps, we could all watch the sunset from the lawn. It is not far."

His sister's tone dripped with an exaggerated sense of innocence, and he knew it could not be genuine. Georgiana was well aware that if Elizabeth agreed, he would not allow Bingley to convey her, and James had already been dismissed. *He* would carry her himself.

Though he knew his sister's suggestion was for his benefit, he was not certain how he liked Georgiana's attempt at matchmaking. He glanced at Elizabeth. *It all depends on how she reacts.*

"Well, I – uh…" Disconcerted, Elizabeth looked to her elder sister for guidance.

Georgiana said, "If we are out at sunset, a footman lights the torches along the path so we may return home safely. I can assure you we will be in no danger."

Miss Bennet made a point of directing her gaze at him before saying, "I know you must wish it, Lizzy. You often walk up the slight hill behind Longbourn to watch the sunset." She again ended her speech with a glance at him.

Elizabeth's mouth dropped open as she raised her eyebrows.

Could Miss Jane Bennet be party to Georgiana's scheme? Why else would she hint that he should carry Elizabeth?

After his display of haughty condescension towards all their friends and family in Hertfordshire the previous autumn, he never imagined gaining the approval of any member of her family so easily… or so soon.

Encouraged, Darcy made his own attempt to convince Elizabeth. "Since Pemberley is situated on rising ground, the view from the lawn behind the house should be a superior prospect than what can be seen from the flatlands of Hertfordshire. I am at your service should you wish to make the comparison for yourself." He bowed.

Elizabeth blinked her eyes several times and looked from him to Georgiana and then Miss Bennet. She then settled her gaze upon Bingley, who was nodding persuasively.

Elizabeth cleared her throat. "Are you certain you would not mind, Mr. Darcy?"

Darcy fought back his smile. "Georgiana is correct; the wheeled chair could not traverse the steps, but it would cause me no inconvenience to climb them while carrying you."

Elizabeth pensively examined his face. He held his breath. Instinct urged him to school his features into a stoic mask, but he refused to obey, though he *did* maintain strict control. While he did not wish to hide his regard from her any longer, he also did not want to frighten her with his eagerness to be of service to her, his delight in the prospect of sharing an experience so meaningful to him, or his anticipation of the opportunity to hold her close to his person.

Elizabeth inclined her head. "If you will not go without me, I have little choice but to agree."

He nodded, resisting the compulsion to thank her profusely. Suddenly, he understood Elizabeth's sycophantic cousin Mr. Collins a little better.

~%~

What were Jane and Georgiana about, making Mr. Darcy feel obligated to carry her to the lawn?

After the way Georgiana behaved this morning when her brother had come upon them in her rooms, she had some idea Georgiana hoped for a match between them. She would try to discourage her from pursuing it again, for such expectations could lead only to disappointment for both her and her friend.

But what of her demure and diffident elder sister, Jane, who had spent her entire life behaving in the most correct manner possible—who taught all her sisters to do the same by example and instruction? Why would *she*, of all people, support Georgiana's suggestion, which was improper in every way?

More than Elizabeth would like, Jane's matchmaking attempt resembled something their mother would arrange.

Darcy stepped around her chair and stood before her.

Despising her dependence on others for almost everything she wished to do, she refused to allow him to lift her from the chair. She held out her hands. He took them into his own.

A pleasant shock of warmth began where their hands touched and spread throughout her body. She obscured her surprise at the sensation by pulling herself up to stand on her uninjured leg.

Darcy's statement from months ago echoed in her mind, *I perfectly comprehend your feelings and have now only to be ashamed of what my own have been.*

If she looked into his eyes, would his shame—his aversion to loving her—be evident there? Unwilling to find out, she examined his neckcloth as he moved closer.

"With your permission, I will lift you now, Miss Elizabeth."

She nodded.

He bent over; one arm slid around her back, the other under her knees. She gasped, crossing her arms over her chest, her clasped hands under her chin. He lifted her as if she weighed no more than a feather and settled her against his firm chest. His spicy scent invaded her senses.

He said, "This would be more comfortable for us both if I had your assistance, Miss Elizabeth."

Confused, she looked up. The wide brim of her bonnet caught under his hat and knocked it off his head. Laughter rumbled through his chest, vibrating against her side. Looking down in embarrassment, she felt her bonnet skim his cheek.

"Oh! I am sorry, sir." She untied her bonnet and removed it, holding it between her hands on her lap.

"Would it be too much to ask…" his voice trailed off.

She met his gaze.

He swallowed hard. "It would be most helpful if you placed your arms around my neck, Miss Elizabeth."

What had she been thinking? Had she not done so to assist the footman with the same task? But that had been easier, for she was not attracted to James in the least. Darcy was an entirely different story.

Tucking the brim of her bonnet between them, she slid her right arm around his neck, reached up with the other to clasp her hands on his far shoulder, and then pulled herself into a more upright position. She raised her chin. His face was now only a hands-width away from hers.

His eyes remained averted as he thanked her and began to walk.

She took advantage of the moment to examine his visage. A slight stubble sprinkled his cheeks and square jaw. He must usually shave twice a day, but since he had only just returned home, he would not have had time. A number of his short whiskers glittered in the sunlight. She smiled in spite of herself. His beard had begun to turn grey.

As he led the way up the steps, she could sense the muscles of his chest, abdomen, and arms as they strained and relaxed with his movements, reminding her that while in his arms, he would know every one of her body's reactions, as well. She made an attempt at steadying her respiration.

He turned his head towards her. His lips almost brushed hers! Her breath caught and her face heated.

Good heavens, why had she agreed to this? How was she to survive being so close to him?

She shivered.

His voice was a husky whisper when he asked, "Have you caught a chill, Miss Elizabeth?"

She widened her eyes and shook her head. "No. Thank you for asking, sir." To voice his name while in such close quarters felt too intimate.

His eyes twinkled with something resembling the amusement he had displayed this morning at her bedchamber door. He inhaled deeply and broke their shared gaze, yet she still could not look away.

After several more delightfully torturous minutes in Darcy's arms, the ground levelled and the path ended. He leaned over to let her down. Her hand brushed across his shoulders as she removed it from around his neck, and she found herself wishing she was not wearing gloves. Keeping her injured leg bent and using his offered arm to steady herself, she gained her footing on her good leg.

A chill passed over her without his warmth pressed fully against her side. She turned her head to hide her blush at the realization. "It *is* a beautiful view."

"Yes, it is," Darcy said. From the corner of her eye, she noted he stared at her.

Why was he making this so difficult?

Elizabeth said, "It feels good to stand for a change." She pointed to a tree a few feet off to her left. "If someone helped me to the tree, I could lean against the trunk."

Georgiana stepped closer, handing her brother his hat. "Your gown would be ruined, Lizzy."

Elizabeth wondered what Georgiana would think if she knew how often she leaned against tree trunks during her walks in Hertfordshire. But Georgiana was correct; this was not one of her usual walking gowns, which were made of sturdier material.

Darcy placed his hand over hers, which was wrapped firmly around his forearm. "It is no bother if you remain here."

She raised her head. There was almost a desperate plea in his deep brown eyes. Did he want her to stay at his side?

Once they descended this hill, their current level of intimacy would almost certainly never occur again. Perhaps she should take advantage of it while it lasted and commit to memory every nuance of these moments. Before she knew what she was about, she had already nodded her agreement.

He smiled and averted his eyes.

She closed her eyes. She should never have allowed Georgiana and Jane to persuade her to do this. It was too much!

And yet, at the same time, it was not enough.

The thought frightened her.

~%~

Elizabeth's eyes were closed, the delicate skin between her brows furrowed.

What was she thinking? Did she regret agreeing to allow him to assist her?

As he carried her, she had examined his features so thoroughly, his blood pounded through his veins. It had been a trial to concentrate on the path ahead instead of allowing his mind to dwell on the meaning of her every gesture.

It was a good thing he had listened to Georgiana and not insisted he be the one to carry her around the house in place of James. Never in his life had he been so tempted to kiss a lady senseless than he had these past few minutes. If carrying her had been a regular occurrence, surely he would have compromised her by now.

Such an event would likely end in a marriage between them, the true desire of his heart, but he knew he would never win her affection if she felt forced to marry him.

When the time was right, he would certainly make an offer, but anything that happened between them would be of *her* choosing, or at the very least, with her permission.

Suddenly, she opened her eyes and stared directly at him with a startled expression.

He had not said that aloud, had he? He swallowed hard, anticipating her response if he had.

With a blink, all concern cleared from her countenance, and she looked away.

He breathed a quiet sigh of relief.

Elizabeth's skin radiated with the resplendent rosy hue of the sunset, and he could not tear his gaze away. She was much lovelier than anyone else could ever be in his eyes.

As the light faded further, his attention was caught by someone lighting the torches in the lower garden.

I hope it is not James.

~%~

Elizabeth was both relieved and disappointed when her usual entourage of footmen met them at the stairs leading to the guest wing. Darcy stepped away from her chair, bowed, and walked away hastily. She stood, leaning on James's arm. Two footmen carried the rolling chair while James conveyed her up the stairs behind them.

Georgiana left them to continue on to the family wing, and Jane walked beside Elizabeth as she was pushed into her bedchamber. As soon as James left them, Jane sat on the bed, looking as if she were expecting Elizabeth to gush with delightful news.

It was just as Elizabeth anticipated—Jane expected Darcy's intimate assistance to lead to an immediate proposal of marriage.

Since Hannah had not yet joined them, Elizabeth asked her sister to help her to the bed so she could prop her injured leg atop of a stack of pillows. Once she was situated and Jane had taken a seat on the edge of the bed, Elizabeth said, "I must beg of you, Jane, please do not continue this matchmaking scheme you have undertaken."

"Matchmaking? Whatever do you mean?"

Unlike their youngest sister, Lydia, who would have voiced such a falsehood without even blinking an eye, Jane was completely unaccustomed to deceit. Elizabeth bit back a smile as she watched her elder sister turn a deep shade of crimson.

"Jane, I was there. I saw your hint to Mr. Darcy, indicating he should carry me up to the lawn. While I realize you felt it was for my benefit, it was not."

Jane abandoned her pretence. "But you said you loved him, Lizzy."

Elizabeth nodded. "I do, but arranging circumstances in that way only makes my situation even more challenging." She smoothed a crease in her gown. "When Lady Bianca was here, she was quite obvious in her intentions. She wants Mr. Darcy for her husband."

Jane said, "But Mr. Darcy does not love Lady Bianca, Lizzy."

"I know. I spent a great deal of time analysing his behaviour last evening, and I could only detect his annoyance with her. But… Oh, Jane… I told you his proposal was not romantic, but perhaps I should have explained more of the particulars."

Elizabeth turned her face towards the window. She did not wish to witness any indication of her sister's reaction to what she was about to tell her.

"After stating the reasons for my refusal—which later, I found were mostly false assumptions—he asked if I had expected him to rejoice in the inferiority of my connexions or delight in the hope of gaining relations whose condition in life was so decidedly beneath him." She shook her head. "Can you not understand it now, Jane? The possibility Mr. Darcy would contemplate a renewal of his addresses is non-existent, especially after spending so much time abroad with his cousin, who is a high-ranking member of his own class. Without a doubt, these weeks in her company could only have reminded him he can have his pick of females from the upper crust."

"What difference could that make if he is in love with you, Lizzy?" Jane asked.

Elizabeth turned her gaze on her sister. "That may be, but the Bennets are not of the upper ten thousand, Jane. When we are in London, we do not attend the same events or know the same people." She sighed. "Even Miss Bingley moves in the same circles as he does, while we have never even heard most of their names."

"But none of this must have mattered to him when he asked you before."

"Now you get to the heart of the matter, dearest Jane. He left me only after declaring he was ashamed of his feelings for me." Elizabeth's voice trembled. "Even if his tendre survived the terrible things I said to him, and if he was able to overcome all his arguments against me when I advised him to use them to forget me, how can I expect him to propose marriage to me a second time? I cannot! Even if he felt for me the deepest love possible, to ask again after a refusal such as mine would be utter degradation."

"But—"

Elizabeth interrupted, "No, Jane. Please, stop. He does not even behave the same way towards me as he did before. After he proposed, I realized every time I thought he was looking at me to find fault, he was gazing upon me with affection. However, since we met again, he smiles and speaks to me in an affable manner. I am no more than a friend to him now. I can learn to be content with that, I think, but if you continue to push us together…" Elizabeth shook her head. "Knowing all this, being close to him all afternoon was intolerable. Please, leave it be."

"I apologize for causing your discomfort, dear." Jane took Elizabeth's hand. "And though I am certain you are wrong, I will do as you ask."

"Thank you." Elizabeth squeezed Jane's hand. "Now, I believe we should both get some rest before we change for supper.

Chapter 28

Darcy awakened with a start. Opening his eyes, he instantly shut them again. Apparently, it had not been a good idea to look out the window before he went to bed last night. Not only had it been too dark to catch a glimpse of the lawn where he had watched the sunset with Elizabeth, but he had not closed the curtains properly. A sliver of dawn's early light shone directly on his face.

He turned away from the glare. Much better.

The previous day had been filled with ups and downs. From Bianca entering the bedchamber where he slept, to finally getting through to her that they would never marry. From Georgiana going missing, to his mistaking where she was found as an empty guest room instead of Elizabeth's bedchamber. From his uncle's health failing and witnessing his aunt and cousins becoming more miserable by the minute, to returning home and having the opportunity to hold Elizabeth close in his arms.

And then, after supper…

He smiled at the memory of such domestic felicity. Even the presence of Bingley's sisters had not lessened anyone's pleasure, as far as he could tell. For the first time since Mrs. Hurst and Caroline Bingley became acquainted with the Bennets, they behaved amiably towards everyone in the room.

He narrowed his eyes and sat up.

Last evening, he simply thanked God and enjoyed it, but something was wrong. Very wrong.

Why would Bingley's sisters suddenly find their good manners when interacting with the Bennet ladies? Were they counting on their changed behaviour to cause everyone to let their guards down?

He sighed, threw back the covers, and stood. If he was to anticipate their next actions, he had best get an early start on the day.

An hour later, as he approached the breakfast room, Georgiana's giggle echoed down the corridor, soon followed by Elizabeth's laughter. Although he could not make out what they said, he stopped to listen to the cheerful tone of their banter.

If only it could be this way forever. Or at least until he and Elizabeth found a good match for Georgiana.

His heart swelled at the idea of Elizabeth helping him chaperone Georgiana during her debut Season. Elizabeth would be there to listen to his sister's opinions of the young gentlemen who would come to court her. Elizabeth would impart to him her opinion of the men who came to ask for Georgiana's hand.

It struck him that the thought of Georgiana's debut into society had always left him in a cold sweat, but this time was different. He might not be looking forward to it, but when assuming Elizabeth would be at his side, he no longer dreaded it. It was simply an eventuality.

With a spring in his step, he continued down the hall and turned through the open doorway of the breakfast room.

Georgiana and Elizabeth looked up at his entrance. He bowed. The ladies greeted him, their faces bright with welcome.

This is the proper way to begin my day.

After offering to get the ladies something more to eat, Darcy filled a plate for himself and took his seat at the head of the table. Georgiana was in her customary seat to his right, Elizabeth sat to his left. Afraid he might be considered dim-witted if he continued to grin for no apparent reason, he hid it by taking a too-large bite of toast so his mind might be distracted with his attempt to chew graciously.

"Georgie was just telling me of your adventures at the pond with your cousins," Elizabeth said, her eyes twinkling with mirth.

Unable to make a response, Darcy raised both eyebrows with expectation. Georgiana would not have told Elizabeth about…

"I did not realize I was a guest in the home of a dragon slayer."

Elizabeth took a sip of tea.

Georgiana giggled. "I still have the hennin hat Father made for me."

"Hennin?" Elizabeth asked.

"Yes, a tall, pointed hat draped with scarves like one sees in paintings depicting fairy tale princesses. Mrs. Reynolds always had a difficult time pinning it up, but she did so in a way it did not come off most times." She blushed.

Finally, Darcy was able to swallow. "I would slay any dragon that held Georgiana in mortal danger."

His heart squeezed painfully as his failure struck him. In truth, he had *not* slain Georgiana's dragon when it threatened. Wickham had endangered his sister, and he had only warned the man off. His cousin Richard had told him time and time again that, had he been there, he would have challenged him to a duel. Richard would have killed him. To this day, Richard could not understand why he had not done so himself.

Darcy speared a strawberry with his fork and chewed it with zeal.

Elizabeth smiled so prettily at him, it took him a few moments to comprehend she had begun to speak again. "Since we had no brothers, I was the protector of the Bennet maidens. Jane and Mary would dutifully accompany me on my walks, and of course we would come across beasts of all persuasions from which I had to protect them."

"I can well believe that as a child, you would have chased away any creatures who dared to terrorize your sisters," he snapped. "As an adult, I have witnessed your valiantly defending the honour of your loved ones by means of the spoken word, more skillfully than any could brandish a sword."

Regret rose in his breast as amusement drained from her face, leaving a deep crease between her brows. She examined her teacup.

Why had he spoken so sharply? He was angry at *himself,* on many levels, but not Elizabeth. His fingers ached to take her hand in an attempt to have her meet his gaze so she could see his heartfelt remorse. He added, "But never unwarranted; never without indisputable justification."

She looked up immediately. He put every effort into shaping his expression into one of sincerity. After a long blink of those beautiful emerald eyes, the distress smoothed from her countenance. He breathed a sigh of relief.

It seemed Georgiana preferred not to notice the exchange. "Speaking of verbal defences, I have heard—from *both* my guardians—that your conversations with our Aunt Catherine were quite entertaining. I hope to enjoy such a sight myself someday."

Crimson suffused Elizabeth's cheeks. She opened her mouth to reply but was interrupted by the entrance of Bingley ushering Jane Bennet and Caroline Bingley, one on each arm. Darcy rose as Bingley escorted his sister to the seat next to Georgiana then guided Miss Bennet to the chair next to Elizabeth.

Bingley filled a plate for each of the ladies and then did so for himself.

Caroline asked, "My dear Georgiana, what have you planned for us today?"

Georgiana's smile was not nearly as heartfelt as it had been a few moments ago. "I was thinking perhaps this afternoon we could go into Lambton for some shopping."

Caroline's face lit up. "A delightful idea! The shopping in Lambton is always superior to that of other country villages. I am certain Louisa will approve." She glanced at Elizabeth. "But it *is* too bad that with Miss Eliza's ankle injured the way it is, she will not be able to accompany us." She said to Jane, "And I suppose Miss Bennet will remain behind to keep her sister company. We shall endeavour to make do without them."

Miss Bingley appeared to be anything but disappointed with the circumstances she outlined.

Georgiana answered, "Oh, but that is the best part of my plan. Lizzy and Jane *shall* be able to come along. I have it all arranged." She shifted her gaze to Elizabeth. "Since the doctor already granted permission for Lizzy to ride in my gig and she is healing so well, he indicated in his note that he felt certain he could allow a trip slightly longer than we have taken thus far."

Darcy assessed Miss Bingley's reaction. She glared momentarily at Elizabeth but schooled her features almost immediately.

"Capital!" Bingley regarded Georgiana and Elizabeth, and then settled his attention on Jane.

"It will be a pleasant outing," Jane said.

Elizabeth grinned. "A chance to ride through the village where Aunt Gardiner spent so much time as a youth will prove quite welcome. Thank you, Georgie."

Georgiana spoke excitedly, "You shall be able to do more than that, if the doctor approves. He wishes to examine you before making his final decision, but he does not anticipate a problem. My brother's carpenter has attached leather straps to a high-walled cart so your chair can be safely conveyed into the village. He rode into Lambton yesterday to measure some doorways, and I now have a list of the shops which have entrances wide enough for the chair to pass through. We can even take tea at the Inn."

Darcy felt himself beam with pride at his sister's thoughtful proposal. That she had done it all on her own was another source of satisfaction. Knowing Elizabeth's fondness for walking, he expected she would, by now, be frustrated at being limited to a chair. A short trip to Lambton might be the perfect diversion for her.

The butler stepped into the room with a silver salver upon which lay a letter. Darcy waved him closer and took up the missive. Richard's handwriting was uncharacteristically messy, giving Darcy an idea of the contents. He broke the seal and read it straight away with a sinking heart.

He had not realized the room had become silent until he looked up. Everyone was staring at him. He cleared his throat. "I apologize, but it seems we will have to delay our outing to Lambton. My uncle, the Earl of Matlock, has moved on to a better place." He met Georgiana's teary gaze. "We should go to Matlock as soon as possible to pay our respects."

Georgiana stood. "Yes! Oh, my poor aunt. My poor cousins. I shall ready myself to leave immediately."

Georgiana preceded Darcy from the room. He stopped across the table from Bingley. "Will you see that the ladies are entertained, Bingley?"

"You know you need not have asked."

"Thank you." He turned to the ladies, settling his attention on Elizabeth. "We shall return before nightfall."

~%~

As Darcy bowed and left the room, Elizabeth turned to Jane and spoke quietly. "Will you ask the footman in the hall to come in, please? I would like to send a note of condolence to Lady Matlock."

Caroline made a noise that could only be attributed to disgust. Bingley turned immediately towards his sister. "Are you choking, Caroline?"

Both Bennet ladies turned to look at the Bingley siblings. Caroline was glaring at Elizabeth without disguise. Elizabeth raised both eyebrows.

Although it was apparent to Elizabeth that Caroline was not in distress, Bingley patted his sister on the back a bit too enthusiastically. Bingley said, "You should not drink your tea so rapidly, sister."

Caroline scowled at him, clearly annoyed.

Jane said to Elizabeth, "There is a writing desk in the parlour off the lower garden. I will take you there myself."

As Jane rose, Bingley sprang from his seat to assist Jane with her chair, but when Caroline made another, similar sound, Bingley resumed patting his sister's back.

Caroline turned to him and exclaimed irritably, "I *would* be perfectly fine if you ceased your attempt at assisting me, Charles!"

Jane swiftly pushed Elizabeth's chair from the room. A footman stepped forward, but Jane waved him off and raced down the corridor to the parlour, shocking Elizabeth. The door closed behind them, and Elizabeth glanced over her shoulder just as Jane burst out laughing. Elizabeth joined her.

When they both calmed down, Elizabeth said, "Finally, you see the truth about Caroline Bingley?"

Jane moved around in front of Elizabeth. "I do… and so does Mr. Bingley. I think she was jealous just now—envious that you hold an acquaintance with the countess close enough to send a note of condolence."

"I am proud of you, Jane! Does her opinion no longer hold weight with you at all?"

Jane smiled. "As long as Mr. Bingley does not take her estimation of me to heart, I will not credit her opinion in the least."

"So he has begun to understand his sister, then? I did not *think* he really believed she was choking, but..."

Jane shook her head. "Last evening, while you all were taking turns playing the pianoforte, we talked." She blushed deeply. "Much of our discussion revolved around why he had not returned to Hertfordshire." Jane bit her lip—a sign she was unsure of how much to reveal.

Though Elizabeth would have given almost anything to hear the details of what they had discussed, she would not press for more information just yet.

The clock on the mantelpiece chimed the half-hour.

"Will you bring me to the desk, please? I do not want to miss giving my letter to Georgiana before she leaves for Matlock."

Chapter 29

While the doctor scribbled in his journal, Elizabeth reached a trembling hand towards Jane, who took it in hers. She felt a little foolish being so excited about the prospect of a short trip to the village. Pemberley's manor house was beautiful, and she was truly enjoying her stay here, but she had never been one to sit still for long, especially indoors. Her daily walks were a means to calm the overactive energies of her body and mind. Given a choice, she would have preferred to spend more of her time outside exploring the estate grounds, and that would have made the time she spent sedately indoors even more agreeable. *If* Providence had brought her here, that is. She reminded herself once again that she would not be at Pemberley at all if she *were* able to walk.

Either way, one of the reasons she had looked forward to this trip to the north from its onset was to experience the places and people she had heard her aunt refer to in the many stories she had shared about her early years there. She knew Jane would have liked to see it, as well, but her sister was too good. She had denied herself any enjoyment of which Elizabeth could not partake.

The doctor closed his book. Jane squeezed Elizabeth's hand.

Mr. Smythe turned to face them. "Since I last saw you, you have progressed further than I thought you would, Miss Elizabeth." He turned to Hannah, who had been present for the examination. "Will you ask Mrs. Reynolds to bring up the crutches Mr. Darcy's carpenter fashioned for Miss Elizabeth?"

Hannah said, "They're in the dressing room, sir." She disappeared through that door.

Elizabeth's mouth dropped open.

Jane clapped her hands with excitement. "Such excellent news."

Hannah returned carrying the crutches.

Elizabeth exclaimed. "I never expected it so soon—not after what you told me the last time you were here."

"I didn't want to raise your hopes. But you must be sure not to overdo, Miss Elizabeth. Keep your right leg bent when you are moving. You may rest that foot on the ground when you are still, but put no weight on that leg as of yet. If your left arm begins to pain you again, you must use the chair."

Elizabeth nodded forcefully. "I will do as you say."

The doctor said, "And do *not* navigate the stairs with crutches."

"I promise not to go up and down the stairs while standing on crutches." She smiled mischievously.

The doctor frowned and raised one eyebrow. "Are you familiar with using these?" The doctor took the crutches from Hannah and crossed to hand them to Elizabeth.

"I am. I will show you, sir." She rose and slipped them under her arms. They were the perfect height. The crossbar was well-padded, as was the hand-grip. Careful not to get them tangled in her skirts, she smoothly made her way across the room and returned. How good it felt to expend some of her pent-up energy!

The doctor nodded.

"Does this mean I may use the crutches in Lambton when Miss Darcy is able to make the trip into the village?"

He scrubbed his hand over his chin. "Perhaps not just yet. I would like you to enjoy yourself, but I do not want you to become fatigued."

"But I *may* go?"

He said, "Yes, you may."

"Thank you, doctor!"

"I am happy to have been of assistance," Mr. Smythe bowed and reached into his bag. He handed Hannah a slip of paper. "Please give this to Mrs.

Reynolds. It is the recipe for a salve in case Miss Elizabeth becomes sore from the crutches rubbing against her skin."

Hannah curtsied. "Yes, doctor." She left the room.

The doctor turned back to Elizabeth and Jane. "Unless I am needed sooner, I shall return in one week. Please give my regards to the Darcys."

After the door had closed behind him, Jane smiled at Elizabeth. "Georgiana will be so pleased by this news."

Elizabeth's mood sobered. "After a trial such as I am sure today will be for our young friend, we shall make a surprise of it to raise her spirits."

~%~

Darcy pressed the Matlock's family seal into the black melted wax and then returned the signet to Richard so he could do the same.

His cousin Reginald—the new Earl of Matlock—rolled his shoulders and stretched his neck. "I believe those were the last of the announcements we are required to make. The remainder of the *ton* shall have to learn of my father's death from the newspaper."

Richard yawned. "And the gossip mill, which works more speedily."

Reginald lifted a letter off the stack. "Mayhap we should not bother to send this to Aunt Catherine. Mother sent a note by express a few days ago, when Father's health took a turn for the worse. She will probably arrive here before this announcement reaches Rosings."

The gloomy atmosphere in the earl's study deepened.

Richard opened his father's table top humidor and offered a cigar to the other two gentlemen, who turned it down. He took one himself. "Darcy, you do understand that since Mother and Aunt Catherine do not get along, our aunt will expect an invitation to Pemberley before the week is out."

Darcy stifled a groan.

Reginald leaned back in his chair and propped his feet on the desk. "And once Anne is at Pemberley, Aunt Catherine will assume there will be a proposal made post haste. Mayhap she will even expect to return to Kent alone."

As Richard cut off the end his cigar, he chuckled. "I would not be surprised if she has anticipated this eventuality and has Anne's trousseau already made up." Richard turned to his brother. "In fact, while we were at Rosings, I once happened past the carriage house. Through the open doors, I could have sworn I spied a cart loaded with trunks."

Reginald smiled.

Because his cousins' teasing was lightening their moods, Darcy had allowed it, but enough was enough. "On numerous occasions, you both have witnessed my informing Aunt Catherine that Anne and I will not marry."

Richard cleared his throat, though to Darcy, it sounded suspiciously like a chuckle. "And we also are aware that Aunt Catherine has always chosen not to hear you on the subject."

Darcy stiffened. He spoke with too much force when he said, "Then her expectations will be disappointed. Even if I was coerced into proposing—which will certainly never happen—Anne has told me she would refuse my offer." He took a deep breath, making an effort to calm himself. "In fact, Anne even suggested I do so and allow her to refuse in front of her mother, but I have chosen to accept the burden of Aunt Catherine's frustration instead."

"How gentlemanly of you." Richard hesitated. "However, are you certain it was not a fear Anne might say 'yes' that influenced the decision?"

In fact, that exact thought had crossed his mind the moment Anne suggested it. Darcy felt his face heat.

Both his cousins laughed loudly.

"Not to worry, Darce." Richard got up from his chair and rounded the desk. "Now that Reginald is an earl, it is entirely possible Aunt Catherine might change her focus to *him* as Anne's future mate instead of you." He pushed his brother's feet from the top of the desk.

As Reginald's feet dropped heavily to the floor, his laughter ended abruptly. Richard opened a drawer, retrieved a box of matches, and returned to his seat.

Reginald cleared his throat and crossed the room to the decanter. He returned with the entire tray, pouring a glass for each of them. The trio sipped their brandy.

Darcy said to Reginald, "You know, I always wondered why Catherine had not settled upon you as Anne's mate to begin with."

Richard answered, "It is because she wants for Anne what she could not have herself."

Darcy jumped up from his seat. "Aunt Catherine wants to marry *me*? Her sister's son?" He directed his gaze at Reginald. "Is that legally possible?"

Richard choked on his mouthful of brandy.

"Not you," Reginald answered. "She has always wanted *Pemberley*."

Richard said, "Do not tell me you never heard the stories of how Aunt Catherine chased after your father, even after he was courting your mother—her own sister?"

When Darcy shook his head, Richard continued, "The way I heard it, our mother spoiled her plans to seduce him into compromising her."

Reginald added immediately, "Which is the reason why she and Mother have never got along."

Darcy gaped at one cousin, then the other. In truth, he had no trouble believing it of her. It occurred to him that his cousin Bianca acted more like Catherine's daughter than her niece. He retook his seat. "I never knew."

As Richard lit the cigar, its tip glowed red.

Instantly, Darcy understood what had caused the light he had seen on the ocean the night he spotted the pirates. It was a wonder he had never thought of it before. He blinked a few times, trying to clear his mind of his distraction and concentrate on the conversation at hand.

Drawing in deeply, Richard blew a stream of blue-grey smoke directly at his brother's face. "Gaining Matlock and a title for Anne just *might* make up for losing Pemberley a second time."

Reginald threw back the rest of his brandy. The glass clunked as he placed it on a table too hard. "You know, Aunt Catherine is correct, Darcy. Rosings *would* be an excellent addition to your properties." He looked at his cousin hopefully.

"I think Darce has someone else in mind for the role of Mrs. Darcy," Richard said, lifting his eyebrows.

Reginald sat forward in his chair. "Oh, do tell."

Darcy finished his brandy and rose. "I should collect Georgiana from my aunt's sitting room and head home. I will see you on the morrow."

As he left the room, he could hear Richard laughing again.

Georgiana had said she wanted to experience Elizabeth's conversing with Lady Catherine. Perhaps she would get her wish, and much sooner than he had thought.

Chapter 30

"Lizzy?" Jane's voice echoed through the library.

Elizabeth looked up from her book and saw her sister standing near the door. Dorothy, her maid, and James accompanied her. Elizabeth glanced at the clock. "Is it so late already?"

Jane nodded. "You *did* wish to go down early so we could be in the front parlour when the Darcys arrived home, did you not?"

"Without a doubt." Elizabeth noted the page number where she had left off and closed her book. "Dorothy, will you bring my book up to Hannah after we have traversed the stairs, please? I believe Jane and I are chaperone enough for each other."

"Certainly, Miss Elizabeth." She took the book and curtsied.

Elizabeth bent, grabbed her crutches, and leaned them against the table next to her chair. She stood. Tucking the crutches under her arms, she made her way towards her sister.

"I cannot tell you how I have longed to be able to cross a room by myself again."

Jane and Dorothy grinned broadly, but James's pleasure was only a light in his eyes. Elizabeth laughed aloud. "I *will* see you smile someday, James."

"Perhaps, ma'am." He stepped aside. The ladies preceded the servants from the room.

At the stairs, Dorothy took the crutches. Jane and her maid went down one flight ahead of James, who was carrying Elizabeth. Once Elizabeth was standing again, she took her crutches. Elizabeth and Jane continued to the front parlour as Dorothy and James withdrew.

"Is it not delightful to be able to make our way down a corridor without an entourage of servants?"

Jane chuckled. Elizabeth supposed her sister could not imagine how it felt since Jane had never required as much assistance as she had these past weeks.

Elizabeth took a seat on a sofa across from the door, where the Darcys would see her upon entering the room. While the wheeled chair was cushioned, the overstuffed sofa was much more comfortable. She handed the crutches to Jane. "Where to you think we should put these?"

Jane examined the room. "Behind the drapes just here?" She crossed to the corner of the room, moved the drapes aside, and leaned them up against the wall. The drapes fell over them.

"Perfect," Elizabeth declared.

Jane found some needlework to keep them busy and handed a few items to Elizabeth. As she concentrated on her sewing, Elizabeth envisioned Georgiana's face lighting up when she saw Elizabeth was not in her rolling chair. She tried not to picture Darcy's smile, as well, to no avail.

Jane reached into the sewing basket and pulled out an embroidery hoop. "I believe this is Miss Bingley's." She examined the stitching. "She is quite skilled."

Elizabeth wondered if she left it there on purpose to remind them of that fact. "Did she ever teach you the stitch she promised to show you whilst we were all in Hertfordshire?"

Jane blinked. "No, she did not have the chance. They were called away so suddenly—"

"Jane!" Elizabeth scolded. "Do not fall back into old habits. She promised to show it to you upon our first meeting her. She had ample opportunity to do so." She shook her head. "Once she saw how skilled you were, it was too much of a risk. You would have done better with it than she ever could."

Jane blushed and busied herself studying the stitch in question, seemingly intent on trying to figure out how to duplicate it. Elizabeth turned back to her own sewing.

Several minutes later, the door opened. Caroline Bingley and Mrs. Hurst stood in the doorway.

"Did I not tell you, Louisa?" Caroline screeched. She took a few quick steps to stand before Elizabeth, her sister close behind. "Miss Eliza Bennet. I have found you out!"

Mrs. Hurst's mouth dropped open as her eyes widened.

"Found me out?" Elizabeth raised her eyebrows. "I am afraid I do not understand your meaning, Miss Bingley."

"You *do not understand?*" Caroline purposely whined. "You understand my meaning completely, you – you impudent little chit. But I will spell it out for you so there will be no mistake. Under false pretences, you garnered an invitation first to Matlock, and then to Pemberley. Meanwhile, you were perfectly healthy all along."

Elizabeth opened her mouth to speak, but another interrupted her, "All this yelling is most unbecoming of any lady."

All four women turned towards the gravelly voice. Lady Catherine de Bourgh's imposing form was stationed in the doorway. Elizabeth noted the lady's travelling clothes were as ornate as the gowns she had worn whilst ruling over her own domain at Rosings Park.

Evidently, she had not yet heard the earl had passed on for Elizabeth was certain she would be all in black if she had. Elizabeth wondered if Lady Catherine had noticed the mourning wreath on the door. If not, it was hardly the place of anyone present to inform her of her brother's death.

In response to the lady's appearance there, the startled expressions on Caroline's and Mrs. Hurst's faces were priceless, but poor Jane appeared alarmed.

Elizabeth pulled herself to her feet. A sharp pain darted up her injured leg, reminding her to shift her weight. Taking hold of Jane's arm to steady herself, she did her best to curtsy. The others in the room followed suit. They all rose from their curtsy as one.

Lady Catherine stomped her cane on the floor. "Miss Elizabeth Bennet, I cannot express my surprise at finding you at Pemberley, but seeing that you arc hcrc, I will have you introduce me to these women."

Each lady curtsied again as Elizabeth introduced them and Lady Catherine raised her chin at each of them in turn.

"This is my daughter, Anne." Lady Catherine gestured to the empty space at her right. Since her mother still blocked the entrance, Anne de Bourgh peeked around her mother's shoulder and bowed her head. Lady Catherine stepped to her left and turned. "Anne, what are you doing? Come into the room."

"Yes, Mother," Anne whispered and curtsied. When she rose, her gaze remained on the carpet.

Lady Catherine crossed the room and took a seat in a high-backed chair, nodding to a sofa to her right. Anne dutifully sat in it. Lady Catherine nodded regally to her left and to her right, granting permission for everyone to claim a seat.

"You there! Miss Bingley." Lady Catherine pointed her chin at Caroline. "What were you saying when I entered the room?"

Caroline rose and stepped forward, appearing quite smug. "I feel the need to protect your niece and nephew, my lady, for they do not understand the danger here. For weeks now, these women have been imposing upon your relations." She made a grand show of sweeping her arm in the direction of Elizabeth and Jane. "Eliza Bennet first deceived Lady Matlock by fabricating an injury, and now she does the same with the Darcys. But as you can see, the first moment the Darcys have both left their home, here she is, without the rolling chair and fully able to walk. If Louisa and I had not come down before we were expected, their design would have gone undetected. It is as I suspected all along. She has used them all horribly."

Lady Catherine rested both hands on her cane and narrowed her eyes at Elizabeth. "My sister-in-law, as well?"

"Yes, my lady. Eliza Bennet was at the Matlock estate when she first *reported* an injury. Lady Matlock, who was in a state of distraction due to the ill health of her husband, invited her to remain there while she recuperated, and she did, until Miss Darcy departed. Out of respect for her aunt, your good niece begged Eliza Bennet to accompany her to Pemberley."

Caroline made her sound like an ingenious conspirator! Amusement bubbled within Elizabeth's breast, but she successfully tamped it down.

"Hmmm." Lady Catherine arched an eyebrow.

Caroline continued. "It is very like what Miss Jane Bennet arranged last autumn, my lady, when we were at Netherfield Park—my brother's estate in Hertfordshire."

Elizabeth heard Jane gasp quietly. She took Jane's hand and patted it, hoping it would quiet her. Elizabeth suspected Caroline Bingley was about to make a fool of herself. It would be better to let her get on with it. Lady Catherine might be a busybody, but she was an intelligent lady. Elizabeth had faith she would see the truth.

Caroline paced a few steps and turned again to Lady Catherine. "As I am sure you are aware from your superior perceptiveness when observing society, beauty can cause men to behave rather recklessly. Even the most intelligent gentlemen are susceptible to deceit when a lady has a particularly attractive face and figure. They attribute purity of heart and superiority of spirit to such a woman, when indeed there is none of either." She squared her shoulders. "At every opportunity, Miss Jane Bennet flaunted herself before my brother. Then, my lady, Miss Bennet invented an illness whilst dining with my sister and me at Netherfield. She remained there for several days, forcing us to invite Miss Eliza to nurse her, as well. The two remained as long as was possible, garnering our brother's sympathies for the elder sister. At the same time, Miss Eliza went to work, brazenly flirting with Mr. Darcy." She clasped her hands before her as she finished her speech.

Jane's hand was now trembling. Elizabeth gave it a squeeze.

Lady Catherine glared first at Jane then Elizabeth. "Is that so?"

Elizabeth cleared her throat and shook her head. "Lady Catherine, it seems Miss Bingley has quite the fantastic imagination. She has attributed deliberate schemes to events that in fact unfolded quite innocently."

Caroline's nostrils flared. "You may have pulled the wool over Miss Darcy's eyes in order to remain here until her brother returned from the States, but you cannot mislead me. The moment we arrived, I tried to warn Miss Darcy as to your duplicitous nature, but she refused to listen, just as Mr. Darcy has stubbornly refused from the start. Meanwhile, you flaunted how well you duped our poor, naïve hostess. And to think you both have the nerve to address Miss Darcy so familiarly." She pulled her face into an expression that seemed as if she had just eaten something sour. "*Georgie. Georgie.*"

Quiet descended over the room for a few moments as Caroline's last words seemed to echo through the chamber.

Lady Catherine raised her chin and looked down her nose at Caroline. "Miss Bingley, who do think you are to be pitying my niece and nephew, calling them stupid and gullible, and assuming Lady Matlock did not know what she was about? Even if her husband—my brother—were ill, my sister-in-law would certainly have her wits about her at all times."

Jane, Anne, and even Mrs. Hurst, sat open-mouthed, their gazes darting from Caroline to Lady Catherine and back again. Elizabeth pressed her lips together, holding back a smile.

Caroline paled as she obviously realized what she had said—aloud, and to whom. She spoke hurriedly, "Naïve... I said Miss Darcy was *naïve*, my lady."

Lady Catherine narrowed her eyes.

Caroline stuttered. "I – I only meant inexperienced. Too trusting—"

"I know *exactly* what you meant." Lady Catherine straightened her spine. "I have heard all about you, Miss Bingley, and about your sister. You are the daughters of a tradesman, always courting my niece and nephew's good opinions, and those of all their connexions. You both take advantage of their generous natures at every opportunity. You delight in making your connexion with them known to all who will listen with the hopes it will open doors to you. Everyone in the upper ten thousand has heard of your antics—trying to win my nephew's heart so he will ask for your hand—but I know for certain that you will never succeed. Darcy is already spoken for." She peered proudly at her daughter, Anne, who blushed deeply.

Before Elizabeth had a chance to think about Lady Catherine's implied meaning, the great lady turned to Elizabeth. "It just so happens I formed an acquaintance with Miss Elizabeth Bennet during this past spring—*after* the events you have detailed for us. During that time, I watched her carefully in the company of two of my nephews, one of whom was Darcy." She returned her gaze to Caroline. "If I thought for one moment that Miss Elizabeth Bennet was guilty of anything resembling your accusations, I would order a carriage this instant and have them both brought to the post-coach in Lambton, informing my nephew of their fraudulent behaviour when he returns from Matlock."

Lady Catherine stood. "Miss Elizabeth Bennet might voice her opinions a little too confidently for one so young, but *she* understands her place in society. However, Miss Bingley, you do not! If you do not behave yourself, I will carry out such a plan with you and your sister, instead."

Caroline backed up a few steps and practically fell into her chair.

A pang of guilt twisted in Elizabeth's chest. When referring to her time spent in Kent, Lady Catherine was correct, but if she only knew what her wishes were *now*, the carriage would be ordered immediately.

"What is going on here?" Darcy's voice boomed from the doorway.

He still wore his overcoat. The butler stood in the hallway, holding Darcy's hat. Mrs. Reynolds was next to him. A moment later, Georgiana entered the room, out of breath and similarly dressed for the outdoors. Elizabeth suspected that upon entering the house, they had heard raised voices and rushed up the stairs to find out what was the matter.

Always proper, Darcy bowed before he crossed the room to stand in the middle of the company. He bowed again to Lady Catherine and Anne. "Welcome to Pemberley, Aunt, Cousin. May I ask to what this *discussion* pertains?"

Bingley stepped into the room, glanced at each face, and finally settled his gaze on Jane. His clothing, and the dusty state of it, spoke of his just coming in from riding the estate. Jane must have signalled him, for he did not advance any further into the parlour.

"Ah, Darcy," Lady Catherine said and pointed at Miss Bingley. "In your absence, I was forced to take matters into hand. Since I have arrived, your *guest* has dared accuse your aunt, the Countess of Matlock, and your sister of being simpletons; you and her own brother of being gullible fools; and Miss Bennet and Miss Elizabeth of being charlatans."

"Caroline said *what?*" Bingley cried out.

Mouth open, Darcy blinked several times and looked at Elizabeth. Elizabeth raised her eyebrows and shrugged one shoulder.

"Is *that* Mr. Bingley?" Lady Catherine asked.

Darcy startled. "Yes. Forgive me." He made the introductions.

Bingley made his bow to both de Bourgh ladies.

Lady Catherine said, "Now that this nasty business is at an end, Anne and I would like to be shown to our rooms. We are in need of a respite before supper."

Darcy said distractedly, "Of course." As he paused, Elizabeth's eye was caught by the mourning band on his arm. Had Lady Catherine seen it, too? "I must speak with you as soon as possible, Aunt. Shall I meet you in your sitting room in a quarter of an hour?"

Lady Catherine nodded.

Georgiana motioned to Mrs. Reynolds, and the housekeeper entered. "Right this way, milady. Miss de Bourgh."

All was quiet for a minute or two after the two ladies were ushered from the room.

Bingley broke the silence. "Caroline, what have you done? Why would you say such things to Lady de Bourgh?"

Now that Lady Catherine had left the room, Caroline sat taller. "I only told the truth, Charles, but I am afraid Lady de Bourgh misinterpreted everything I said. For example, just look at Miss Eliza!"

Everyone turned their gazes to Elizabeth.

Elizabeth smiled and gestured towards Georgiana. "It was to be a surprise for you, Georgie, when you returned." She glanced at Caroline. "Had I known it would cause such a commotion, I would not have asked Jane to—" She turned to her sister. "Jane, will you show them, please?"

Jane crossed the room and retrieved Elizabeth's crutches.

Elizabeth said, "The doctor came whilst you were out and gave me permission to use these instead of the wheeled chair." She rose, tucked the crutches under her arms, and took a few steps. "I apologize that my partial recovery was the catalyst for such a distressing scene. I suppose I should have slid the crutches under the sofa."

Caroline stood, harrumphed, and stomped out of the room. Mrs. Hurst curtsied, excused herself, and followed her.

Darcy began to laugh. It became contagious.

When all had calmed themselves, there were congratulations from everyone about Elizabeth's state of healing, and then Bingley spoke.

"I apologize to you all for my sisters' accusations. I should go speak to them, I suppose," he said, though he did not seem to be in any hurry to leave, first seeing to Jane's well-being and comfort. Finally, he excused himself.

As Bingley left the room, Darcy went above stairs to change. Georgiana stayed behind with Elizabeth and Jane. "Lizzy, with all the confusion lately, my Aunt Matlock forgot to have the last of the mail received from Longbourn brought over to Pemberley. I believe the footman was to give it to Hannah to put in your rooms. There are several letters and a parcel."

"Thank you, Georgie." Elizabeth furrowed her brow. "Hmmm… I wonder if I left something else at Charlotte's house."

Jane did not do well hiding her yawn.

"I think you should rest before supper, as well, Jane," Elizabeth said. "When either of you are ready, you may find me in the library, reading my letters."

Chapter 31

Since Darcy did not have time to change his clothing before meeting with his aunt, he stood as still as possible while Hughes brushed the dust of the road off Darcy's pants and coat.

"Hughes, have you heard anything from Lady Catherine's servants as to whether or not she is aware her brother has passed on?"

"No, sir, I have not," Hughes answered. He put down the brush and went to work on tying a fresh cravat at his master's neck

"Make it simple, Hughes. I shall return for a bit of respite and to dress for supper after I have spoken to my aunt."

"Yes, sir." Hughes finished the job. "If you wish, I will go down to the kitchen to see what I can learn and report back here in a few minutes."

Checking his pocket watch, Darcy shook his head. "It is unnecessary. I must go to Lady Catherine now." Remembering what Richard had said about Anne's trousseau, he sighed. The way this day was progressing, Richard just might be correct. "But talk to our staff and get an idea of how much luggage my cousin and aunt have brought along with them, will you?"

~%~

Elizabeth accompanied Jane and Georgiana to the stairs.

Georgiana said, "Oh! I forgot to ring for James."

Confident all the other guests were busy elsewhere and they were keeping the servants well occupied, Elizabeth asked, "Would it be terribly shocking if we did not bother James this time? It is only one level."

Jane said, "Lizzy! The doctor told you not to try the stairs with the crutches."

"I was not planning to use the crutches, Jane. Well, not in a conventional way, at least." Elizabeth bit her lip.

Jane's eyes widened with realization. "No. You would not do such a thing at Pemberley."

"Now I *must* know," said Georgiana. "Please, show me."

Jane closed her eyes and turned around. "If Mama ever asks…"

"You can honestly say you did not see me do this," Elizabeth finished for her.

Elizabeth clip-clopped over to the stairs and sat down to one side. With her crutches in her right hand, she lifted her right leg straight out and placed her left hand on the step above where she was sitting. Using the crutches, her hand, and her good leg, she managed to ascend the stairs one step at a time.

Georgiana clapped her hands. "Do not tell my brother, but I did something similar three years ago when I was injured, but only when he was not at home to witness it."

Elizabeth slid one crutch towards the second staircase, stood on the top step, turned around, and holding the railing, she tucked the other crutch under her arm to assist her up the last step. She then moved across the landing and repeated this series to ascend the second staircase. When she was standing again, she progressed away from the top of the stairs and brushed off her skirts.

"You can look now, Jane," Elizabeth called out. She turned to Georgiana. "I twisted my other ankle a few years ago. Doing that helped disperse some of the energy which I have always been used to expending during my daily walks."

Georgiana nodded. "I understand completely."

As Jane caught up with them, she asked, "Shall I ask Hannah to bring your letters to the library?"

"Yes, please do. Ask her not to forget the parcel, please." She noticed Jane trying inconspicuously to check the back of Elizabeth skirt. "Don't worry, Jane; I will change before supper. And I promise to allow James to take me down later."

"Of course," Jane answered, but her relieved expression spoke volumes.

Georgiana and Elizabeth exchanged an amused look.

~%~

Elizabeth entered the library and sat in what was becoming her favourite chair, sliding her crutches under it and the table to her left. She reclined with her right leg propped up on an ottoman. Expecting Hannah to arrive soon with her letters, she closed her eyes.

Lady Catherine's voice echoed in her ears. "Darcy is already spoken for."

Eyes flying open, Elizabeth bolted upright in the chair.

The way Lady Catherine had turned her gaze upon her daughter after uttering those words prompted a shiver to travel up her spine. And Anne— the way Anne blushed!

Elizabeth's stomach sank, and with it, the anticipation which had sparked the day she had met Darcy again in London. No matter how she resisted, the dream was ignited anew by Georgiana's recital of all Darcy had said about Elizabeth in his correspondence with his sister, and then blazed into a roaring flame the moment she met him again here at Pemberley.

He *would* have had ample time to make an offer to his cousin during the two weeks between her own refusal and the day he had left for America. It was done in many families of the *ton* to keep their wealth and property within the bloodline. After all, even though the Bennets were not amongst the *ton*, her own mother had expected Elizabeth to marry her cousin, Mr. Collins, so Mrs. Bennet could live out the rest of her days at Longbourn, and the estate would someday be inherited by Mr. Bennet's grandson.

But why had Miss de Bourgh and Mr. Darcy not made an announcement as of yet?

Their uncle!

Yes, she could imagine they would not announce their engagement while the earl was so ill. Now that he had passed on, she expected they would wait again. Knowing Lady Catherine, Elizabeth was sure the announcement would take place the moment the mourning period was over.

How could she have allowed herself to hope?

I must extinguish all my expectations once and for all.

Her eyes filled with tears.

A noise to her left caused her to look up. Hannah stood only a few paces away. Elizabeth had been so involved with her thoughts, she had missed the girl's entrance.

Elizabeth removed her handkerchief from her pocket and patted her cheeks. She sniffled. "Thank you, Hannah. You may leave them on the table."

Judging by Hannah's frown, Elizabeth knew she would not get off that easily.

"'Tis there anything I can get you, miss? Some tea, pe'haps?"

Elizabeth smiled the best she could. "No, thank you. Sometimes we just need a little time alone, do you not agree?"

Hannah nodded.

"Will you come for me when it is time to dress for supper, please? I am sure to feel better by then."

"Yes'm." Hannah left the room.

Mayhap my letters will distract me from my troubles. She blew her nose. *The parcel first, I think. They are always good news.*

She opened the outer wrapping. Inside was a note and then a second layer of brown paper. The address written on the second wrapping consisted only of:

Miss E i e
Longbour Hert

She opened the note.

> *Dear Lizzy,*
>
> *I hope this letter finds you recovering quickly. You and Jane are dearly missed.*
>
> *As for this parcel, with an address written such as this, it is a miracle it found its way to Longbourn at all. Please write to whomever sent it and instruct them to write out the entire address from now on.*
>
> *Give my regards to your sister and to Miss and Mr. Darcy.*
>
> *Papa*

A mystery, indeed!

Elizabeth opened the wrapping to find yet a third sheet of brown paper. It was almost as if she were peeling away the petals of a rose.

Now the way the address was written made sense.

The writing on this layer had obviously been exposed to water. The only letters remaining legible were the ones someone else neatly rewrote on the second layer of paper. This wrapper had been torn, and it seemed some of the contents were missing, for the paper was folded over to lay flat within the second wrapper. If folded correctly, Elizabeth judged it should have held about twice as much as it did now.

Carefully, she unwrapped the third layer of brown paper. Inside was all foolscap, with writing on both sides. The sheets of paper at the top and the bottom of the stack were completely indecipherable, but as she flipped through the pages, the damage grew less. The words on the sheets towards the middle of the pile must not have been wet through because the writing on them was clearer. The handwriting was familiar, but the words seemed scribbled, as if the author was thinking rapidly and wrote quickly before their ideas escaped them.

Author... Oh, poor Ruth! It must be the book she wrote and wished me to read. I hope this was not her only copy.

Her heart broke at the condition of the pages.

Since the manuscript made it all this way, and even though she would not be able to follow the entire story, she felt obliged to give her friend Ruth the benefit of reading what she could.

Sorting through the pages, Elizabeth paused at a page that was almost entirely legible. This was definitely not Ruth's hand. The handwriting here was neater and even more familiar than the other pages she had seen so far. It looked almost like... no, it could not be Mr. Darcy's writing. The words at the top of the page caught her eye. It began in the middle of a sentence:

to the churchyard on Gracechurch Street.

She gasped. It *was* from Mr. Darcy!

Why would he send her all this? And through the post?

Perhaps she should not read any more.

Her respiration increased.

But he must have wanted her to read it. Why else would he have sent it?

> *My heart ached as she apologized for what she had expressed during our previous meeting. Although I was honoured she sought me out to vent her conscience, I never meant for her to feel the burden of self-reproach. True, her arguments were based on mistaken premises, but all-in-all, she said nothing about me that was false. In fact, her judgements of my character were closer to the mark than I was prepared to acknowledge at the time.*

I went to her without a doubt of my reception. By the very manner of her refusal, I was properly humbled. Her words shewed me how insufficient were all my pretensions to please a woman worthy of being pleased.

It has been a lesson hard learned, and yet it has been most advantageous.

That day in London, it was difficult to speak to her confidentially as we were in public. Members of her party were nearby, and others were passing us in the street. I am unsure as to how well I relayed the information I wished to impart. Not knowing whether or not she understood might drive me mad before I return to England.

I can still feel her delicate hand resting on my arm. As we walked along, I longed to tell her that somewhere within my soul, even that evening at Hunsford Cottage, I knew she was correct, but my mind was not ready to accept the accuracy of her insight. I wanted to tell her that afterwards, as I wrote the letter I had given to her the following day, I thought I was angry with her, but looking back, I now know I was angry with myself. When I left Hertfordshire, I missed her quite dreadfully, but that sensation doubled after I left Rosings Park. Day and night, I had been haunted by her. In every crowd, I would hear her voice and turn to see if I could catch a glimpse of her lovely countenance. On every breeze travelled a hint of her sweet scent. In every candle's flicker, I only saw the light dancing in her fine eyes. My dreams were filled with her smile and the sound of her laughter.

Elizabeth's heart was racing too fast to continue reading. She averted her gaze away from the page.

Did she imagine all this? Was it indeed written about *her*?

I have just read over what I have written thus far. It is good I did not say any of this aloud. She would have run from me!

Elizabeth shook her head.

Still, perhaps I should have found a way to speak more plainly. I regret not telling her all that was in my heart. I should have told her the manner of her refusal was the best thing that could have happened to me. I have grown and changed because of her. How much I owe her!

Elizabeth's eyes misted. Did he honestly feel this way?

This voyage of mercy to America has come at an inopportune time, and it is most unwelcome. As I travel further and further away from her, the ache in my heart grows. It is selfish of me, but I fear she might meet another man before I return, and I will miss my chance at proving I have taken her advice to heart. But as my mother used to say, I must look for the good in all things. Therefore, I hope to make use of this time alone aboard ship. From the time we left England, I have had little to do other than agonize over all that occurred between the two of us since our first meeting in Hertfordshire.

This was written while he was aboard ship on his way to America? Was it his journal? If so, she should not read any more. She closed her eyes. *But he sent this to me.* She opened them again, turned the page over, and continued reading.

In turn, I have examined my life up until the moment of my proposal. I have come to several disheartening conclusions. There are so many things I would like to share with her.

I have been a selfish being all my life, in practice, though not in principle. As a child, I was taught what was right, but as an only son—and for many years, an only child—I was spoilt by my parents and was never taught to correct my temper. Although it was proper for a son, sending me away from home to attend school only deepened these faults.

Being of an ancient family and the grandson of an earl, the sons of even the highest members of the peerage were persuaded to befriend me. As a result, my sense of self-worth was puffed up. The good principles instilled in me from birth were tainted by my increasing pride and conceit. I learned to be selfish and overbearing; to care for none beyond my own family circle and others of high rank; and to think meanly of the rest of the world's worth compared with my own.

Such I was, from eight to eight and twenty, until the lady who owns my heart rejected me. Such I might still have been but for her reproach. She has done me nothing but good.

Elizabeth wiped at a tear as made its way down her cheek.

Ever since I have undertaken this excursion into the examination of my character, I have reviewed the way I treated the ladies and gentlemen in Hertfordshire—and yes, even <u>her</u>—attempting to view my behaviour through another's eyes. The remorse I feel about my conduct is consuming at times. This exercise has proven a life-altering experience.

The pain in his words caused her tears to flow freely now. Would another man admit to such things? How could she ever have judged him so harshly?

During this journey, I have had the opportunity to watch and interact with individuals whom I would have shunned, even scorned, before these revelations. I have learned much from them. Each of them, from every station in life, deserves a great deal more notice and respect than I would have given them in the past.

Every day, I pray I redeem myself and grow closer to being worthy of her. I pray that when I return to England, God will allow me the opportunity to show her I have taken her advice to heart. I pray that someday she will accept me.

Elizabeth gasped and covered her mouth with her hand. Did he intend on renewing his addresses?

Chapter 32

But had not Lady Catherine said—

A movement to her left attracted her attention. Her heart stopped.

Darcy stood a pace away from her, blushing a deeper crimson than she had ever seen upon a gentleman's countenance.

"Mr. Darcy!" Her face grew so hot, she could only imagine her colour must have risen high enough to rival his.

He handed her a handkerchief. "I came to get a book…"

She stared at the cloth a moment before he moved it closer, and she accepted it.

"It was a mistake," he uttered so quietly, she barely made it out.

Elizabeth's throat tightened. She could not make a sound.

He shifted from one foot to the other. "That is, I did not mean for my journal to be sent to you. Or to anyone."

She cleared her throat and found her voice, though it was hoarse when she said, "I apologize for reading it. I thought the pages were from my friend, Ruth. She is writing a book." She closed her eyes momentarily. She owed him the full truth. The next was said with more volume. "At least, that is what I thought at first, but… well," She took a deep breath. "When I started reading the page, I confess I knew it was not Ruth's." She stared down at the paper, which was still in her hand. "But I could not stop myself."

When he did not reply, she looked up. His expression was so full of anticipation, she had to speak again. "I only read this one page, sir."

"Ah," he whispered, nodding.

She lifted it up to him. "Do you wish to see it? So you know what I have read?"

His gaze flitted back and forth between her face and the page. Moving slightly forward, he stepped back again. "I probably should, but at this precise moment, I am not sure I want to know what I wrote to make you cry."

Her mouth dropped open. "Oh! No, you misunderstood, sir. Sometimes a lady's tears are not negative in nature."

Darcy turned the ring on his last finger so rapidly, Elizabeth thought he might cut himself. He stared at her unblinkingly. "*Not* negative?"

She waved the page at him. "I think you should read this. If someone had read a page from my journal, I would die of curiosity."

He blinked several times before taking the paper from her. When he scanned down to the bottom of the second side of the foolscap, he released a long breath. His gaze snapped up to meet hers. "Were they?"

"Were they what, sir?"

"Your tears. Were they *not* negative?"

Elizabeth took a deep breath. Every word on that page spoke of his love for her. This was her chance to undo all the damage she had done in the past. Could she do it? Could she tell him she loved him? Would he respect her if she did? She hesitated a moment longer. His heart had been bared. She must expose her own.

"My tears… my thoughts… my feelings were—*are* not at all negative, sir."

Darcy closed his eyes and swallowed hard. She had not realized he held his shoulders so stiffly until he relaxed them. When he opened his eyes, all the tension left his expression. He dropped down on one knee before her and took her hand in his.

"Miss Elizabeth Bennet, will you do me the great honour of becoming my wife?"

Consumed with joy, she was about to accept when she remembered her resolution of never making another impulsive decision again. As she

Wendi Sotis

paused to think her answer through, Lady Catherine's announcement from earlier in the day pushed her happiness aside. "What of your cousin?"

He raised his eyebrows. "Bianca has no claim on me."

Elizabeth blinked. "I did not mean Lady Bianca." She paused. "Are you not engaged to be married to Miss de Bourgh?"

Darcy's gaze never left hers. "Lady Catherine *imagines* Anne and I desire a union between us as much as she does. It is not so."

"So you are not engaged, sir?"

"That remains to be seen."

With a tilt of her head, she furrowed her brow.

His eyes sparkled with a hint of mischief. "You have not answered yet."

Elizabeth could not hold back her smile. "Then you *are* engaged, Mr. Darcy."

He took in a deep breath. "I must know. Was it the page from the journal that changed your mind?"

She shook her head. "Upon reading your letter, I realized I had seriously misjudged you." Darcy ran his thumb over the knuckles of the hand he held, sending a shiver down her spine.

He grinned crookedly. "I thought you said you only read the one page?"

"I was speaking of the letter you handed me at Rosings Park, sir. Am I to expect another?"

He chuckled and gestured to the stack of papers she had been sorting through. "Did you not find one enclosed with this?"

"Not yet." She pressed her lips together. "Shall I continue looking through it?"

He blushed again. "I think not. I will go through the pages and give it to you when I find it."

"*If* you find it. I judge about half of it missing."

Darcy paled significantly. "Missing?"

"Yes, the wrapping was torn."

He looked down at the papers and frowned deeply.

She squeezed his hand. When he again met her gaze, his frown disappeared.

"There was nothing in my journal identifying either of us or anyone else. A few place-names…" He shook his head. "But there is nothing I can do about it now. The maid at the hotel in Virginia did not speak English well and misunderstood her instructions. Finding the letter addressed to you atop of my journal pages, she mailed the entire stack to you. I meant only to give the letter to you if I ever saw you again. I do not even know why I addressed it."

Elizabeth mouthed a silent "Oh." It did make more sense now. She bit her bottom lip. "Regarding the letter I *did* receive from your own hand at Rosings Park, I must inform you that after reading it several times, my feelings changed completely."

His astonished expression almost made her laugh.

"You mean…"

She nodded. "I would have accepted had you asked again when I met you in London, *before* you left England."

Several emotions crossed his features. He chuckled quietly. "And even so, I am glad I did not ask then. I believe I know myself more completely now." He smiled widely. "And I will make a much better husband."

Happiness bubbled within her. "Will you remain on your knee all evening?"

He rose, helping her from her chair. Forgetting about her injury, the pain that accompanied her placing weight on her right leg caught her by surprise, and she stumbled and flailed. He steadied her.

She did not realize her hands were on his chest until she felt the beat of his heart hammering through his coat against her palm.

"I will not allow you to fall, Elizabeth."

The emotion in his voice as he called her by her Christian name caused her knees to give way. He caught her in his arms. She leaned against him. Her stomach fluttered.

"Did you re-injure your ankle?"

Unable to speak, she leaned back to look in his eyes and shook her head slightly. She could not tear her gaze from his. His spicy scent nearly overwhelmed her senses.

He leaned forward just a little and hesitated. His gaze wandered over her face, stopping briefly at her lips. Unconsciously, she licked them.

His gaze snapped back up to her eyes. "May I kiss you?"

She nodded, angled her head back further, and watched him bend towards her. She closed her eyes in anticipation. His lips pressed gently against hers. He pulled away an inch or two as she opened her eyes. He was smiling.

"I never thought—" His voice caught. He swallowed hard. The hungry look in his eyes made her insides quiver.

Sliding her hands up his chest to his shoulders, she moved up on her toes and brushed her lips across his. "Neither did I," she whispered near his mouth.

"Elizabeth." His breath swept across her cheek. His hands cupped her face, first one thumb skimmed across her lips, then the other. One hand slid down to cradle her neck. She leaned her cheek against the other and closed her eyes. His fingers traced her chin and jawbone as his lips drifted across her cheek and forehead. Each of her eyelids received a kiss before he returned his attention to her lips once more. His chest heaved as he gathered her against him. She pressed the side of her face against his heart.

"Thank you," he murmured. "Thank you for accepting me, my dearest, loveliest Elizabeth. I will do everything I can to make you happy."

"You already have, Mr. Darcy."

He tightened his embrace, resting his cheek on the top of her head. When their breathing slowed, he pulled away and looked down at her. "Will you call me by my given name when we are alone?"

She smiled. "Yes, Fitzwilliam."

A shudder passed through him, and he kissed her again.

A high-pitched squeak came from the direction of the door, followed by quick footfalls and the bump of the door closing.

Darcy turned away, leaving his arm around her back to steady her. Nobody was there.

Elizabeth said softly, "It must have been Hannah coming to tell me it was time to change for supper." She chuckled. "We probably shocked her."

"She will understand when we make the announcement."

"But we cannot announce our engagement until you speak to my father... though it might be a good idea to inform Hannah after what she has seen."

He smiled wickedly. "And I am glad she did. If Mr. Bennet denies his permission, I will simply explain how thoroughly I have compromised you just now and use her as our witness. That will convince him to change his mind."

Elizabeth giggled. "I do not think you will meet with any resistance. I have told him how I feel about you."

He raised his eyebrows. "You told your father?"

She nodded. "My aunt and uncle know as well. And Jane."

He looked at her with such wonder, it took her breath away. "Georgiana?"

"I think we should tell her and Jane as soon as possible. I did not confide my feelings to your sister, but I believe she guessed."

He nodded distractedly. "Well, at least your father will be expecting me when I show up at his doorstep. I shall leave the day after the funeral."

Elizabeth could feel her face fall. "So soon?" She did not wish to be separated from him just yet.

He placed a finger under her chin and tipped her head to look up at him. "Would you rather I wait until you are able to travel? Georgiana and I can escort you and your sister to Longbourn."

"That would be perfect."

She blushed as he stood staring at her.

"Excuse me. I am still in awe that you agreed to marry me."

She grinned. "I honestly did not think you would ask again. Especially after I saw Pemberley. I thought you would have come to your senses by now."

"Come to my senses?"

"Of course, my mother has educated me in running an estate, but I am sure Miss Bingley and Mrs. Hurst *explained* all about Longbourn after their visiting Jane. My father's estate could practically fit inside this library alone." She gestured to the room.

"But I have every confidence in your abilities." He hesitated. "Does the size of the estate frighten you?"

"A little." She beamed. "But I have confidence in my abilities, as well."

Darcy's rich laughter echoed throughout the chamber.

The clock chimed the half hour and Darcy glanced in that direction. "It is time to retire to change. If we are late, supper will surely be delayed," he said. "Let us not get on the wrong side of Mrs. Reynolds or cook so early in the engagement. I shall escort you up to get dressed for supper. Please take your seat for a few moments."

She did so.

He collected all the pages and handed them to her, and then slid her crutches out from under the chair and table.

She took the page from the top, which was the one she had read. "May I keep this one?"

He examined her face for a moment and nodded.

She folded it and placed it in the pocket of her skirts. "Will you ring for James, please?"

He grinned and shook his head. "James will no longer be carrying you around, my dear."

He leaned over and lifted her from the chair.

Elizabeth laughed. "What of my crutches?"

"I will hide them. It would be my privilege to carry you whenever possible. There is much time to be made up for. I was jealous of James."

She tilted her head. "Were you?"

"Absolutely."

She reached up to caress his cheek. When he arrived home, he had a bit of stubble there, but now it was smooth. "There was no need, Fitzwilliam."

"I was jealous just the same." He turned his head and kissed her palm.

"But what of your other guests? Do you not think they will talk if their host is carrying me around?"

"Let them." He took a few steps across the room.

"What about when you are not with me?" She asked.

He stopped. "Perhaps you are correct." He returned to where the crutches were now leaning against a chair and put her down. "You may hold them while I carry you." He handed them to her and swept her off her feet once again.

She chuckled. "I can walk to the stairs, at the very least."

He ignored her suggestion.

"Carrying me everywhere will tire your arms."

He moved towards the door once again. "Impossible. You are not heavy at all."

The door swung open. In the entranceway stood Caroline Bingley and Lady Catherine.

Caroline raised her arm, pointed at them, and said in her most dramatic tone of voice, "*This* is the type of behaviour I warned you about earlier, Lady Catherine!"

Chapter 33

Caroline turned to Lady Catherine. "You can see for yourself it was *I* who told the truth. Now she has deceived you, as well. Eliza Bennet will stop at nothing!"

Anne poked her head around the corner of the door frame. Her eyes widened, and she pulled back into the corridor. Familiar with her mother's temper, there was no doubt Anne was avoiding the inevitable explosion of her mother's wrath.

Lady Catherine pushed past Caroline, nearly knocking her down. The door banged shut behind them. His aunt was glaring at Elizabeth and him. Her nostrils flared.

No one was going to take this happiness from him. Not his aunt. And certainly not Caroline Bingley.

"Do you not think you should put me down, sir?" Elizabeth asked quietly.

Reluctantly, he gave in to her wishes. Taking the pages of his journal from her, he made certain Elizabeth gained her balance on the crutches. "I may be forced to explain…"

She nodded.

He resumed his progress towards the door, slowing his steps to remain next to Elizabeth on her crutches.

When the two ladies did not move from the opening, he bowed slightly and said, "Excuse us, ladies."

Both remained in place.

"Do you not see what she will do to secure him?" Caroline harrumphed. "When I came in earlier to look for a—" Her eyes searched the room. "A *book*, they were wrapped in a passionate embrace, and the harlot was kissing him."

Anger churned in Darcy's chest. He narrowed his eyes at Caroline. "It seems Miss Bingley entered the room during a private moment following Miss Elizabeth's acceptance of my proposal of marriage."

Caroline paled.

"That is impossible. Utter nonsense!" Lady Catherine exclaimed. "My wishes, those of your poor departed mother, and all your family and friends will not be prevented by a young woman of inferior birth, one who is of no importance in the world and wholly unallied to the family."

He growled, "I warn you, Aunt, I will not allow *anyone* to insult my betrothed."

Lady Catherine paced a few steps further into the room, then turned and pointed her cane at him. Darcy faced her.

"Darcy, you have always known that you are destined for your cousin."

"Again, you are mistaken, madam," Darcy said firmly. "Whenever we have discussed this subject, you have not listened, but you *will* hear me now. I am my own man. I do not have to rely on anyone to make decisions for me, especially regarding my own happiness. Miss Elizabeth Bennet has accepted me. She and I will marry."

His aunt examined Elizabeth closely. She allowed several moments to pass as she seemed to come to a decision and calmed herself.

"Miss Elizabeth Bennet." She paced before them. "I assume no one knows about this agreement except those of us in this room. There will be no dishonour to either of you if you withdraw your agreement to the engagement immediately." She turned to Caroline. "I am certain Miss Bingley will not repeat any of what we have discussed."

Caroline shook her head almost frantically.

Elizabeth arched a brow. "Why would I do such a thing, your ladyship?"

"If you marry him, you will be censured, slighted, and despised by everyone connected with him. Your alliance will be a disgrace; your name will never even be mentioned by any of us."

Elizabeth stood a bit taller beside him and raised her chin. "I would be surprised if anyone was bothered by my decision other than you, your ladyship. In fact, *two* of Mr. Darcy's own family have hinted towards a match between us these past weeks. Even if what you say does become truth, I expect to find exceptional happiness in being married to Mr. Darcy. I do not imagine ever having a reason for complaint."

Darcy's heart swelled with affection.

Lady Catherine's colour rose higher. She was so incensed at this point, Darcy imagined smoke coming from his aunt's ears. "Miss Bennet, if you were sensible of your own good, you would not wish to quit the sphere in which you have been brought up."

Elizabeth raised both eyebrows this time. "In marrying your nephew, I should not consider myself as quitting that sphere."

"Your mother is the daughter of a tradesman. Your uncles are tradesmen still." Lady Catherine hammered her cane onto the floor in exasperation.

Caroline backed away and stood against the wall near the door.

"Your nephew does not object to my connexions, your ladyship. In fact, my aunt and uncle *in trade* were guests at Matlock recently. They were treated with the greatest civility and respect by the countess herself, *and* by her sons."

He said, "We will not bend to your will—"

"Mother?"

Everyone turned towards the voice. Anne stepped through the doorway. She walked to stand before her mother.

Lady Catherine stretched her arm and pointed at Darcy. "Tell him, Anne. Tell him how you have always counted on becoming Mrs. Darcy. It has been your only hope. Your dream. Demand that Darcy follows through with our plan."

Anne's eyes widened. After a moment or two, she spoke in a voice so quiet, Darcy had to strain to hear her. "It has not been *our* plan—only yours, Mother. I have been telling you for years that I will not marry him."

"But Anne," Lady Catherine said, her eyes open wide. "I thought you only said this out of fear he would not do his duty and propose. If—*when* he asks, you will certainly accept!"

Anne shook her head. "No, mother. I would not."

Lady Catherine's nostrils flared again. Her tone was desperate when she exclaimed, "You will obey me, Anne. You *both* will respect the wishes of my recently departed brother—"

Anne stepped closer and placed her hand on her mother's arm. "Mother, you may have forgotten I was in the room at the time, but I happened to have witnessed several conversations between you and my uncle the last time he visited Rosings. Uncle Matlock was clear that Fitzwilliam and I both deserve to be *happy* in our choice of a marriage partner. He refused to force us to marry if we wished otherwise."

His aunt scowled. "Darcy! If not for yourself, think of what your marriage to this – this *girl* would do to poor Georgiana. The scandal of such a match would be hers, also. She will never marry well if you do not."

He reached out his hand and took Elizabeth's. "Please, Aunt, put an end to this display and wish us joy."

Lady Catherine huffed out a breath. "I am most seriously displeased." She shifted her attention to her daughter. "With *all* of you. Yours is a generation of selfish ingrates." She stormed from the room.

Wordlessly, Caroline slipped out the door.

Anne smiled up at Darcy. "I *do* wish you joy." Her gaze shifted to Elizabeth. "Both of you."

"Thank you, Miss de Bourgh."

Trying to regain the feeling of elation from earlier, Darcy asked, "You said you noticed Georgiana's attempts at matchmaking, but you mentioned *two* of my family to my aunt. Who is the second?"

"I believe your cousin, Colonel Fitzwilliam, was casting a favourable light in your direction even before you returned to England." She arched an eyebrow. Darcy took in a quick breath.

Anne held out her hand to Elizabeth, who took it. "If Georgiana and Richard approve, you now have *three* allies amongst the Fitzwilliams. Welcome to the family, Miss Elizabeth."

~%~

Supper was a quiet affair as Lady Catherine, the Hursts, and Caroline took their meals in their rooms, and Mrs. Annesley was out for the evening visiting friends.

Elizabeth would not allow the scene with Lady Catherine and Caroline to spoil her mood. She could not stop smiling. She felt as if she were the sun, and her happiness touched everything around her. Her elation had caused Hannah to grin from ear to ear as she rushed Elizabeth through her preparations before supper. And James… almost. She was beginning to doubt she would get him to smile before she returned home.

A realization came over her, and she sighed happily. Soon she would call Pemberley *home*. She had all the time in the world to achieve that aim.

Darcy leaned towards her and asked quietly, "Seeing that Anne already knows, I would like to tell Georgiana and your sister tonight. But since Bingley is present, I thought I should ask…" his voice trailed off.

"Jane knows me too well. When I met her in the sitting room before we came down, she guessed immediately. Apparently, I was beaming with joy."

Darcy's smile widened.

She glanced at Bingley then returned her gaze to her fiancé. "Judging by the way Mr. Bingley has been smirking at us, I suspect Jane let it slip to him while we were in the drawing room. We should tell Georgie as soon as possible."

"Then I will do it now," he said and rose from his chair. All conversation came to an immediate halt. He held up his wine glass to Elizabeth. "I would like to propose a toast to Miss Elizabeth Bennet. This evening, she has made me the happiest of men when she agreed to become my wife."

As Darcy took a sip from his wine glass, Georgiana squealed and sprang from her chair. She rounded the dining room table faster than Elizabeth had thought possible and threw herself into her brother's arms.

"I knew it!" Georgiana cried and looked up at her brother adoringly. "Thank you so much, Fitzwilliam, for the prospect of such a wonderful sister."

Darcy laughed. "I should be thanking you, Georgiana. It was *you* who brought her home."

Georgiana turned to Elizabeth and embraced her. "I am so happy," the younger girl said.

"No one could be happier than I," Elizabeth said.

Georgiana turned to hug Jane, "You will be my sister, as well."

Jane answered, "In addition to the three you have not yet met."

Georgiana stepped away and put her hands to her cheeks. "Seeing my brother this content and the expectation of having five sisters – it is just too much!"

After the couple accepted joyful congratulations from Bingley, Jane, and Anne, Darcy said, "I must ask you to keep this between us for now. As soon as the doctor gives permission for Elizabeth to travel, I shall escort her and Miss Bennet to Longbourn where I shall ask Mr. Bennet for his blessing."

Bingley clapped Darcy on the back. "I plan to escort my family to Hurst's family seat tomorrow, and I will continue on to re-open Netherfield Park. Darcy, you and Georgiana are welcome to stay with me. Miss de Bourgh, if you wish, you may accompany them, as well."

Anne said, "I appreciate the offer, Mr. Bingley, but I believe I will be leaving Pemberley with my mother tomorrow." She blushed. "We will stay at Matlock until we make the trip to Rosings in a few days."

Bingley bowed his head slightly and turned to speak to Jane.

When attention was firmly away from Anne, Elizabeth said quietly, "I am sorry our happiness has caused a breach between you and your mother."

Anne sighed. "Her disappointment will pass." She paused. "*Eventually*. If only she had listened to what Fitzwilliam and I told her so many times, this would not have come as such a shock to her." She shook her head. "I hope that now she will enquire as to what my preferences are instead of making mandates regarding my future." Her tone was wistful. "It will be a pleasure not to have all of her sentences preceded by the phrase *when you are mistress of Pemberley*." Anne giggled.

Elizabeth was surprised by Anne's speech, and even more by her laughter. There was colour to Anne's face Elizabeth had never noticed before. The threat of an unwanted marriage had taken its toll on the poor girl. When in the company of her mother, Anne had always been silent. The more Elizabeth thought of it, the more she realized Lady Catherine barely left time in her usual monologue for anyone else to speak.

Darcy smiled. "You just might get to visit Town and entertain as you have always wanted, Anne."

Anne's eyes sparkled as she nodded.

Elizabeth guessed at why Darcy furrowed his brow. Lady Catherine had done her daughter a great disservice by keeping her in Kent and shielding her from the world. Even if Anne was older than most debutantes, a lady with a dowry even larger than Georgiana's—which would include the estate of Rosings Park at some point in the future—would never experience a shortage of suitors.

Yes, Anne would be wooed by many a fortune-hunter.

Darcy and his cousins would have to keep a close watch on Anne so no men took advantage of her naivety. If the worst should happen, Elizabeth knew Lady Catherine would blame *her* because Darcy had married her instead of Anne.

Would he have married Anne if he had never met her?

A pang of guilt rushed through her.

Darcy reached for her hand under the table. "It is not your fault Lady Catherine did not prepare Anne for society by keeping her under her wing at Rosings all these years."

Elizabeth's mouth dropped open. "How did you know I was thinking just that?"

His gaze swept over her face. "I could see it in your eyes."

~%~

After supper, the gentlemen chose to accompany the ladies into the parlour. Bingley escorted Anne and Georgiana out of the dining room. With one crutch for support, Elizabeth took Darcy's arm with the other. He offered the other to Jane.

Instead of taking it, Jane held up a letter. "Mr. Darcy, my father wrote this before he left Pemberley for Longbourn. I was instructed to give it to you in the event this happy circumstance occurred, as I knew it would."

Darcy took the envelope from Jane, and she left the couple alone.

He stood staring at the missive for some moments, wondering what it could contain.

Elizabeth asked anxiously, "Will you not open it?"

"I confess I am afraid, based on the memory of my behaviour whilst in Hertfordshire, he will have already refused his permission before I even request it. I would much rather speak to him in person, so I can convince him how much I care for you."

Elizabeth shook her head. "If that were the case, I believe he would have waited until you solicited his permission in person." She applied pressure to the arm she was holding. "Please, Fitzwilliam? I would like to read what he said."

Darcy braced himself for what might come, broke the seal, and angled the letter so Elizabeth could read along with him.

> *Darcy,*
>
> *If you are reading this letter, not only are you one of the most intelligent men in England, you are one of the most fortunate, for it can only mean you have offered a proposal of marriage to my daughter Elizabeth, and she has accepted you.*
>
> *Since my Lizzy has confided to me her feelings on the matter, and she is still unable to travel due to her injuries—which was a condition of Jane's handing you this letter—I must trust my sister-in-law's opinion that you do, in fact, hold a real and lasting affection for Elizabeth.*
>
> *Although no man could truly deserve her, I hereby grant permission for you and Elizabeth to marry.*
>
> *I expect a note from you and one from Elizabeth as soon as is possible so I can inform my wife of this news and save you and Lizzy from the brunt of her enthusiastic response. I am certain she will begin planning the wedding in the next moment, so if you have any preferences, please include them in your missive.*
>
> *I expect you to make my Lizzy happy, Darcy. Do not disappoint me.*
>
> *Yours, etc.*
>
> *Thomas Bennet*

"Thank you, Papa," Elizabeth breathed as she leaned her head on Darcy's shoulder, hugging his arm.

"Elizabeth. I cannot believe it." Darcy kissed the top of her head. "We have your father's permission."

She smiled up at him. "We are now officially engaged to be married, Fitzwilliam."

Darcy could not help himself. He took her in his arms and kissed her soundly.

Chapter 34

Shortly after Darcy and Elizabeth entered the parlour, Bingley was called away. More than a half an hour later, whilst the ladies were deep in conversation, he returned, meandered over to Darcy, and sat beside him.

"Darcy?" Bingley coloured.

"Is something wrong, Bingley?"

"First, I would like to apologize for my sisters' conduct since they arrived at Pemberley. Especially Caroline's. I forbade them to come down this evening. Hurst remained above stairs with them to, shall we say, keep watch over them. After Caroline's behaviour the past two days, we were both afraid of what she might try next. It is why Hurst suggested he take his wife and Caroline to his family's country house, far away from you and Miss Elizabeth. Where she could do no harm." He ended on a sigh.

Darcy cleared his throat. Though he now disliked Bingley's sisters more than ever, Bingley was still his friend. "You mean her behaviour concerning my aunt?"

Bingley pulled at his cravat. "Yes, well, that and, you see… both Caroline and Louisa had retreated to Caroline's rooms for many hours this afternoon, making us suspicious. It was lucky Hurst thought to check the outgoing post for anything Caroline was sending out."

Darcy's temper began to rise. "What has she done, Bingley?"

"She wrote letters to several friends in London. About you and Miss Elizabeth. We retrieved the envelopes, and Hurst opened them." Bingley cringed. "They were quite – erh – *compromising*."

Darcy stiffened.

"We fear there might have been other letters sent before the batch we caught. My sisters say there were none, but Hurst and I are not sure we trust them." He took a breath. "I am sorry. As you know, this affects me, too, and we believe that was part of their goal. They think I will abandon my suit with Miss Bennet if their family is disgraced."

"And they expect I will renounce Elizabeth." Darcy closed his eyes and took a moment to calm himself before speaking again. "Keep the ladies company whilst I speak to Mrs. Reynolds. She will know for certain whether they used the post earlier in the day, or even yesterday." He rose and left the room.

As he walked through the kitchen in search of Mrs. Reynolds, he was met with many smiling faces. Although gossip among the servants was frowned upon at Pemberley, he knew the news of the master becoming engaged would be exempt from that rule. Obviously the footmen in the dining room had passed on what they overheard during his announcement earlier.

Finding Mrs. Reynolds in her office, Darcy entered and closed the door. She examined him expectantly, her eyes bright with questions and a smile on her lips, waiting patiently for his proclamation.

He blew out a deep breath.

Mrs. Reynolds had been more like a mother to him and his sister than a servant. Although he was sure she would understand, she did not deserve to be on the receiving end of his anger at Caroline Bingley and Mrs. Hurst. She had earned the right to be one of the first to know about his engagement, no matter what disaster had come up in the interim.

He nodded. "Yes, Mrs. Reynolds. Someday soon, Miss Elizabeth Bennet will become the next Mrs. Darcy."

Mrs. Reynolds's face lit up. "Congratulations, Mr. Darcy! Miss Elizabeth is an excellent lady. Every member of the staff will be overjoyed to hear this news."

"If they do not know already." He chuckled. "Now, I have a question of great import. Do you know if Caroline Bingley or Mrs. Hurst have sent any letters out in the post recently? Especially since my aunt arrived?"

"Give me a few moments, sir, and I shall find out." She exited the room.

A Lesson Hard Learned

Darcy paced her office.

Mrs. Reynolds returned. "As it turns out, sir, earlier, Miss Bingley's personal maid handed letters to one of the chambermaids in the guest wing. But it seems, just previously, the maid overheard a conversation between Miss Bingley and Mrs. Hurst about what they had written to their friends. She decided on her own she did not like the subject of their discourse, and so she did not post them."

Darcy let go the breath he was holding.

Mrs. Reynolds took several letters out of the pocket of her apron and handed them to Darcy. "I apologize, sir. The chambermaid will be dismissed immediately."

Darcy smiled. "Do not let her go, Reynolds. She deserves a bonus of double her monthly salary, instead."

Mrs. Reynolds's eyes widened.

"And burn those letters immediately!"

Mrs. Reynolds blinked several times. "Yes, sir."

"Please advise the maid that, in the future, she should not delay. She should explain any problems to you immediately, and you will speak to me."

"Yes, sir."

He leaned down and kissed Mrs. Reynolds on the cheek. "Thank you for hiring an able staff."

The housekeeper was blushing when he left the room.

When Darcy returned to the parlour, he encountered Bingley standing in the corridor just outside the room, waiting for him.

Darcy said, "They both sent out messages, but a loyal maid overheard them discussing what they wrote and held them back. They are being burned as we speak."

Bingley let out a long breath. "How did I end up with such deceitful, manipulative sisters, Darcy? We had the same upbringing, but I never would do anything like this."

Darcy shook his head. "Sometimes I believe they were cut from different cloth than you."

Bingley said, "Just in case something did get through, I have an idea. If any of what my sisters said were true, I would never ask for Miss Bennet's hand, would I?"

Darcy answered with amusement in his voice, "It *would* be a perfect vindication."

Bingley said, "Actually, I had planned to make an offer this evening, but when I learned you had asked Miss Elizabeth to marry you today…"

Darcy patted Bingley on the back. "You did not wish to ask her so soon after I had done so with her sister?"

Bingley nodded. "As soon as I heard your news, I decided to make my offer once we had all returned to Hertfordshire. But now, do you not think it would be better if I made an offer tonight?"

"Go to it, Bingley. Miss Bennet and Elizabeth are so close, I do not think they would mind becoming engaged on the same day." He raised his eyebrows thoughtfully. "I will be leaving at daybreak to escort Georgiana, Lady Catherine, and Anne to Matlock to stay with my Aunt Adelaide during the funeral service, so I will not be able to see you off tomorrow. But this provides you with an opportunity. Anne and Georgiana will retire early." He smiled. "I will find some excuse to speak to Elizabeth privately, giving you a few moments alone with Miss Bennet."

A wide grin spread over Bingley's face.

Darcy said, "I wish you luck, my friend, though I do not think you need it."

The two shook hands heartily and re-entered the parlour.

~%~

An hour later, after they had said their farewells to Anne and goodnights to Georgiana, Elizabeth followed Darcy into the corridor.

"I need your opinion on this…" He paused. "This *chair.*" He walked over to a bench and rested his hand on the back.

"The chair?" She furrowed her brow. "What about the chair?"

"Do you think it should be reupholstered?" he asked. "Perhaps all the chairs in the corridors should match?"

She examined the chairs. They already did match.

A movement made by the footman standing nearby caught her attention and she realized it was James.

She returned her gaze to her betrothed and tilted her head. "What is this really about, Fitzwilliam?"

Darcy turned to James. A hand gesture dismissed him.

James bowed and, as he walked past them, she noticed James was smiling. She had done it!

She hoped the gesture was a sign of his approval of her soon becoming the mistress of the estate, and that the opinion was shared by the entire staff.

When James turned a corner, she took a step towards Darcy. "Ah, so you were trying to get me alone, were you?"

Darcy moved closer, wrapped his arms around her, and pulled her against his chest. She tilted her head back.

"Partly." He leaned in, but not too close.

She angled her head so her mouth could be easily reached, but he did not bend further. She arched a brow. "Partly?"

"Mmmm hmmm." He bent another inch and stopped.

Her anticipation grew. She licked her lips.

"I will miss you tomorrow," he said. "What will you do?"

"I will write to my father, for certain."

He bent a bit more. "I will write to him as soon as I retire this evening and ask Hughes to give it to Hannah so you can put it in the post with yours on the morrow."

She studied his lips.

"What else will you do?" he asked.

"It will be only Jane and me during the day. We will think of something. We always do."

The corners of his lips turned upwards. "I am certain you will have much to talk about."

She nodded slightly and brought up her chin so her lips brushed his. He hesitated no more, caressing her lips with his. Her shock as he deepened the kiss lasted only a moment, for she was a quick study when acquiring skills she enjoyed.

After a minute or two, Darcy ended the kiss and gathered her against his heaving chest. When she caught her breath, she began to understand the reason he had called her out of the room. She pulled away slightly to look up at him.

She smiled brightly. "Mr. Bingley is proposing to Jane!"

Darcy laughed. "I will never be able to surprise you with anything, will I?"

She shook her head. "My family has rarely succeeded in surprising me. There are always patterns of behaviour that give them away."

"I will enjoy such a challenge." His lips grazed hers briefly. "I believe we have given them enough time."

"Are you sure? Mr. Bingley sometimes takes a while to get to the point."

"Yes." His chest expanded. "I do not trust myself alone with you any longer than this, Elizabeth."

Though his statement and the hungry look in his eyes caused joy to flutter in her chest, she felt her face heat.

"Come, let us see what Miss Bennet's answer is."

Darcy knocked and hesitated. Bingley and Jane were moving apart as he opened the door. Jane blushed furiously, but her eyes twinkled with joy when she met Elizabeth's gaze.

"Jane!" Elizabeth cried.

Jane rushed to her sister.

"I am so happy, Lizzy."

Elizabeth hugged her the best she could while holding crutches.

"Two daughters engaged in one day! Mama will require smelling salts for certain!" Elizabeth quipped.

Jane laughed. "Papa may need to borrow them."

~%~

So occupied was Elizabeth in thinking about all that had happened during the previous day, she could not sleep. Though she would have liked to have gotten dressed and gone downstairs to wish her affianced, Georgiana, and Anne a safe trip to Matlock, she did not want to bother Hannah or James so early. Instead, she donned her robe and a shawl and made her way to the window seat to witness the sunrise. She pushed open the large panes of glass and leaned her back against the wall.

Even though the stars were still shining, certain members of the Pemberley staff were already busy. From here, she could see the coach-house and stables—far enough to avoid the smell of the horses, thank goodness, but close enough for Elizabeth to observe the flurry of activity. Since the window was high on the wall, only her head and shoulders were exposed, and she felt safe to remain where she was.

Absentmindedly, she began loosening her plait and then moved to retrieve her brush from her dressing table. The least she could do was make Hannah's job easier later by brushing out her long mane now.

The de Bourgh's luggage was loaded on a large cart and began the journey towards Matlock.

The company of Lady Catherine would not be missed, but Elizabeth would have liked to know Anne better—*only* if her mother were not in attendance, as had happened last evening.

The de Bourgh coach was pulled from the coach-house, and horses were hitched up, then it was brought around to the front of the house.

The Darcy coach was wheeled out next, and several stable boys led out horses.

Elizabeth pulled her shawl more tightly around her and sighed. Darcy would depart for Matlock soon.

Although she would have Jane for company today and there would be a multitude of staff present, the house would feel empty without him. And Georgiana and Mr. Bingley, of course.

At least Elizabeth would see Darcy again this evening. Poor Jane would put on a strong facade, but Elizabeth knew her sister would grieve for the loss of her fiancé's company until they met again in Hertfordshire. By then, Bingley would have spoken to their father. Elizabeth was certain he would approve the match.

As the sky began to brighten, the Hursts' coach was brought out of the coach-house, and a man started sweeping it out.

She could go her whole life without seeing the Hursts and Miss Bingley again, though that would not be the case because Jane would marry into the family.

One of the horses reared and landed badly. A boy ran into the stable. A man Georgiana had introduced as the lead groomsman came out, calmed the horse, and examined the horse's legs. The boy rushed around to the front of the house.

After a minute or two, the boy returned, trailed by another figure.

Elizabeth grinned. It was Darcy. Since there was no chance someone was watching her, she examined his fine figure as best she could at this distance. Oh, how handsome he was! Such broad shoulders and an athletic physique. She still could not believe this man was to be her husband.

He followed the boy across the yard, spoke to the groomsman, and then examined the horse's leg. Darcy shook his head and gestured in the direction of the stable. Another boy came out and handed something to the groomsman, who knelt beside the horse. He rubbed a salve into the horse's leg before bandaging it. The groomsman led the horse away and a few moments later, another was brought out. Darcy turned and began to walk away.

He seemed very tired. A twinge of worry and guilt pinched at her. Darcy had been through so much lately—the sea journey, his uncle's passing, his aunt's and Caroline Bingley's disruptions. A nagging sensation at the back of her mind reminded her she should include her own first refusal among the list. Her guilt deepened.

She had been selfish last night. Knowing he had to leave at dawn this morning, why had she not insisted he retire early?

As he approached the house, the sun broke the horizon.

Darcy looked up and his gaze caught hers. His frown and worry-lines smoothed. Elizabeth waved. Darcy removed his hat and bowed formally. As he straightened, he glanced behind him at the men working on the carriage and then raised his eyes to her again. Distracted by something she could not perceive, he looked towards the front of the house. He nodded, and she thought he sighed. He raised his eyes to her once again. She blew him a kiss. His smile filled her heart with joy. He mouthed, "Thank you," placed the hat on his head, tipped it, and walked on.

When he passed out of sight, Elizabeth realized she had been smiling so broadly, her cheeks hurt.

~%~

Two hours later, Elizabeth stopped at her writing desk to retrieve the letters she had received yesterday but not had the time or inclination to read as of yet. She slipped them into a pocket and clip-clopped her way to the sitting room to meet Jane. Elizabeth expected Bingley to be the only other occupant in the breakfast room this morning, so she was determined to keep herself busy in order to offer the couple a bit of privacy.

Hannah preceded her and opened the door, then rang for James. The sisters waited in the corridor near the stairway. With James's help, they made their way to the breakfast room. Bingley stood on their arrival. Elizabeth sat in a different seat than usual, further down the table, using her correspondence as an excuse. She knew neither were fooled, but their expressions seemed grateful. Bingley made up plates for both ladies, and Elizabeth turned her attention to her letters.

She knew they were outdated—Georgiana had previously told her they were delivered at Matlock just after she had moved to Pemberley, but with the earl's illness, they had been forgotten.

One was from her friend Ruth, which she opened immediately. Ruth stated she would not be able to send her manuscript until the autumn, as she had left it in her bedchamber in Town and her family was now visiting at their aunt's country estate. Elizabeth chuckled and wondered what she would have thought if she had seen that letter before she had opened Darcy's package.

The next was from her sister Kitty, informing her Lydia had borrowed a bonnet of Elizabeth's and left it in ruins. At the time Kitty had written, Lydia was trying to make one of her hats look like it, decking it out with ribbons taken from Elizabeth's ruined one.

The third... goodness! It was the letter Darcy told her he had written. He had obviously taken his time writing this one, given that his penmanship was impeccable. There was no return address, but after re-reading the note he had handed to her at Hunsford, she was quite familiar with his usual handwriting. Judging by its undamaged condition the brown paper on the parcel must have been torn before it was wet through, and the letter must have fallen out.

She sat staring at it for several moments before remembering he had told her he would give it to her if he found it among the journal pages. Since he intended she should read it, she broke the seal.

In it, he explained all he had not been able to say that day in London, but in much more reserved terms than he had in the page of his journal she had read. He apologized for the poor judgement and lack of manners he displayed during his shameful excuse for a proposal at Hunsford cottage at Easter, as well as the bitterness in his previous missive, explaining he had taken her response to heart. It ended with a statement saying it was of vital importance to him that she know he was attempting to mend his ways.

She smiled to herself. All in all, the intent of the letter was similar to that of the page from his journal, but she was glad she had read the journal page. In doing so, she received a glimpse into his heart in a much more intimate way than the tone of this communication allowed. She decided to put it in her keepsake box, folded within the journal page. It would serve in the future as a reminder of the difference between the formal and precise manner of address he used in his letters and his internal passion.

His passion for her.

A shiver passed up her spine.

The sound of scraping furniture against the floor returned her attention to the others in the room. Bingley helped Jane from her chair. It was time for Bingley's family to leave Pemberley.

Chapter 35

Darcy slipped into his Aunt Adelaide's sitting room to check on her before he and the other gentlemen left for the funeral service. Anne and Georgiana sat on either side of the countess, each holding one of the older lady's hands. He had accompanied the ladies about a half hour earlier when they paid their last respects to the earl before the coffin was closed. It was a difficult moment, and all three seemed as if they had continued crying well after they had quitted the parlour. Bianca had been with them then, but she was not here now.

He did not notice his Aunt Catherine was present until he stepped further into the room.

Lady Catherine said, "She is an obstinate, headstrong girl; selfish and insensitive. She has no sense of propriety or delicacy of feeling." She glanced at Darcy, turned up her nose, and looked away. "I cannot believe my nephew would forget what he owes the family—what he owes to Anne—and has allowed himself to be drawn into the traps of her arts and allurements. Anne and Georgiana will surely agree with me."

Darcy stepped forward and opened his mouth to defend his lady love, but Lady Adelaide held up her hand to stop him.

Lady Adelaide turned to Georgiana. "What do *you* think of Miss Bennet?"

Georgiana seemed terrified to speak in front of Lady Catherine, but she sat up taller and said in a clear voice, "I highly value her camaraderie and am pleased with the prospect of having Lizzy as my sister."

Lady Adelaide nodded and turned to Anne. "And your opinion of Miss Bennet, Anne?"

Anne shrank into the sofa under her mother's glare, but then she looked at Darcy and seemed to find her courage. Still, her voice was small and weak when she said, "I am proud to call Miss Elizabeth my friend."

Lady Adelaide levelled her gaze at her sister-in-law. "In case you did not know, Catherine, I happen to have hosted Miss Bennet at Matlock recently. What you say about her is the complete opposite of what I *know* to be true. In addition, Richard holds Miss Bennet in the highest respect. Even Reginald met her and found her delightful." She said to Darcy, "Personally, I found Miss Bennet to be a lovely young lady. I approve of her completely."

Darcy's heart swelled with affection for his Aunt Adelaide, Georgiana, and his cousins.

His Aunt Catherine chattered on. "You and your sons were out of your senses with worry and grief regarding my brother's debilitating illness. You could not see clearly and did not recognize the degrading qualities in the girl. She is as *I* say."

Darcy almost laughed for just after he had arrived at Pemberley yesterday, as he approached the room where Aunt Catherine was scolding Caroline Bingley, he heard her voicing the opposite opinions of both her sister-in-law and Elizabeth.

Lady Adelaide sat a little taller. "Catherine, do you forget to whom you are speaking? I have never been out of my senses for one moment of my life, whether grieved or not." She waited a few moments before going on. "It just so happens even my dearest husband liked Miss Bennet. Though he never met her himself, he wished to hear about the lady who was injured on our grounds and her relations who were staying with us. I made daily reports to him on all my dealings with them." She switched her gaze to Darcy. "And when Richard told us he thought Darcy was interested in the lady, my husband gave his blessing should Darcy ever propose."

Darcy approached Lady Adelaide, took her hand, and bowed over it. "Thank you, Aunt, for passing on that information."

Lady Catherine hissed like a feline and rose from her seat. "That girl is a temptress. She has seduced my entire family!" She took a few steps then turned to her daughter. "Anne, be ready to leave Matlock in the morning." She left the room.

With the slam of the door, his Aunt Adelaide wilted. "I am sorry to say this in front of you, Anne, but Catherine is one of the most complicated women I have ever dealt with." She closed her eyes and rubbed the space between her brows. After taking a moment to recover, she said to Darcy, "If your Elizabeth can hold her own against Catherine, she will be able to handle any lady of my acquaintance."

Darcy agreed. "Is there anything you need before we leave for the church, Aunt?"

She shook her head. "No, thank you. I am not sure where Bianca has gone, but I have faith my dear nieces will see that I am as comfortable as possible."

~%~

Several hours later, Darcy wandered the halls of Matlock in search of his sister so they might leave for home before the evening light dwindled. Under no circumstances did he wish to be forced to stay the night. He was in desperate need of Elizabeth's presence.

Bianca stepped into the corridor from her mother's sitting room. He stopped and bowed to her, and then asked if Georgiana was inside.

"Yes, she is with my mother, but Fitzwilliam—"

He held up his hand. "Bianca, it has been a difficult day for all of us. Please…"

She took a step forward. "I only wanted to wish you and Miss Elizabeth joy, Fitzwilliam."

Still suspicious, he thanked her.

She turned to walk away and then turned back. "My father and I had a long talk soon after I arrived here."

Unsure of what to say in response, Darcy nodded.

"Father told me something which surprised me." She stared at the handkerchief she held in both hands. "He said he wished I would find love,

278

for he felt it is the only thing of true value in life. He said in the end, wealth, position, and rank meant nothing." She met his gaze. "It has given me a great deal to think about."

"I am happy to hear it, Bianca."

"I am sorry for the trouble I caused, Fitzwilliam. I am shamed by my behaviour."

Exhausted and ill-equipped to detect whether she was telling the truth at the moment, he simply nodded. He moved in the direction of his aunt's door. "Excuse me."

"Of course," she said and continued down the corridor.

He breathed a sigh of relief and entered to collect Georgiana.

Time would tell whether there was hope for Bianca.

~%~

For the next few days, Darcy breakfasted with the ladies and spent a few hours catching up with estate business that needed his attention.

Elizabeth blushed as she thought of the few times he had found her alone for brief interludes. The time was spent in bliss and harmony, so much so that Elizabeth wondered when the other shoe would drop. She was much relieved when it did not.

One day, Mrs. Reynolds entered the sitting room where Elizabeth was writing a letter while waiting for Jane to go down to breakfast. She said the doctor was on the estate to see a tenant who was ill and asked if he could examine Elizabeth a day early. Elizabeth agreed.

An hour later, Elizabeth and Jane met Darcy and Georgiana at the guest wing's staircase. Elizabeth was using only a cane.

"Good morning, ladies," Darcy said with a grin. "I heard the doctor was waiting for me in my study."

Elizabeth smiled back at him. "As you see, I have shed the crutches and may now use a cane. I also have permission to try the stairs this morning."

Darcy looked away for a moment at the staircase and then back again. "Only if you hold the banister with one hand and my arm with the other."

Elizabeth nodded. "I will not complain."

Slowly, they made their way down the staircase. She felt herself beaming when they reached the bottom. Once the ladies caught up with them, they all continued down the corridor towards the breakfast room. "I am sure the doctor will also tell you he has given me permission to travel." She lowered her voice so only Darcy could hear her. "Jane is beside herself with happiness. I suspect she is most anxious to see Mr. Bingley again. He should be at Netherfield by now, should he not?"

"I believe so," he answered as they arrived at the breakfast room. He proceeded to help the ladies into their chairs then excused himself, promising to return as soon as he spoke to the doctor.

A few minutes later, he returned. "I will be happy to talk to Mr. Bennet in person," he said to Elizabeth after he took his seat. "Having his permission granted by letter does not seem real. How would you feel about beginning our journey the day after tomorrow?"

Elizabeth said, "It sounds perfect."

"I shall send an express to your father and Bingley today to inform them of our plans."

Chapter 36

Five days later, the Darcy coach pulled into the drive at Longbourn. The Bennets stood on the drive to greet them, along with a visitor, Bingley, whose wide grin could only be matched by Jane's.

Nodding, Bingley handed Jane from the coach. Her father approached and said a few words to Jane. The way her face lit up before she turned into her father's embrace informed Elizabeth that Mr. Bennet had just given his permission for Jane to marry Bingley.

Darcy stepped down next, and he assisted Elizabeth and Georgiana, after which he made the introductions of his sister. Mr. Bennet surrendered his eldest daughter's hand to Bingley and approached Darcy. The two gentlemen shook hands.

"I am pleased your elegant equipage was able to traverse the miles safely and bring my two eldest daughters home, Mr. Darcy," Mr. Bennet stated with a light tone, though his eyes were suspiciously glossy. "The next time either Jane or Elizabeth arrive at Longbourn, it will be as married ladies."

Darcy's demeanour relaxed after receiving the confirmation Elizabeth knew he needed. "Thank you, sir. I am the happiest of men to have received your permission to marry Miss Elizabeth."

"That is just what Bingley said to me not a quarter of an hour ago, though about Jane, of course," he chuckled.

He held open his arms and Elizabeth stepped into them. "Thank you, Papa."

Her father kissed her forehead and whispered, "Be happy, my Lizzy."

"I will, Papa. I am sure of it."

When he finally released her, he turned away from the group and blew his nose.

Georgiana backed away a little when Mary, Kitty, and Lydia began all at once to congratulate both couples, their voices loud and boisterous.

Surprisingly, Mrs. Bennet was still standing off to one side, staring at her family and visitors as if she were in shock. Elizabeth moved towards her. "Mama, are you unwell?"

She patted both cheeks with her handkerchief and shook her head. "I am very well. Very well, indeed, Lizzy. Here I am, seeing it with my own eyes, and I still cannot believe it. Two daughters engaged to be married—and to such fine gentlemen as these!"

Mr. Bennet invited them all indoors. The Darcys begged to be excused, though not before Mrs. Bennet secured them all to dine at Longbourn the following day.

Quite reluctantly, Bingley offered to escort his guests to his home.

Laughing, Darcy explained he knew how to get to Netherfield. He turned again to Mr. Bennet. "Would you mind if we took a turn around your garden, sir? I would like to stretch my legs a bit before we re-enter the coach, even if it is only for three miles."

Mr. Bennet raised his eyebrows. "Certainly, be my guest."

Mr. and Mrs. Bennet returned to the house whilst the others headed for the garden. Elizabeth was prepared to walk with Georgiana, but since she seemed happily engaged in conversation with Mary, Kitty, and Lydia, she attached herself to Darcy's arm, leaning upon him heavily.

"Are you able to walk this distance?"

"I shall be fine as long as you are here with me."

Darcy slowed his pace, taking full advantage of their increasing distance from the others to speak softly to Elizabeth, "I will miss you this evening, and every evening until we wed."

Elizabeth gazed up into his eyes. "I have become accustomed to hearing you wish me good night and seeing you at table as I break my fast."

"I long for the day that wherever I go, I can take you with me, Elizabeth."

She stopped walking and turned to face him. "Six weeks?"

That hungry light shined from his eyes again, and it made her insides quiver. "Six long weeks until our full mourning is at an end." He sighed.

Her ankle was stiff from the ride, and Darcy suggested they take a shorter path. They soon caught up to the others.

With one last look at Elizabeth, Darcy helped his sister into the coach. She waved to Darcy and Georgiana as they pulled away.

When the coach made the turn at the end of the drive and moved out of sight, her father came up beside her and offered his arm. "You seemed to need an arm to steady you. I do not want to see you injured again." They turned to walk to the house. "It is good to have you home, Lizzy."

"It is good to be home, Papa."

He arched a brow. "Is it? I thought you might be spoilt staying so long at Pemberley."

She smiled up at him. "I am not saying I will not someday think of Pemberley as home, but certainly not yet. Longbourn will always be my first home."

As they entered the house, Mrs. Hill wished her joy, and then informed her there was a bath waiting. Because Jane was still walking in the garden with Bingley, she wondered if Elizabeth would like to bathe first. She happily agreed.

As she turned towards the stairs, she heard her mother's exclamation echo through the house, "Two daughters engaged!"

Her father chuckled and said, "I will be in my bookroom, Hill, and not to be disturbed—unless, of course, a young man comes for one of the other girls."

Her ankle pain now pulsing with her heartbeat, Elizabeth waited until Hill and her father were out of sight before sitting down on the stairs and making her way upward, one step at a time.

~%~

Six weeks later, Mr. Bennet escorted both Elizabeth and Jane down the aisle of Longbourn church to their waiting bridegrooms. Their double wedding had been greatly anticipated, and many of their neighbours were in attendance for the ceremony, more likely than not so they could tell their friends that they had witnessed such an oddity.

However, there were a few present who had travelled from near and far to see the happy beginning for two couples in love. Mr. and Mrs. Gardiner would not have missed the event they had had so much to do with bringing about. Bingley's sisters were, of course, in attendance for their brother's wedding, but their blatantly false smirks did not fool anyone.

Though they both wished Darcy's Aunt Adelaide and cousins could have attended the wedding, later Darcy confessed to Elizabeth that when the minister asked whether anyone knew a reason why they should not marry, he was glad they decided to wed during Lady Catherine's full mourning period.

The wedding breakfast was a grand affair. All were grateful the weather was fine, for Longbourn was so packed with guests, many felt the need to step out into the cooler garden, perfectly shrouded in dappled shade at this time of the morning.

Before too long, it was time for the newlywed couples to leave. The guests lined up along the drive to wave them off.

There were many smiles and a few tears shed as Elizabeth's entire family renewed their plans to join them at Pemberley at Christmas. Georgiana clung to her brother as she promised she would be well staying with Aunt Adelaide at Matlock for a month. Darcy and Elizabeth's original plan was to tour the Lakes for their honeymoon trip, but because her ankle had still not recovered completely, they settled on going to Pemberley. Instead, they would take Georgiana to the Lake District with them after the spring planting at the estate.

Once on the road to London, where they would stay the first night of their married life at Darcy House, Elizabeth turned to Darcy. "I had forgotten the date, but Jane reminded me earlier—it was a year ago today we all met at the Assembly Ball."

He took her hand and slowly pulled off her glove one finger at a time. "A year... is that all?" He brought her hand to his lips and kissed every finger, then her wrist.

Distracted as he did the same to her other hand, Elizabeth took a minute to respond. "Yes, one year. So much has happened since then."

"I am so glad it did." He leaned towards her and stopped an inch from her lips.

"So am I." Boldly, she moved forward the last inch, brushing her lips against his as she whispered, "Husband."

"My wife," he breathed before kissing her thoroughly.

When he pulled away, she was dazed. Recovering, she said, "You have been holding back, Mr. Darcy."

"I still am, Mrs. Darcy." His hungry expression made her shiver.

Not knowing what to say or do in response, Elizabeth laid her head on his chest and snuggled into his side. "This is the first time I have ever been truly alone with a man."

His voice rumbled through his chest against her ear. "Well, I do hope I am the only man you have been alone with, but, the first time, Elizabeth?" He paused. "What about when you and I were alone in the library at Pemberley?"

She gazed up at him. "There was always a chance a servant or another guest would come in, so I did not feel unsafe."

His breath caught. "Do you feel as if you are in danger now?"

Elizabeth pulled away slightly so she could see him better. "No. You are my husband. I trust you implicitly."

Darcy fidgeted a little in his seat, though Elizabeth did not understand what she could have said to make him uncomfortable.

To fill the silence, she said, "I could never understand why an unmarried lady needed a chaperone in a moving coach, anyway. What more could possibly happen than a stolen kiss?"

He grinned rakishly. After a few moments, his smile faded. "You are serious in asking that question?"

She nodded. "Of course."

A strange look came over him. "If it were not our wedding day, I might show you," he said under his breath.

Elizabeth glanced around her, and, thinking about what her aunt and mother had explained married couples *do* when alone, she blushed deeply. She moved away and looked up at her husband with wide eyes. "In a *coach*?"

His rakish grin returned. "I am certain it has been *attempted*, at the very least."

When she realized her mouth hung open, she snapped it shut.

Darcy laughed. "It was just an observation, Elizabeth. Fathers and brothers must think of all possibilities when charged with the protection of daughters and sisters. In time, you will think along the same lines, for example, when safeguarding your own daughters from unworthy gentlemen."

She examined her hands, which were now in her lap, embarrassed she was so incredibly naïve. "I suppose so. I just never thought of it in quite that way."

With two fingers, he raised her chin. She looked up.

"Does it not make sense that I am overjoyed—even relieved—to hear you have never had the *need* to think of it?" he asked.

She blinked several times. "Yes, I guess you would be."

He gathered her into his arms and gazed deeply into her eyes. "Please never hold back your thoughts or actions. You can trust me, Elizabeth. With anything."

"I do. Already, you are the perfect husband."

"And you are the perfect wife." He kissed the tip of her nose. "Have I ever told you how ardently I admire and love you?"

Smiling at his repetition of the opening phrase of his first proposal, but in a much different tone than it had been said the first time, she brushed her lips against his. "I love you, too, Fitzwilliam. I know we shall be very happy together."

"We shall be happy, Elizabeth. That we shall."

Just the beginning…

Finis

I hope you enjoyed *A Lesson Hard Learned.*

Please consider leaving a review on Amazon.com.

Thanks!

Wendi Sotis

THANK YOU

Gayle Mills and **Robin Helm** for their fabulous editing expertise;

FTHRW Critique Group for all their suggestions;

The **Beyond Austen** readers for their feedback, which kept me writing;

Christina Hovland for her read-through of the final product;

And of course, **JANE AUSTEN** for inspiring me!

About Wendi Sotis

Wendi Sotis is a graduate of Nassau Community College and Adelphi University, and holds a degree in Psychology. Following the birth of her triplets in 2000, she decided to stay at home to raise them.

Having always been an avid reader and adoring fan of Jane Austen, when her triplets were independent enough that she could find a little time to herself, Wendi searched the internet where she discovered a treasure trove of "fan fiction" written by fellow *Janeites*. At first, experiencing Austen's stories from several different characters' points of view caught her interest, but then she branched off into reading sequels, "what if" stories, and modernized versions of Austen's tales.

Though she had always aspired to become a writer, Wendi did not make a serious attempt until one day, after awakening from a dream, her imagination began churning up a tale to surround it.

Wendi continues to write while living on Long Island with her husband, Matt, who paints her covers, her son, and two daughters.

Contact Wendi through the following venues:

Website: www.wendisotis.com
Facebook: http://www.facebook.com/pages/Wendi-Sotis-Author/231869130201504
Twitter: https://twitter.com/#!/WendiSotis
Forum: http://beyondausten.com

Books by Wendi Sotis

Adapting characters from Jane Austen's much loved tale, this novel takes Elizabeth Bennet and Fitzwilliam Darcy on a much different journey than Austen did in Pride and Prejudice in this sweet Regency novel.

Through their fathers' friendship, Elizabeth Bennet and Fitzwilliam Darcy meet as children. Over the years, their feelings for each other grow and they promise themselves to each other, but unfortunate circumstances and interfering family members seek to keep them apart.

Will misunderstandings and mistaken impressions divide Elizabeth and William forever?

While staying true to the characters of Jane Austen's much loved tale, this novel takes Elizabeth Bennet and Fitzwilliam Darcy on a much different journey than Austen did in Pride and Prejudice.

Although family and society expect Fitzwilliam Darcy to ignore his heart and "marry well," soon after entering Meryton, he falls in love with the woman of his dreams. The problem is, while she is perfect for him in disposition, the lady is far below him in everything that matters to his peers and relations: wealth and connexions.

Past experiences have convinced Miss Elizabeth Bennet that marriage with a gentlemen of high social standing would be out of the question. However, against her better judgement, she cannot turn away from the man she loves, and enters into a friendship.

Fate, mystery, and intrigue bring them together again and again in Hertfordshire, Rosings Park, coastal Broadstairs, and London. Will Elizabeth and Darcy listen to their consciences and continue on simply as friends? Or can they overcome the confines of duty, the malicious designs of others, and their own scruples, and allow the yearnings of their souls to guide them, instead?

A sweet Regency romance blended with mystery and adventure.

Since ancient times, every Halloween, the ritual of Sanun is performed, freeing the dead to interact with the living for one night. One Evil Soul discovers a way to hide from the Return, remaining on Earth to meddle with the fates of the living. As the centuries pass, It begins to search for the High Priestess, intending to force her to do its bidding, no matter the cost.

Appearances can be deceiving, even in Regency England. To most, Elizabeth Bennet is simply the second daughter of an insignificant country squire, but in truth, she is High Priestess and leader of an ancient cult secretly co-existing alongside British society. Confusion reigns when she learns that the man she despises, Fitzwilliam Darcy, is her Soul Mate, assigned to protect her from Evil. Can they work together to preserve the future?

A sweet, magical, Regency romance, inspired by Jane Austen's Pride and Prejudice.

While taking a solitary ramble on her father's estate, Elizabeth Bennet finds an injured woman, cares for her, and helps her return to her gypsy camp. For her exceptional kindness, Elizabeth is awarded a blessing, bestowed through gypsy magic.

Forgetting the incident, Elizabeth thinks it merely odd when she begins to receive drawings in the mail with no return address - until she recognizes these same scenes as they become true events in her life.

Through the blessing, circumstances bring Elizabeth and Jane Bennet to Ramsgate, where they meet Georgiana and Fitzwilliam Darcy, along with a charming young man named George Wickham.

Will Elizabeth's efforts to reshape future events alter her destiny?

 Building contractor William Darcy doesn't trust women. Elizabeth Bennett, an architectural intern working on his latest project, wants nothing to do with such a rude man. Because of a magical blessing inherited from an ancestor of a similar name, Elizabeth begins to doubt her sanity when her cell phone receives pictures predicting future events. After Elizabeth uses the photos to save William's sister, the wall between them begins to crumble.
When William witnesses Elizabeth viewing a series of prophetic photos, he becomes involved, as well.
Will their shared experiences become the foundation of love?

Foundation of Love is a sweet, Jane Austen-inspired romance with a bit of magic / paranormal. A contemporary sequel to The Gypsy Blessing, which takes place in Regency England, it can also stand alone.

~%~

In this sweet Pride and Prejudice-inspired romance, William Darcy has finally torn himself away from work to join his sister at their vacation house in the Florida Keys.

There, he meets his sister's new friend, Elizabeth Bennet, the housesitter staying next door.

A light, fluffy, feel-good short story/novella. No graphic love scenes

~%~

A woman awakens in a hospital room, injured and surrounded by strangers. The car accident is a blur, and her mind is nearly a blank slate. The name on her driver's license reads Elizabeth Becket, and she's enrolled at a local college, but none of this feels right. Her college application claims she's a writer—are her vivid and frequent nightmares a story conjured up in her imagination or could they be memories of her former life?

The only thing she knows for sure is that an urgent sense of danger casts a shadow over her entire existence.

Irresistibly drawn to Fitz Darcy, the man living next door to her new apartment, her soul longs to trust him. Is he safe to love, or is he part of the frightening events her subconscious is fighting so hard to keep buried?

A contemporary mystery romance with a clever nod to Jane Austen's Pride and Prejudice.

~%~

Shortly after Elizabeth Bennet refuses Fitzwilliam Darcy's offer of marriage, he becomes convinced her reproofs were correct and determines to become worthy of her love. His attempt to arrange a "chance" meeting is successful and they cross paths in London.

Soon afterwards, Darcy sails for Virginia to retrieve his newly widowed cousin, who has found herself stranded in a country on the verge of war with her native land. Once there, he suspects her sights are set on him as her next mate. Even worse, his journal—which details his feelings about Elizabeth—is accidentally posted to Elizabeth. Can he return to England, convince her he has taken her opinions to heart, and win her love before she receives it?

The impulsive Elizabeth Bennet is injured while touring a Derbyshire estate with her aunt and uncle, and circumstances find her at the home of Georgiana Darcy while she recuperates. While there, Elizabeth realizes she is in love with Darcy, but will he arrive home and assume the worst about her after finding her living at his estate?

Look for *The Pact*,
A non-Austen Regency Novel
Coming to Amazon soon!

Continue reading for
a sample.

Wendi Recommends

Books by Robin M. Helm
Yours by Design Trilogy

Guardian Trilogy

Coming Soon from Robin M. Helm

Understanding Elizabeth

Jane Bennet's illness is much worse than expected, and she must remain indefinitely at Netherfield. Her sister Elizabeth joins her, and in her distraction over Jane's health, she tucks her private writings in a book which she leaves in the parlour upon returning to her chambers. Darcy, unable to contain his curiosity, reads Elizabeth's thoughts and is shocked to learn her true opinion of him.

Will Elizabeth's carelessness prove to be a hindrance to romance, or will Darcy's awareness of her feelings help him to understand her more completely?

"You owe me," Bertram Aldridge, the Earl of Westbury, slurred almost incoherently. "I saved your lives on the Continent."

Robert Colton exchanged a wary glance with his friend and cousin by marriage, Garret Sharrington. Both heard these words often.

Westbury slouched far enough to rest his head on the seat-back and blinked as if attempting to focus on the gentlemen on the bench across from him. "You owe me," he repeated.

"That we do, Westbury." Sharrington knocked three times on the roof of Lord Westbury's coach to signal their readiness to depart. He waited until the noise of the horses and wheels would drown out their conversation if the driver was listening. "What can we do for you this time?"

"Ten thousand."

Colton's eyes widened. "Pounds?"

"Not for my sake, but for my family's." Lord Westbury's face crumpled with a pained expression. "I must pay the impost takers by the end of the month or it will be twelve."

Sharrington shook his head. "We knew your gambling debts were serious, but..."

"I thought I could win back enough to pay my debts," Westbury stated much more intelligibly.

Colton was not surprised at the earl's miraculous recovery. When he was in trouble, pretending to be inebriated was common, but he could not keep it up for long.

"I've already mortgaged the house in Town." Westbury rubbed his hand across his face.

"How *could* you?" Colton curled his upper lip in disgust. That meant his debts had been much more than they were now. "What of the estate?"

"Burchard Park is entailed and cannot be mortgaged. Had I been able to do so, I would never borrow from the impost takers and risk their unreasonable premiums. I need funds, and I need them before the week is out. Westbury House has been in our line for generations. The mortgage is due..."

Sharrington caught Colton's eye. Entailing Burchard Park had been a smart move by Westbury's father. Colton sighed, nodded, and turned to look out the window. No matter how he abhorred it, the time had come to end this.

"We have two propositions for you, Westbury." Sharrington shifted in his seat. "I believe they will benefit us all. As you may know, my daughter Victoria's dowry is twenty-five thousand pounds." Sharrington raised his eyebrows. "It seems Victoria has taken a fancy your son."

Westbury sat up straighter. "Twenty-five thousand should be just the thing—for now."

Sharrington held up a finger. "But I insist on a condition of the contract. Lord Eagleton will be in control of Victoria's dowry funds. All of it. *He* will pay off your debts."

The earl agreed, and then turned to Colton. "And what will you do for me?"

Colton frowned. "I will not do anything for *you* directly, Westbury, for I know very well you will gamble it away and your family will be eventually left with nothing. However, I will take pity on your grandson, who will inherit the earldom someday. How old is he now?"

"Percival James is seventeen."

Colton fought back the urge to retch. Even the idea of what he was about to offer made him ill. He forced the words out of his mouth. "My father left thirty thousand pounds for each of my daughters' dowries."

He hesitated, thinking the plan through one last time. Should it be Penelope or Celia?

Every day, Penelope became more like her mother. Whatever man took her would end up as miserable as he was, and he would not wish that on such an amiable Aldridge boy. He also could not saddle good-natured Victoria with Penelope as her daughter-in-law. His elder daughter would despise her cousin for marrying the man who already had a title. She would do everything in her power to make Victoria's life difficult.

Meanwhile, Celia was a sweet girl—his pride and joy. It pleased him to know she would become a countess someday, for she would do the title justice. It was quite possible Celia would have a happy life.

Yes, it should be Celia.

He took a deep breath. "When you draft the marriage settlement between Lord Eagleton and Miss Sharrington, you and I will draw up another contract, as well. Victoria Sharrington is my wife's cousin, and she is quite close to my younger daughter, Celia. Celia will be presented at Court during the winter after her seventeenth birthday. The contract you and I will sign will state that five years from now, on Celia's eighteenth birthday, Percival James will take possession of Celia's thirty thousand pounds. Since it is not legal to sign a marriage contract as they are underaged, it must be a gentlemen's agreement between us that they will marry."

Good Lord, what did I do? He prayed Celia would someday forgive him.

Westbury was silent for several minutes, then nodded. "I agree. In return for your generosity, I will never gamble again."

Colton's nostrils flared. "We have heard that before." He leaned forward slightly. "Once these contracts are legally endorsed, you will never make demands for payment of a life-debt again."

"Correct." The earl nodded. "Your debts to me will be paid, and I will *not* gamble again. You have my word on it."

Westbury extended his hand first to Sharrington, who shook it readily.

When the earl turned towards him, Colton searched Westbury's eyes. His former commander might tell untruths in normal conversation, but when he gave his word, it was as good as any legal document.

He reached across the aisle and took Westbury's hand.

The pact was sealed.

~1814 - Four years later – Burchard Park

"Whoa." Percival James Aldridge slowed his horse and glanced around. Responding to its owner's anxiety and perhaps the same noise that prompted James to stop, Horatio pranced, perked up his ears, and stepped backward in agitation. James leaned to pat the horse's neck. "Easy, boy."

Both man and beast turned towards a repetition of the sound. After dismounting, he paced softly towards the area where the noise originated. A squeak came from the bushes off to his right. James closed his eyes and let out a sigh of relief. He addressed the grouping of shrubberies, "Is someone there?"

One bush in particular moved more than the others.

Horatio huffed and lowered his head to graze. Much as James recognized the sound, the horse must have distinguished the scent of the lurker and knew there was nothing to fear.

"Miss Colton, is that you?"

Celia stood up but did not turn to face him. She spoke in an agitated tone, "Yes, Mr. Aldridge."

"Why did you not answer the first time?"

Not yet seventeen years old, she still wore her hair loose about her shoulders. As she shook her head, her long curls bobbed across her back, tumbling down to brush her slim waist. She turned slightly, stepping into a ray of sunshine that filtered through the tree branches and illuminated her. Angelic was the only term he could think of to describe her. The light exposed strands of rich strawberry in her golden hair which were unnoticeable in the shade. He swallowed hard and fisted his fingers, which lately always itched to touch her whenever she was near.

Celia's voice distracted him from his thoughts. "I – I hoped if I did not answer, you would go away."

She turned to face him as he made his way around the bushes. Trails of tears streaked the dust covering her face. The pristine white gown he noticed earlier in the day was now muddy and torn. A bandage of sorts, crimson with blood, was tied around a sleeveless arm. Fear and concern flooded through him. "What happened, Miss Colton? Did someone harm you?"

Her right hand moved to cover her upper arm. She blushed. "I tripped and fell."

James moved closer and reached out to her, but remembering himself, he froze. "May I examine your injury?"

She nodded.

As he unwrapped the bandage, he bit back a gasp. The wound was deep. "This needs to be cleaned, or infection might set in. Come." He took her other elbow, led her to Horatio, and pulled two flasks from his saddlebag.

She held her arm straight and looked at the gash. "Earlier, I cleaned it with water from the stream and placed crushed yarrow over the gash. I believe it slowed the bleeding. After chewing on some willow bark, it doesn't hurt as much as it did."

He stood blinking at her a moment. "Still, I would like to proceed. I am sorry, but this will sting."

She nodded. "Do what you must, sir."

To distract her from his ministrations, he asked, "How did you learn about yarrow and willow?"

"My nanny was from Scotland. She took me for walks in my father's woods and taught me which plants could be used to heal, which could be eaten, and which were poisonous."

"Good to know."

"But she also told me that moss grows on the north side of the tree. It does not seem to grow on the north surface here for some odd reason, or I would have been able to find my way to the manor house before now. Deeper in the woods, some trees had moss growing on all sides."

"Moss will grow on any surface in shady areas." He poured water then brandy over the wound. Though she flinched and hissed, she did not cry out. He wrapped a clean handkerchief around the gash. As he secured it, he asked, "May I ask *why* you did not wish to be found?"

Her eyes began to fill with tears, and she looked away from him. "I – I did not want to face Lord Westbury. I was afraid..." Her voice trailed off as a tear escaped and rolled down her cheek, making a new path through the dust.

James raised his eyebrows. "Afraid of my grandfather? But why?"

She sniffed and turned her head further from him while shaking it slightly.

"Celia?" He took her chin between his fingers and tilted her head up to face him. She kept her gaze directed downward, her long, thick lashes shielding her eyes from his view. "Are you and I not friends?"

She nodded slightly.

"Please... what has my grandfather done to frighten you enough to keep you from returning to Burchard Park for so many hours?"

Celia whispered, "Lord Westbury did nothing. It was my own clumsiness. I went out walking only so I could think clearly. I had to find a way to tell him... to explain. He is so ill. I did not wish for the shock of what I did to cause his condition to worsen."

He pulled out a second handkerchief from his saddlebag and moistened it with water from his flask, then handed it to her. "For your face."

She coloured and wiped at her cheeks. When she looked at the cloth, she raised her eyebrows. "I did not realize I was so dirty.

He held out his hand for the handkerchief. "May I?"

Celia nodded and directed her gaze at his neck cloth as he wiped at an area she missed on her chin.

"Believe me, Miss Colton, my grandfather has lived a life fuller than most. Nothing *you* could do could possibly shock him."

She looked up, and his heart stopped—as it always did whenever her intense emerald eyes held his gaze captive. Celia might be young, but even covered in dirt, she was still the most beautiful girl he ever saw. Heaven help him, if she were older, he would...

It was not until she turned away that he realized he began to lean towards her. To cover his act, he plucked a small twig from her hair and took two steps backwards.

He cleared his throat. "I have no sidesaddle, but I once saw Victoria make do with my father's when her horse was injured and the beast would not allow us to remove her saddle. Although Horatio is not used to a lady riding him, he is so well-trained, I think he would be fine having you sit unevenly on his back. I shall lead him."

"If there were a second horse for you to ride, I would be happy to ride Horatio, as he and I are good friends. I daresay, I will hold you to that offer someday, sir." She smiled and raised her chin slightly. "However, today, I am quite well enough to walk."

"You have been walking a good part of the day, Miss Colton, and you are injured. I would be shirking my duty as a gentleman if I should allow you to walk to the manor house from here."

"If I tire, I will let you know."

The stubborn set of her jaw was familiar enough to know she would not submit. Hoping she would agree to ride soon, he conceded to her request.

Taking Horatio's reins, he held out his arm to her. "Let us begin. My father's wife was quite worried for you when I left the manor house." He looked at his watch. "I have been gone for more than two hours. I imagine she is in need of smelling salts by now. Grandfather sent every available man to search for you."

Celia took his arm and they began walking.

Remorse was plain in her voice. "I did not mean to worry Lord Westbury, my cousin, or anyone else. I had no thought of staying away so long, sir. When I fell down the embankment, I became disoriented and must have walked in the wrong direction. Whenever we have ridden out this far, I simply followed Cousin Victoria, Lord Eagleton, or yourself."

"You do realize if I did not stop when I did, you might have been out here all night."

She shook her head. "A little while ago, I sighted the Ridge and knew which way to go from there."

James did not answer. It was a miracle she was not injured more seriously in her fall. What would have happened if an unsavoury character came across her before he had?

After a few minutes passed, he said, "I know Grandfather gave you permission to walk out alone, but perhaps it was with the unspoken understanding you would remain within sight of the house. I do hope you will do so from now on." He raised both eyebrows. "And do not think you are fooling me with all this misdirection. You still did not answer my question. What made you leave the house in the first place?"

Agitation tinted her voice as she answered. "Clumsiness, pure and simple. I spread Lord Westbury's map on my writing table without moving the inkwell to another table first. The ink spilled across the top quarter of the page. Lord Westbury may never find it now."

He cocked his head to the side. "Of what map do you speak? What will Grandfather never find?"

She covered her mouth with her hand and furrowed her brow. "I let slip too much already, sir. Your grandfather swore me to secrecy on the matter. I believe it is meant to be a surprise for your father, you, and your brother."

Understanding dawned. "I give you my word, I will not reveal what you tell me."

Finally, she answered. "Lord Westbury gave me the document the first summer I came to visit with Cousin Victoria. Across the top are verses... no, more like riddles that must be solved. Each one leads to another portion of the journey." She blushed. "Lord Westbury asked for my help in unravelling the riddles so he could find... *something* that was buried somewhere at Burchard Park long ago."

James nodded. "May I ask whether this treasure was buried by the second Earl of Westbury?"

Celia opened her eyes so wide, he feared they might pop from her head. "Yes! How did you know?"

He avoided her question. "You have worked on this problem for years?"

Celia nodded. "Only during the summers. I was not comfortable taking it with me from Burchard Park, though I did copy down all the verses so I could work on them whilst away from here. Once I found the answer to a riddle, I needed the map in order to find something pictured on the grounds that corresponded with that word. Some of the puzzles had more than one answer. It is not as easy as one would think."

James smiled. "Your perseverance is to be commended, Miss Colton. You have shown more patience than any Aldridge ever has." He gestured toward two riders in the distance. "Will you excuse me, please?" He took several steps away from her and whistled several short spurts, then waved his arms. The two men changed direction and began riding towards them. James led Celia to a tree stump. "Sit and rest while I ride to meet these men. I should like to give them the news that you have been found relatively unharmed so they can return to the manor and inform my step-mother. Do you still feel up to walking or shall I ask them to return with a cart? It is at least another hour's walk from here."

Celia sat and slumped slightly, then straightened her back. Never having seen her display anything but the perfect posture, that slip confirmed his suspicion of her complete exhaustion.

"I am willing to walk." She paused. "However, if one of the men would be so kind as to meet us on the return path with a horse equipped with a sidesaddle, I will ride the rest of the way from wherever he finds us."

He turned away from her, for he knew he could not hide the triumph he felt in this small victory. "I shall return shortly." He bowed slightly and mounted Horatio.

~%~

Celia watched her companion ride towards the others, whom, even at this distance, she recognized as two of Lord Westbury's stablemen.

Goodness! Although she was happy to spend so much time alone with James, as she called him in her thoughts—for he despised being addressed as Percival, his true Christian name—she had no idea that being away from the house for a few hours would have caused such a fuss. Granted, she *had* been lost and injured during her adventure, but she would have found her way without assistance... eventually. Perhaps if Victoria did not suffer from heightened emotions during her delicate condition, her cousin would have more faith in Celia's abilities.

What did James mean when he said that she possessed more patience than any Aldridge? Should she inquire when he returned, or should she wait to speak to the earl? The older gentleman made the map sound like a secret. When she mentioned it, she had no idea James would know of what she was speaking. But James's comment made it seem as if he knew all about it. Curious...

Confidences she understood, for James and her friend, Miss Regina Buchannan, had shared many with her, but she, herself, was unused to *this* sort of intrigue.

If she told Regina about any of this, her friend would laugh. Regina always teased her, observing that what should have been inconsequential happenings, and were for others, always became complicated for Celia.

Meanwhile, Regina strolled through the entirety of her seventeen years without conflict or impediments.

Part of the reason could be attributed to the differences in their mothers' dispositions. Mrs. Buchannan was an easy-going, amiable lady who made certain her offspring had every advantage in life. As long as her children were happy, Mrs. Buchannan was completely content.

On the other hand, her own mother was continuously demanding of her daughters. Yes, they were provided with the best of everything, but also, she insisted they employ the most rigorous masters in every subject available to ladies, and even a few areas of study that were unusual for ladies to explore.

When alone, her mother often mentioned she groomed each of her daughters to be worthy of marriage to a peer.

To her mother's delight, her plan worked wonders for Celia's sister Penelope, who inherited their mother's ambitions.

Celia had hoped her mother's desires would have been quenched by Penelope's marriage to a baron, for although Celia put everything she had into her lessons and did quite well, her own wish was for something her mother could not support.

The event of her sister's marriage seemed only to re-energize the social climbing yearnings of her mother, who then doubled her efforts with her younger daughter. Even though Celia would not be presented at Court until this coming Season, once a week for the past two years, her mother insisted she devote hours preparing for her royal presentation—practicing to walk, curtsy, and back away from the Queen, all the while dressed in her sister's formal court gown, complete with hoops, train, and ostrich feathers in her headdress.

And now! Now, Mother was determined that her younger daughter should aim higher than her sister... in fact, quite frequently in the weeks leading up to Celia's leaving home for her annual summer visit at Burchard Park, her mother hinted at her hopes for Celia's marrying James, who, upon his grandfather's death, would become a viscount, and along with his father's passing, an earl. She hoped that, God willing, both would occur far in the distant future.

While it was true that her desires matched her mother's in the object of her future marriage, Celia wished to marry only for love. And although Celia's heart yearned for him, James did not love her... at least, not in the way she wished.

She wondered whether her mother would cease making these remarks if she knew the pain she inflicted every time she brought it up, or if knowing Celia's secret would only cause her to become more forceful and determined. She suspected the latter.

Celia studied James conversing with the stablemen on the other side of the meadow.

She sighed deeply. From the moment she first saw him at Victoria's wedding breakfast, James had held a special place in her heart, and her fondness had only grown in strength ever since.

Realistically, she understood her dream of someday marrying him would never come to pass—so hopeless was it that she never even told Regina of her feelings for him. At first, James had looked at her as if she were almost a sister, then later, a friend. She knew she would never be anything more than that in his eyes.

She often bit back jealousy as he told her about the ladies he had admired at soirées in Town or at house parties in the country. If he recognized her feelings for him—of how these conversations pinched her heart—he would think of her affection as a silly childhood infatuation, and he would cease to confide in her altogether. And she could not bear seeing pity in his expression, of that she was certain. No, she would have him feel comfortable conversing with her on almost any subject, no matter what she had to endure in the process.

James remounted Horatio and began his return. The stablemen rode off in the direction of the house.

James sat a horse better than any gentleman she had ever seen, but then again, he excelled at everything. Depending on what the situation demanded, he was stronger, faster, kinder, or more pleasant than any other man, and he was certainly more gentlemanly at all times.

Celia sighed and shook her head to clear her mind. It would not do to be thinking of this subject when he approached!

"What shall I do about the map?" she thought aloud and worried her bottom lip.

It would not be a betrayal of Lord Westbury's trust should she listen to James if he chose to bring it up again, and so she resolved to offer no additional information, though it would be better if James did not speak of it at all.

He approached and dismounted. "Did you have enough of a rest, or would you like to wait here for the stableman to return with Buttercup?"

Celia smiled as she always did when she heard the name of the horse that was hers to ride whenever she visited. The name made it sound as if the horse was a placid old mare, but in fact, she was quite spirited. "We shall walk. I do not wish to delay our return and cause Cousin Victoria additional worry."

~Meanwhile, at Malverne Manor, home to Baron and Baroness Bellerose

Daniel Kenilworth stepped into the parlour, looking for diversion. Spying the baroness and her mother, his eyes widened, and he turned to slip away from the room before he was noticed. When he heard Mrs. Colton mention his good friend by name, he froze in place to listen a few moments longer.

"I predict Mr. Aldridge will be *caught* even before the Season begins. You know very well Celia is quite beautiful—as are you, of course, Penelope. But Celia has a particularly full figure, which I have noticed most gentlemen admire. If she does as I instructed, using all of her feminine wiles on the poor man this summer, he will not stand a chance... the same as you did with your dear baron, my dear. I am expecting a letter from Victoria any day informing us that Celia has been compromised. In fact, I have already composed my reply. I will insist they marry even before the beginning of the Season—to save face, of course." The older lady sniffed. "After all, the disgraceful gossip that went along with the earl's tomfooleries ended with his accident, and their family has finally regained respectability. I am confident they will not risk throwing it all away with another scandal."

"Are you certain she will do it, though, Mama? Celia is not... she does not *think* as we do. She may not have even understood what you expected if you did not lay it out in detail. She seems a bit dense when it comes to these things."

Mrs. Colton narrowed her eyes. "She is *my* daughter. Of course she understood, and she will do as I have ordered, the same as you did."

The baroness clapped her hands and smiled. "It is exciting to think my sister will one day be a countess! She is at Burchard Park now?"

"Yes, and so is Mr. Aldridge. She would have joined us here next month, but Victoria asked that she remain as a companion during her confinement, and that only works in our favour. I understand the child should come any day now. I just received a letter from Victoria saying she and the viscount have asked Celia and Mr. Aldridge to be godparents."

"But Celia will meet us in Town in the autumn, will she not?" The baroness asked. "I planned to have my modiste provide her with a few gowns for the Season."

"You are very generous, Penelope. She should be in London by October, at the very latest. With the gowns we both shall provide towards her wardrobe, Celia will be well dressed this Season, and quite ready to begin her marriage to Mr. Aldridge. Truly, I am thinking of it as more of a trousseau than anything else."

~

At the click of a door closing, both ladies turned see who had entered the room. Nobody was there.

The baroness opened her eyes wide. "Do you think someone came in while we were talking and just now left? It would not be good if we were overheard. Who do you suppose it was?"

"Most likely a servant." Mrs. Colton shrugged. "It really is of no importance, my dear. With our close connection to the family, if it gets out we have our hopes set on Mr. Aldridge for Celia, it should come as no surprise. We did not mention the contract."

Penelope narrowed her eyes. "Does Celia even know of the contract? She does not act as if she does. "

"She does not, dear. As you said, she has different ideas than we do." Mrs. Colton raised her chin. "Your father had the expectation that Celia would enjoy her debut more if she did not know her future was already decided for her. Of course, I thought the scheme foolish, but as your father lay dying, he forced a promise from me." She pressed her lips together as if her last words had been sour.

Penelope whispered, "What was it?"

"I promised I would not tell Celia of the contract until the summer after her first Season, which is when it is specified they shall become engaged."

"Perhaps I could tell her—"

Mrs. Colton interrupted, "I cannot advise you to do so, Penelope, for your father thought of that, as well." Her expression transformed into a smirk. "In any case, Mrs. Buchannan informs me Celia often speaks to Regina, Mrs. Buchannan's daughter, of marrying only for love—of all things."

Penelope shook her head. "I knew she had some fanciful ideas, but that is ridiculous! Only in novels do people marry for love."

"You know how childish Celia can be at times." Mrs. Colton waved away the thought. "But I do believe your sister will do as I wish, though not for status or connexions, as others would do. From watching her expression when she speaks of Mr. Aldridge, I have come to believe she actually fancies herself in love with the gentleman."

Mrs. Colton waited until her daughter's giggles subsided before continuing. "I must depend on Celia following her feelings—and soon." She paused and raised both eyebrows. "Our attorney advises me the ceremony must take place before *their* attorney finds the clause that may be seen as a way out of the contract."

Penelope's eyes widened with her gasp.

Mrs. Colton nodded. "Even though the contract is to their family's benefit as well as ours, I have watched Mr. Aldridge when I have accompanied Celia on her visits to Victoria's estate. He is a stubborn man who values his independence above all else. I have little doubt that if he learns of the clause, he will take advantage of it. He does not wish to be told what to do."

Watch for *The Pact* to be released

soon at Amazon.com

Made in the USA
Monee, IL
07 February 2024

53092135R00184